JOH
THE PARTISAN

JOHNNY
THE PARTISAN

BEPPE FENOGLIO

Ω

QUARTET BOOKS

First published in Great Britain by Quartet Books Limited 1995
A member of the Namara Group
27 Goodge Street
London W1P 1FD

A catalogue record for this title is available from the
British Library

ISBN 0 7043 7078 6

Typeset by Contour Typesetters, Southall, London
Printed and bound in Finland by WSOY

Translator's Note

Beppe Fenoglio introduces English words into his text in what appears to be an arbitrary fashion. In many cases the result is bizarre; no attempt has been made to correct his usage. His English insertions are italicised throughout.

Preface

Beppe Fenoglio was born in Alba in Piedmont in 1922. Conscripted into the army he saw no active service. In September 1943 he found himself in Rome at the moment when the monarchist government, breaking with its German ally, made a separate peace with the Anglo-Americans. In the period of confusion and indecision that followed the Italian armed forces disintegrated and like thousands of others Fenoglio made his way home. In due course he joined the partisans and took part, mostly in a monarchist formation, in the armed struggle in Piedmont. After the war he joined a wine firm and spent the rest of his life in its undemanding employ. His main energies went into writing obsessively about the partisan war which he described with a notable lack of heroics.

Fenoglio was not a member of the literary establishment of postwar Italy. Many of its most important figures had also come out of the Resistance but they were of the Left. As a monarchist, Fenoglio was politically unfashionable and published little in his lifetime – a volume of short stories, a novel on peasant life and a novel based on his experiences in 1943. After his death in 1963 he left a large amount of work in progress. It was from this literary legacy that *Partisan Johnny* emerged in 1968.

The work exists in three versions. One surprisingly is in English, a language in which Fenoglio had read extensively (chiefly seventeenth-century authors) and used eccentrically with what are often embarrassing results. The other two versions are later and in Italian. Both are incomplete. Both cover with variations the same ground – the partisan war in a district of Piedmont called Le Langhe and a courageous but futile gesture – the occupation of Alba by the partisan forces in October 1944. The present version is an editorial conflation of the two versions. In them Fenoglio developed his highly personal style which is rich in neologisms and in anglicisms (which naturally disappear when rendered into English). It is a style which is admirably suited to his hard-headed, pessimistic account of a period in modern Italy which became a rich source of legend and hagiographies.

STUART HOOD

Johnny the Partisan

I

Johnny was looking at his town from the window of the little hillside house his family had rushed to rent for him in order to hide him away after his unexpected, unhoped-for return from distant, tragic Rome, through the sevenfold meshes of the German net. The spectacle of the local 8 September,* the surrender of the barracks with an entire regiment in it to two German armoured cars *not entirely manned*, the deportation to Germany in sealed waggons had convinced everyone, family and *hangers-on*, that Johnny would not come back: in the best of cases he was travelling to Germany in one of these same sealed waggons, having left from some station or other in central Italy. Johnny had always had an aura of a vague, unfounded but *pleased and pleasing* reputation for being unpractical, of having his head in the clouds, of thinking life was like literature . . . But Johnny had burst into the house very early in the morning, sweeping like a disgustingly dirty gust of wind amid his mother's swooning and his father's sculptural amazement. He had undressed like a whirlwind and dressed anew in his best civilian suit (the old vicuna one), walking to and fro in this rediscovered elegance, comfort and cleanness, while his parents followed him madly in his brief circuit. The city was uninhabitable, the city was an antichamber to the Germany he had escaped, the city with its brave proclamations by Graziani,** which had been crossed a few days before by floods of disbanded troops from the Italian army in France, the city with a

---

* 8 September 1943 – the date of the Italian armistice with the Allies and the German take-over of Italy.
** Field-Marshal Graziani (1882–1955), commander-in-chief of the armed forces of Mussolini's puppet republic, had issued calling-up notices.

German detachment in its main hotel, and continual irruptions of Germans from Asti and Turin in trucks which filled the deserted grey betrayed streets with terrifying screeching noises. Absolutely un-inhabitable for a disbanded soldier but one still subject to Graziani's proclamation. Enough time for his father to run off to obtain permission from the owner of the little hillside house, time for him to snatch up haphazard half-a-dozen books from his bookshelves, and to ask about his friend who had returned, time for his mother to call after him: 'Sleep and eat, sleep and eat, and no wicked thoughts' – and then up on the hillside, into hiding.

For a week he had eaten a lot, slept even more, nervously read bits of *A Pilgrim's Progress*, Marlowe's tragedies and Browning's poems, but without any sense of relief, with an annoying feeling that things were getting worse. And he had seen a lot of countryside, as something internally refreshing, a lot of countryside (sometimes whole quarters of an hour and more on a single detail in it), trying to exclude from it the signs and marks of human beings. The house was stupid and pretentious but it rose on a crest in the livery of autumnal love, perched dominantly over the bed of the river where it left the city, running between low banks like a constant stream of lead, solemnly muddied by the first autumn rains. *In the stillness of the night* its noise clambered up the crest with a rustling noise to the windows of the house as if for an ambush. But Johnny loved the river, which had seen him grow up, and along with it the hills. The hills loomed all round, crowded in all round, more and more autumnally blurred, in a musical swirl of slow vapours, sometimes with the very hills nothing more than vapours. The hills loomed over the riverine plain and over the city, gleaming unhealthily under a blemished sun. What stood out were the large shapes of the cathedral and the barracks, brick-red the one, smoky the other, and to Johnny observing them both seemed absurd monuments.

The autumn days, although autumnal, were unbearably long; the gains made from sleeping by day were quickly eroded by nocturnal insomnia; now he spent the nights smoking, crossing his legs and reading deeply. *So mornings were diseased and nightmared.* The landscape disgusted him now that the pleasure of rediscovering his native and vital countryside was over. Reading disgusted him. It was as if that surfeit of food and sleep cancelled out his whole military life

– at the end of a week he no longer knew how to set about stripping a machine-gun, something he could do blindfold a week before. And that was bad, something inside him pungent and *icefying* warned him that it was bad, weapons would enter his life again, perhaps by the window, despite any strenuous decision or solemn vow to the contrary.

He felt the lack of the radio morbidly, acutely; at least for the moment his parents had not been able to do anything about it. He began to crave to hear the voice of Candidus* *gluttoning on his own accent.* Almost every day his father came up *for several requests and annotations* and to tell him the local and national news, those whispered and those broadcast. From his opaque, iredeemably non-narrative voice Johnny thus learned of the liberation of Mussolini on the Gran Sasso thanks to Skorzeny** (he was snatched like a *palio* flag, they weren't even capable of shooting him in extremis, not even of hiding him safely), of the setting-up in Germany of a national Fascist government, of the announcement made by Pavolini† of the massacre at Cephalonia†† over Radio Rome – handed back by the Germans (Johnny saw with extraordinary clarity and closeness the high official's alien face and thought icily, like lightning, of his physical elimination). In town, his father told him, nothing was happening and precisely for that reason people were less and less trusting, they shut themselves up more and more in themselves, unhealthily. 'Who is in charge of public order?' The carabinieri were on duty but with evident reluctance, lately with obvious iciness. Who else had arrived from the collapse? the most far-flung – Sicco from France, Frankie from Spoleto, someone from the Brenner – 'think of the men taken by surprise in Greece, in Yugoslavia, not to speak of Russia –'. Gege was dead – you mean you didn't know? – the coffin had arrived from Montenegro back in the summer. His family

---

* Candidus (John Marus), a celebrated commentator for the BBC's Italian Service.
** Otto Skorzeny, commander of a German Special Forces unit rescued Mussolini by plane from the Gran Sasso, the mountain in the Abruzzi, where he had been confined by the Italian government.
† Pavolini – Fascist Minister of Popular Culture, later secretary-general of the Fascist-Republican Party. Executed by partisans in 1945.
†† 10,000 Italian troops on the Greek island of Cephalonia held a plebiscite and refused to surrender to the Germans. 9,000 were massacred.

maintained he had fallen in action but everyone knew he had ended up a suicide, he had shot himself in the mouth. So that was Gege – the absurd vet, the man who had set him on the road to *dreamboyness*; after Gege there would be no one any more who ran with his arms like seagull's wings.

His cousin Luciano had returned safely from Milan by a night march through the *deep* of the rice-fields of Vercelli parallel to the autostrada on which the German convoys roared. Now he was at home, yes of course, in the house just outside the town gates, on the slopes of the hill on the top of which Johnny lived. His father left again: 'And don't move from here for any reason. Hold out. If you don't want to think of yourself, think of us, of your mother. She agonised these last days.'

But that very evening Johnny decided to go and visit his cousin at a time that was darkly auspicious, cutting across the soggy hill. He could no longer bear the nightmarish solitude and the unchanging view of the earth crumbling away in the damp dark like a fistful of sand under an inexorable silent stream. He walked blindly. But how did men manage to reconquer like that positions overwhelmingly lost, to win back all their capacity to command, to punish and kill, to force to submit to their martial law, and with scanty, laughable weapons, enormous masses of men and infinite expanses of land.

His cousin had not changed at all – only an accentuated thinning of the hair broadened his already immensely wide brow. The military habit of mind seized hold of Johnny and forced him to imagine his cousin in officer's uniform but he could not complete the portrait. Instead on the contrary, he could see in him an instinctive, ironical contrariness, like a small boy with his long black stocking up to his thighs, automatically, illogically suggesting Silvio Pellico.*

'I was on duty at the Central Station on 8 September and the first two Germans who arrived in a truck, we did for them properly – It was very easy almost the punishment for their incredible cheek in turning up, two of them, to seize the station at Milan. There were civilians along with us including a lawyer. Really and truly, a dream of a situation, intoxicating, like the Five Days.** And take note that the

* Silvio Pellico (1789–1854), writer and patriot imprisoned by Austrians for twenty years.
** The Five Days in May 1848 of the resistance of the people of Milan to the Austrians.

4

lawyer was anything but young, a little old man, he had put himself under my orders exclaiming "Cedant togae armis"* and fired, personally, and it all looked to me like a carnival, fancy-dress affair. Then you turn round and you see no one round about any longer while the Germans are gathering strength more and more. A shame to have to throw away a brand-new uniform, throw it away to save your skin, it had cost such a lot at the Military Store.'

His aunt was mumbling over the knobs of the radio, Johnny remembered this ancient acquistion of theirs, they had bought it on purpose to hear the première of Mascagni's *Nerone* – his uncle was mad about music, they had invited the whole family to hear it and sit in front of the set.

His uncle, a mountain of a man, a *jelly*, under the flagrant sentence of the flesh, squealed with fear, *hand-menaced* his wife who was adjusting the volume knob. In an unexpected falsetto he asked her if she wanted to end up like a man who, surprised by a Fascist patrol listening to Radio London, had been arrested and held for nights in a mysterious dungeon with his naked feet in freezing water. Johnny expected Radio London but heard a different signature tune and then the announcement of the Voice of America. Cousin Luciano *grinned humorously* the moment he was out of the circle of light, the aunt stated clearly: 'We prefer the Voice of America. We are fed up with these English – they are bastards like all of us in Europe. The Americans are different, aren't they? Cleaner.'

The American announcer had a fine voice, fascinating in its dashing vibration – *twang* – but the news was *under his voice*. The great landing at Salerno,** initiated with the prospect of a swoop on Rome, had become bogged down on the first ridges of the coastal hills. Luciano who had followed the affair at home said they had actually run the danger of being thrown back into the sea and in any case had ended up little by little in positional warfare and Johnny said that the German division they had seen passing through Savona must have played a big part in it. There was no point, you could see at a glance that they were the kind of people who knew their job. The distant memory magnified them for him – titanic soldiers purged of filth.

* Latin – Togas give way to arms.
**The Allied forces landed at Salerno, south of Naples, on 8 September 1943.

There followed a commentary by Fiorella La Guardia.* Who is that? The mayor of New York, just think, his highly up-to-date aunt, who lived only for the Voice of America to come on, informed them. 'He is an Italian, an immigrant, someone of our age. Imagine how far he had to travel to end up being mayor of New York.' The voice of La Guardia exploded in the loudspeaker – it was intolerable to Johnny with its coarse Anglo-Sicilian inflections, a repellent hybrid of raven-black Sicilian sweat and Anglo-Saxon asepsis. He spoke with bursts of violence, stripping the words – it felt as if the chips from that stripping process rebounded dry, wounding, against the grille of the set. The voice highly *pitched*, inspired it wasn't clear whether by contempt for his former fellow countrymen or mortal hatred for the Germans: for him everything was easy, immediate, clear-cut, mortal. He shouted: 'A-ttack them! A-ttack them with sticks and knives!'** Johnny and his cousin leapt to their feet out of indignation and contempt. They shouted in their turn: 'Attack them with sticks and knives! But he hasn't seen the tanks of the Hermann Goering division! If that is the mayor of New York! The Americans at Salerno have a lot more than sticks and knives but they can't advance a step! Idiot! Lousy idiot! Peasant!' The aunt had got up, silent and rigid and puffed up with unreserved, martyrly, silently aggressive admiration for America and things American, including La Guardia. Then she calmed down and sat by the set again, her ear intent on disentangling and treasuring La Guardia's last yell while the uncle, all his gelatinous mass atremble, hissed to her to turn it off, that what was important had already been said and heard. She paid no attention to him, shrugged at the sweating agitation of this lump of a man with the whistling breathing of an obsessive child, and turned the knob at the fading of the last note of the musical close. Johnny and his cousin were walking up and down the narrow kitchen in infinite rage; they halted together under her critical and loving gaze. She raised into the light her worn silvery head and said: 'It is terrible to have sons of your age at this time.' Johnny felt touched, he said to himself that he ought to begin to think of his parents, to bother more about them and their spirits; now he realised to the full his father's ageing.

* Fiorello (Little Flower) La Guardia, Democratic mayor of New York.
** La Guardia's Italian is highly Americanised.

6

He took his leave, Luciano said to come back the first safe evening when he had nothing better to do; the aunt nodded in confirmation with her usual spirited sobriety, but the uncle said goodbye with stammering coldness. 'Come and see me one afternoon, Luciano,' Johnny had whispered but the old man heard and said *spelling*: 'Luciano isn't moving from here – he's never going to move away again.' But his cousin came out to accompany him along the hill road which was seething with *frappé* darkness. And they did not say a word to each other.

The first autumn seemed to be on its deathbed. At the end of September thirty-year-old nature was writhing in menopausal *fits* – a dark sadness fell on the hills drained of their natural colours, a drabness to take one's breath away in the leaden flow of the drown-dead river, lapping at its low banks with treacherous sludge, between the distant low poplars, black and seemingly (to his *surmenagé* eyes) multiplying like a pack of cards in a juggling act. And the wind blew with a frequency that was out of season with an unnatural velocity and force, that was decidedly demoniacal in the long nights.

From the window Johnny scanned the asphalt-grey straight stretch of road that ran downhill townwards, reaching the very obvious frontier with the cobbles of the town. Movement and traffic had visibly become less frequent, epidemically so, and the little there was had sensibly speeded up, the passers-by seemed almost to have accelerated comically like characters in Ridolini's films* and in the ridiculousness of it there was a clandestine touch of (viperous) fear.

He clearly saw, at a great distance, his father coming up to the house still on the suburban asphalt; the fatigue, the *non-joy* of his walk struck Johnny. He followed him along all the exposed stretch, his heart melting at the love and devotion of the old man. 'It is terrible in these times to have sons of your age.' Each of his steps spoke of anxiety and abnegation and the son, high up and distant, felt he would never be able to repay him, not even by a hundredth part, not even by staying alive. The only way to repay him, he thought now, would have been to love his own son as his father had loved him: he will get nothing out of it but the balance will be struck in life's great

* Ridolini, Italian name for Larry Sernon, Hollywood director and actor in many silent films.

ledger. He trembled with the desire and the intention to receive him well, adequately, but as his father disappeared from his sight, starting on the first steps up to the house, Johnny automatically with *grinning* anxiety wondered if had brought cigarettes.

Yes, but not such a good ration as usual and a bundle of newspapers. Johnny convulsively lit a cigarette and flattened out a newspaper. The game was going on, Fascism was slowly but surely recovering with an organic quality that one would never have recognised in it. The newspapers were falling into line, the ephemeral editors of the interregnum* having been swept away, the ones who had written the leading article about liberty, the salutary tragedy, the rapprochement to the eternal, indispensable Western values. A photograph of a reorganised military unit, Graziani's men, who had gone back on their oath to the king to keep faith with the *foederis arca germanica*:** they looked athletic, extremely efficient, infinitely more so than similar units of the late Royal Army, very modern, *Germanlike*, all with smiles of exploding faith, with a lousy visual effect, openly, deliberately fratricidal. But the acme was contained in the photograph of Ettore Muti's legionaries,† who carried ultramodern weapons along with the old fancy-dress of the march on Rome,†† tommy guns slung over black ski-tops, with the tin badge of the skull. But, on examination, unbalanced units made up of old men and children, veterans, raw recruits and mascots.

Johnny raised his eyes from the paper to his father. He was sitting with a certain suppressed unease on the *cheap* wicker chair, his head wavering slightly in the discreet light of the *rapidly decaying* afternoon. Fear, despair, gloomy thoughts, conferred on him the stony configuration of Eygptian or Aztec man: the elementary feelings that had come to the surface froze into an ancient iconicity, cancelling out – Johnny noted – centuries of progress in his bearing.

He immersed himself in the paper again. Fascist power once again

---

* The interregnum between the fall of Mussolini in July 1943 and the establishment of his puppet regime in Salò in September that year.
** The German ark of the treaty.
† Ettore Muti, a Fascist boss assassinated in 1943 who gave his name to a notorious antipartisan formation.
†† Mussolini took power in 1922 after a 'March on Rome' (by train in his case).

controlled the great cities from which it would spread out into the small ones and into the countryside like a patch of asphyxiating oil. All the papers underlined in particular that the workers were going along with the edicts, they had all gone back to work and were doing their job regularly. So they were reorganising, they would be tough, take a long time to die, and in this reorganisation and this resistance to final death, Johnny saw not so much the bovine face of the Duce liberated by Skorzeny as the face of Pavolini and of many others like him, never seen but now easily imagined, like prints you could run off . . .

He let the newspapers slip to the floor, swooping down anxiously like shot birds, 'Anything new in town?' His father quickly re-composed himself for the fatigue and the nobility of speech. Nothing impressed and yet pleased him like speech. 'Nothing apart from that it seems two trucks of Germans and Fascists have arrived at the hotel. Is it true that one of these evening you went down to your uncle's house? That was very bad of you. You are not to move from here. You need patience but you are not to move. Think of us at home thinking of you up here and this is a little comfort to us in our worries but you . . .' 'I am going mad here!' 'Eh?' shouted his father in angry fear. 'I am going mad up here! Up here alone! and also because I don't see what danger there is in coming down to town for a minute.' 'You don't see the danger? you are mad. Just because nothing has happened so far! But so much will happen that we will never again have dry eyes because of it. And what do you think life is like in town that you so much want to come down? In town we live like mice, we have hardly any friends any more, no one trusts anyone else. We no longer trust even the carabinieri on duty, we tremble to meet them. And if we speak a bit you can bet there will be talk of spies. The Fascists are raising their heads again. Do you know the son of the party secretary has gone to be a cadet in a new Fascist school? Do you know that the lawyer and his son have enrolled in a black brigade?'* 'How am I supposed to know up here?' but suddenly the *idée fixe* of physical elimination seized him, struck him like lightning. He could so clearly see himself as judge and executioner of his fellow countrymen, no his fellow citizens, there he was executing them for

* The Fascist militia.

9

those ridiculous party uniforms. They had not gone and put on uniforms and armed themselves because of the English, they had done it because of themselves, of the Italians, the others. Well, the Italians would kill the lot of them; thanks to an Italian hand they would not be cannon fodder for the English. 'Have you seen my teachers? Do they come to see me?' 'I haven't seen them again but of course they'll come. But sincerely I am not too happy about your seeing Professor Corradi. He talks too much, without taking any precautions, and then everyone knows he is a Communist.' Corradi? a Communist? But what did it mean, what did it entail exactly to be a Communist? Johnny had no idea apart from the close relationship with Russia. 'Off you go now – it's getting late,' and Johnny watched the unnatural evening fall on the plain, putting out all the gleams on the roofs of the city like a snuffer. As for the hills they were sinking in the purple. 'Yes, but promise me and your mother that you won't stir from here any more. If you want to stretch your legs you have your hill at a sensible time.'

Johnny promised and watched his father go downhill accentuating the congenital curve of his shoulders because of the path which blurred in the dark.

Because of a sudden feeling of cold he went back in. He felt around him and in him a precarious state, a miserable state because of which the whole of him was finely splintered, pauperised, frighteningly reduced compared to a normal human dimension. And a sexual urge, sudden and overwhelming, came to complicate everything, to bring everything to the pitch of crisis. He would have to go down into the town for that reason as well at the cost of finding Germans and Fascists in the dusty démodé little parlours. The business struck him as dirty but irrefutable, with the deadly squalor of a surgical intervention. That inflated his human misery, made him appear to himself as a repellent bag of wind swollen with serious triviality.

He sank headlong into foreknowledge and foresight of the evening and the night. A furious but not vicious fit of smoking would rapidly squander his already reduced tobacco ration and insomnia, because of the excess of sleep during his *rehabilitation*, his senseless and vortiginous thoughts, the sexual urge which would certainly re-emerge dentate and acrimonious. He said to himself violently almost whispering: 'Remember when you were a soldier? You were desperate because of the lack of solitude, you were almost on the point of vomiting because of life in common. Do you remember the dreams you had when they gave you close order drill or Fraglia stuffed your head with the mechanism of the machine-gun? You dreamt of being alone and *disengagé* in a room more or less like this opening on to a view of the river and of the hill and translating peacefully some English classic or other.' Now all these premisses and possibilities existed, arms and men were collectives far away, beyond the hills, beyond the river, in the great imaginary cities, in the immense misty and shivering plains . . .

Almost miraculously he found in his grasp the volume of Marlowe's tragedies. He sat down with enforced, grimacing determination, opened and flattened out the book at the beginning of the *Famous Tragedy of the Rich Jew of Malta.* He would translate it, spend the evening translating it; not with the eye but with a pen, he would put it on paper with an elementary, minute and firm hand; calligraphy as a life-raft.

> Albeit the world thinks Machiavel is dead
> Yet was his soul but flown beyond the Alps
> And now the Guise is dead . . .

He leapt to his feet, high above the focus of misery, of impossibility, shut the book with a sharp bang as if he wanted to crush between its leaves all the lice of this misery of his. He climbed up to the floor above, barely closed the window open on the late Piedmontese evening, on the aquatic vibration of the foliage in the wind. He lay down in the cold sheets, which were immediately but fallaciously soothing, hoped to fall asleep at once and to find himself waking in late morning but as if to the greatest of miracles – *I want a woman, I need a girl – he pleaded beyond the ceiling* but then as if to purify and guarantee his entreaty – *I want but to get her young tasteless breathing!*

II

He was so close to the girl from the hill, so unmoving that he could almost microscope the jasper flecked with gold of her pupils and yet her voice came to him as if through numerous filtrations. 'Was that nice?' *she stammered.* 'Tremendously. You are . . . you are amazingly good.' But then Johnny raised himself and cried out: 'But I don't feel like a man!' She *goggled.* 'You're not being fair to yourself –' and again John repeated louder and indifferent and deaf to the girl: 'I don't feel like a man.'

They had come down from the hill to the river through the gap between the two railway *tunnels* in a sad orgy of yellow. Whenever the path was easy and *unhindered* Johnny fell behind her intent on her one plait, a thick heavy plait of a colour from which *by that vision* Johnny understood what the English mean by '*auburn*'. The girl was very slightly younger than he and wore her plait as a sign of enchanted, prolonged adolescence. A last autumnal sun was present drawing bluish gleams from the metallic surface of the river and lingering on the poplars as if on the locks of old, old women. You could hear the sporadic call of an invisible heron and all the water was silent except where from the high cliffs every so often a slide of tufa fell away. She said: 'If I weren't a woman I would like to be a woman. And a woman again. And another woman again. But if I couldn't be that I'd like to be a heron.'

Then she began to recite '*My moment with you is now ending*' but with an implicit though gratuitous reference and then Johnny was assailed by consciousness of her sex and was with her and in her and not what he seemed to have felt all afternoon, her as something external, something abstract, perhaps suspended in midair like a spirit, but something concrete and low, real, waiting for the caress of his hand, like a confirmation and a possessing. And she *disclosed like a rose* aiding Johnny's work with skilled minimum movements.

Now all was silent, the heron mute and the tufa that slid down from the high recesses of the rocks seemed frozen, only the water had found its voice and sighed as if its entire substance were a sigh. But there was no *gale* for their unprotected bodies. And Johnny repeated, slowly and more painfully: 'I don't feel like a man!' 'Let's go home,' she said, 'up the hill. Let's go home and put on *Covering the Waterfront.*'

But they did not have time to rise to their knees.

The drone of the planes arrived steathily like a natural component of the immense symphony; but it grew; it enucleated and diversified, *boasted* of its mechanical nature and the two machines (English? American?) appeared distant, low, mad, skimming the hills beyond the river. They dived on the bridge, then pulled out and up as if after recognition of its intactness and importance, flew along the river very low, rose up above the couple to leap over the cliffs but, even when they pulled out, all the leaves and grass trembled and the couple as well. She rose up on her knees and covered herself, her terrified fingers ineffective. Johnny pulled her into the shelter of the low bank stretching his hands over the rest of her naked flesh. 'They're coming back but it has nothing to do with us. It's the bridge they're after. *Damn'em.*'

Their drone re-echoed as if falling headlong along the line of the cliffs, they shot like arrows in another pass parallel to the course of the river. Again the whistling ruffling of the branches, the maddened grass lashing them in their blind prone position, then Johnny saw them from behind, their tails ten metres above the surface of the water, murderously aiming at the bridge. They sent on ahead a downpour of machine-gun fire as if to clear their view and then they dropped their bombs. One fell on the glassy mirror of the water, the other on the shore in a *flourish* of boulders but immediately afterwards two tubers of creamy dust, exceptionally firm, flowered on the bridge to mask the certain, hideous wound. The planes were already hovering above the hills beyond the river, placated and light as if deprived of their sting, already merged with the unfathomable air, while from the right bank there rose the strident chorus of the astonishment, of the pain of the town. She finished dressing *with unsteady hands*. 'I don't want them to have destroyed the bridge,' she said. But there it reappeared between the rents in the reluctant dust-cloud, the third and fourth of its six arches demolished. *Damn them!*

He broke his promise one evening in early October, the gloom on the hills something to flee from like a cholera epidemic. He went down into the town like a surprise attack, choosing in the dark the must unusual and safest approach. Just at the edge of town a darker shadow – gigantic – detached itself from the uniform shade; and Johnny took his hands out of his pockets. But the colossus merely wanted a light. Johnny gave it one turning his face away from the halo of the little flame so as not to be seen or to see. And so he saw at the foot of the railway embankment a moving and wriggling bundle, a woman wriggling in the first cold. That shapeless lactescent patch gave him a tremendous feeling of unease but he held straight on far from the brothel district.

The streets were rigorously deserted, rigorously neglected as far as men were concerned, only the belated light from the sky drew dull reflections from the paving-stones. He walked along hugging the walls, in this way he sometimes heard emerge from the sealed houses tired voices, sometimes desperate even in their suffocated state, always with a grumbling sound as neurotic as it was precise. Fleeing across the square he saw his own house for a second with, in it, his unknowing and trusting parents perhaps *making the best of enjoying their own solitary wake* simply as their reward for their sacrifices for Johnny, disciplined and sensible on his safe hillside. He accelerated greatly to tug himself free of the umbilical cord of remorse, to remove from his sight the front of his house so precarious and almost it seemed collapsing in the darkness.

He made for the café belonging to Guido's father in the modern main square *signalled* by the shafts of light that filtered from the worn blackout. The place was run down as if deliberately neglected, the number of staff drastically reduced, the display cabinets for the wines and liqueurs grinned through their numerous, too numerous gaps. Two couples were playing at cards, arranged so that both had an eye on the door; mute and determined, they were playing as if it were a punishment. Guido's father came towards him with an air of straightforward recrimination and reprimand on his funereal face. 'Did Guido come home after 8 September?' 'He had seven days' leave and his mother and I managed to have it extended. He was at home on the 8th, he was very lucky . . .' 'Where is he now?' The café-owner sucked his whole bloodless face into his mouth. 'In the hills, but where?' 'Will you give me an ersatz coffee?' He said No with his head, he wasn't doing it out of spite, Yes, he wanted to put him out immediately but he was too good a friend of his father's. 'Just tell me if you have seen Professor Monti?' Monti ordinarily *mealed* at the *main hotel* and then looked in at his café for his 'coffee'. But habits had been upset after the armistice. Fortunately he was to be found at the Albergo Nazionale, a hotel in the old town with a starburst of safety exits which completely lost themselves in the mazes of the medieval town and from there in the open fields by the river. Johnny left for his new destination thinking with sad relief of the solemn and happy nights of high summer in which he and the others, today's dead, the prisoners of war, those in hiding, the men who were boys when he was a boy, played at tag all over the town and round about the Albergo Nazionale was one of their main *resorts* while the other generation was with the women of its generation in the hiding-places on the river banks and in the hills . . . He walked at a good pace with an uneliminable remnant of the military *gait* and he felt as if he were going not through a town but over an ant-heap humming with subterranean life yet spasmodically intent on the sounds and noises overhead.

The professor was at the Nazionale in the furthest-away room which communicated with the old stables and from there through a *zig-zag* of lanes to the banks of the river. When he turned round at the sound of Johnny's anxious step the scant light lit up Monti's glasses out of all proportion. Monti was not alone but with Y, a kind of friend, and totally taciturn – a soldier, he had only got away from Alessandria where he was serving at the transport depot – so not worth spending a narrative line on. Monti had got up with his mountaineer's bearlike bulk straightened out by years of living in the plains. He gave him a philosophical hug, saying how pleased he was to see him in the flesh again, thus destroying the foreknowledge of communication. They sat down while Monti with polemical euphoria forbade him to relate to them his escape from Rome. 'I won't talk about it,' said Johnny, 'I'll confine myself to offering a drink in full and complete settlement of any of my debts to fortune.' But they didn't want one because there there was nothing drinkable left. 'If I were dead,' said Monti, 'I would have used Phaedo's words* for you – in Hades before my time – wonderful things' and they all laughed *harshly*.

There followed an irksome and miserable silence and Johnny hid his disappointed *appallingness* by the long, meticulous process of crushing his cigarette in the ancient and chipped advertising ashtray while out of the corner of his eye he took in the arrears of fatigue which slackened Monti's profile, one that sparkled unnaturally even in repose with dialectical intelligence and philosophical discipline, leaning on his broad, excessively hirsute hand. 'And Corradi?' Johnny asked at last.

A noise of a motor vehicle shook the narrow street outside violently, earthquaking the walls of the little room. All three remained in suspense with their hard mouths softly suspended in that moment of apprehension, then the motor moved off, now it had only the innocuous and petulant resonance of a modest gas-fuelled vehicle perhaps terrified by its own noisiness.

'Corradi may come or not,' said Monti. 'Is it true he's a Communist?' 'Always was,' said Monti quickly as if in apology. Johnny was unable to apply the nature of Communist in a way that fitted that little *liceo* professor who was familiar only with Baudelaire and D'Annunzio. And Y seemed to resent the subject. 'You have to know,' Monti went on, 'that even at the university they called him Corradyev.' Johnny asked if he had not been influenced by his experience in Yugoslavia against Tito's partisans. 'Certainly. In fact I shall never forget what he said when we saw him again at the *liceo* on leave from Yugoslavia. "You should see the *liceo* in Zagreb. Everybody off and away, the rector, the professors, students and beadles, all partisans!" Then in town here he chiefly kept company with four soldiers from his regiment – four Communists. I remember one in particular – from Tuscany with a square beard – very black, a sculptor in civilian life, I think I may say that he was better as a model

* Phaedo – the Socratic dialogue which discusses the immortality of the soul.

than as a sculptor. At all possible times they were always together on the second bench in the public gardens and sometimes Corradi invited me too. But he called them comrades and only addressed me as a friend. Note the conceptual distinction.'

A pause during which with narrowed but blazing eyes he seemed to stare at Corradi's image in space with a terrified sense of repulsion as if faced by some well-known man who had voluntarily had himself inoculated with leprosy. Monti on the other hand seemed to have plunged forthwith into a sad state of absorption but he shook it off to say in a loud voice that made the little room shake: 'Oh there's something very interesting! do you know that on 25 July* they – I mean Corradi and the four soliders – hoped that Badoglio** would not have the situation under control? yes, because in this way the essential conditions postulated by Lenin would come about: when a government collapses it must be the people that rise up and seize the imperium . . .' 'But it was a vain hope,' said Johnny, with a bitterness that surprised himself. 'I was never so bored as on the night of 25 July when I was on public order duty.' Then Monti said no more, he turned his wrist to bring his watch into the *mainstream* of the light and said: 'Corradi won't come now. It hasn't been his evening. We had better go too.' He was the first to rise – arthritically. 'The moment I get home I shall read my Kierkegaard for an hour or so, and then sleep until tomorrow which is so distant and miraculous.' Johnny remembered and said: 'Are you still on Kierkegaard?' 'My boy, Kierkegaard can easily take up a lifetime.' And Y: 'I am eavesdropping – but is it healthy to devote oneself to Kierkegaard in these days?' Monti sighed at the ineluctability of a professional performance: 'Look – Angst is the category of the possible. Hence it is an extension into the future, it is composed of myriads of possibilities, of openings to the future. On the one hand, Angst, it is true, throws you back on your own being and from that comes bitterness but, on the other hand, it is the necessary "*Sprung*" – that is the leap into the future.'

* 25 July 1943 – the date when Mussolini was dismissed by the Fascist Grand Council and fell from power.
** Field-Marshal Badoglio, who became head of government on the fall of Mussolini and proceeded to treat with the Allies.

Corradi was to be seen '*some days after*' with Monti and a knot of ex-students under the colonnade of the old café – with in front of them ersatz apéritifs and above them a splendid October sun, all in harmony and cheerful in apparent synchronism. And Corradi darted a furious look with his glasses at Johnny as he arrived. He was as bespectacled as Monti; but in Monti's case the lenses were revealing, magnified the pupils with crystalline limpidity, whereas Corradi's lenses had a clouding effect on the observer, the pupil faded into a mysterious blob. Moreover he had become more massive, but also more agile, it seemed, and his head had assumed the rotundity and profiled *allure* that was leonine. *Shook hands an acheful intensity and pleasure.* And Johnny gazed at him with a new fascination: he saw him as if he were in uniform, a priest, at all events someone apart. But Corradi started up again as formerly – that is to say making a noise being fun. There still remained in him that certain cutting edge of intellectual cynicism which had made of him an idol at the *liceo*. And suddenly it seemed odd, almost offensive to Johnny that Corradi should think he was more at ease with these four distant soldiers than with his colleagues and students.

They had met in the old main square in full sunlight and at the little tables of the top-ranking restaurant although the danger had not only not diminished but certainly increased. Although it was well known that in the big cities there were no – or hardly any – draft-dodgers, the Fascist newspapers were trumpeting about the resto-ration of the glorious old barracks, the mass reappearance of the glorious old grey-green,* and from Tuscany there had fallen like a thunderbolt the news that a draft-dodger, dug out of hiding, had been shot within twenty-four hours. The news hung over Italy like a gigantic black cloud: everyone now understood what the Fascists were prepared to do, the case was terrifying as a *breach of code*. But that is what they were up to.

'Naturally,' said Monti, grim-faced because of the external re-flection of his inner depression. 'It just needs a Fascist armed with an old gun to turn up in some place and it is easy for him to enrol all these youths and form them up in columns.'

'But we all know the remedy by now,' said Corradi with a new

* The colour of Italian army uniforms.

voice – one in which some pith had been inserted in his proud but grating *liceo* voice. Monti did not speak, evidently they had been arguing shortly before. And so Corradi went on: 'All it will need is for any one of these draft-dodgers – also armed with an old gun or a bill-hook or a penknife to lie in wait for the Fascist on his bullying way and fall upon him. From behind, naturally, because one must never confront a Fascist face to face, he must be attacked with the same precautions as a man has to take with an animal. You jump on him, kill him and drag him by the feet to some spot to bury him, rub him off the face of the earth. And it would be advisable to carry with you a little brush with which to cancel for all eternity even his last footprints in the dust of our streets.'

'That is what these days is called a partisan,' said an ex-student. 'You're still the first and best,' Corradi said to him while a gleam of sarcastic satisfaction sliced through his foggy lenses. But they were all – each one for himself – intent on weighing this new word, so airily suspended – new as an Italian acquisition, so tremendous and splendid in the golden light. And Corradi went on: 'It all comes down to agreeing on the true meaning of the word partisan,' casting such a *sideways* glance at Monti that his pupil squinted right out of the lens. And Monti said with plaintive emphasis: 'A partisan is and will be anyone that fights the Fascists.' Corradi darted a circular glance at all those who had instantly accepted Monti's definition. Then he said: 'Every one of you is unfailingly certain to become a partisan in the end. I am not saying a good partisan because partisan like poet is an absolute word rejecting all gradations.' Johnny glanced at Monti, finished drinking his apéritif with *heavy repugnance.* And Corradi said: 'Let's carry out an examination – of the scholastic kind, if you like – on the partisan. Can we accept Monti's definition whereby a partisan is someone who fires a well-aimed, decisive shot at the Fascists? Johnny, you catch sight of a Fascist or German and you prepare to fire at him in all cases in honour and *fulfilment* of the definition. But a "but" presents itself – by firing at him and killing him it can happen that a few hours later a Fascist or German column bursts into the place or the neighbourhood and as a reprisal puts it to fire and sword, killing ten, twenty, all the inhabitants of that place. In the consciousness of such a possibility, would you, Johnny, fire just the same?' 'No,' said Johnny vehemently and Corradi laughed behind his glasses. 'Let us continue along this path which is strewn with difficulties but instructive, would you agree, Johnny, if your father were a Fascist and an active Fascist to the point of being able to compromise your safety and that of your partisan formation, would you feel able to kill him?' Johnny bowed his head but someone else said with a certain *stammering* heat: 'But, professor, you are only giving extreme cases.' 'The life of the partisan is made up only and entirely of extreme cases. Let us proceed. Johnny, if you had a sister, would you use that sister of yours, would you use the sex of that sister of yours to ensnare a Fascist or German officer and have him brought for the business to a reasonably comfortable place where you are already lying in wait to eliminate him?' No one uttered that No which in any case had already shouted itself in the desert-like silence and then Corradi moved his hands rapidly as if he were crumbling something. But Monti with an effort sat up straight. 'The professor means that one cannot be a partisan without a precise ideological infrastructure. Freedom in itself does not seem to him to be a sufficient ideological structure. In the last analysis the professor means that one will not be a partisan if one is not a Communist.'

'Indeed,' said Corradi. 'Otherwise you will be merely Robin Hoods. Johnny, allow me to forecast that you will be a splendid Robin Hood. But as Robin Hood you will be infinitely less useful, less serious, less praiseworthy and, note this, a less fine figure than the least Communist partisan.' Monti *goggled*. 'You know, Corradi,' he said with deathly calm, 'you disgust me. You disgust me as a Jesuit would.' 'And you are infantile,' said Corradi with the same loving-deathly calm. 'And you are all infantile, all of you,' said Corradi, shaking his leonine head and making a gesture to brush them all aside like an adult with a bevy of tiring children. But one of them said: 'I don't understand, professor, why you are so angry about it. We will kill Fascists and does a Fascist killed by a Robin Hood not greatly serve the Communist cause?' And then they broke up because Y said, in a *hoarse* but deeply felt humorous tone, that they were running the infantile risk of all being captured while they were conducting a disquisition on the essence and teleology of the partisan by the first Fascist suddenly to appear round the corner of the café with a rifle slung on his shoulder. And Monti turned round once more and said with his tired face made more so by his neglected beard, 'Boys, don't let us lose sight of liberty.' 'And what about these famous arms to ambush the Fascists with?' Monti *goggled.* 'Corradi has some. On 8 September Corradi buried all the weapons of his unit. He can arm a group right away.' But they shook their heads. 'None of these weapons will be mine. I won't follow Corradi. But then what about weapons?' 'The weapons have got to be taken, for example by disarming the carabinieri!' And he left them in a state of stupefaction, with the enormity of the suggestion. How they had to *brace up* to overcome, tear up the complicated organisation of a force that was by tradition an age-old guardian, to snatch from it the necessary weapons which were dedicated to public order . . .

Johnny went down into the town again and always at night at the exact time when night was born, but he did not see Monti or Corradi again and perhaps did not even seek them out. One of these nights he was irresistibly drawn to the cinema and went in with a certain presentiment of *mettle.* They were showing *Blind Venus* with Viviane Romance, still in *sexy shape* flanked by the intolerable, alien and serious face of Georges Flamant. The place with the usual air of decay that went with any management, with a dusty shabbiness even on the screen, was almost deserted and in the intervals of light the scanty audience looked at each other *frowningly* as if reproving each other for this folly of the cinema under the threat of Graziani's proclamations.

Johnny was sitting in the balcony, high above the scanty stalls. At the point where the storm and the sexual fury of Captain Flamant die away together there was a desperate *stampede* in the foyer, a suffocated, desperate intake of breath, a harsh voice of command and ferocity, something akin to the dull explosion of a sudden outbreak of violence. A spectator got up with an immense noise, shouted 'Fascists' who had burst in to carry out a search, threw himself at a wall, at a barred safety exit. The noise in the foyer continued but they had not yet burst into the auditorium now deserted by those who had slipped through the safety exits which were actually down there and Johnny thought in agony at the mischance of having chosen the shut and locked balcony rather than the safe haven of the stalls. The others were furiously attacking the walls and the door, which held out, thundering under their blows. The projectionist had cut the film without turning on the light in the auditorium. Johnny found himself

21

up against the parapet above the distant stalls which awaited him with death among the seats or with frightening, equally capturing, equally *death-sentencing-and-allowing* fractures. But he had decided to jump rather than allow himself to be taken. He had straddled the parapet and found himself headlong over the terrible and rescuing floor, with its terrifying mouth with its teeth of iron and stone and wood. But he did not loosen his hand from the last piece of iron because it was not the Fascists but only some sort of attempt to rob the till. Everything that was sudden, treacherous, that exploded into shouts was Fascist.

Johnny left the cinema at a run imagining himself to be mortally pale and feeling like *jelly*. He took his way up the hill, angry with himself, *remorseful* as far as his parents were concerned, all along the steep path, mentally dismembering the body of Viviane Romance who now seemed to him to be a filthy alluring bloody Fascist. He would not go down into town again, he thought as he climbed the hill in the violet night, if he will leave the hill it will be only to climb a higher one to the archangelic realm of the partisans.

III

The pistol he certainly had. Yet feeling it flat and heavy and so magisterially shaped in his inside pocket he did not at all feel that something had been added to him, and he felt it to be alien and irritating and by no means the solidly cast weapon of his dream. He went along the semi-deserted tedious streets; now people of his acquaintance no longer stared at him – neither at him nor the other deserters or draft-dodgers – in the friendly, thoughtful recriminatory way of the first few times, now they stared at him with boredom and distance, with the air of 'have it your own way so long as you keep it well away from me' – so he walked along thinking of nothing but where to hide it till the great day came since it had never formed part of his thought – nor perhaps his abilities – to have to use it now, at the first corner. Yet he walked with a new feeling, a feeling of being different from everyone he met; the chance was a thousand to one that none of them travelled with a pistol over their hearts, their hearts beating as if astonished against its flat and icy surface, and it seemed to him that this abstract and hidden hardness of the pistol and its fatal nature must be reflected in his walk and his face. He must 'look' different. But then when his alert state of mind reminded him that it was simply a matter of transporting a weapon from one hiding-place to another, the difference vanished like an extinguished light and he appeared to himself as grey and passive as the reflection of everything else in the late-November afternoon.

He turned off towards the outskirts of the town and then straight to the river: he wanted wanted to go halfway down the bank between the bridge and the white rocks to smoke a cigarette (the last of the afternoon's programme), kneeling in the grass which was already withered, his eyes piercing the invulnerable veil of the waters. But when he *stepped* on the farthest part of the bank the mangled bridge, its laceration still fresh and, as it were, bleeding in the cast-iron sky that was immediately close, irresistibly attracted his eyes. And so too the sight of the new ferry at work. So he went up river to within some fifty paces of the ferry landing-stage.

There were people on the pale shingle, which was unusually dirty, because of the fascinating and suspenseful novelty of the ferry, seemingly breathing with anxious throats little gulps of medieval air. The ferrymen worked with composure and emphasis, with identical self-satisfaction, and with the same self-satisfaction those ferried across disembarked as if from a singular adventure. Johnny piled himself a seat of stones, round stones splashed with exsiccated mud, sat there and lit his cigarette: he would make it last as long as possible, he would smoke it at the same slow pace as was everywhere – in the passing of the waters, in the work of the ferry, in the passing of the labile clouds in the dilapidated sky. And he watched till the air was so hazy that the very precise though truncated bulk of the bridge had a completely blurred outline as if pitying that great wound and the evening air began to ripple and accelerate the dark water and make the overhanging poplars groan.

There were few people left now with Johnny, lingering on the grey-coloured shore, and in a lull in the wind the silence was such that one clearly perceived the loud splash – almost *slamming* – of the midstream water of the river against the red anti-rust sides of the ferry as it floated along. When on the road beyond the river they heard, with a deceptive fluidity and tenuousness of sound, the noise of a longish convoy of trucks. It was difficult to count them exactly because of the screen of poplars but there were more than twenty trucks and their colour as well as the colour of the men mounted on them, like the way they flowed, was German. Two or three people on this side of the river recognised them, *scrambled off to the town*, the pebbles of the shore leaping away centrifugally beneath their mordant and hasty steps. Then a man who was standing near Johnny got up slowly – some kind of worker of indefinable age, with on his head a beret which seemed to have been squeezed there at birth so closely did it fit him with greasy precision and irremovability, came closer and said: 'But are they mad over there to run away like that? Don't they know yet that the Germans fire at anyone who runs away?'

Johnny said – but with a frightened lack of interest: 'That's true – it's better to stay where you are, play it that way . . .' He felt warm on his face the worker's appreciative and at the same time perplexed glance. But on the other bank the Germans did nothing at all as if the people on the opposite bank, centrifugally scattered, had not entered their field of vision; they seemed intent, touristically, on the sight of the bombed bridge and the ferry immobile in the middle of the river, Johnny could gather from a distance the anguished suspense in the minds and muscles of the *aware* ferrymen and ferry-passengers. A youth lost his head and dived off the craft feet first then emerged and swam with ease in the main current, following it into the distance, as if he did not yet consider it safe to land on the shingle occupied by Johnny. Then in a murmur the worker at least advised stooping down a little and he and Johnny squatted on the shore, indeed the worker lit half a cigarette and smoked it hiding it in his cupped hand as if not to be caught redhanded. The Germans continued their contemplation and there was no sign in their distant gestures of irritation at the unexpected obstacle but only a contemplative air, that of tourists. 'If the Germans were coming our way, thank God for the English who wrecked the bridge,' said the workman. Then Johnny turned his gaze to the far end of the *mainstream*; the man who had escaped by swimming was already on land far away, *scrambling* on the last visible stretch of shore towards the dark of the woods on the banks. Now the Germans had started up their engines which had a hint of mystery about them, the enmity and the strangeness even in the vibrations of the engines both Johnny and the workmen felt, and then they set off again just like tourists who have completed an artistic visit according to programme. And it was very soon that they saw the tail of the convoy on the open road going towards Turin. Everything moved – people and the ferry and the air itself as if coming to after a hibernation. Johnny got up as did the workman somewhat rheumatically saying: 'They weren't after us. They stopped to look at the bridge – the result of their enemies, the English. But they're going to have to come sooner or later – they're certain to come overland.' He had along with the air of a town-bred mechanic a certain all-enduring air, a kind of invincibility, such a certain presage of spring that follows winter, that Johnny was grateful to him. But when the man made a sign to leave together for the town (the invitation was in his walk not spoken in words) Johnny shook his head, said with a grating voice that he had to go south. And did so circling round the widest part of the town on the banks of the river and then taking it from the south; seemingly comatose in the dusk, with a squat look jellified by fear, like his old uncle, as if only now assailed by the echo of that sudden German apparition. The very bulk of the Romanesque campanile of the cathedral *looked jelly and under height-level* no longer the eternal token of general survival and on the fading clock-face the hands, the shadow of the hands said six.

He went back home; his parents were already eating supper, on the stairs he heard the (dejected) rattle of the cutlery. His father confined himself to shaking his head at his rashness but his mother attacked him for this way of exposing himself to perdition with voluntary heedlessness and then Johnny discovered the only way to calm her, instead of minimising the danger, he said calmly: 'I saw the Germans.' The couple remained with their cutlery in the air far from their melancholy meal. 'They were a whole convoy, they stopped for a good twenty minutes on the other side of the bridge. They did absolutely nothing.' 'And where were you?' swallowing down their astonishment that the Germans did nothing. 'At the river – on this side.'

He prepared to eat with the least desire in the world. His father said that his friend Bonardi at his ex-petrol pump on the northern edge of the town had a nocturnal visit from the partisans. They were looking for fuel, they contented themselves with two half demijohns of solvent which was simply all his friend possessed. 'What were they like?' asked Johnny with his heart in his mouth. Everything was possible except that they should be men like everyone else. His father reported with his voice more muffled that they were dressed in white, all wearing the blouses of Alpini ski-troops. 'They must be stragglers from the 4th Army – people who couldn't or didn't want to get home. And according to Bonardi they are no angels. They wouldn't believe that he had no petrol and threatened and ill-treated him. Bonardi says they frightened him as much or more than the Fascists and Germans.' He shook his head. 'There will be violence on both sides and we are all at sea.' And then Johnny thought of the desperate sadness of being old like his father and Bonardi, old and white-haired and rusty men amid the unleashing of agile, proud and ferocious youth such as they were in the prehistoric spring of 1915.* He simply could not bear the idea induced in him of his father caught in that maelstrom and threatened and ill-treated whether by one side or the other. He looked at his head drooping over his plate in desolate recognition of age.

His mother mentioned the oath of allegiance to the Republic.** Some people had already taken it, a pure formality – a trip by train to the headquarters in Bra, the oath, a handshake, all in an atmosphere devoid of virulence – one of strict comradeship, in complete *fair play*. Some people had already taken it, that was something one knew in spite of opportunistic secrecy: a lawyer, the head of an elementary school, a surveyor with the prospect of a Todt† contract. 'They can go to hell if they are expecting an oath from me,' said Johnny *out of his munched bread*. But his mother said tonelessly: 'I didn't tell you to advise you to take that road. Besides it doesn't apply to you yet. Up to now they want the oath from officers. And you didn't make it to officer.'

'What are you going to do now?' they asked when they saw him rise. He replied that he was going to look around for Professor Monti. 'I really have to keep up some contacts, something is coming to a head and it is impossible – and illogical – to keep to oneself,' and then he was going to sleep but in the bed in his house. His parents' heads drooped over their plate but they did not react, they were abandoning themselves to the vortex of chance.

The moment he went out a hard pressure on his chest reminded him of the pistol. He turned round to get home and hide it but did not do so because of *puzzlement* about its hiding-place which was not to be solved rapidly and so he kept it on him. It seemed it must give him a *grim thrill* that would make his depressing nocturnal wanderings tolerable. *He was not quite sure to meet Monti, to be willing to meet Monti.* In the shadow he passed a town policeman, so

---

* The date of Italy's entry into World War I.
** The Republic of Salò – Mussolini's puppet government in the town of Salò on Lake Garda.
† The Organisation Todt – the German agency used for the construction of fortifications.

miserable in his useless uniform, and so conscious of it, with in his *unofficial* (almost furtive) walk all the consciousness of his miserable uselessness.

He went to the Albergo Nazionale which he knew the professor had fallen back on after the Germans sporadically *haunted* the *main hotel* in cold that seemed to erode the paint. But he found Monti first, on that very same street, he recognised him in the dark by his shuffling gait due to his arthritis, which was exacerbated by the first cold snaps. And he was accompanied, a tall and slim young man, very mechanical and compact in the way he moved his arms and legs. It was Sicco and he was moving his pipe, which had gone out, from one corner of his mouth to the other. 'And Corradyev?' whispered Johnny. 'He's away already – near Bra – to organise his red group.'* Johnny's heart gave a leap, immediately repressed by the compact chill of the pistol. But for Sicco he would perhaps have talked about his pistol – even shown it. Monti said: 'But for this damned arthritis of mine I would have been with him this evening already. With my prejudicial distinction still holding good. But the interesting thing is to begin to fight, then later we'll see. I have to wait till the spring,' and he said it as if it were the first spring after *Doomsday*, 'always provided that I get reasonably better in the leg.' 'Why over towards Bra?' Johnny inquired, his mind returning to those places seen and passed through so often on the way to Turin and back, the red hills on the left of the highway, good soil for limekilns, all in cliffs and *canyons*, clad on top by a green that burnt as brightly as if the red beneath trebled the brilliance of the green giving a compounded *eye-catching* spectacle of masked earth. 'Anywhere is good, Johnny. When I go there I shall make for the Langhe.** Maybe because my father's people come from there.'

The professor announced that Sicco had something interesting to say and more to do. And Sicco began to speak, he would certainly speak with his syllabled precision and a terrible economy of gesture, something goose-like in the rhythmical jerks of his thin neck. He said: 'Tomorrow with the first train I am going to Bra to take my oath like a good boy . . . Wait before you insult me, Johnny. With the

* A Communist group.
** A hilly zone in Piedmont which became a famous centre of partisan activity.

afternoon train I shall be in Como and will obtain a bilingual permit and Ausch . . .' 'Auschlanding,'* Monti corrected. 'Armed with that I shall start to act for the Committee of Liberation as representative of the Liberal Party.' 'Good,' said Johnny and 'Good,' said Monti adding: 'You people on the Committee will have terrible moments – of a kind not even the fighting partisans will have.' Sicco nodded modestly, barely closing his lips on the mouthpiece of his pipe, he seemed ready for those moments without the least apparent apprehension.

Then Monti lamented the effect of the cold on his legs, *the black, houndlike mute of cold raiding the frosty pavé* and Sicco proposed that they withdraw to a little out of the way café which was fairly safe but, as he himself admitted, not very attractive, dirty, with a few card-players who played with ferocious determination with the gaps on the shelves grinning sarcastically. And then Monti with a wonderful shift of *humour* proposed the elegant brothel as the most advisable *hall* in order to exchange some liberating small talk with the meretricious Aspasias,** 'the most loyal women in the world', without the least preoccupation with sex. The other two went along with this. Sicco only begging them not to stay too long because he had to take the first train in the *appalling earliness* of tomorrow morning. What brought him closer to Johnny – infinitely more than in the past – was the quiet sober way he looked forward to the oath, the certainty that he would preserve the same polite and distant air in front of the Fascist officers who would receive his oath, thus providing him with the tools most adapted for the better carrying out of his voluntary anti-Fascist task. Monti said: 'And there won't even be any need to be too frightened about being trapped in the brothel. If the Fascists arrive, I am of the opinion that they won't do anything to us, the brothel solidarity of Italian males will prevail and we will end up by forming a nice collective group outside of and beyond all politics.' Laughing they went to the elegant brothel.

It was completely deserted and with no hope of customers – so much so that the young ladies were completely and normally dressed in ordinary clothes and were playing poker and smoking in

* There is no such word in German.
** Aspasia – the famous Athenian courtesan.

the dining-room. The Milanese lady of the house greeted Johnny warmly, paid her moderate respects to the professor and quite coldly to Sicco who never stopped sucking at his little cold pipe. She was clearly worried by the turn things had taken but the very nobility and antiquity of her profession seemed to inspire her to reticence and dignity in her jeremiad until at the end she allowed herself to express her feelings in the same sweeping terms and with the same abandon as any small shopkeeper facing a crisis. The first extremely severe blow had come with the armistice and the disbanding of the armed forces, no more gentlemen officers, no more NCOs; the second and more serious one, not so much in its volume as in its trend, the decline in visits from civilians. 'They are finding it elsewhere, they are finding it elsewhere as never before!' she complained. 'The war's to blame. And no one thinks of morals any more, there's no religion any more and all of them – girls and married women. Out there there's free love and any amount of it. And we are making do . . .' 'With each other,' Monti concluded.

The women did not appear demoralised, they were playing with *souple* nonchalance, smoking with rapid short puffs like little pecks, only occasionaly darting sideways entirely unintentional glances at the guests. Until Sicco dropped his pipe, got up to his full height and gave a sign to the blonde at the head of the table. 'Forgive the breach of convention,' he said, 'but – but the fact is that they've got so many clothes on.' 'I understand and excuse you,' said Monti, 'it could be the last time.' And Johnny added: 'The embrace in the shadow of the guillotine. *With the big blonde.*'

The small one with the dark hair, the tiniest and least professional of the two left over, laid down her cards and produced a packet of R6. The murderous sideways glance of her companion cut short her offering gesture. Monti said: 'You're smoking German stuff' lightly. And then her companion exploded – a big clean-cut Venetian with eyes that were by nature excited. 'She has a boy-friend in the Republic,* she has.' 'Whore,' said Johnny with a liquid smile, very gracefully. And the Venetian girl made a move to hit her with the back of her hand. The madame intervened with an outburst soon reaching a high *pitch*: 'Young ladies, don't let's start again. Stop it, you cows.

* Mussolini's Republic of Salò.

You're here to work. It's not having anything to do that puts these silly ideas in your heads.'

The girl from Venice said: 'I saw her friend, I did, there's no use her saying no. At the station in Bra, changing trains. A shit-face. I've never seen the likes of him and I've seen a few in my thirteen years. He fancied himself – thought he was tough, always with his hand on his revolver half out of its holster. Next time tell him to put the pistol away but not so far that you can't pull the trigger.'

The brunette held her head low offering it to the smoke emerging from her cigarette as if in a sacrificial inhalation and fear visibly shook her thin shoulders. 'What gets up my nose,' the big one went on, 'is that I was friend and protector to her, I took her into my bed every night and cuddled her for hours. You know about it,' she said to the madame, 'you always suspected something. And this creature has a friend in the Republic. But the day will soon come when a partisan will rub him out. Yes, yes, I'm not afraid that you'll report me because I'll always manage to take you by the crotch and split you open to the top of your head like a piece of wood.' Johnny looked at Monti because of the shadowy signal which reached him from his hand that was now suspended in the halo of the lamp. 'Ladies! Ladies! I am one who goes about crying Peace Peace. The vagina must not be the victim of any tragedy. One cannot command the vagina to have responsibilities nor can they be attributed to it. My prayer is that this special war, which will see endless deaths of every kind, will come to a conclusion at least without anyone having to die because of her vagina. God grant that the slaughter may be only of men and that the vaginas may with impunity, without discrimination, fortify the combatants, comfort those about to die, and be at the last the victors' total prize.'

'Disgusting!' the Venetian girl summed up looming over the silent and pained brunette like a fleshy boulder. And the madame, grateful to the professor, said: 'The professor, because he is a professor, has spoken like a book. Just think about your work and your earnings, that thing you have has nothing to do with politics and pricks don't wear uniforms. If you have ideas, keep them to yourselves.'

The Venetian said no more, merely repeated the gesture of a slap with the back of her hand but this time with a certain tenderness in the way it remained suspended, a particular care, which indicated

31

that that very night she would take her into her bed again and cuddle her until the dawn. But at that very moment they noticed that Sicco and the blonde girl had come down a few minutes before and the girl said with an uneducated and *faltering* voice: 'I always pray for the partisans. Every evening I say a prayer for the partisans,' and at her clear statement there was a quivering and something like a flutter of wings in the close still atmosphere of the brothel. And Johnny felt that it was painful not to be a partisan yet and to be excluded from the fruition of the whore's prayer.

They shook hands before separating, Monti to his philosophical vigil, Sicco to his short perhaps nightmarish sleep that must be cut short at five in the morning for the icy and smoky station and for the train that was to bring him face to face with the Fascist officers, who were as mythical as their partisan antagonists.

Johnny left for a gloomy night leading to a *goalless*, empty and quivering day that would not end. In the heavy sky where the stars were pricked out as if on velvet a plane was groaning with an infinite awareness of its minuscule size, constantly on the edge of a crash. It was the plane of unknown nationality perhaps *waged* and piloted by a modern aeronautical Captain Nemo* which, popular rumour said, machine-gunned all the lights that broke the blackout, in a fanatical insistence on absolute darkness.

* The commander of the vessel in Jules Verne's *20,000 Leagues under the Sea*.

IV

Next day early in the morning Johnny went up into the attic to bury the pistol, his brain *sickening* as he imagined how long it would remain buried. As he climbed up the inaccessible treacherous little stair to the gloomy corrugated slope of the low roofs, he thought back to his childhood when the attic was the most satisfying and adventurous of his *indoor resorts*. The musky overhang of the roof, the barrier of beams and joists, the very coarseness of the walls, the dense, undisturbed population of wasps and beetles, the presence here and there of tin and sheeting as part of a general armour-plating, the still and tepid air shot through with the buzz of the wasps as if swarms of arrows had been let loose, the absence and the downright unthinkability of women, all contributed then to make him think of and see the attic as a congenial setting for adventure or at least as one place in the world where there was nothing else to do but be vigilant and fight. Sometimes he installed himself in the guttering of the dormer window giddily high above the cemetery dominating the massive walls of the cathedral and with overwhelming ease imagined himself, identified himself with a defender (his congenital Hectorean preference for the defence) who from a vantage-point repelled a multiple assault. He could, all things considered, think of firing at and killing white men but it was something that cost him a twinge of conscience which in the end had a negative effect on his aim; then he went on to the Redskins and the Afrian negroes but things still weren't perfect and *heart-setting quiet*, and were only set right by the application to the assailants of the most vivid and atrocious *warpaints*. But now it's a question of whites, he said, while he placed the pistol wrapped in cottonwool and cardboard in the hollow of a beam and covered over the filling without apprehension

– indeed rather with a certain kind of pleasure inspired by his imagination as a handyman. But it was all poisoned for him by the thought that he was burying a pistol which he would find useful some day or other.

In the attic there was an abstract and artificial void – the cold of a refrigerator. He came down the little stairs again recalling how accurately the steps had fitted his childish steps; now during the descent his foot hesitated because of the slight difference of height in each one of them and their headlong steepness.

His father had just come back from shopping with the air of a housewife at once depressed and stubborn. His mother was unwell, the world war seemed to lie heavily on her liver; she hardly moved about any more, she hardly did anything any longer without keeping her tightly shut hand on her incurable side. But today his parents' depression was abysmal, all-embracing, defying all attempts at concealment. Johnny wanted to hear from his mother for he felt an aprioristic irritation at his father's narrative slowness, which was at once constitutional and intentional, and at his unconscious hermeneutic methods. Today his mother was struck *speechless* by something other than the pangs of hepatitis. Now his father's handsome, expressionless face was opening up for a revelation. 'Last evening you saw a column of Germans, you said.' 'I saw it and told you so.' 'And do you know where they were going? You don't know? To B . . . You went through B once with us when you were little when we had the 509 . . .' 'And what did the Germans do in B . . .?' 'A reprisal.'

For the few deaths that the partisans had inflicted on them from positions among the boulders round the village, next day they had burnt, killed, rounded up, pillaged . . . 'Two priests as well – one of them in a burst of fire into the flames which would have killed him anyway.'

For Johnny the vision of the day before, emerging sharply, became horribly blurred, while the sight of the authors of the reprisal was still very sharp as they looked quietly out over the sides of their trucks, gazing at the landscape like tourists during this unprogrammed twilight stop. And his parents' crystal clear inclination to curse *in primis** those heedless partisan marksmen playing at fighting the

* Latin – first and foremost.

Germans was horrible. His mother began painfully to sort out the shopping. 'Not even God will keep them away from us, Johnny, go back to the hill at once.'

Something happened very soon, in the first days of December, even if it was something that was half diplomacy and half violence. That day Johnny was fortunately out of the house at his cousin's to relieve him marginally from the killing boredom of a reclusion that was strictly invigilated; his uncle was strangely, morbidly unapprehensive, absorbed in his hundredth re-reading of the unabridged *Les Misérables*, the only constant theme which took him back – him the retired, conservative businessman – to his betrayed left-wing socialist youth. They were looking through the misted windows down the frozen-hard slope, as far as the pale walls of the town, the box of the radio shaking, waiting as if mesmerised for the Voice of America; every so often the uncle raised his enormous head from the worn pages of his book of books and announced in a voice tremulous with admiration for the previous century and irritation with the present: 'Victor Hugo. Writers like that were born only in my day –' and the two cousins hastened to say they agreed *to stop him not to break* the buzzing activity of their brains which were overall and overempty.

Everything happened in those moments which were at once somnolent and neurotic within the cubic confines of the city. To apply Graziani's proclamation in part a strong body of armed Republicans arrived suddenly from Cuneo to arrest those draft-dodgers who had not even deigned to reply to the proclamation. In view of their absence, which was both to be expected and complete, and finding it desperately necessary not to let things slide with all the immense consequences for the future, they extended the political responsibility for the distant draft-dodgers to their parents at home and with the help of sullen and terrified carabinieri took the members of their families to the local prison, *dozens of them*, and then awaited the inevitable result of psycho-sentimental pressure. In the early afternoon the Republicans left the cowed city, leaving the responsibility for the detention with the local carabinieri reinforced by a squad detached from Bra.

At about six o'clock a letter penned in Johnny's mother's elementary ataraxic hand arrived at the house in the country. He absolutely was not to stir, not come down into the town which was terrified but seething, the carabinieri terrified and yet very tough, and to ask his aunt for hospitality until further notice.

Johnny at once went downhill in the serotine shadows with the excitement of drawing close to the great mystery box of agitation. The trees planted round the walls were shaking unnaturally with a terrible stormy sound. Behind him he heard a hasty step on the asphalt and turned towards it. It was Luciano who had escaped from home, he too seeking to regain his stature as a man; he was at his side in a second, silent, determined and faithful. The others had broken the rules of the game, a whole age-old code; they were going to see what was happening, to protest, to wipe out the infraction.

The streets on the periphery were absolutely deserted and silent, but from the centre of the town there filtered through a confused hum, like something fermenting, and yet extremely heartening. And it was mysterious and heartening to retrace the footsteps of the Fascists on the town's cobbles. Awareness of the inevitable use of force completely possessed them, rope-strong, cheering, toughening. Johnny was furious at the thought of his buried pistol, which he could recover only from behind his parents' threatening and tearful blockade. His cousin said: 'I have my service pistol.'

In the streets of the centre a flickering, fencing, rat-like movement of people – all of them young. They joined up with them, no face particularly well known, but all youths and townspeople; they were angry with the carabinieri on whom they heaped all the epithets and insults of popular tradition, adding a new one, infinitely more weighty: 'Traitors'. Almost everyone had a weapon, pistols big and small, very modern ones and bits of ironmongery, and some displayed at their backs the bubonic deformation of the hand-grenade. The immediate understanding, an understanding of the blood, that went beyond the shouts and hates, was intoxicating. The oldest of them, well under fifty at any event, while all the others *planned* the attack on the prison and the liberation one way or another of their imprisoned family members, continued to curse the carabinieri, with a congenital hatred for all police forces but with a cheerful feel like shouting at a fair.

Everyone was talking at the same time and yet everything miraculously flowed together in a rapid, perfect accord. The majority were armed with family heirlooms or with the earth-covered legacy of the 4th Army in its torrential flight. In the square the commander of the town police rose up, fat, given to hypertension and cross-eyed, slow-footed in his shuffling high boots, all his badges of rank gleaming in the falling night. He raised a hand and said with the most paternal of voices: 'Disperse, boys. Boys, listen to me, disperse. It isn't an order, you understand, it is advice from the father of a family. Go home, boys.' A general laugh of complete hilarity shot through slightly with a certain vein of rancour answered him but the man staggered under it: the nice man who handed out fines at the football matches, the prince of the town police force such as it was, interposed his *petty* uniform as a *stop* to anyone who might spit in a determined way on braid worthy of a general. The insult gave strength to his voice and re-established his *staggering* figure a little, suggested to him a half-command in place of the advice he had uttered: but then from the nocturnal group there emerged a boy – certainly a rat from the working-class houses (that mixture of lazzaret and casbah by the malodorous stream) – out in front of him there stuck an incredibly big nineteenth-century pistol which, when the hammer was cocked, gave an exaggerated, chilling click. The stripling pointed it at the official solar plexus, ordered him to about-turn, *marshalled him* with the pistol in the small of his back up to the doors of the town hall, stuck him in the guardhouse (that *remembrance* of the air-raid wardens) – 'And don't you dare stick your nose out again.' Everyone gave a brief dry laugh; now it was the turn of the carabinieri.

They marched on the barracks, without ever turning round, with marvellous indifference about their own numbers. People leant out of doors and windows, irresistibly dislodged from a morbid and voluntary lethargy dating from 8 September. From every door young people joined up with the great mainstream, older people approved in *grim* silence, others counselled prudence and cunning with prudent and cunning voices. In the main square other groups were advancing from the cardinal points of the compass, they flowed together and coagulated in silent synchrony. The boy who came alongside Johnny's elbow shouldered a hunting rifle of great value and Johnny was once more overcome with rage at his absurdly concealed pistol.

They took up all the last street before the barracks, at once elastic and compact, their outer edges skirting the empty spaces, almost touching the faces (casting glances, sexually excited) of the women at the windows. A boy, at the head of them all, marched along brandishing a megaphone.

The barracks was set jewel-like in a compact block but now looked like the most solitary building in the world, a lunar fortress, black and close-sealed, and its sombre shadow was sharply projected in macabre fragments on the street which was white in the December moon. They arrayed themselves in front of it, packed together and bottled up in the four metres of the street, which was suddenly closed off at the end by the palisade of the football ground. Finding, consolidating his place or *footholding*, Johnny thought that if the carabinieri were to fire a volley under the impulse of hate or fear there would be a massacre. And Luciano said so in a loud, unflawed adult voice. But no one commented or moved away, each of them in that cul-de-sacked phalanx. Meanwhile the unknown boy had already put the megaphone to his mouth, raising it like a weapon against the thick railing in front of the façade of the barracks ringing its *front-garden* – an absurd and unexpected green beauty spot on its grim face.

'Carabinieri!'

The voice rebounded from the walls and the gratings on the windows – more lethal and terrifying than a point-blank volley, the megaphone amplified the boy's voice, distorted its power. But a perfect silence isolated and fortified the barracks even more.

'Roy-al Carabinieri!'*

Once more no reply came but from the blind gratings one could guess at weapons traversing like branches in the wind.

'Carabinieri, I am speaking to you. I know you can hear me. Carabinieri. It was a disgusting trick by the Fascists, you know it as well as us and we only want to wipe it out. Come on, carabinieri, give us the answer we are expecting.'

Nothing, still nothing, until a boy lost patience and slung a hand-grenade over the railing, aiming at the barracks wall. But it fell far

---

* The Carabinieri Reali had the king as their supreme commander and therefore technically at least did not come directly under the Fascist regime.

short, it struck a young cherry-tree in the garden with a red halo so that it appeared momentarily as if under X-rays. Then from a minaret of the barracks there came a burst of machine-gun fire, warning, high, which splattered against the distant wall of the football ground. They *dropped* in the very white, frozen dust. A man snatched the megaphone from the boy, slipped along in the shelter of the little wall of the enclosure, flourishing the megaphone on high like a periscope. His voice was adult and not even the distortion of the megaphone robbed it of its innate dialectic, of its native diplomacy.

'Carabinieri, you want to seal your fate. The machine-gun didn't affect us one way or the other. We aren't little boys – we are PARTISANS, partisans from the mountains, who've come down into town to wipe out the blot – we too have machine-guns, carabinieri, and cannons and an armoured car. If you force us to attack we'll finish things off in a minute. But then you'll have no more excuses. Got it, carabinieri? We are partisans. Among us there are carabinieri too, your fellow-soldiers.' He finished and turned round with an anxious face, amazingly asking for a judgment on his bluff.

They heard the silence crackling, the electric sizzling of the atoms of the silence, then they heard a click at the door of the barracks and what came out was a figure rendered almost invisible by the intensity of the moonlight. He was carrying an electric torch, with it he illuminated his whole person to show his officer's uniform; with a desperate crackling of gravel he advanced to the fence. The man with the megaphone went towards him. They could hear him speaking undecipherably but toughly, they saw him roughly hold back the officer when he advanced towards the group. Their words came across dry and incomprehensible like gusts of wind from the marsh. They were unable to come to an agreement because they parted in opposite directions with the rhythmic step of those about to duel. Turning round the man said at the top of his voice: 'All ready! Bring forward the armoured car!'

At the crisis of the bluff the carabinieri surrendered. The rebels invaded the garden, the carabinieri with no visible arms on them arranged themselves with feigned indolence against the barrack-wall, lighting cigarettes with angry unsteady hands. In a minute, in this glow of cigarettes, they became aware that it was not a case of real partisans from the mountains but kids, for the most part, kids in contravention of the law who would be terrified and wet their pants at a ferocious face and a loud voice, armed with ridiculous family relics. Then they sank their heads on their chests and kept them there but it was not sufficient to mask the shame and the rancour, the anguish of the bluff. Johnny who had *relented* at their fate as salaried defenders of law and order, hardened his heart again at that shameless revelation. But he intervened when one of his side, a man over thirty, attacked a carabiniere, smoking and miserable, like all the others, and gave him a punch and a kick. 'Leave him alone!' 'I gave it him for my father.' 'And what did I do to your father?' the carabiniere lamented. 'You did nothing. But other carabinieri, carabinieri like you, arrested him for a theft he did not commit and to make him confess beat him on the chest with little sandbags. From that day he didn't stop coughing till he died!'

It was something that struck Johnny like a dagger, making him appear to himself as a man not of flesh and blood but of cardboard from the pages of books. But there was no more time, *all-calling* the bulk of the people made towards the prison with as a nucleus the officer and three carabinieri. The officer walked as if blind, as if he of necessity had to trust himself to the guidance of the grip in which he was firmly incorporated, and was already gasping noisily.

Up to now it had all looked like an everyday event: a gang of boys in a certain town had played merry hell solely and simply to set right a nasty situation in the above-mentioned town, but more than halfway to the prison they struck up with prodigious spontaneity and synchronicity the *Hymn of Mameli** as if to announce themselves from afar to the prisoners and the warders. After a while the carabinieri too joined the chorus but perhaps they were moving their mouths soundlessly.

They blocked the alley between the prison and the nearby church, continuing the hymn, hearing it taken up and repeated from within the walls, while the officer knocked at the nail-studded door. The warders were not to be persuaded not even after examining the officer through the spy-hole: they thought they had to read the opposite from what the officer said under the pressure of the pistol.

---

* A patriotic song dating from the Risorgimento, written by Goffredo Mameli, who fell fighting the Austrians.

The hymn died away hoarsely to give way in the throats to a shout of impatience. The warders opened up, squeezing themselves against the walls so as not to be overrun by the triumphant *stampede*, the dozens of prisoners were already gathered in the grim courtyard and on the stairs out of disgust with their cells and their poor state. They embraced and kissed each other. 'Johnny, kiss my mother, please, because I want to see you do it,' said one of the draft-dodgers. Johnny did so while claps rained on his back. All those set free were careful to say loudly that the warders had been good and kind, understanding and very humane. With a strangled voice the officer said to everyone and no one in particular: 'Watch out, for goodness' sake, watch out that the common prisoners don't get out!' The prison guards, whining, wagging their tails, little sweating men from the South, slipped out and in all directions, taking advantage of territory familiar to them from which the majority were precluded, their hands clasped, cursing their duty and orders, blessing the idea and the event and those taking part, *snivellingly* begging those who spoke in dialect to express themselves in Italian *for their ears' sake*.

Against the saltpetrous and evil-smelling wall one of them was talking: 'It had to be done and was well done. But there will be consequences. The Fascists cannot overlook it or they're lost. We must expect a large-scale reprisal within twenty-four hours. They can't do anything to the officer but you can take an oath that back in the barracks he'll be on the phone and making his good little report to the Fascists.' They looked at him out of the corner of their eyes, exhausted, drooping, unmartial, and felt that he would gather his last energies to do just that. 'It's best if everyone goes and sleeps in the hills or at the very least finds somewhere else to stay.' And to keep out of sight all day tomorrow.

It was all over, there were few of them left now, straining to hear the departing, *subsiding* paeans of victory and of liberty. They left the narrow courtyard so that the gate could shut on the common criminals and the warders. *They tottered a little* with pleasant weariness after the first great revolt. It had really been a great shake-up and the officer had been the portrait of an Italy erect and indestructible for centuries. Incredible but true. 'I'd come with you for a little, but I'm tired,' said his cousin. 'Come tomorrow and spend all day at my place on the hill.'

He went homewards more slowly than he had ever walked with a fatigue upon him and within him which forced him to smile, abundantly, stupidly. In the proud cold of the Northern December he moved as if encapsulated in a bell-jar with the temperature of last May. At home he drank a glass of water in one breath, its coldness revived him completely as if from an agitated sleep. In the corridor he was met by the breathing of his parents, alternating, smooth. He stopped and stood for a long time under the spell of their gentle nocturnal breathing, 'I have never listened to their breathing, that breathing which one day will die away.' They were sleeping so well while he lived his life and attacked the public forces of law and order and their buildings, practically armed, the better armed when and where unarmed. He could rely on the soundness of his father's sleep but not on that of his mother always sleeping with one eye open. In fact she called to him at the door of their bedroom; without rising she asked him what had gone on, she had heard a great shouting, great singing and clapping, but perhaps it had been an illusion. 'What happened?' 'Nothing happened.' 'And yet –' 'If anything happened we'll know tomorrow.' 'Tomorrow morning –' 'If you sleep tomorrow morning will be there in a minute.'

He lay down feeling himself weigh on the yielding bed as never before, never as at that moment did he have the clear (plastic) sensation of his enormous weight, of his terrifying concreteness as a man.

In the morning the whole town was talking about the forceful action of the previous evening and as if the stimulated fantasy prevailed all the merit and responsibility were attributed to authenic (however phantom) partisans from the mountains, actually equipped with an armoured car (who had not seen it standing dynamically static at the gates of the town with its gun traversing?) and headed by officers from the Alpine troops – among them a certain Lieutenant Johnny. 'Were you there?' asked his mother but with the slightest note of interrogation. Johnny waved his hand to indicate the trifling nature of his intervention and his scepticism about the consequences. At that moment the town's chief bailiff, a man of the old ecclesiastical school, very clever and prudent and balanced, who was only waiting for everything to come to an end in order to refound the branch of the PP.* He wanted to speak to

* PP – Partito Popolare, the Catholic party suppressed by Mussolini in 1926.

Johnny's father but had no difficulty in speaking in the presence of the whole family, such a distinguished and admirable and . . . unfortunate family. The bottle of rhubarb cordial shook and tinkled in his mother's hand when the old man spelt out 'unfortunate' but now the old man smiled and excused himself with a wave of his white hand. He said they must expect a reprisal for the events of the evening and he knew that the reprisal would be turned into the simultaneous taking as hostages, for an indeterminate time, of a score of citizens. The list had been drawn up and handed to the appropriate person by the old Fascist lawyer Cerutti before enlisting in the far-off black brigade* in which he was renewing his youth. Everything was arranged, he knew the time when the various arresting squads would set out. 'Very well, thank you, but –' said Johnny's father impenetrably. 'You are the fifth on the list,' the bailiff then said but with a voice that minimised things, 'Me!' 'My husband!' 'My father?' 'Why?' 'Socialist.' 'Me!' 'My husband a Socialist!'

Johnny had an attack of hysterical laughter spilling over into enraged weeping. His father a Socialist! All right, according to his father, on the very few occasions when he had broached the assassination of Giacomo Matteotti,** it was something that had always stuck in his throat; the twilight portrait of the Martyr and 'the idea which does not die inside me' were perhaps the only things which from time to time had the enormous capacity of moving him fantastically but . . . Socialist! His father was struck dumb, perhaps merely concentrating on calling up in a distant mist the old vicious face of the lawyer, Cerutti, but his mother had an attack of deep anxiety and hepatitis. The bailiff intervened soothing and bland, his voice rendered more pleasing and cheerful by the rhubarb cordial. 'Please don't have an attack, for heaven's sake! It's not a trifle but not a tragedy either. Pay attention to me. Make the little sacrifice I commend to you. All three of you go up into the hills, to the little villa where your son found refuge after 8 September.' The three of them raised their heads together at this idea of his which was explained by his being the man from the diocese. 'It is very possible that you will

* The black brigades were the Fascist militia.
** Giacomo Matteotti, the Socialist leader and member of parliament murdered by Fascists in 1924.

43

have to stay there for not more than a week. Shut the house up well and I promise to come at once a day to see that nothing has happened to you. I promise.'

It was decided on the spot, his mother decided with her totalitarian faith in men who were para-ecclesiastical and who to her were the infallible masters of worldly wisdom. 'Only I and the vicar-general will know,' said the bailiff. 'It is my wish that the vicar-general should know too,' said his mother with her unconscious genius for protocol. 'I hope you may not have to stay more than a week but do not leave without my advice – wait for word from me,' and he eluded their thanks, recessionally.

Johnny recommended to his mother to take only snowboots: and intuition that was stronger than him uttered it but this was not a match to set alight the nitroglycerine of his mother's intuition, she was entirely deafened by her concentration on the programme of packing the suitcases. Johnny climbed lightly up into the attic and withdrew the pistol.

At one in the afternoon they were already on the hill after a quiet and tiring trip punctuated only by his mother's financial preoccupations. 'Our money is going much faster than expected.' His father said: 'You can make money again – no one has managed to make a new skin!' Said Johnny: 'Don't worry about the money. When it's all over I shall work. It should be all over by the summer.'

The little house had a new air, having gone wild. And everything around had an new feel, totally hiemal, the river and the plain and the hills, all presaging a cemetery without springtime resurrection. The town appeared through the unmoving vapours of the mist, greyish with apprehension, in the coma of black waiting. It had such a funereal aspect that it was a consolation to be out of it. As for Marida, their spots, the hedges and paths and the nooks in the hill:

> *When yellow leaves, or none or few, do hang*
> *Upon those boughs, which shake against the cold,*
> *Bare ruin'd choirs, where late the sweet birds sang . . .*

He felt sorry to see his mother with her hepatitis labouring to make a bed for him too – that bed which – but for self-betrayal at the last moment – he would never occupy. But could he tell her?

The afternoon and the evening rushed down, Niagara-like.

Everything died except the dark and the wind, a strong wind which sawed at his mother's nerves. She had a need for Radio London at once adrenalin-stimulating and stupefying, she had a crisis because of the lack of the radio. His father however was comfortably finding a place in the new psychological situation with his obscure and sinuous adaptability. They went to bed very early, his father rubbing his hands in an access of energetic physical euphoria and in a bath of inviolable safety, saying with an incredible voice rendered infantile and lilting: 'How lovely to lie in bed with that wind out there.'

Johnny had said he was going to stay for a little and read but when every noise died away *upstairs*, he set aside the book by Marlowe and *elbowed down* to write the letter, moved by its brevity and *business-likeness*. It was meant chiefly for his mother and was a hurt although a minor one; he could not even bear the thought of being present *de visu** at the duel in her between creative love and the possessive. It was *heartrending* to think what her morning would be like on the *dreary* hill faced by that letter (even if too short and distant) which would perhaps be her only *life-piece* for what remained of her life if for him . . . the adventure ended badly. Then he ran his finger over the page as if to leave a further sign of himself, for its certain opening by his mother later if . . . But his mother was a strong and brave woman and *mainly from her he knew to draw things for his opening adventure* and moreover a steep vein of religious pride.

For the last movements he trusted to his soft footfall, rigorously muted, a cultivated gift of his. Everything went well, the pistol already on his breast, but now monolithic, like a muscle incorporated in him and already active. Only his snowboots he went outside to pull on in the howling and intoxicating wind.

He left for the highest hills, the ancestral land which he would help in its unmoving potential, in the vortex of the black wind, feeling how great a man is when he is in his normal human dimension. And at the moment when he left he felt himself invested – *nor death itself would have been divestiture* – in the name of the authentic people of Italy to oppose Fascism in every possible way, to

* Latin – face to face.

judge and to act, to decide militarily and as a cititzen. Such supreme power was intoxicating but infinitely more intoxicating was the consciousness of the legitimate use he would make of it.

And even physically he had never been so much a man, herculean he bent the wind and the earth.

V

It was four in the afternoon and Johnny was in the high hills, sombre in the blanket of snow with no more gleams as if corrupted by the incipient *dusk* with its mottled arsenic-yellow leprosy. Murazzano was in front of him and since he believed the village to be at the farthest edge of the Langhe his heart fell. Further than the Langhe he did not intend to go so as not to break from his ancestral sphere, and up to Murazzano he had come across neither hair nor hide of the partisans, who did exist but were as abstract as the North Pole.

Evening was falling fast and weariness assailed him with a predatory and logical grip. He had been travelling since the morning on foot on snow and sheet-ice except for a short distance halfway up the hills in a bus – a mobile hut of misery and icy cold. Then on foot again towards the *top hills*. The very few people he met on the road, men whom approaching danger and innate distrust made sharp and *snivelling* at the same time, walking like him with their chins tucked in to their chests to make a smaller target and reduce the sadism of the cruel wind, were already casting glances at him as if they already recognised in him a partisan. At a certain point on the bus only three of them were left: Johnny, the driver and an elderly carabiniere. The driver was no more up-to-date and knowledgeable than an old carter; the carabiniere was a squat and morose man visibly, ostentatiously unarmed, with a beard a few days old sprouting on his solid cheeks. Not a word passed between them.

Four was striking on the campanile of Murazzano, the only object – along with its tower – to emerge from the low misty shroud which enwrapped the Lazarus-like village. Johnny *oathed, sighed*, then marched on to circle round the little hill behind which ran the last straight street of the village. He seethed inwardly and then was

47

struck cold by the thought that this evening, the evening of the day – the fateful, paeaned day – when he entered the ranks of the partisans he was going to knock at the door of an inn for a night's lodging, still not a partisan, but still some wretched traveller. And what if the innkeeper, having scrutinised his face, which had already changed, were to shut the door in his face . . .?

But when he had circled the hill he immediately saw a large building, square with a wide circle of cement cleared of snow, identical with the style prescribed by the regime for all the granaries of 'the Italian people'* and on the round terrace a lorry loading, *swarmed about* by uniformed and armed men, only one of them watching with feline indolence the road Johnny was taking. These were partisans! He was not misled by the preponderance of grey-green in their mended and patched-up uniforms, indeed some of them were completely clad in grey-green but it was not the Fascist grey-green. The Fascist grey-green – because it was Fascist – had automatically taken on a different *shade* as if the Fascist wearer had made it lose its nature, its colour saturation and its brightness. These were partisans *and sunshine reshone over all the dusk-domed world* . . .

Johnny dashed towards them with such élan that he aroused the suspicion of the man facing down the street. He was in complete grey-green, therefore as miserable as a common soldier of the Royal Army in critical surroundings, while the misery and suffering of his life as partisan imprinted an age like Methuselah's on his face, which was half buried in his shabby balaclava. He was a cowed creature prey to the cold and Johnny noticed that to unsling his rifle and cover Johnny he took enough time to be killed three times over had he been a Fascist. He gave the Who goes there and then Halt with a desperately Sicilian accent which escaped from his teeth as if from the mechanical grip of a knitting machine so that Johnny was taken aback, was amazed and incredibly angry. Everything had to be so northern, so Protestant . . . His perplexity cost him a second and more

* The building is a store set up by the Fascist regime for the compulsory collection of grain from the peasants – as such very unpopular with 'the Italian people' of Fascist rhetoric.

vibrant warning while some of the men busy loading turned round ready to support their comrade.

'You are partisans!' said Johnny without the least questioning inflection. He had to give an account of himself in that electrified atmosphere and perhaps he had never succeeded in being so concise and exhaustive. 'I want to join the partisans with you.' The men had turned back to loading: the men from the North all looked like workers or peasants as far as could be seen from their muffled garb – something between country and skiing clothing – and all were armed but wretchedly so. 'I want to join the partisans – with you!' The men were loading sacks of grain and huge, disgusting slices of lard. In the door to the depredation and the storehouse stood an old man, dishevelled by the wind and fear, evidently the guardian and person responsible for the store. He was saying: 'Don't take it all – leave me part of the stuff so that I can keep in the Fascists' good books when they come to check up on me. Like this you are ruining me – like this it will look as if I didn't make the least resistance and so am on your side –'

Johnny passed from the snow of the road to the cement of the round terrace, as if the cement represented his investiture as a partisan; now he was very close to the truck, brushed against by the men as they came and went loading. The Sicilian noticed his transition and marched over towards him, irritated and vindictive: 'Who told you to go in?' 'Can't I yet?' whispered Johnny. And then a partisan, a little dark boy, so thin that his thinness accentuated the disproportionate quilting of a *full-sized* winter fur jacket, turned round sighing and as he turned presented Johnny with his full face, an integral text of Lombroso's* criminal symptomology, and with a gesture that was almost angry signalled to Johnny to *join them. And Johnny paced another pace, ringing on the investiture-concrete.* 'But, Tito, what do you know about him?' protested the Sicilian his words more than ever coming out of his mouth as if from a textile mill, his speech as it were lacerated by the teeth of a machine. 'Oughtn't you to make him wait, talk about it with the commissar first?' The word *shot ineffectually* for Johnny in the atmosphere which was already

---

* Cesare Lombroso (1841–1946) considered delinquency to be due to biological degeneracy.

dark and crystallised. The small one with the Dillinger-face* denied
the authority of the commissar, his superior with an identical sign
with his head, spontaneous and mechanical like a tic, and Johnny
finally joined the partisans almost stepping on the corns of the
perplexed and dissatisfied Sicilian. And he made his way into their
midst in the wake of the little partisan who had accepted and
guaranteed him individually. And in the press he clearly saw the red
stars sewn on the jacket collars and the peaks of the caps of most of
them. He was registering how each one of these men, his new
companions, was abysmally inferior to him in physical distinction,
just as if made of different flesh and bones, when the truck made a
grumbling noise and started off. It was driven by a partisan in
complete fireman's uniform with a coarse Ligurian accent, that too so
disappointing and depressing . . . Johnny watched the uncertain
manoeuvre certainly no more euphoric than the guardian of the
collective granary who was now left to his plundered state and his
responsibility *in capite*.**

The truck manoeuvred to attach a trailer which up to then had
remained invisible to Johnny behind a corner of the granary. The
partisans – a score of them – stormed the truck to install themselves
in it and thus avoid the trailer which was very precariously attached to
the machine. Three partisans, three Sicilian soldiers as identical as if
mimeographed, resignedly approached the trailer and climbed in
with the irrational clumsiness of their old dragging uniforms. Thus
an unspoken racial separation had operated; from his place in the
truck Johnny examined the three Southerners who were now taking
up position with belated accuracy the better to stand up to the jolts
and the centrifugal force. The road, as much as could be seen of it in
the chaotic *dusk* proclaimed itself, to say the least of it, to be
acrobatic. In the truck the men, trampling on the viscid slices of lard
laid out on the floor like sliced dogfish, sighed at their imminent
passive role at the hands of the driver. 'Where are we going?' asked
Johnny of his sponsor, 'To the base,' replied Tito with an indifference
that took for granted the term which Johnny had not yet digested.
Following Tito's finger the base was a village shaped in a bizarre way
like an ancient boat set on the crest of a high hill as if on the breaker

* Dillinger – a famous American gangster of the thirties.
** Legal term describing a tenancy.

of a stormy sea that had been suddenly halted. A cobweb of evening vapours wrapped itself in a wandering way round its lifeless houses, sometimes entangled in the campanile, sometimes fading away into the darkening sky. The hill of the base was immense, wide and mammary, falling away in great cliffs to the valley bottom which was already nocturnal in the scrub and broken ground. Johnny's heart sank, melted, so it was no longer any more firmly consistent than the surrounding snow corrupted by the arsenical, untimely, deceptive thaw. But what did one expect the partisans to be like? Archangels – these people?

The truck set off towards the road which in the visual snatches one could guess was linked to those tourniquets unravelling on the great steep drops of the base-hill. And soon, against the dark, against the cold, against the business of being a partisan, the men on board struck up *Bandiera Rossa*.* A violent and *disjected* chorus, the verses not well known and equally so by all, therefore crammed full of individual interpolations which combined however to increase the threat of the song. They were Communists, that's what they were; but they were partisans and that could and should be enough for him. '*Commies, Red Star – but so far as they fight Fascists*,' he thought in English with special *relish* polemicising with the raging song. The term 'commissar' came back to his mind with a solid and vivid sharpness like a red placard against a white background of snow. Something like or identical with that political functionary in the wake of the Red troops which the Fascist war correspondents called politruk.** '*I will see afterwards*,' Johnny said to himself suddenly annihilated by fatigue. But the mental *emblankment* was not such as to exclude attention to the driver and fears for him. The road was impossible and the fireman drove on it like a drunken champion or a bewildered amateur; Johnny, like every other man on board, felt himself to be living only for the moment and their exposure to the inevitable catastrophe. In that statue-like state of trepidation he stared at the three Sicilians bouncing in the serpentine trailer, clinging on and alone like *marooned* sailors.

---

* The Italian version of the Red Flag which calls for land and factories, no war, Communism and liberty.

** Politruk – Russian for 'political instructor'.

The road bit in; exhausted and mordant too was the immensely high hill, streaked with shadows of deepest black on a spectral bank of snow; the darkness rose up to the topmost peaks as if to an inescapable ambush, at each corner the village of the base disappeared and reappeared, assuming a horribly phantasmal quality in the fast-falling night.

The disaster happened in a unique unforeseeable stretch that flattened out between to extremely steep banks. The truck skidded, the cable held firm with a desperation more human than metallic, the trailer with its three passengers who were being thrown about skidded along the bank, righted itself, seemed to save itself, then the cable came away with a horrible groan, the trailer went adrift and bounced; at the last second of equilibrium two men dived out on the right side, the third, Johnny's opponent, jumped on to the bank and the side of the trailer crushed his back. The men banged rhetorically at the little grated window of the cabin, the fireman braked, went on in a fearful serpentine way for a few more metres.

The Sicilian had died at once, by the light of matches they could see on his back the horrible, jagged gash. His two fellow-countrymen stood stiffly over him like two funeral candles already. Tito said: 'Can we leave him here till tomorrow morning? I'd say so – in any case no one can help or harm him.' In Tito's voice there was a profound respect, almost a touch of protocol as between one sovereign state and another. The two men, completely overwhelmed, assented with their sharp, dark chins, only removing the dead man's rifle and boots: this last despoiling act they carried out with piety that was at once respectful and determined as if to forestall a specific Northern act of jackalism. Then they set off up the mountain again while Johnny said to himself that he had learned that with the partisans one didn't only die because of the Fascists and it chilled him more than the terrible wind which was now entirely nocturnal.

Something else happened before arriving: the man from Liguria crashed a gear and the wheels did not bite on a slope and the big truck slipped backwards. They all got out. Someone stuck his jacket or fur doublet under the wheels so that they would bite again: all this in an atmosphere of fatalism, of fatigue and unshakeable determination, the wind whirling away the men's curses and almost their bodies. 'Bloody Fascists,' said Tito quietly with his *dry* and compact voice which not even that wind was able to *disject*. That was it – one had to blame only the Fascists, not nature nor the Ligurian driver, nor the truck. The latter started up and came to a halt a little further up hill to wait and take the men on foot on board once more, its loud hum the only indication of itself in the overwhelming night. They caught up with it immensely slowly, on the open stretches the wind bent you in two like an iron bar concealed in the dark at the height of the *solar plexus*. Walking to the truck John asked Tito about the leaders. 'You'll see them.' 'Where are they?' Tito jerked his head towards the two reddish globes penetrating the smoky vapour which coincided with the village base. 'And what are they like?' Tito did not reply but Johnny had noticed the *bluntness* with which he had received and transmitted the word 'leader'.

They got down in the village in the *theatrical setup* of ghostly shapes which was the village rendered concrete only by the quiet and dirty burning of reddish lights from houses of the civilians. The windows were Lilliputian, chipped and low down at street level with that characterisitc *feature* of Alpine villages. The cobbled street was steep and very uneven even under a thick layer of snow where this had not frozen. Johnny simply prayed that morning would come, perhaps the morning would make him see everything differently, would *rescue* him from that black wave of misery and risk which now completely submerged him.

He went in with his fellow-travellers and had supper of bread and meat in a big bare room in the intensely white acetylene light that hung swaying. And as he ate he observed the others to find himself confirmed and made more miserable by the discovery that none of them was remotely of his class (physical and or otherwise) unless a day or a little more than a day of that desperate animal-jungle life stamped on them all – even on a building genius – that bestial mark. The others paid no more attention to him after turning round to examine indifferently with a bovine turn of the head and a slow gleam in the eyes the new arrival announced to them. Johnny was now trying with wearying pertinacity not to lose contact with – not to mention sight of – Tito; this small youth with his Lombrosian physiognomy was after an examination all round still his favourite, the only one with whom Johnny could feel *matey*. And his recognition of this caused a tremor of amazement now that Tito was completely and clearly visible in the pitiless light of the acetylene lamp, his head freed from his peaked cap.

He had an exaggeratedly small nose but one planted malignantly in the exaggerated pits of his eye-sockets, a forehead irregular and covered with lumps and devoured, as it were, by the thick and vulgar plantation of black hair that was without sheen with a few streaks (already unnaturally white) as repellent as dead snakes, bloodless and imprisoned in tar. His mouth was twisted and his chin receding. His whole body was neurotically tiny and must be abnormally hirsute. And yet there flowed from him a paradoxical directness, a *dryness* and a cordiality that made you rub your eyes. And he was, by his own admission, just nineteen; and the discovery assumed vast proportions for Johnny and for the first time made him doubt his own twenty-two years. He could not feel older than Tito, indeed he could not but feel a stripling in comparison with him.

Tito got up from the table and came over to him, knitting his thick brow at the automatic promptness with which Johnny had copied every one of his gestures and movements. 'I'm going to sleep,' he said, 'and you'd better follow me. They're detailing the guard now and you who're new would be on it right away. And I don't expect you want that very much tonight.'

They slept in a greyish-white building outside the village – an even bigger ship moored on the black crest of the void. The darkness was unable to prevent Johnny from discovering that it was a church: the snoring of men and the rustle of straw filled the nave. Outside the wind raged as if it saw the possibility of breaching the wall of the church. Tito said: 'Yes, it's a church. But deconsecrated.' 'How long has it been deconsecrated?' 'They deconsecrated it the day after they found us sleeping here. You see we have a lot of things to settle with the parish priest.' Immediately afterwards Johnny heard the sharp snap of the cut wire and the dry scattering of straw. Tito worked in the dark with an acquired sureness and ease; in the dark everything was reduced to an acoustic rather than a tactile fact. Tito advised him to bury himself in the straw and then Johnny reacted *out of too much thankfulness.* 'You don't have to think you must treat me like a nanny, Tito. I've been in the army, you know.' Tito had never made the acquaintance of the army but it seemed to Johnny that in the realm of acoustics his correction had not had the slightest effect. And was this little noise one of scornful arrogance? And the very young people, the twenty-year-olds like Tito knew and judged the army only in the aftermath of 8 September, so it was natural that they thought it was kind to comment wordlessly – at most with raised eyebrows – on anything to do with the army.

But it was a good idea to continue the conversation, almost to force it to continue; this prevented Johnny from finding himself tête-à-tête with other heavier and more real thoughts. 'What's the matter with the parish priest, Tito?' 'Does religion mean anything to you?' 'Let's say that relationships between man and man are more important,' said Johnny. Tito hesitated a moment, and in his minimal pause the snoring had the note of a death rattle, the groans from the straw seemed to indicate the acme of mortal collapse. 'The priest – the priest is – an idiot,' Tito concluded with sad *abruptness.* Johnny *goggled bitterly.* 'He's a character who doesn't know how to adapt.' 'Is that possible,' observed Johnny, 'in a Catholic priest?' 'He's like,' Tito went on, 'most of these damned carabinieri. What goes against the grain is not Fascism, what goes against the grain is that power has passed to us. And they get themselves killed, they get themselves killed and we kill them, but you'll find out that there's nothing sadder than putting an idiot out of this world.' 'And has the priest understood now?' 'It seems not. They don't trust him – that's for sure but –' Johnny *was getting so accustomed to acoustic sight* that he could 'hear' Tito shake his head. 'I know what it is,' Tito went on later, 'It is that red flag with the hammer and sickle opposite his church – you'll see it tomorrow – that drives him mad and will bring his death.' He said the last word with such indifference that Johnny felt himself encouraged to ask him the most intimate question. 'Are you a Communist, Tito?' 'No I'm not,' he exploded. 'I am nothing and I am everything. I am only against the Fascists. I am in the Red Star because the formation I came across was red – what they have going for them is that they organised it and presented it to me who was looking for it so much – more intensely than I have looked for anything up to now. But in the end if I am alive just let them come and tell me that I am a Communist!'

That was how it was, Johnny said to himself, feeling he was losing *the edge* of the realisation so bitter and important now and which expressed itself in him in English: '*I'm in the wrong sector of the right side.*' Tito suddenly wished him goodnight and the polite wish sounded *appallingly* anomalous in those surroundings.

No sooner was he alone with Tito lying there a continent away, than *those* thoughts attacked him as if they had only been waiting for Tito to disappear, for Johnny to be bereft of a witness and an ally. '*I'm in the wrong sector of the right side,*' he repeated to himself. But there must be other formations in the hills – 'Blue'* formations, that was it, in which he would not be so painfully aware of the qualitative gap, no longer have a motive for that superior sense of difference which at the moment caused him such distress, tortured him, as amid the obscene laughter of a triumphant fraud. His eye, radar-like in the concrete darkness, appeared to illuminate and scrutinise the surrounding humanity, inferior and miserably abandoned in its leaden slumber. It was with these people that it was his fate to fight – and die. If captured en masse with these people he would have to share all the wall or the ditch and the Fascist lead.

He became aware of an immediate feeling of danger. Up to that morning or better until yesterday he was in a fluid position, which could be shielded from any mortal impact by means of fictions or subterfuges or cunning twists with a reasonable margin of probability of survival, but now it was signed and sealed, if captured he would no longer have the slightest *chance* and the minimal right to a discussion, he had taken his place in the great dualism at the price of immediate, undebated execution.

The dark was sinister, the roar of the wind sinister, as if it were exposing the dark shelter to a dazzling irruption of a sentence seen and illuminated and of a massacre made easy by way of justice; the dark and the wind both contained and directed an equal charge of ambush and of risk *momentarily prior to just-seen death*. The abandoned sleep of the others did not reassure him, on the contrary it was like the collapse before the unbearable *show* of danger. They were so many corpses awaiting the *coup de grâce* which protocol demanded. He hoped that exhaustion, so legitimate and slothful, would overcome him, overcome him until late in the morning. But the fatigue, announced by so many heralds, did not come marching into the field of battle in serried ranks, and Johnny rose, stumbling

* Monarchist formations.

horribly, and advanced to the shadow of the door, *rough and tenacious in denegating egression.*

Outside, the darkness was complete but much more reassuring than its sister within, Johnny *paced some paces in the concrete void*, and it was reassuring, encouraging, euphoric, to feel that in the darkness as if one were on the brink of the void, which could be reached by a sole step against headlong danger and death. He found a nook, he huddled up and in that nook, victorious over the immensity of the raging wind, he lit a cigarette at the first go. To the *scratch* and the cosmic evidence of the reddening point of light the dry rustle of a frozen uniform replied. The sentry moved up to him and it was one of the two Sicilians. 'You have proper cigarettes? Ah you're the new one. Give me one. You light it for me.'

Johnny lay down again, light-headed with insomnia, comfortably smoking against the blind wall of the church that gave on to the void – a wall so rough that his skin could feel it even through his clothes. He asked the Sicilian if he had long to go on his spell of duty, he felt so well that he yearned to take his place. 'I don't have a fixed spell. I stand down when I simply can't go on any longer.' 'What does that mean?' 'Tonight it wasn't my turn at all but I went on duty and am on duty just the same. You see I come from the army, you'll have understood that. The boys here don't go on sentry duty, the silly buggers. They go on sentry duty and ten minutes later they come back to sleep or go somewhere else and so no one is a proper sentry. You're amazed, eh? you're shocked. But I won't sit there without a sentry and if no one goes on sentry duty I do at the cost of wearing myself out. There are too many kids among the partisans and too few real soldiers with military experience. And what you would really need are people from the army. Unfortunately almost all those who have been in the army don't want to know about it any more. Just look and see if there is a real army officer about the place.' 'There will be some,' said Johnny, 'but in other formations, maybe they don't want to hear of "red brigades".' But the Sicilian said: 'And where are these other formations? Can you point them out to me?' 'No, otherwise I wouldn't have ended up here.' 'Maybe other formations will come but for the moment there are none as far as I can learn. Tell me where there is a formation with real soldiers and real ex-army officers and I'll go there even if it were in the teeth of that traitor

Graziani.' 'And yet they do exist,' said Johnny but simply as a sober wish for himself and for the insistent soldier. Then he prepared to go back in, happy and grateful for those hints which slyly and irresistibly were pervading his body with an attack of total somnolence. He went back into the blind block within, seeking in vain but with gratitude Tito's prone form.

In the morning everything was infinitely less bad. A discreet but spacious sun cleared the snow, almost restoring its virginity, and gave colour to everything, actually gave a shine to the polychrome uniforms of the partisans. And from the whole village there flowed a normal bustling noise, cheering because normal, which ended up by sounding almost festive, given the period and the situation. Women were already going about to and from the bakehouse and the fountain, looking at and being looked at by the partisans with smiling cordiality, even if their smile was a little forced at the corners of the mouth because of the presentiment of what the partisans might cost them, their men and their roofs from one day to the next.

'What do we do today?' he asked Tito with a certain *business briskness*. 'We are bored as usual,' said Tito soberly. And Johnny was amazed. 'You are bored?' 'You'll soon learn that when you're not in action being a partisan is the most boring job in the world.' 'And can't you go into action every day?' 'You can ask the headquarters staff whom you'll get to know this very day, I think. Ask the commissar Némega or Captain Zucca* or Lieutenant Biondo.'** Johnny noticed that Tito pronounced the ranks with scathing though highly indirect irony.

They were just passing in front of the headquarters, the former municipal office. From its façade hung in an enormous, plethoric cascade a red flag with hammer and sickle, and it overflowed from the balcony in extra heavy folds which looked dangerous to the mere touch. Johnny was struck and filled with admiration at the same time but he whispered: 'Idiots! A Fascist officer would see it from Rome with his field-glasses.' They passed in front of the church – closed, *nay* sealed with an air about it that was at once bitter and offended and vengeful, *as fearfully and hatefully resenting on her ruddy façade* the distant gleams from the red flag.

* Zucca – pumpkin – the nickname for a bald man.
** Biondo – a *nom de guerre* like the others: the Blond.

Now they were walking towards the highest point of vantage on the absolutely naked and slightly shiny cliff. And Johnny's eye ran along the range of the immense hill which seemed to him to be Polyphemus' wife squatting there and posing. His gaze was lost abysmally as the hill fell away stepwise to the valley bottom, to the pinewoods and the scrub around the frozen watercourses – even kilometres away any possible Fascists would have to look naked.

'You who've done the officer training course,' said Tito point-blank, 'what do you think of it?' 'Of our position?' In agreement Tito closed his hairy hand which was *circularising* the landscape. 'Magnificent. Except that –' Tito anticipated the shared criticism with a *grim* smile of satisfaction. 'Except that –' Johnny concluded, 'we can't deceive ourselves that we are an armed island. I haven't seen anything at all yet but we can't be too well off for arms and ammunition. So this magnificent position could become our pyramid tomb if the Fascists – or worse the Germans – surround us at the bottom.' 'Perfect,' said Tito, 'and why is that? Because up here they are going about things against commonsense. Here they are setting up garrisons like in the regular army, here they think in terms of ground occupied like in the war of '15. Bloody fools! they'll make us all die because of their damned stupidity! Partisans are dia-metrically opposite – even a child would understand that. We must be invisible – we must act and disappear again, never settled in one place, always *ubiquitous*, few of us and never in uniform. We must be able to sacrifice the uniform – but try to tell them that! You'll soon see what a carnival of uniforms there is. We must give a stab in the back and disappear, melt away and return to the attack in the same mysterious manner. The surviving Fascists must have the impression that their dead have been killed by a tree, by a landslide, by . . . something in the air, they must go mad and commit suicide because they never see us. But no – bloody fools, they set up a proper garrison and dream of the day when things have got to the point when parades are possible.' Johnny sighed. 'Certainly it's a very difficult job and the Italians are doing it for the first time.' 'Yes, but we will die because of these mistakes and because of the very nature of the Italian people the lesson will not be learned. I go out of my mind because of all this and at this moment am convinced that the best thing that can happen will be to get out of it alive. But we are so much at the beginning and the end is so distant that none of us will see it.'

Nevertheless it was melancholy in sexual terms to think of oneself as dead, buried in a corner of that immense hill while out there in the exploding spring one's successors, the heedless, *disparaging maybe* triumphant successors, in other uniforms, with other arms, other mentalities, grasped victory.

Several partisans appeared on the ridge, taking no notice and unnoticed in their turn, one had stuck on his head a sombrero which was extremely strident in that arctic landscape and therefore immediately its trigonometric centre. They launched a hay-sledge on the vertiginous slope and had fun.

It was hardly nine o'clock. 'Time simply doesn't pass with the partisans.'

Johnny and Tito *made again* their way through the village, Johnny thinking with intermittent anxiety of his summons to the HQ which could not be long delayed. The village was so tiny and also so divided up into sectors that the partisans seemed to be swarming and so that the embryonic brigade had a strength of some forty men. At one end of the village a partisan was cutting up a calf for rations. Johnny was cheered in an animal way, being aware of a voracious hunger *as new for a new dimensioned man*. In the sunlit and crystalline air the exposed flesh seemed polished: the butcher, incredibly bloodstained, and furiously tense in that inexpert task guided by purely visual memory, turned round at their passing with unconcealed annoyance. He was a peasant, a young one, who had taken the plunge into the partisans in the first days, as if in a joyful and ferocious revolt against his destiny of enslavement to the earth: leonine, with an extremely narrow forehead, in his icy eyes only a single gleam amid the outpouring of his ferocity. He seemed to resent extremely the *goalless walking* of the two partisans, one of them new with the unequivocal look of a townsman, who were passing by his *all-serving* labour with a grimace. Tito greeted him with unconcealed condescension; he replied at first with ridiculous shyness and then with a hoarse outburst. A few paces further on Tito said he couldn't stand peasants: 'I mean in partisan formations. I would like only students and workers in the partisans. People who do a clean job and by jobs I mean killing and a clean job because as they kill they are always in a temper, you understand. Not so the peasants; the peasants enjoy it and so they take their time over it and so in a muddled and messy way as well. They kill shouting and hitting like with the trapped fox which was causing damage in the field or the henhouse, you understand? And the man like the fox has to die a thousand deaths.'

They walked past the HQ once more. At one of the little windows just clear of the motionless heavy wave of the huge red flag a little man appeared and as much of him as emerged from the sill was perfectly clad in the uniform which the Fascists had brought into fashion. It was enough to bring on a heart attack to suddenly see that Fascist cap adorned with the Roman sword sticking out but the face beneath it was so clownishly disarming and sly, so tremulous and at the same time so conscious of the fact that the same trembling was a shield, that the fit of orgasmic astonishment died away – as happened with Johnny – in a semi-comic personal rebuke for that impossible excitement. As Tito related, this was the first proper Fascist prisoner captured by the brigade *somewhere outside* Mondoví and his appearance was so enormously inferior, the circumstances of his capture so shamefully easy, hunger so evidently what had inspired him to enrol, that it had seemed contrary to every manly law to proceed to an execution. He had been living as a prisoner for three weeks, washing up twice a day, his fate sealed only if a partisan death occurred, he being an inadequate sacrificial offering. And Johnny thought that even faced by the executioner's weapon he would not stop moping and mowing like Totò* with the diabolical, tremulous, deep-down plan to make the executioner drop his weapon because of convulsive laughter. From his little window out of which he always looked, the dishes having been done, he did not let the least of the partisans pass by without raining down on him the most flowery greetings and without calling him 'boss' – which he also did as Johnny and Tito passed.

He withdrew only when the Southerners passed, his chief enemies because of their common South. They wanted to shoot him, had offered themselves as executioners, in a taciturn olive-coloured determination to wash this stain from the coat-of-arms of the South but they had found no support – not even from the commissar Némega.

Johnny was called to the HQ late that same morning. Waiting for

* Totò – a famous contemporary Neapolitan comedian and actor.

him were the commisar Némega, Captain Zucca and Lieutenant Biondo. Captain Zucca was wearing an immaculate white waterproof coat over a civilian suit and had on his head an officer's cap with the badge of the Bersaglieri.* If he was an officer he was certainly the coarsest and most *menial-looking* officer of the late army. This was not very important, Johnny had long found his way about in natural hierarchies, but he could not help feeling the shock of an excessive and unwarranted attribution of rank. The captain in uncertain and laborious self-imposed Italian asked him for confirmation of *his being* an officer cadet. Then he said that in a month's time he could be platoon commander, naturally after passing certain tests.

Lieutenant Biondo was certainly not a lieutenant – in the army by his own admission he was newly promoted sergeant. He looked like a handsome and younger copy of Johnny's old sergeant – the same extremely healthy thinness, that same pale and determined face, the same natural *daintiness* in his by no means lovingly kept uniform but lacking the blind respect of rules and with a spirit of initiative which the old sergeant not only did not possess but which he would have found in very bad taste. And Biondo with relief and admiration for Johnny, who was waiting, confined himself to agreeing with an uncomfortable nod of the head to his admission to the partisans. Then the two 'military men' left in joint haste, half because of the expected boring nature of the commissar's usual disquisitions and half because of an uncomfortable inferiority complex and a sense of uncongeniality, which was not only a question of rank, with the commissar, Némega.

Commissar Némega was thirty, well off, middle class, a slim and not very strong figure and yet *dainty* and a head which greatly ressembled – apart from the wrinkles of vice – that of Osvaldo Valenti.** A most refined hilarity shone in his face as if at the success of the mistake, as if at the realisation of and commentary on the fact that he had trapped with an ordinary net and in vulgar company a precious fish. 'So at last we can count an intellectual in our ranks, an element from the upper classes,' he had a polished, affected voice

* Bersaglieri – literally marksmen – a famous regiment.
**Osvaldo Valenti – film actor, member of Fascist anti-partisan formation. Shot by partisans in 1945.

which he was libidinously pleased with and which he used with quite undisguised skill. 'Do you know any foreign languages?' 'English.' 'Well?' 'Like a *lord*,' said Johnny in order to strike at him in the spirit of class. 'It will be enormously useful to us,' said the commissar, sweetening his dry statement of instrumentality with the purple tones of that voice of his. 'Not now, but later the Allies will help us.' 'You are mistaken.' 'Why on earth?' asked Némega with the most plaintive air yet attained. 'I don't see the English supplying Communist partisans.' 'I am informed that they have done so for Tito and are doing so now.' 'Yes,' Johnny admitted but without a sense of having lost a move; the whole thing felt to him to be in a tone of nauseating academicity.

'Besides you look to me like the scribbling type. Well, not now but when our brigade has come of age and is the most powerful formation in all the Langhe we will print a newspaper for the men, for our sympathisers and people in general and you will be one of the editors of that newspaper. Certainly not the leading articles but you can do partisan colour pieces.'

Johnny *shrunk violently*. 'I will not do anything of the kind. I left my pen at home and with it syntax and grammar. So long as I am here I do not intend to take anything in my hand but a rifle.' 'Even if the rifle fitted your hand infinitely less well than the pen?' *hinted* Némega with the terrible fluency of wasted violaceous instrumentality, '*I expect and confide in a very next proof*,' said Johnny. Némega let this pass thinking of the time that remained before them; no other face in Johnny's expert memory held more of that sense of the final victory over everything and everyone. The thought, then . . . the objective of getting the better of Johnny seemed of interest to Némega who was at the peak of his desire. Now he had moved away from the mayor's desk and moved towards the door with steps at least as cunning and studied as his voice, tricking Johnny into thinking it was his release. But he went on: 'As war commissar I give a course in Marxism. It is not offered to all the men in the brigade obviously and I do not delude myself either about the fruits I can gather from certain elements who are admitted to the course but I should be greatly pleased at your attendance and attention.' Johnny *refused flatly* and his No provoked a steely glint in the commissar's pale eyes. Besides his voice and his step he was able to modulate his glance as well, 'I did not come here for any courses, except a course for training in possible new weapons, the ones you hope for from the English. I am here because of the Fascists – and only that. All the rest is for what comes later.' 'What comes later,' said Némega, 'is something you will learn all you need to know about precisely by following my course.' 'I'm not interested.' Némega flapped a hand, tiny and strikingly *forceless* except for a *minute-long* grudging clasp. *He confided in the future, as Christians.* 'However I won't get grey hairs from you. You are committed, thank heaven, at least on the level of language. Can you guess how long it is since I had to look for a word?' 'Really, I'm in the wrong sector of the right side.'

VI

And action did not come to hurl you down from that peak which was gradually obsessive, to free you from the gnawing dissatisfaction, from the partisan's gloomy boredom, to carry you off one day at least from Némega's practical sphere of influence, to link you if possible more closely to Tito.

People were not idle, on the contrary they were obliged to carry out real performances of strength and endurance, not half a day passed without their being called out to pull the truck which was stuck at some point on the impossible road and the reconnaissance marches and the trips for provisions become more frequent. In charge of supplies was a man already in his forties, the oldest member of the brigade called either Mario or Sergeant-Major. He was surprisingly like the perfect askari* at Porta Pia** whom Johnny remembered out of all the nightmare of Rome's 25 July, but the inflection of his voice was as Northern as one could desire or deplore. Although, according to Tito, he had never been in action, the sergeant-major was, along with Biondo, the only owner of an automatic weapon – an English Sten,† the first of the unending series to come later and how the sergeant-major possessed one at this time was a fairly-tale worthy of the researches of the *Intelligence Service.* Although he did not use it he did not lend it either, and there was not even any hope of getting it from under his dead body. If there was,

* askari – literally an African soldier but here just a long service one.
** Porta Pia – the district in Rome where Italian troops resisted the Germans. Johnny was there in an earlier account.
† Sten – a very sturdy, simple sub-machine-gun often dropped to partisan formations.

there would have been a Homeric scrum round his corpse with nothing Achillean* about it to judge by everyone's visible lust for that Sten.

Sometimes Johnny along with others escorted the sergeant-major on foraging expeditions. People gave in and handed over reluctantly, regretting what they offered, taking the requisition chit and looking at it as if at some fabulous object, and almost no one held back from providing the impassible sergeant-major, who noted in silence additional addresses of people who could provide more or better stuff. Was this the slow forceps-birth of fiscal conscience in Italy? thought Johnny.

One day he escorted the sergeant-major along with another partisan, Geo, even taller than Johnny and with a general air of having TB, to requisition a calf from a landowner. The old man was an epigone of the ancient race of the mountains, there was about him something ragged and dirty and noble in a gypsylike way: all wrapped up in stinking rags but round his neck he wore a scarf of pure silk tied with a gold ring. Abraham-like he was sitting in the middle of the kitchen surrounded *in state* by all his generations of women. Mario planted himself in front of him, prosaic and *businesslike*, bitterly superior like an NCO in the colonies in the presence of some baroque tribal notable. Johnny and Geo *eyed the women*: it was strange how noticeable was the clear gap of a generation: the women were either in their sixties or fifteen years old. The old women were frightened and puzzled; the young ones relaxed and curious. The old man was ready for them, he indicated the next-door byre with his bristly hand, but asked what he got in exchange. 'I shall sign a requisition chit for you,' said Mario producing his notebook with shameless casualness like a tax official. The old man did not interfere but watched with watery eyes the course of Mario's pencil on the paper as if that writing really did not in any way register the fate of his calf. Mario tore out the chit with lightning skill and with a *slap* offered it expressionlessly to the old man who took it in his deformed hands and suddenly turned his illiterate eyes away from it and said to the sergeant-major's face: 'This

* A reference to the fighting in the *Iliad* round the body of Achilles' lover Patroclus.

is worth nothing – with this I can't even . . .' and he tore it up with those hands of his. Perhaps there was a sign from Mario which Johnny did not catch but Geo was on top of the old man, taking him by the silk scarf. He leant over him like famine over stinking, ugly obesity. The women did not intervene not even with the expected sobs, they confined themselves to embracing the girls, almost drowning them in the waves of their skirts, which were solid and stank of the goat-pen. Johnny, who had oscillated for a moment between contempt for that sudden brutality and disgust at the calculated, ugly avarice of the old man, was pained by the old man's extreme solitude. But at that moment Geo slackened his grip on the neck which had turned purple beneath the *unwashed* patina. And the sergeant-major used the familiar form of address: 'You made a big mistake not to believe in the validity of these chits of ours. They are guaranteed by the Italian people which is your people too. After the war they will all be honoured down to the last cent. You had only to put my chit among all your dirty papers in the sanctum where you keep your dirty money and in the end you would have found yourselves refunded down to the last cent. But not now – now we are going to take away your calf without leaving you a chit. That way you'll learn. And you will be lucky if I forget this and tear out the proper chit when I come to requisition the second of your four calves.'

Sometimes there were alarms but all false; the partisans scattered again, half relieved, half disppointed after having swarmed on to the vantage-point with their eyes roaming – and at the same time mesmerised – over each piece of ground, over every spot possible for the Fascists' feet or wheels. The Fascists still had other things to think about, they were organising; later they would come up to crush them all with one foot; for the moment they had withdrawn to the plain which was full of mists, in the bitter febrile activity of organising, sometimes suddenly raising their burning eyes from the grey, exciting sea of maps, of plans and projects, to the marvellous lofty vision of the finished operation, the partisans lying in their blood-pools, dangling from a thousand branches, people crawling, on their knees, ambushed, rising up from that horizontal position only because their arms were stretched out in the Roman salute.*

* The Fascist salute – Fascism claimed to be the heir of the Roman empire.

Némega himself was almost invisible, for whole days and nights he did not cross the threshold of the commune, which was the sanctum of his thoughts: sometimes Johnny, passing by on menial, armed tasks, heard in the school (a big bare dusty room like a Waldensian* meeting-place) the drone of his voice – tired and didactic as if it were not worthwhile with that audience to deploy the scholarly and modulated voice which partisan Johnny would have deserved.

Captain Zucca disappeared more and more frequently, now he was generally absent. He went off with his sanguine coolness, having simply removed his military cap, perfectly decent and plausible under the anonymous wrapping of his white raincoat, its button-holes stripped of the little red stars. As he began to be obsessed with the hilltop Johnny learned to envy Zucca: Zucca went down to see the civilians, took the bus, jumped down from trains, lived in civil society, however risky it might be, every yard of it a pitfall. Johnny was morbidly weary of turning in at seven in the evening so as not to share the wretched low-beamed room in the inn where breathing was impossible, where each evening the partisans not on duty packed themselves in and in that stowage-space some of them made out that they could play cards comfortably, where everything was rationed, space and breath, below the existence level. The civilian houses were sealed tombs, entry was rigidly and tacitly precluded by the very terror of the occupants and Némega approved of the separateness from the civilians, so as not to induce in his men nostalgic memories, reminiscences, comforts. And outside a black wind whistled eternally, as if it sprang from the very roots of humanity's mad heart.

Johnny felt dirty, horribly so, he had quickly acquired an automatic, frequent habit of *ripping* at his skin like a hysterical reaction to the sticky immobility. Unlike most of the others he washed every morning, breaking the ice with an axe in a little pond near the observation post, but it was no longer any use, the murderously cold water, except to cleanse one's face of the nocturnal incrustations, of the poisonous patina of fermented straw

---

* An old Protestant sect from Northern Italy *v.* Milton's Sonnet XV 'Avenge O Lord thy slaughtered saints'.

and other people's breath. His hair, which was by now very long, weighed intolerably on his neck but what he found more repugnant than its weight was its woolly rubbing. He was not yet ready to face the partisan barber who, in the very middle of the little square, with a disgusting air of a pantomine executioner, cut hair with a tailor's scissors following the rim of a bowl which the patient held miserably in place on top of his skull with his own hand with the repellent psychological result of appearing to aid and abet his degradation. Tito, a Tito who was in a state of crisis to the point of voluntary tactiturnity, read his mind and only said: 'Fascist bastards!' It was already a relief – in fact a plus and something decisive – that Tito always slept alongside him, to think that the rattles and the tossing and turnings and the bad smells were at least Tito's.

Nor did the intense cold do anything to cause that feeling of discomfort to hibernate; Johnny observed that quite a few comrades had taken to scratching their fingers, at first in secret bouts, their eyes rolling with the effort and their relief, then in an open, blaspheming systematic campaign. Not even solitude, which was granted only by stints of sentry-go, allowed him to have thoughts – oh how disconnected and fleeting – that went beyond that sovereign physical preoccupation – '*I'm feeling so beastly, so beastly!*' – so he lamented to himself, passing his free hand from his weapon to his face in terror at finding incorporated there – and no longer even surgically removable – that patina of animality, of sub-humanity which was reflected in the faces of others, of those who had been partisans for a month before him. Perhaps all the others too had climbed up with a human, civilised face like his own; and that month before him had squashed and dehumanised it in the way that had struck him so much upon his arrival, which had made him think of a nightmare landing in a fraudulent rabble of beggars and brigands. He often felt now the need to recall, to evoke his so-distant civilian world and as an exorcism it came to him spontaneously to intone, during his hours of guard duty, a song from those days, a superior redeeming song. That night he *crooned long ago and far away*, hoping, willing that coming out of him it would affect him like a balm, melancholy but effective. The notes died in the turbulent wind and came down blindly in some ravine under the weight of consciousness of their own shortcomings, of their own absurdity.

He went to Lieutenant Biondo for a pass. Time to go down to Murazzano and come up again – Murazzano, the village least distant from the base and a place for *petty* holidays in normal times, with a chemist's and a small shop for little luxuries. Biondo passed him on to Némega with a kind of admission of lower rank which was more in sorrow than in anger. And Johnny quivered in the presence of a responsible military officer who had to be dependent on the commissar for a trifle like a pass for a couple of hours for one of his men. Johnny marched to the commune; the soft snow was *no carpet* for the painfully rough surface of the street. Neméga was at the door of his sanctum as if he had just appeared there, *airy*, rendered insubstantial and at the same time weighed down by a surfeit of intellectual work. 'Commissar, can I go down to Murazzano for a couple of hours?' 'What to do?' 'Shopping. A few articles needed immediately for reasons of hygiene.' 'Such as?' 'Talcum powder, soap, eau-de-cologne.' Némega flatly refused. 'I feel very dirty and out of sorts. I'm certainly not intending to run away,' Johnny fanned the flames. 'I know, the men would be very happy to have their first *chance* to chase a deserter. But you will understand that for the same reasons I ought to grant everybody a pass. Don't think you're the only one to feel dirty and out of sorts. But that way it wouldn't be a partisan brigade any more but a crowd of servant girls going shopping.' Johnny shook a finger behind his back as if he knew he had the whole unit drawn up behind him. 'What would you say to a fine collective outbreak of scabies?' 'Right, let me tell you it has been foreseen but foreseen as one of the least of problems. So you wanted the pass to buy comforts, let's say. Tell me, Johnny, did you come up here to us with a kitty?' 'Naturally.' 'That's bad, *mister*. This points to a glaring failure of a partisan state of mind, a substantial, inferior concept of partisan life. It's like carrying a civilian suit in one's kitbag, you understand me. You ought to have come into the hills like us without a cent. You would have understood everything much more and done your duty more fully. And when you go out requisitioning supplies you wouldn't put on a squeamish air and look soft-hearted and superior, which is what our quartermaster tells me about you.' But then he added in a conciliatory way as if he had read in Johnny's eyes the bitter realisation that he, Némega, was poisoning the hard partisan life which Johnny had overcome minute by minute. 'You'll manage to do your bits of shopping. We're going to move soon and there won't be a day without action any more. You'll make a trip to the nearest village and buy everything you think you need. Oh, I was forgetting,' and he said it in a way that meant it simply could not escape Johnny that he had forgotten on purpose, as a studied, malignant reprisal. 'I was forgetting – have been for quite a while, to tell the truth, that there's one way in which you can passs your spare time, that you can practice your English up here. I see you are pricking up your ears. We have among us two prisoners who have escaped from camps. Sorry, they are not pure-blooded Englishmen. They are South Africans. A paracolonial substitute,' he commented with a *twist* of his thin and highly coloured lips. 'How come I have never seen them? Where are they?' 'They live like cave-dwellers. By their own choice,' he added hurriedly. 'In homage to the worldwide anti-Nazi, anti-Fascist coalition I wanted to take them into our unit and had even thought up their *noms de guerre*. Don't laugh – they would have been *Victory I* and *Victory II*. But they didn't want to know, they simply refused to fight. But since they depend on us for their rations I put them in the kitchen as mess-orderlies and they made no objection. You're sure to find them in the kitchen.'

As he marched to the kitchen Johnny came across Regis. 'Why didn't you ever tell me that we have two South Africans?' he said rudely. 'Sorry, but who the hell cares about the two South Africans?'

The mess kitchen was housed in a long, low hut towards the *wild* centre of the village; you got there by an overgrown path which the thick snow barely concealed. As he ploughed through it Johnny imagined it in high summer with its enclosed life of nettles and wasps and lizards in the perpetual but ineffectual rise and fall of the wind. But in high summer, thought Johnny, he would be there only if dead and buried.

At the door he met the regular partisan cook, a forty-year-old with an equivocal look but lively and active coming out for water balancing two pails. Asked about the two South Africans he replied in an anodyne manner that the two Englishmen were inside.

In a corner that was mildewed and shadowy Johnny could make out two broad backs clad in khaki – not the classical khaki of the motherland but a slightly different khaki of an inferior olive green. The uniforms were on their last legs but all mended and patched with a certain desperate care, with tenacious almost snobbish punctiliousness. Their big heads, connected to the torso by bull-like necks of a greyish complexion were *clipped* with a certain monkish crudity and humility. '*How territorial do they both look,*' thought Johnny bending over them. They were peeling potatoes, thawed out and with purple patches, they were working with systematic *grinding* slowness, with a pathetic attempt to achieve economy and output.

Johnny spoke *abruptly.* '*A bit unwarlike, isn't it, peeling potatoes?*' They turned round slowly, looked up without the least surprise at hearing their own language, in a moment they resumed the rhythm of their peeling. The one with the older and more *imposing* look who said his name was Burgess simply asked if Johnny was a partisan too. '*Yes. What army service then?*' '*Artil'ry.*' '*Where were you caught?*' '*Marsah Matruh, 1942.*' '*By Graziani's troops?*' '*Rommel's,*' Burgess corrected rather emphatically. '*Where was the camp you ran out of on armistice day?*'* '*Near Vercelli,*' said Burgess miraculously contriving to suppress all the vowels in the name.

'*Near the rice marshes,*' said the other with a voice that was bizarre in its immaturity. He had the same build as Burgess, almost the same age, but gave indications of complete moral flexibility, a childish lack of defences, which shone from his liquid, adolescent eyes. He was called Grisenthwaite, Johnny had to have it repeated and finally he fell back on spelling it. Grisenthwaite obediently spelled out his name and then, '*Have you got a spare razor blade for me?*' '*Sorry, I haven't. The chief here tells me you are unwilling to fight. May I know why?*' Naturally it was Burgess who answered. '*We have enough of fighting, me boy, cause we've been through too much fighting, big big fighting in the sands. Myself I'll never put my finger on a trigger whatsoever. Nor will my pal here, Grisenthwaite. The fighting engine's broken inside us. Furthermore . . .*' '*Speak straight, Burgess.*' '*No, that's all. I think.*' Johnny said slowly, heavily: '*Men, you are wreckedly here, aren't you?*'

'Yea,' from Burgess and a confirmatory nod from Grisenthwaite. They were so direct and open in their feelings that Johnny became annoyed. '*Stop your damned peeling on, will you?*' They obeyed with a sort of automatic alacrity. '*How did you feel in the camps?*'

---

* 8 September 1943, when Italy made peace with the Allies.

Grisenthwaite's eyes drained with a flash of nostalgia and Burgess with a change in his metronomic voice: *'Not badly. Fairly well, I'd say. Left out smoking,'* and Grisenthwaite nodded his head. *'Tobacco shortage?'* Johnny inquired. *'No tobacco shortage. We received RC** *packages quite regularly. 'Twas a bias of the Italian camp-commander. He was not particularly Fascist but he had got his own ideas about war-prisoners. Positively war-prisoners are not to smoke, he would state. Something like a branded chastisement...' 'And you?'* *'We once struck but he undemorded.'*** *'Blockhead.' 'Kind of a fanatic,'* said Burgess meekly. And Johnny produced his packet of cigarettes. *'Have a pair,'* but the couple shook their heads and Burgess said: *'Why to rouse again an unmaintainable vice?'* Then he sighed and said: *'Had we known we would never have left the camp.'*

'We ran through the marshes,' Grisenthwaite put in unexpectedly, *'knee deep into muddy water.' 'Had we known the following,'* Burgess continued with suffocated remorse, *'we should have stuck quietly at the camp. But the war looked at a few days' maturity. Damn ourselves,'* he exclaimed and then settled back once more into gloomy *moroseness* bending down to take up knife and potatoes again. Grisenthwaite *eyed the re-entering cook, not at all interested. 'Say, me boy – the Fascists – er – you call them republicans now...'* *'Yes?' 'What are the Fascists going to do to us if and when they recatch us? Will they shoot us on the spot or simply lock us in their camps again?'* Johnny glanced down at Burgess, a big vein was beating on his thick neck, which was naked and strained, as if stretched out for immediate execution. Johnny said: *'They won't shoot you, I think, provided, of course, you're not caught redhanded, with weapons on hand, I mean...'* and faced by their deprecating reassuring mime hastened to add: *'I know, this will never be. They will simply lock you up again. So be easy.'*

---

* Red Cross.
** Presumably Fenoglio's invention from the Italian 'demordere' = to give in.

VII

While the Fascists still did not appear some new recruits arrived, impelled up from the misty plain by Captain Zucca's unselective hand. From the little wall at the command post in the first sun of the last winter Biondo, Johnny and Tito looked them up and down while they waited to be received by Némega or hung about, fearful and perplexed and left to themselves after their interview. Biondo lamented that they did not have sufficient arms for the basic nucleus not to mention taking on new people the most fully equipped of whom turned up with a starting pistol. Tito made it clear once more that for him the whole system was wrong – they were trying to begin where Yugoslavia taught that they ought to end up. 'There's Némega's political hand in this. The Communists, just like the Fascists, proclaim the dogma of numbers as power. The brigade has maybe forty armed individuals but is perhaps eighty strong.' Johnny recalled a recent confession by Némega at a moment when Némega seemed alcoholically excited, certainly committing an act of treachery towards himself, a puritan of lucid, mad inhibitions, anti-nicotine, alcoholless, innocent of amphetamines, he had got to the point of grasping Johnny's arm with Johnny *shrinking* openly and said to him with lips that were softer than usual, too wide open: 'What I dream of, what I shall have is a division of a thousand Garibaldini.* A thousand. I can see them passing in front of me, all in leather jackets. You will ask where I shall get a thousand leather jackets. Some of them I shall order, the rest the men will have to get for themselves. They will go down into the cities, they will attack the

---

* The Garibaldini were the Communist partisans – Garibaldi embarked on his invasion of Sicily in 1860 with 1,000 men.

drivers, the mechanics, everyone who wears a leather jacket professionally. A thousand men all alike in the most modern uniform, the most brilliantly modern uniform you can imagine. Beret of black oilskin, jacket of black leather, breeches of grey cloth and black gaiters.'

Johnny went into the bakehouse, received his crisp roll, so exquisite and basic that anything to go with it would have ruined it; but this time he did not stay there with his shoulders against the hot wall of the oven. Nibbling at it, he went slowly to the flat place at the look-out, his eyes deep in the mists of the little valleys and ravines where shortly before the mist had been thickest, unmoving, clogging; now every cavity and piece of broken ground seemed to be freeing itself like an ear from the tampon of cottonwool. He sat on a boulder that was half-naked, in a state of dripping nudity because of the thawed snow, and thought of the spring on its way, of the icy water of the thaw a foot deep and running in torrents on the paths, the white passive space which would disappear because of a greater movement, the greatest possible movement by themselves and the Fascists. After being treated by the snow the earth would be dry and elastic, better adapted to be host to the great game. The snow, if on the one hand it represented a safety cushion, on the other it meant, brought with it the most horrible, the most rigid of deaths, if circumstances, luck, brought about the abolition of the safety cushion. Johnny could not get out of his head Biondo's story of the death of the first man in the brigade to fall, *trampling* in a field of virgin snow, having walked unconsciously towards Fascists and Germans as they marched along a road that had been cleared of snow, he had found himself like a fly in honey, so certain a prey that they had actually exaggerated how badly they aimed, they hit him when they were tired of their game, his red blood was bright on the snow, almost artificial like the pink syrup that crushed ice drinks up.

Two, three bursts of machine-gun fire rang out in the valley – the ear judged it to be two slopes away. The rattle of the shots was delicious to begin with but as the open space lifted the echo to the peaks, to the village and beyond, the noise became rending and shattering, tigerish. It was the Fascists at last: it was something to hear them even if the best remedy for the sense of excitement would have been to see them. 'What are they firing at?' asked Johnny running over to Biondo who was as erect as a pillar amid the wave of the surrounding partisans. They were the only partisans within a huge radius – who could they have been firing at? Némega said, plausibly, that they were firing at civilians fleeing from discovery by this unexpected, early-morning raid. The distant machine-guns far down the hill *went out again* in the unravelling mists. Némega had got things right; men, men *raided* the farthest slope, cloaked civilians, in flight. But they were fleeing along the crest of Monesiglio so that none would come up here to cast light on things, to give details.

A column of forty men was formed with all the personal arms available plus the machine-gun which this time would necessarily sing. It was carried – in one piece – by Pinco, a giant childishly jealous of it, although his relationship to the weapon was limited to its herculean transport. Biondo would operate it in the field in Pinco's passive devout vicinity . . .

As he went down the thawed path Johnny noted that – unless there were some hidden away – the machine-gun had eight magazines and not all of them full. The Fascist machine-guns were crackling down there at short intervals, with a certain demonstrative tone, which pointed however to abundant ammunition.

Johnny shivered in the viscid and icy grip at his ankles of the water which the thaw had turned into a torrent. Since the slope was too steep and treacherous for a straight-line descent they were snaking down so that Johnny every so often had before his eyes a curve of the partisan snake. They were descending calmly and smoothly, they seemed to be concerned only not to slip for metres in the mud of the thaw, the relative distance from the camp allowed them still to carry their weapons casually, they carried them so loosely and slung round their necks like guitars. Most of them were bare-headed, a few had berets, a couple had balaclavas. The Fascists must have helmets pressed low on their heads, certainly had them; and so for Johnny in its preliminaries the battle took on the form of a clash between helmets and bare-heads. Now Johnny was going downhill, melancholy and calm, placing as best he could the feet which were carrying him from no man's land to the ground that was on fire under the snow. They went through a chestnut wood – it did not offer the least feeling of shelter or hiding. Just beyond the wood, in its grim nakedness like a collection of gallows, a fleeing civilian, low and hunched like a hare, turned his head quickly just to see the partisan column instantly there and *imposing*, like a ghost, he changed direction at a run with a groan of total fear, indiscriminating, blind to Biondo's hand raised in a signal to halt and confer.

The machine-guns were silent, now only a few rifles went off, sporadic and virulent, like test-firing. The partisans were now climbing up the last slope, looking at it benevolently and confidently as if to propitiate its soil and its footholds and its patches of cover. No one spoke although everyone's mouth trembled with the need to speak, the necessity of uttering a joke at least. Sometimes, without losing step, Biondo turned round with a tranquil air that was firm, almost painful. He was so paradigmatically the dreamt-of chief that there was almost the fear that it was only really a dream, which was necessarily bound to fail clamorously when put to the test by facts. A chief like Biondo was too fine for he was perfectly equal to the trust he inspired.

They were astride the last slope, at a signal from Biondo they spread out in echelon, the machine-gun in the centre looking more like a palladium than a weapon. Johnny and Tito lay down side by side in a square between two trunks, clear of snow, they felt the ground soft and sweet, not too yielding, the ideal ground for lying in a first dialogue with the spring earth. A partisan ran ahead of them to stretch himself out at the vertix of the triangle. Tito chased him away with a hissed insult. The man moved aside on his elbows, turning his face round – which was childishly sulky and on which the sulks cancelled the surge of excitement. The Fascists were firing their rifles invisibly. But it seemed to Johnny that a certain bullet of theirs was not entirely unaimed, from the last *hissing* noise it seemed aimed at him, he thrust his face down into the earth, then he rose up again, uneasily, along with Tito. The latter was gazing at the lack of anything visible in front of him with screwed-up eyes and lips, his pre-occupation gave to his Lombrosian face a concentration, a firmness that preceded a crime.

The Fascists were nearer now, perhaps hidden by the evergreen thickets and the houses where they must be wandering about in the courtyards. Their nearness, once ascertained, gave Johnny a repellent sense of intimacy which could be resolved only when firing opened up.

They exposed themselves inevitably: their point sections were framed in the clearings, free, unleashed, unworried, their helmets extremely *sun-catching*. The whole partisan line fired, Johnny too, and almost blindly, without wishing to hit, only as if wishing to rip apart that suspended mirage-like atmosphere. The patrols rolled unhurt into the woods and the heavy firing began.

The bursts of the invisible machine-guns cracked high up in the branches. Johnny turned on his side and waited, calm and prepared; after that first precipitate round he would fire only at sight, with a guarantee of success. He could see no one; who were his comrades firing at? Tito too was examining the *firing line* from side to side as if to discover and appropriate the secret of their target. And the partisan fire was extremely thin and in the centre Biondo seemed to be on the point of stopping it. The Fascists were firing abundantly, convinced they would win with the pure volume of their fire, their aim was very concentrated, always high but excellently laid down on the sector. The machine-guns were singing full-throated but they did not make too much impression with their air of aiming at everyone, of not wanting to hit anyone unless it was everyone. The rifle-fire on the other hand was *agonizing* with that tense sarcastic air, *better knowing*, of wishing to hit you, you and only you.

The clock struck in the bell-tower of the nearest village, eleven, with the same peal as ever. Johnny had grown old, exhausted as if by that one shot fired. The damp was invading his body like a cancer. Then he got bored, he was actually annoyed by the excessive menial intensity with which Tito insisted on watching the left-hand sector of the wood in front.

Then in the roaring silence the Fascists made themselves visible once more. They drew near for the crushing moment of contact, they flew across the open patches like lizards over little walls between men sitting here and there. The grey-green of their uniforms drew the fire like no other warlike colour; in the suckling wood their helmets had become opaque to a tearful *lustrelessness*. Johnny prepared to fire at the ones in the open, at those bounding up, but after two of his shots lashed the innocent earth behind the camouflaged ghost of a *leaping* enemy, he settled into the wearing wait for a sure shot. It was exhausting, like holding back from play at the roulette wheel turning indefatigably . . . Tito had not fired yet. When he did fire he did so with a start and a haste that froze Johnny's blood as if he had been allowed time only to register his own death. But he had time, a whole luxurious, almost voluptuous time for the bull's eye. The boy was dancing thirty metres away, blinded by his own courage; thin and elastic, intoxicated by his own courage, by his martial cunning, and by woodland nature. Johnnny fired at him without effort, without ferocity, and the boy fell, slowly, in the same way as Johnny slowly rose on his elbows in a kind of ascension and suspension before his first dead man. Dazed and excited, head and chest uncovered, he followed the last twirl of the man he had killed on the soggy grass. He went down suddenly *bruising* his nose on the ground under the fire from an automatic rifle, raging and systematic, almost 'thinking' of managing to extract him from the protective earth and raise him up into the naked air as a certain target. He lay with in his ears the crack of Tito's carbine and the great *ouverture* of Biondo's machine-gun, and in every part of him the chilling certainty that his hair had been parted by the burning track of the millimetric second round from the automatic rifle. But his hand shook and he did not manage to verify this.

Then he fell into a kind of torpor in which the shots echoed *touffues* and cottonwoolled; he shook off the torpor to fall back into a real state of boredom. He would even have decided to light a cigarette except that it would have cost him a movement which would have violated for a moment his perfect, sweet closeness to the earth. He looked at what remained of his ammunition as if it were something absolutely inexhaustible. Then he roused himself; the Fascist volleys were continuing but high up and innocuous and yet compact, calculated, precise and mechanical, as if let off not by a body of men but by a single great mechanism with set times for the discharges. And the Fascist were no longer visible as if they had plunged into a sudden deep trench.

Suddenly in the centre Biondo brought the machine-gun into action, letting off a burst so furious, frenetic and desperate that even Johnny and Tito at their distance from him understood that he had come to the end of the last magazine. Biondo had slid away from the butt, Pinco came over to it, gigantic to the point of appearing to be standing up although he was on all fours and Biondo whispered something in the ears of the men in the centre. It was clear that he was breaking off contact and it was something that both relieved

Johnny and terrified him; it would be the worst moment if the Fascists gained the open ground between the two slopes. Johnny turned round to examine the ground to be crossed with a kind of desperation; it was partly patched with snow and otherwise looked slippery. The men *scrambled to their feet* as if on ground that had an electric charge, firing a frantic glance at the Fascist front, the sight of a helmet no longer a target but a trumpet call for flight. But helmets did not mushroom so the men were still only dashing about on ground that had an electric charge. Biondo was moving about behind the centre of the line which was already broken, on its feet. Tito was shaking with excitement and distress. Johnny concentrated on looking ahead, he looked down to where his man had fallen; he was no longer to be seen. The Fascists, still invisble, were still firing strongly and annoyingly.

Biondo was now giving the flanks the signal to retreat. His mask became sterner at the lack of attention from the men on flanks, he rose up to his whole height to make his gesture more forceful and striking. Then the centre suddenly fell back, the men barely stooping so as not to shorten their stride on the slippery ground towards the interminable exposed breast of the second slope. Someone had fallen already, instinctively people thought under the Fascist fire, but he had only slipped, there he was getting up again splashed with mud, gripping his recovered weapon. The Fascist fire continued to be high but on the slopes of the breast it would be very accurate; when Biondo with a sudden move to the right and a hawklike cry changed direction and drew them all far from the slope towards a ravine which opened up in welcome and offered a safe haven. Johnny's heart sang and laughed; everyone's heart did the same as they entered the ravine, letting it swallow them up joyfully. It was a hell of mud, it stank of rotten leaves, the vegetation that curved over to conceal it like some abortion of nature dripped horribly but it was welcome safety. Johnny stopped for a moment against the entrance to the ravine and looked to the earlier spots. The Fascist helmets were flowering there like a spontaneous and stereoscopic bed of mushrooms, *gaping* and gazing at the deserted hill, mockingly. Then they turned their gaze towards the right place but held back at the sight of the grim and mysterious mouth of the ravine. They aimed their rifles at it waiting for their comrades to swell their numbers from behind. Then Johnny *swirled in*, ran right through the ravine, rejoicing in the constant trickle of water, violating the mud, and rejoined those who were already climbing up in the cover of the hill, calmly, measuring their steps so as not to slip. Further up the climb became worse, to slip meant a loss of scores of steps, but they made up for it by throwing themselves forwards and clinging to the end-poles of a huge, poor vineyard. Every so often the slope formed a saddle, they had a *glimpse* of the space between the two hills, which was swarming with Fascists, reduced to dwarfs by the distance, rendered ridiculous by the way they skidded about pointlessly on the slippery earth. From a little saddle high up Johnny saw that the Fascists were again taking up position, keeping their distance and taking precautions. They must be officers, the ones who were threading their way through the main body which was now motionless and halted, officers who were reckoning on the return of the partisans. There were about two hundred of them now dotted over the wide expanse, unmoving, and although it was noon they seemed to be wrapped in the cellophane of twilight. Now their trucks also came into view on a stretch of pearly-grey road manoeuvring with a kind of resignation and fatigue.

Johnny shouldered his rifle better, treating it with a sort of affection and receiving from it in exchange a kind of contact, a suffused animal warmth. The others had halted in the immense courtyard of a litlte poor farmhouse, the inhabitants eyeing them from the micrscopic windows, leaving all their space and belongings to the partisans who had given battle to the Fascists without getting the worst of it – on the contrary. The courtyard floor was open to infinity as if it rose on a truncated peak; the men stood there silent, calm, each by himself. Most of them were queueing patiently at the well to drink freezing water in that amorphous temperature, the creaking of the pulley was a peaceful noise. Others were walking about thoughtfully on the rutted courtyard, their heads markedly bowed, others were sitting on the low wall or on stone-flags, examining or seeing to their weapons.

Johnny went on to the courtyard happy and anxious to mingle with the men, with all of them, no longer with the instinct to pick out Tito and stay close to him. Tito was in the very centre of the courtyard with his rifle at his side, he was meticulously tidying his stockings and breeches. When he saw Johnny he winked to him joylessly but with a profound air; but Johnny did not go over to him, every one of these men, even the most brutish of them, seemed to him to be a Tito, and what is more a brother. Because of the humidity of the scene of the encounter many were coughing, all of them cleared their throats from time to time and the pulley of the well creaked. Johnny's heart opened and melted, he went all round the courtyard to make himself participate with and be aware of every man. They were the men who had fought with him, who were on his side and not on the other. He was one of them: the humiliating sense of a gap of class had completely dissolved within him. He was like them, handsome like them if they were handsome, ugly if ugly. They had fought with him, they had been born and lived – each with his own origin, games, work, vices, solitude and ways of going astray, to find themselves together in that battle.

Lieutenant Biondo was seated lightly, his horsy legs very wide apart, on the dominant stretch of the low wall, he gazed *lazily* into the very distant *melting* distance where the Fascists were slowly withdrawing. Now he was looking intently at a cigarette – because it had been kept in his trouser pocket during the battle it was all out of shape and was losing tobacco from numerous tears. Johnny passed him one of his own which was only squashed. Then suddenly he moved away from him again so as not to have to speak to him. He would have said to him: 'You are only a sergeant, Lieutenant Biondo. You commanded me splendidly. Yet we could not expect you to be a true commander. For men on their own, young and ill-equipped like us, it was enough for you to be commander in the sense of giving the signal for battle to begin. But, sergeant, you were a true commander. You commanded in a masterly way.'

He laid down his rifle and sat on a free bit of wall, very high up. Fatigue attacked him, treacherous and sweet, and then a feeling of stiffness. Then in his backbone the wave of fear came spiralling up, long and slow, the wave of fear of the battle he turned over in his thoughts. The same thing must be happening to the others because they were all a little bent, withdrawn, as if to follow the same wave in their backbones. A battle is something terrible, afterwards it makes you say (as with many puerperal women) never again, never ever again. And yet Johnny knew he would stay to fight all the battles fate held in store, battles imposed by the partisans or the Fascists, and he *felt* the battles would go on being fought in that very same war when he and Tito and all the men in the courtyard (and now there seemed to him to be a lot of them, an army) were under ground, cut down in one battle and safe from any other battle.

The men were so motionless and absorbed, so statuesque even with all they had come through within them, that the peasant children who came among them were silent and *haunted* as if in a museum.

VIII

An informer reported that the tobacconist in Marsaglia had received his supply of tobacco and a requisition squad was formed. It was a mission that was greatly coveted because apart from the uncertainties of the personal requisition it represented a pleasurable escape, in the winter coma, down a long stretch of thawed and snow-free road unlike the other side to the north which was still deep in snow. Marsaglia was two steep hill-faces away from Mombarcaro, two slopes bathed in sun, among a mosaic of snow-covered patches which gave the *thrill* of navigating an archipelago and with its medieval castle and its tree-clad bastions and its general look of being walled into the Middle Ages gave the impression of a landscape – a paradoxically northern one – in the manner of Salvator Rosa.*

Along with Johnny – with a kind of inner surge of physiological primaverility – there set out Tito, Geo with his consumptive air, and a partisan (one of the new ones), a poor product of the crossing of Ligurian and Piedmontese stock, antipathetic and contemptible at first sight. On enrolment he had proposed as his *nom de guerre* Stalin but Némega had rejected it with austere impetuosity almost as if to forestall a desecration. Then he had fallen back on Fred and the name Fred he wore sewn on his red scarf thanks to some mountain girl he had hired or flattered.

At the moment of departure Geo had brought up the old headache about weapons. He said loudly that a squad of this kind ought to have the automatic weapon, that it was time the stay-at-home sergeant-major made his Sten available, no one in all conscience could any

* Salvator Rosa (1615–73), painter of wildly romantic scenes.

longer lay *stress on the personal nature of weapons.* Johnny and Tito, who had already set out in front, had to stop and then turn back to the centre of the village because the argument had spread and the partisans were taking part, some on Mario's side and some on Geo's. *Stung,* Mario said loudly that they were talking about a ridiculous mission, a 'shopping expedition' by orderlies and a request of this kind for a mission of this kind must necessarily be a cover for some illicit business. Biondo took Geo's side, Némega intervened in the uproar and was perhaps on the side of the sergeant-major. Then Biondo offered his sub-machine-gun but no one could accept his sub-machine-gun from him; as Polo said, said it was like borrowing the pen of Dante Alighieri and then Némega persuaded Mario and the Sten passed from the latter (sulking childishly) to Geo, who was extremely tall and aesthetically skeletal, with flushed cheeks, on his inexorable way to becoming the perfect double of John Carradine.*

Johnny and Tito *goggled* and set off again. They walked *leisurely but strongly,* Tito ahead with a certain air of a poor Jew from some Polish ghetto because of the lambskin coat into which his diminutive body disappeared. Geo followed sulking incurably, sulking at Mario, sulking at himself and even with the weapon which, now that it hung on his arm, seemed no better than a modest rifle. Fred brought up the rear, floundering horribly where it had thawed *getting* severely reprimanded by those ahead for his splashes. Johnny walked along with his eyes fixed on Tito's pleasant silhouette, which was given a humorous air by the skin overcoat, but in reality shut off, his mind under siege. He was thinking about himself, about the degree of his intellectual survival, he felt he was dangling over an abyss when in one *text* he realised that he remembered nothing about aorists.** 'All this will come to an end and I shall have to get down to Greek from the start and won't be able to do without Greek for the rest of my life.' It was a horrible boring business – even now you could feel sick at that distant labour. Perhaps it was better to die among the partisans: incredibly what it was about was a proper bourgeois set-up. 'All this

* John Carradine, American actor, whose gaunt face led him to be cast in many horror movies in the thirties.
** Aorist – one of the past tenses of the classical Greek verb which denotes a simple past occurrence.

will come to an end' and then he decided to enjoy it, this march, in this gelid air, with his rifle on his arm, in that victorious sun, towards the delightful place where the tobacco would be requisitioned. And he found himself reciting *Sumer's icumen in* in a voice that was involuntarily intelligible so that Tito turned round, intrigued and interested; it was wonderful the way his delinquent eyebrows crossed each other, and turning towards the front again he sank into the snow he had not sighted.

Before the last ridge, amid a backdrop of bare trees, Geo said he could not resist the temptation to try out the automatic rifle – Did they understand? he had never fired a burst! Johnny remarked that it would mean giving the alarm to the people in Marsaglia, forcing the men to creep into freezing holes or run for their lives on naked ridges in the crude light. 'Who gives a damn about them?' said Fred, infected by Geo's temptation. Tito remarked that then they would have to give an account to Mario of the missing rounds. 'Up the sergeant-major. Are we supposed to be still in the army? In any case I'll only let off a couple.' And he cocked the rifle with contemptuous restraint. 'You've never fired a burst and you think you can control it – the first time you try? You'll let off half the magazine before you know.' But at that moment Geo pressed the trigger, there were six or seven shots at the intact trunks. It was as if the whole world had been raped by them, the four of them stood there on tiptoe with bated breath as if confronted by a miracle that had taken place and then disappeared to provide a testimony for the believers. Then Tito shook his head and let out all his held-in breath. They set out again, Geo already asking what he would say to Mario, tacitly begging them to rack their brains and come up with some reason for firing.

The burst of fire – an *earl* burst, a *prince* of a burst exploded from behind the ramparts of the castle. Tito was struck down with his rifle slung, perhaps it was that piece of wood and steel that made him fall so stiffly, like a pole. Johnny watched his collapse with interest, while the trail of the burst of fire *fluttered* his jacket. Then he looked over at the ancient wall where the Fascists were emerging, erect, slow, *masterful*, levelling their rifles again with extreme slowness and *nonchalance*. Geo was walking towards them as if hypnotised or in ritual march holding out his borrowed weapon. You had strenuously to resist the contagion of that ceremonial march of surrender which was at least as hypnotising as Tito's little heap. Amid the swarm of musketry which left the wall with a paradoxical *flopping*, and an innocuous sound and tore the air apart ferociously, with the Fascist marksmen moving about – outside the wall now but as if their feet were weighed down – Johnny felt all the blood in his brain like a frenzied impulse to escape. He fired blindly at the wall and turned back. He bumped right into Fred who was unhurt and bewitched, both fell with a crash. Johnny did not rise again but rolled back the way they had come a millimetre at a time on the sticky earth, each time he rolled over he hazily saw a tiny rise in the ground fire, eight steps away, a corrugation in the earth. But he would never reach it rolling with that rhythm, and when as he rolled he became aware that he was facing the Fascists he closed his eyes tight so as not to see a Fascist over him, grinning at his *endeavour*. The earth around him exploded with a gentle *flopping* noise but close and frequent. He heard neither voices nor shots, Geo had perhaps surrendered already noiselessly, everything had happened according to a mute procedure.

He was on the corrugation in the ground, he clambered over it sideways, convinced that he would fall down a hand's breadth, so as to have a minimum of cover. And instead he fell a metre, painfully; it was a botched manoeuvre cushioned by a thin layer of snow. The bullets *thudded* against the front of the ridge with a watery *flop*. Then Johnny made a sudden move to the right on his elbows towards the point where he could see it joined the ravine. Someone was following him but he did not need to turn round, it was Fred, certainly Fred. The Fascists had not advanced for the capture or for a closer spray of death, they were firing from fixed positions with excitement and yet with a certain detachment like people firing at a moving target in a fair. Now they were firing just ahead of them, standing still and putting their faith in the ultimate goal – to hit them as they exited from the scene into the mouth of the ravine.

Johnny's boots were tunnelling in the mud, he slowed down while his knees melted with the intolerable fatigue of the change in speed. And Fred bumped into him blindly, Johnny shouted, then they plunged into the ravine as if from a springboard of bullets.

What flowed there was the deadly water of the thaw, it bit at their ankles and blocked their way suddenly. He turned round to see Fred, he was breathing down his neck, his whole mouth fleetingly garnished with yellow vomit. They heard a little ill-tempered and petulant noise exploding in the distance. The ravine led by way of a small ridge to the road which runs down from Marsaglia to the plain. That was the source of the noise; a rudimentary, handmade armoured car was coming slowly down as if going about its own peaceful business, but Geo was bound to its turret with his feet in the air and his head downwards, his untidy hair brushing against the opaque bonnet.

The stripped branches no longer leapt. Johnny and Fred got up and marched up through the icy water that looked like anisette, up towards where the ravine became deeper and the water plunged into a whirlpool in the tufa. They were exhausted once more, they sat on a projecting rock with water up to their knees, looking sideways along the deserted hillside. Fred wanted to say something *but he only grimaced*. No human voice but the grass and the boughs spoke under their hands and their feet, as they advanced. It was better to die like Tito, in his own time and his own place, with terror so sudden and brief as almost to cancel out the awfulness of the penetrating bullet. He was envying Tito like this when he was forced to raise his eyes to the ridge where the shadow of the Fascists had risen up. A voice – distant and very high – seemed to be rebuking them, urging them on. Among the branches what was most striking was only and above all the shiny green material of their helmets, shiny and repulsive like the solid shell of unpleasant insects, and a low, almost jocular murmur of voices from Emilia engaged in the search.

Johnny rested his eyes on Fred's side which must be as massively obvious to the Fascists as to himself, he examined the turgid flesh so close to an easy shot. '*They're going to kill us in water. I'll see my own blood getting off on the tide.*' He sighed and slowly, sadly raised his rifle in the direction of the ridge. At that moment Fred came back to life to bring a hand down on this rifle-barrel and force it down with the barrel humiliated in the water. He was seized with fury at Fred but stopped because out of the corner of his eye he saw the Fascists carrying on uphill, he caught sight of their lower legs wrapped in the filthy army puttees, their leaden boots pounding uphill, no longer with much zeal. Johnny *gaped* at the miracle of invisibility and to vomit the heart-burn that flooded his mouth. Fred merely crossed his arms on his chest.

But then they realised that the others had stopped fifty paces uphill and now were coming back, at wide intervals, and each one in his turn threw a hand-grenade, a German one, into his shadow. Johnny caught sight of the first which flew slowly into the emptiness of the ravine and exploded in the middle thirty metres away. The second, the third came closer. Then Fred first gave a moan and then opened his mouth wide to shout at the top of his voice. Johnny plugged it and to be sure pushed him down into the water and immersed him up to the neck. Then Fred lay down in the water at his full length but his big behind stuck out ready to be sliced, conspicuous and ridiculous. Another grenade burst ten metres higher up wounding Johnny with some splinters of rock. He merely lay back against the wall of the ravine, it was the most exposed of positions but he could not huddle himself up like an animal and in any case there was no escape. He received on his left cheek the *grand slam* of the last bomb uphill, but it was merely air rendered virulent by its displacement. The next one would be the one, the historical one – but it exploded too far down hill, it bit low down in the trunk of a poplar; Johnny *stared* at the laceration.

So death would come when they passed for the second time up the opposite bank but it did not happen. Shortly afterwards they heard a confused noise of off-duty voices from the Fascists walking fast towards the flat ground where Tito lay, voices at rest, *ungrudging* it seemed at their lack of success.

Fred looked at him, showing his face, which had become gaunt in a second, at the hypotenuse of his shoulders, dripping with icy water, his lips white and his irises colourless. Johnny wanted to smile to him, tried it, but no part of him obeyed him any more. Fred came out of the water on all fours swimming towards his rifle which was filthy with mud, staring at it with sceptical eyes and yet as if it were a goal. Johnny saw in him, apart from the filthy clothing, a body ravaged by pain and terror, infinitely more miserable and filthy than his clothing. And he was like Fred, identical.

They set off with their rifles slung, shuffling in the water, unstable, their eyes lowered and unseeing, *frissonant* horribly. For some minutes Johnny had been trying to shape a smile addressed to himself; for some minutes Fred had been contorting his face, doing violence to his mouth so as to force an utterance from it.

They reached the lower slopes of a big hill, bare and dry, drained of colour, which appeared to Johnny, always credulous, to be a lofty expanse of asphodels. But they were alive. There ran across it, almost clinging to the naked soft slope, a sabbath air to which the backfiring of the Fascist motors added *restfulness*. They walked on with legs over which they had no control over peaceful ground, forgetful of everything, unconscious of everything except the dull effort which their bodies made to become entirely normal again. At last Fred threw himself on the ground with a wail, he rolled to and fro there for a long time like an active epileptic. Johnny stood leaning on his rifle like a shepherd's stick watching Fred as if he were a dog lashing out at the ground of its own accord, mad with the joy of living or because of fleas. Then Fred, still rolling about, wept liberally and noisily enough to awaken the echoes in the mountain. And then Johnny remembered Tito and thought of him but as a man dead centuries ago. Meantime Fred had recovered the power of speech after his reaction and lamented Tito incoherently, *babbling* in a piercing voice.

They were making – but this was unconsciously – for a farmhouse halfway up the steep hill, which was hidden almost till they reached it by the stout wall that formed a terrace round the courtyard. From the first rifle fire the inhabitants had been scrutinising all the ground in their view and only now with the partisans well in sight and recognisable raised their heads above the rim of the wall. And came to meet them, stiff and serious, across the muddy courtyard. *Children with them.*

For Johnny nothing was ever again so questioning as that rigid silence of theirs with children clinging to their trousers. Fred began: 'They have killed our comrade and captured another. Our comrade Tito is dead. Tito is dead.' And when the others asked where and how then Johnny too joined in and told of the ambush and with a childish gesture – exactly that of children asked for a grown-up explanation – stretched a hand out towards the distant plain, which was clouding over beyond the grim *ridge* and that was where the peasants turned their gaze but in their pupils there was the terror of a discovery they had already made. Nothing was to be seen, only lack of movement and early mist. Johnny surprised himself by saying in the same tone as Fred: 'They killed one of our companions and captured another. Our comrade Tito is dead. Tito is dead.' Then an old woman detached herself from the wall of her sons and sons-in-law, shifting a suckling grandchild from one breast to the other with ancient dexterity and said: 'And I have a son missing in Russia.'* Fred spread his arms in a cross to the empty sky and said: 'Be thankful he is in Russia. You see what happens to us who are in Italy.'

The children with shapeless faces, hanging from the paternal trousers as if from an unstable pulley, every so often kicked out to get their balance again.

Johnny felt something sly and long run down his spine just as after the battle but infinitely slyer and longer. Battle in the open was tremendous but the ambush infinitely more so. His brain was stammering: '*I'll get out of this all. I can't abide it. I won't never 'gain go through this all. I've had really too much of this all.*' So in order not to look like an epileptic in front of those extraordinarily intent and concentrating peasants, Johnny rose up with a fierce jerk and ordered Fred to follow him home without Tito and Geo. It was about two in the afternoon and they *groped* in the dusk in the nausea of terror. Once when he lost his step and was overtaken Johnny saw that Fred had one trouser leg where the scissors of a bullet had sliced it, and the slit showed his drawers of thick wool and an incredible purple colour.

The truck was waiting spluttering at the top of the hill, the sparse recovery squad spread in the back, the hungry machine-gun on the cabin, the driver waiting for Johnny to emerge from the doctor's house. Johnny and Fred, sulky convalescents, looked at the scene; they were not part of it, they had given Biondo all the information necessary for the recovery. At last Biondo came out again with a folded sheet and the doctor's wife – scarcely visible – followed him to the doorstep; she seemed to be giving him warnings which Biondo *acknowledged* with his curt urbanity. Biondo jumped up

---

* The Italian Army Corps sent to Russia by Mussolini was surrounded and suffered huge casualties.

into the cabin and the truck set off in neutral.

Two hours later they could hear its loud purr at the bottom of the hill. Johnny cut short his feverish pacing up and down and lined up with the people of the village who were already all collected in the little square. *Most shrunk from the front-line seat*, almost all of them as the noise of the truck drew nearer began to suffer, pressing a hand on the solar plexus or the mouth, some beginning to pant. To prevent them from seeing anything the children had been shut up in the houses and in the intermittent sound of the motor one could hear the noise as they tried the shutters and doors to get a chink through which to see the square.

The truck came on, confronting the last slope with a scream worthy of Sisyphus.* Johnny looked for a last time in the opposite direction and saw the church *gaping* for the service it could not refuse, the truck *landed*, the men ran up and lowered the side and they saw what had to be seen. Tito was enclosed in the sheet – the doctor's wife with her fingers on her lip looked at the red mould which had blossomed on her fine double sheet – shut away hermetically like someone who had died in the mountains or at sea. In the porch of the church Biondo removed the hood and exposed him to the waist. *He sailed in front of Johnny*: what he saw there was the seal of eternity as if he were a Greek killed by the Persians two thousand years before. The sockets of the eyes were deep, the skin already reduced to pure trembling cartilage, feeling the breeze, and the mouth lamented the absence of kisses of a thousand years ago. His hair absolutely motionless and heavy, the hair of a statue.

They did not lay him down in the church on the cheap trestles but on the first step of the sacristy and a woman shouted: 'Don't leave him on the stone, poor boy! Stone is bad for him even his head is on the stone! Run and get a cushion!' Némega and Mario, now without his weapon, saluted with clenched fists, the majority of the partisans did not move, the priest shuffled his feet in the nave. From the right the Sicilian soldier marched on with a rhythmical step as if in a procession bearing in the hollow of his hands two or three bloodied stones. 'Look at them, look at them, all of you, men and women, they are stones bathed in his blood,' and he took them over to the

---

* In Greek legend Sisyphus was condemned to roll a stone uphill for eternity.

retreating line of civilians like relics and the women actually crossed themselves.

From the steps Lieutenant Biondo made a sign to the people to approach in vain, they stood nailed to their places. Then he spoke, he who considered his friendly gesture to be enough, and said with his pedantic voice, 'Come closer, come and see our Tito, see how they killed him. They killed him the way you kill your rabbits –' and he repeated his *approaching* wave but in vain. Only the doctor wanted to go up but he was not in the front and he tried in vain to slip between the wall of the first ranks which was solid, rendered insensible by horror. So that he took a few minutes to make his way round the square and emerge at the church near Tito. He was very shortsighted and had almost to kneel over him, he seemed to be searching with his nose rather than with his fingers the open gaps. It was then that a shout rose up into the sky like a rocket which filled everyone with horror as much as Tito did. It was Polo, the peasant partisan, who in the very middle of the square had bent over on his knees, and was turning up his sleeves and with his rumpled hair hung over an imaginary basin. 'They have killed Tito, who was our comrade! I want to wash myself in their blood. I want to wash myself up to here,' and he pointed to his biceps and was now washing himself in a horribly natural way.

Sergeant-Major Mario took a step for the archives and *unobtrusively* but *efficiently* took a photograph of Tito with the kind of little Kodak you buy from a stall. In the dark yawn of the nave the vestments of the priest *gleamed*; he was *shuffling his feet as ever* at the door. Thus Némega declined Mario's invitation to the funeral oration and the priest came out with his loyal army of two little servers, his face distorted by the duel between his ritual duty and his bitter resentment. But immediately after the service Némega had a red flag wrapped round the coffin which had been procured at the last moment – the kind commonly used for country burials much more like a box than a coffin with miserable handles. But the priest had already turned his chasuble towards his church.

'What have you done? Tito was in no way a Communist,' said Johnny to Némega, *trampling* together in the *mud* to the cemetery. The other turned to him with a *sharp* whisper. 'Isn't it the flag of his unit? And if you are referring to the clenched fist salute is it not the salute recognised by his unit? Be clear that Tito is a dead Garibaldino, he is a dead Communist. The red flag legitimately and duly wraps the body of a fallen Communist.' He stopped because they had reached the very grave straddled by the athletic and idiotic village sexton. The end of the procession had come with lightning speed. Johnny would have liked to walk on into infinity, a corpse that was *praesente et movente.**

Tito was lowered with all speed and hastily buried. And looking at that fresh grave Johnny said to himself that however soon the war ended that new grave would always seem to him immensely distant as if at another pole. The partisans were already turning back with a certain *grim appreciation*; they had seen the treatment reserved for him; he could go.

To take up the routine again, without Tito. Sentry duty, eating, sleeping, action, stasis, without Tito. And the prospect, the certainty of falling and of being immediately, automatically a dead Comm-unist. Négema had gone on sadistically: 'When the war is over Tito will be a thread in the great skein on the Italian balance which afterwards we will present to the people in our blood-stained right to power.' Despair drove him to where he felt the most repugnance – he mixed with the majority of the partisans in the evening in the inn, in asphyxiating layers, amid their gamey smell, *missing Tito horribly.* Later Némega came to him, tunnelling his way through bodies, ill-tempered and anxious to please, inevitably but squeamishly leaning his elbows on the filthy table. 'You're very low, Johnny. You are missing Tito, and you are depressed by the fact that you got away and he did not in the same situation. I never understood what points of contact you could have with Tito – try not to feel bad about it too long. But it won't happen. Because new people are arriving. Captain Zucca is doing great propaganda work getting people from the plain and next spring they'll come up in huge numbers. And not only workers and peasants – people from your class will come up too otherwise what are we to think of the middle class?'

'The middle class,' Johnny answered, 'has already come up into the hills – it is in those famous blue formations** I keep thinking

---

* Latin – present and moving.
** The non-Communist monarchist partisan formations

about and where I am destined to end up.' But he said it without conviction, without a cutting edge, opaquely *despondent*. Only a catastrophe could disintegrate the Garibaldi Brigade but Johnny at that moment lacked the physical courage to cope with a catastrophe.

That same night, while still in the inn, the news came that Geo had been shot by the Fascists in Ceva, the very day of his capture, in the barrack-square. And Johnny wondered if Geo's last *footstanding* had coincided with the shadow of one of the many footprints left there by Johnny during wheeling close order drill.

IX

The Allies were behaving disappointingly round Montecassino* and the only one pleased seemed to be the commissar Némega. For months the radio had been going on about nothing but the unopposed Russian advance: the leaders – including Johnny who was included because of what was recognised as his 'higher education' – listened to it in the house of the local doctor, a microscopic oasis of semi-urban civilisation in the mountainous desert of Mombarcaro, in the drawing-room saturated with solid darkness where the polychrome disc of the set shone like the crib in the vast night of Bethlehem. The doctor had decided to offer them hospitality and to entertain them, he had gambled the risk of compromising himself in this way with the partisans against what was now an unbearable lack of company capable of conversation at even a minimum level. And now he had got to the point of arguing openly, bitterly with the commissar. The doctor was for the Americans, body and soul, he maintained that on a closer historical examination all the other belligerents would look half-size. 'I am saying and will maintain that in this conflict America has committed something like fifty per cent of its resources and energies. Just imagine the day or the occasion when America will throw them in one hundred per cent' – all this while his wife in a state of *suspense* – rapidly overcome – moved about among them with a perfumed train, her feet radar-guided in the intact darkness, distributing little cups of sugarless brew, while Sergeant-Major Mario followed her with eyes like gleaming lenses in the dark, in desperate frustration.

* A crucial German mountain position round the monastery of Montecassino blocking the Allied advance on Rome.

One evening they brought the doctor the present of a bottle of commandeered liqueur which their host put into immediate circulation. Perhaps it was the alcohol, perhaps the comfort of the drawing-room or something else, Némega let fly with heart and voice, *gave vent* to the Communist programme. The radio, which had just been turned off, had confirmed the Russian advance and the problems of the Allies on the Gothic Line.* 'We have great hopes of the East,' he said. 'Tito can beat all the speed records including that dreamt up by von Conrad in 1918 on the Venice–Milan line. We can legitimately hope to liberate Northern Italy autonomously and to meet the Anglo-Americans on equal terms when they have crossed the Po looking for Germans most of whom will be already destroyed or imprisoned in Italian Communist camps.' They could hear the painful *creaking* of the doctor's *swivel-chair* and Némega thrust his sadistic face forward into the iridescence of the dial. He wanted – had to carry on to the end. 'As early as 9 September† we Communists set out with a maximum and a minimum programme. The maximum one consists of the Communist revolution as the corollary to and crowning event of the struggle for liberation. Failing that, and this is the minimum programme, we will take part with conventional methods in the competition for a parliamentary majority.' Johnny said: 'Right – I pray that you are limited to the minimum programme. I'll be for you and you for the minimum programme.' He was increasingly uncomfortable with those red stars which – once a priviledge on the first caps – now shone on all of them as an obligatory general order of things and everyone sewed them on without objections though without a smile, they were the most natural and satisfying thing to set against the Fascist badge! And the joke was that the only or the principal source of supply was the nuns in the neighbouring villages; they made them up with a certain crude and loving care and lack of precision, and the quartermaster Mario maintained that he would not dare – could not even think of avoiding payment or paying late.

The brigade was now about one hundred strong with perhaps ten

* The fortified line in the Apennines the Germans fell back on after the fall of Rome.
† The day after the Italian collapse in 1943.

men with military experience. Sometimes the echo of a shot, neutral, distant and arcane, cut through the silence of nature and the high hills amid spring's gestation. The partisans basking in the first sun and in their state of armed inactivity, turned their heads more and more lazily towards the mysterious source of the noise and Johnny raged with dissatisfaction and shame. In the immense battle line of the world war he had allotted himself a few metres of sterile earth in the mountains, concentrating entirely on a mob of Fascists who could presumably emerge from one or two little Piedmontese towns here and there on the compass. His inability to find a replacement for Tito certainly played its part but 'Where are they, what are they doing – people like myself?' Johnny asked the roads, the paths on the precipitous crests, the mysterious *not giving* plain. Tito he once sought out in the churchyard, once when he could no longer endure – to an unhealthy degree – that lazy basking community, *grim* and slobbering. But on the mound of the grave he was unable to establish even the slightest dialogue with Tito *underlying*, indeed for all these minutes he was seized by a literary *fit* which was certainly frivolous, perhaps sacrilegious, certainly extremely unpleasant: '*watched the moths fluttering among the heat and harebells; listened to the soft wind breathing through the grass...*' He ran away in headlong shame. Even the improvement in nature troubled him now, reawakening the demands of his body. During the winter he had put up with it as if in an armed Lent but now all the humours were stirring within him and, not purging themselves in the eruption of pus that was action, they poisoned him completely. Now he dreamt long and frivolously and exhaustingly. He dreamt of himself dressed in vicuna smoking with Mimmis and Gherits, conversing at his best, making love with all his might, listening to Anglo-Saxon music in a fine salon, in a bitter-sweet atmosphere of *comfort*, everything and everyone around him making their *keenest endeavour to civility.*

The distant girl from Carrú* turned up at the base with her old golden *infula*,** her polemical masculine stride, and the stockings of other times but now worn and threadbare. *Glanced* murderously

* Not mentioned before, she presumably comes from an episode not included in this edited version of the MS.
**Latin – a band of wool worn by priests and Vestal virgins.

at the peasant women lying in wait and terrified at their *lilliput-windows and strode into command*. She stayed there all afternoon and night. He chanced to comment on the event to Johnny Regis, a worker from Turin, whose gnomic taciturnity Johnny greatly appreciated along with his absolute lack of smell in that feral world. Regis sucked in his thin lips and shook his head with pointed sagacity: he said these were not places for women, he absolutely could not bear to see them there, it was easy to foresee that things would go badly with partisans who accepted, introduced women. Another interjected – someone not seen before – with *a haggard & passionate* face, he said loudly that he was ready to have nothing in common with headquarters but what he could not put up with was that the bosses were fucking, this being the only case in which he claimed his rightful share. But after a while the girl came out with the stride of someone preparing for a long journey and nothing in her betrayed love – the extraordinary indecipherability of women! – and made her way energetically, almost with an air of rebuke, through the *puzzled* partisans.

The next morning the truck was ready at the very top of the hill with Lieutenant Biondo in new boots of thick leather, hurrying his men on with his hand. Johnny stopped at a distance, he had a stomach upset that morning: the first action after and without Tito terrified him, he watched the men clambering on board the truck like *an unreliable, shruggingly rejectable* collection of strangers. He was about to opt out for the first time, to report sick, but Lieutenant Biondo looked hard at him from by the cabin door with knitted eyebrows and a sad mouth. Johnny looked at him as if he was seeing his hair turn white that very moment and moved towards the truck with a complaining step.

The lieutenant took him into the cabin with him. And Johnny soon felt better. The wind of their journey, even the dominating and responsible position in the cabin, the silent and understanding closeness of Biondo, *rearranged his frame*, he could begin to think well even of the invisible men in the back, and gladly looked up when at each skid in a bend there came down from the cabin-roof the mouse-like *tapping* of the machine-gun's tripod. Biondo was calm to the point of being absent, silent to the point of apnoea, so that it did not even occur to Johnny to ask him about the operation.

But at last he did ask him for it seemed at that point unnatural and almost a fault not to do so. Biondo, still staring ahead at the road which slid past under the belly of the truck said they were going down to Carrú: the girl had reported the return of the political secretary* to give substance to his threats of shootings, burnings and deportations – did Johnny know that the girl's two brothers were in Germany having been denounced by the secretary? So they were going to kidnap the Fascist secretary, perhaps he was closely surrounded by a squad of men from the Fascist headquarters in Cuneo. 'Ah, a police action.' 'This needs to be done too,' said Biondo with sober *dislike*.

In the plain the snow had quite melted, the fields were spangled, the roads had a cold gleam, everything was swept by a tonic ventilating current of air, the sun *literally flapped* on the slim campaniles, speaking to Johnny of a humanity that simply belonged to a different ice age. He immersed himself in the landscape, he imagined what he wanted to do and could do with whom, all the way along that shining road parallel to the stream (visibly of Alpine source), under these avenues of poplars so silvery cold and alive, in the little caffé-latte squares of little villages so obviously at peace. His heart *sobbed for instance of peace* and so he saw little or nothing of what happened at the crossroads. He saw as if in a dream the aerodynamic blob of yellow coming from the right and, with eyes shut, heard its crash into the partisan truck. When he opened them again he saw, parallel to his chest, the burnished barrel of Biondo's tommy-gun, resting on the windscreen of the truck and heard the men behind *thudding* to the ground.

Johnny got down to the ground clumsily and laughed in the crystalline air. The Germans were emerging from the crash, they got themselves up so *shocked* that no one found it necessary to insist on hands up: the partisans themselves were crowding round, excited, and as it were disarmed by the chance happening. Germans captured in a road accident: Biondo himself, with his sub-machine-gun hanging down, *looked helpless before the lotto-event*. One of the Germans was the first to come to, he towered over the partisans who were already going through the knapsacks, deaf to the demands to

* That is of the local Fascist Party.

100

put his hands up, pointing childishly (and wailing in a falsetto voice) at the interior of the car. The driver and another soldier had escaped without injury but an officer *yet twisted at this place, pointing at his disabled leg.* There was no way of moving aside the Germans who had emerged, they seemed to be entirely *nonchalants* about the partisans, in fact had every appearance of wanting to take charge of the rescue operation; but now the partisans had cooled down and with guns at their chests forced them away from the smashed vehicle and they moved away saying in a filial way: 'Herr Major!'

From the beginning the machine-gun had commanded the road from which the yellow blob had shot out in case it were the advance guard of a whole column, but from the beginning to their eyes the whole road *wringed in its desertedness.* Biondo was very angry. 'A nasty business. We didn't need it. However things turn out, whatever Némega decides, we'll soon have them on top of us.'

By now the Germans seemed to have become conscious of the collision which had been transformed into an ambush and capture by Italian irregulars but their distant eyes wanted their major who was just being extracted. With white lips he strangled his lament at the fracture allowing scarcely a tiny sound to emerge. He was in great pain and the cold sweat broke out on his grizzled temples, slowly, lasting, and concrete like dark grapes. He was laid delicately on the grassy bank, *a tiny dapper man,* much smaller than his gigantifying uniform. 'Can you speak German?' asked Biondo who was extremely uneasy. 'Nein!' *snapped* Johnny. The major was talking his own language but as if under hypnosis, with slow rambling words.

They could not miss the appointment in Carrú so Biondo ordered them to turn the German car upside down in the ditch, which the partisans did with childish fury; three of them had already put on their heads the strange, toylike caps of the *big-craped* German soldiers. The car settled down in the bottom of the ditch, showing its dusty-oily belly, it had the air of a monstrous tortoise, and looked quite hostile, as if saying it had been built and tested in hatred of and for war against the Italians. The three soldiers were called over, they lifted their officer in a filial gesture and transported him to the other side of the watercourse to a sparse thicket. The partisan lorry was testing its *roadworthiness,* disinterestedly. And Biondo ordered everyone on board except Johnny and another, snub-faced René.

'You're the only one I can trust completely in a case like this. Wait for me for a couple of hours. You are sufficiently hidden from the road. If they make the least false move or if they stop their cars on the road you and René will kill them and cut up across the hills.' Then he went to the lorry with three P38s* hanging from his belt.

Nothing happened in that couple of hours, the Germans did nothing but see to their officer, speaking in pure German but slowly and affectionately, to the great irritation of uncomprehending René who a couple of times *ineffectually burst out* with 'What are they saying, German pigs?' Johnny guessed that they were only speaking about the fracture – the leg seemed to be entirely *disabled* under the unusual, *indicative* creases in his trousers. Beyond that they seemed indifferent to their unequivocal capture, they must be placing comforting reliance on the rules of war: the sign of the red stars gleaming on the berets did not even make them scowl.

The truck came back sooner than hoped. Biondo had had the idea – and time to do so – of getting a mattress on which to lay out the major who refused, thanking him in Italian, the drop of cognac which Biondo had found for him as well. The partisans looked on neutrally at this display of chivalry and good manners. When the truck dug its way out, at the lurch Johnny had to get some immediate support and it was then that he saw the man, the Fascist.

His *tomorrowless* age was about fifty, he was dressed with an elegance rare in these times, in the style of a bourgeois *minute-man*. He had a bronzed complexion which terror and despair turned into a *rotten grey*. His physique – although he tended to overweight – retained a sportive and subversive *allure*. With hairy hands he clutched the side of the truck and during the whole journey never raised his eyes from the floor, from the earthy mass of the partisans' heavy boots. The Germans, from the other corner of the truck, glanced at him for a moment, very probably *grasped* his nature and situation but did not betray any feeling, almost certainly he was of no importance to them, they continued to *nurse* their major – so diminutive now if one looked down from above at him lying there.

The Fascist bore no signs of struggle or beatings, his capture must have gone off very smoothly, and he knew he was going on this

---

* German pistols.

tremendously speedy truck towards his execution. No one guarded him particularly as if he were already harmless and not worth paying attention to – like a corpse. The partisans neither prodded nor plagued him, as would certainly have happened given the probability of a less drastic fate, they confined themselves to extending to him, offering him, occasional glances which were slow and very serious. Regis told Johnny what had happened. The man was dining in the best hotel in Carrú at his usual table in a corner that dominated the entrance with a big pistol (*by the by* who had grabbed it?) beside his cutlery. The girl got Biondo to lend her one of his new German pistols and managed to cover him from the window which was half open on to the midday sun. He spat out what was in his mouth and *sprung* up with his hands in the air while his napkin slipped to the floor down his trembling legs.

At the base he would have been the prime attraction but the four Germans completely supplanted him. The village *went in exceeding flutter* all *gaping* at the sight of the Germans and at that of the partisans who no one would have credited with such a coup; the people had to be chased back into their houses *militari manu*,* only the doctor stayed on and confirmed the fracture. A woman was called back: she should speedily prepare something delicate and substantial for the wounded German. The men who had not been at Carrú moved in waves towards the room with the Germans to catch a glimpse of them. Némega put up with it for a little then he had them rudely cleared away by Biondo and the men withdrew, reluctantly, swearing and grumbling, recalling Fascist behaviour, with an air of mutiny. The commissar did not even make an effort to conceal his painful situation, he seemed *cross* with Biondo for the collision. 'A very bad business, the very worst that could happen to us at this moment. We are still in a stage of getting organised, the ideal thing would be to deal only with the Fascists and not even very often. It's easy to see what will happen. I know the damned Germans. Damned they are but they never let go of their men.'

A new voice said: 'It's very true – the Germans never let go.' Johnny turned round and found himself faced by a new man – a *supercilious* person of about thirty with thick soft moustaches

* Latin – by armed force.

English in style and colour, stylish in civilian dress and without the slightest trace of being a partisan. Johnny noted that he kept close to the leaders and took care not to find himself mingling with the rank and file. He spoke with a soft, self-satisfied Lombard cadence, but his eyes had a metallic gleam. Sergeant-Major Mario informed him that this was Antonio, Antonio the saboteur. At this description Johnny and the others turned towards him again as if to seek for and find on him the badges and charismatic signs of his special skills. 'He must be a first-class element,' whispered the sergeant-major. 'He brought two suitcases full of instruments for his job. And fine suitcases.' Antonio the saboteur knew they were talking about him and walked across in the middle distance *fluttering in his strict-contained airs*.

A woman, the one chosen as cook, passed through the partisan guards holding in front of her a bowl of strong broth for the German major with the partisans *leaning* in the wake of that rich smell. Regis shook his head and sobbed a laugh. We Italians were always the same, always with a complex about the Germans. Consommé for the poor German major who has a sore little leg which he got working for the Italians. 'We'll bump them off,' said one of them without the least element of doubt. But another broke in: 'We're mad if we kill them!' 'Because they don't bump us off?' *snarled* Regis with a waspishly humorous tone that had no time for babytalk. But the other did not give in: 'If they were SS – but they are from the Vermast.'* 'Some difference! What do you know about it anyway?' 'I know the uniforms.' Regis shrugged dissatisfied. These four Germans were causing a disease, the very houses seemed to tremble from a telluric shock because of their explosive content.

By a kind of polemical association of ideas Johnny looked round for the Fascist. 'Have they dealt with him already?' 'Who?' 'The Fascist.' The job, Regis knew, wouldn't take place before evening and indeed the Fascist came into view, ghostly at the bars of the ground floor. 'Who'll deal with him?' Someone said they were waiting for the Spaniard, the *delegado militar*,** who had been on the look-out for an execution for some time. 'I have only one religion,' said Regis, 'it's

* The Wehrmacht, which had a separate command from the SS.
** Spanish – the military representative attached to the formation.

104

not to kill except in battle. My heart tells me that if I were to do it I would come to the same end.'

Regis shook himself all over excitedly like a dusty dog, and his opponent from before said: 'I agree about him provided they deal with the Germans as well, all four of them. Meantime I'm taking him a cigarette' but he didn't move. Johnny said: 'Why don't you take him a whole packet. But remember that without the dead, theirs and ours, nothing would make sense.'

The day was becoming special, extraordinary in a *fitfulness* like a gust of wind that shook the men having first taken hold of them. In mid-afternoon a squad which had gone out along the road to Liguria came back with an enormous truck and trailer with a MI* number-plate, fresh from the factory, *shining out of* springtime paint. They had held it up and requisitioned it *sur place* on the immensely long, *bleak* crest of Montezemolo. Its only driver, a big Lombard with a strong accent, was getting into a state because of the unexpected happening and its consequences. He kept watching the partisan driver who was looking at the *parlour-like* cabin like a savage at the deck of an unguarded white ship and at the same time was arguing with the partisans on the ground, asking what on earth he would say to his bosses (his proprietors, he said) and with a mad gleam in his eyes looked at the sergeant-major who in a cold bureaucratic manner was opening up his requisition pad. The truck and trailer were manoeuvred by the same impatient partisan driver into the street between the little square and the arch; it filled it hermetically. The driver was invited to *a meal* and went off protesting in his loud thick voice: 'You can imagine, lads, whether I am on your side or not, I even fired at the Germans on 8 September but what am I to say to my proprietors?' The partisans praised and calmed him.

A little later, travelling from the north-east along the crest and the valleys, there came unusually heavy rifle fire, which slit open the whole sky, with as counterpoint the roar of mortars. Biondo and Johnny went to that acoustic meeting-place, they sat on a solitary bank, on the cold and not very yielding grass, which a flock had just left, with on their faces the sweetness of the overripe afternoon. 'Is it in the Belbo valley?' asked Johnny. Biondo nodded. With his eyes

* That is to say Milan.

fixed on the mother-of-pearl distance, at the lofty sky which must be over the battle, a witness sworn to secrecy, they listened for a long time, smoking and scarcely moving. The din pleased Johnny who felt and was marvellously well. The same went for Biondo who – very paradoxically for him – shivered with pleasure. 'Have you ever heard the German flame-thrower firing?' Johnny replied No revealing a *hint* of deprivation. 'It has a very strange noise, like the whirr of wings of a bird coming out of the branches. I heard it at Boves. It is . . . fascinating, because of the fascination you don't take cover and get killed.' Then it was over down there and for them too; they went back frowning and chilled. Something was being got ready for the Langhe and for their partisans and their accomplices.

In the evening the low thick clouds were forming pack-ice in the sky, from the ground floor the Fascist emerged, went on between the Spaniard armed with his envied Llama* and an unarmed partisan, undoubtedly a peasant, certainly responsible for the grave. The peasant drove the Fascist on like an animal but with a light touch and understanding. They took the low road towards the crumbling quarry on Monesiglio. No shots were heard but they interpreted it this way – the shot from the Llamada had coincided with the first stroke of the Ave in the campanile.

In the night Biondo took extraordinary security measures, he tripled the guard and Johnny from excitement skipped sleep and passed the time off duty on his feet. They were all electrified, oscillating between disaster and a miraculous success, under a chaotic sky, which filled them with indistinct, contradictory presentiments.

So in the morning they found themselves worn out and full of aches and pains, with drawn faces and unsteady eyelashes, forgetful of the four Germans no less than of the dead Fascist. But the morning promised a wonderfully fine day and from the clear sky, the clear air, the ground softly pulsing under the tender sun someone uttered the hope, for all and out loud, that nothing would happen.

An alarm signal from below rushed them all to the northern bastion. Up the winding road, there climbed – scattered and slouching – a formation of partisans; out in front the familiar purplish

---

* A kind of rifle.

106

uniform* from a distance visibly soiled with earth, with dew and rents, set *colonial-like* in the gaunt wall of its Slav bodyguard. With the others Johnny clambered up on to the medieval arch among the first lizards to see them pass beneath. They had borne yesterday's battle, then they had disengaged, had passed half the night just clear of ground lost and then had made for Mombarcaro to join forces because it looked as if the Fascists did not wish to break off the action – rather to extend it.

The admirers of the Russian** of the first visit asked loudly about his fate. The leader answered with his soft but sonorous voice: 'Valodkia is dead. We left him there. A bullet in the forehead. I never saw anyone fight like him – as if he were drunk.' He made his report smilingly, with a broad and genuine smile, with a gay excitement as if for him it were a game or a *fictioned* sacrificed by film extras. The Slavs† filed past weary and wooden; at their last step they threw at the top of the arch decked with partisans their serious *impressive* glance – that of men who come from a real battle, with their cartridge pouches gaping half-empty, around the whole of their thin bodies the indissoluble magnetic field of grazing bullets.

The great meeting took place in the little square, their commander frivolous, but insidiously frivolous and equivocally brilliant as always – 'I lost seven men including the Russian,' he said lightly, the only thing that increased the burden of his regret being that there had not been more. He went up to Némega with a drawing-room effusiveness, his arms held out limply, asking him for hospitality for a few days and cooperation for all eternity. Némega returned the embrace – his *shrinking* hands slack on the repulsive purple cloth drawn tight over the well-nourished shoulders – and assured him of everything. Biondo scowled and then let loose the men of quartermaster's staff to requisition some calves.

The leader from the foothills then presented and lauded his band's latest acquisition, an ex-member of the Foreign Legion, congratulating himself on the choice composition of his formation:

* A reference to some episode not included in the present edition of the MS.
** The Russians who fought with the partisans were usually escaped prisoners of war or deserters from German labour battalions.
† Yugoslavs like these were usually ex-POWs.

all collector's pieces. The legionary was a tall *lanky* individual, ill-formed, but with a homoeopathic face all regularity and decision. He was prestigiously armed with a Skoda parabellum, the first they had cast eyes on, and such a piece of equipment as to impress even Biondo who was so resistant to the mania for fine weapons. It was a short and massive sub-machine-gun, designedly amorphous, with horizontal reinforcing pieces, with the silver barrel hung about with bits and pieces and pierced in an oriental manner. 'How did you enlist in the Legion?' '*Force majeur.* I had punched an officer of the Militia* in a cinema in Turin because of a film that was dirty propaganda. If that criminal of a projectionist hadn't turned up the lights in the hall I could perhaps have got away. Enforced clandestine emigration and . . . the Legion.' Unexpectedly his voice was full and mature, always sarcastic, the only well-toned muscle in his unco-ordinated body.

The leaders having withdrawn to the command post everyone clustered round the legionary as earlier round the Russian. Johnny went over to the Slavs who were a clan on their own, silent and looking askance even at their comrades. One after another they went over to the parapets above the cliffs examining the position. Then they sat down with their creaking legs and examined their rifles which were in a terrible state because of water, powder and fire. They began to complain, addressing jeremiads to each other in ciphered monosyllables. They asked Johnny for oil to clean their guns but Johnny was *helpless,* then one of them indicated the shop to him. One of them made a collection, went to the shop and came back with a big bottle of *cheap* brilliantine exhumed from a sleep of ages on a dusty shelf. They would never have contaminated their thick hair with it – their wild, dull dry hair that rustled like stalks, humming in the light wind. They cleaned their weapons with the brilliantine under the eye of Johnny, perplexed but admiring and *remorseful.*

Their Italian commander emerged from the command post and came over to them. He smiled to them in his open and ambiguous way, he said well done to be working so hard to deal perfumed death and handed a cheque in lire to the one who seemed to be their elder and chief. He pocketed it impassively and impassively shook on his

* The Fascist Militia – the episode is clearly prewar.

pole of a body his shirt and trousers, both reduced to a weft. '*Nema greba, nema pantaluna*,* boss.' 'I'll see to it, we'll see to it. The first time we go through a big village with a good shop.' 'Doglian?' 'Yes, Dogliani.' He was baroque, effective, absolutely unacceptable, but perhaps he had *pulse*, he seemed to be *in love with his men* but like a soldier of fortune.

At that moment the burst of fire from the Skoda crackled from the inn. And it seemed to Johnny that the house became deformed outside because of the turmoil taking place inside, then it disgorged one of Biondo's men shouting for the priest. Then the immediate but *shrinking* scrum at the door was cleft by René with his hand on his temples and shouting indistinctly he fled towards the *ravines*. Regis emerged in pursuit of him, shouting for help, for them to help him to catch up with René before he killed himself. René's receding yell was lasting, infinite.

Johnny shouldered his way in. The host was babbling, blinding against his chest his waitress-daughter in convulsions, the partisans were squeezed against the walls and looking at a table where three men were twitching, mortally hit. The legionary's parabellum was in its place on the round table, still pointing at the three men, innocent and tigerlike. The legionary had laid it down there to do card-tricks for the public and René had been unable to resist the temptation to have an admiring look at it, to touch it with his worker's hands; the burst of fire had gone off in a heavenly way.

The three men, two of Némega's and one belonging to the man in purple were sitting and still twitched without moaning. They were bleeding furiously and one had been hit in the mouth and completely disfigured, his eyes untouched, enormous, astonished, drained of colour by pain. Not dead but dying, stupidly beyond all salvation, Johnny saw in them the sudden misery of dying flesh, the skin already like clay, the shagginess of their beards already frighteningly nasty and animal, every bit of their flesh losing its quality vertiginously. The doctor and the priest arrived but the doctor did not make way for the priest not even ten minutes later.

Johnny barged out again to wait outside for the sentence: his feeling of dejection forced him down to sit on the road. Above him a

* Serbo-Croat – No shirt, no trousers.

partisan of whom Johnny glimpsed only the faded *bagging* trousers said: 'We are a crowd of irresponsible kids.' 'That's right, and the little we manage to do is by a miracle.' Johnny was coming round slowly. Then the doctor came out to announce that although horribly wounded all three could be saved, even the one hit full in the mouth. The truck swayed at the top of the descent to Murazzano with its floor covered with tenting, the wounded now groaning were loaded on board and laid down. Biondo jumped up on to the parapet and shouted down to René and his pursuers: 'Come back all of you, they're not dead, they're not going to die.' The truck *shot-down*.

Regis popped up again in a gap in the parapet as if at the mouth of a well, breathless. 'Johnny? We were complaining about boredom but this is too much.'

X

In the late afternoon – the truck had returned from Murazzano and the sun was setting headlong leaving on the tops of the Alps *cheap* and smoky clouds like newly dead embers – Némega, the commissar, had the men of the two groups gather on the wide, purplish field under the church-dormitory. He wanted to harangue them with that voice of his which was so unsuitable, full of caesuras, finicky. From that unexpected and all the more welcome fusion he read good omens for the greater and inevitable union of all partisans – the men stamped their feet on the dewy grass and shivered in the evening wind. Now Némega went on with a partisan lesson to be drawn from General Time and the men either thought about other things or concentrated their gaze on the commander in the purple uniform who merged with the background of the field – the only one who stood outside the ranks with Némega rocking with a fixed smile on legs clad in dandified boots.

Johnny looked away and suddenly among the evening mists which had already triumphed in the plain he heard like a drill the rude noise of the German trucks and then, triumphing over the blanket of mists, their diabolical white and red headlights. Someone gave a shout and the groups scattered uphill almost as if the Germans were at the bottom of the big meadow. Up above people stopped and looked down from the parapet. Someone counted the lamps out loud and with them the trucks and as the number rose his voice became muffled with despair. Such a deployment of forces for their two men and a dog. Clearly the operation on a grand scale had been dictated and rendered necessary by the capture of the high-ranking German officer and by the news of the juncture of the two rebel groups.

111

In the dusk Lieutenant Biondo had the two machine-guns sited on the last two bends on the road from Monesiglio and *manned* the deep trench of a ditch between the church and the command post. The men slipped into it cursing themselves for not having dug it deeper and more adequately when they had nothing else to do. Johnny looked either way along the muddy ridge and saw that one in three in the trench was brandishing a pistol. He shouted to Biondo to take him with him to the machine-guns but Biondo ran off unhearing. In the trembling noise of the wind one could hear the terrified whimpering from the houses of the villagers who now knew themselves to be the epicentre of the reprisal.

Biondo, when he reappeared stopped at the machine-guns to check their line of fire and Johnny jumped up towards him from the trench. But Biondo was not a pessimist; for him that column was too monumental to have them as its objective – according to him it was a big convoy that had stopped on the road to Liguria. 'You mean we're not worth it?' said Johnny this time but appeased by the ascendance and experience of the lieutenant. 'Némega thinks so too,' said Biondo.

Two hours passed in the long, swampy shivering cold of the trench. The lieutenant's opinion, if on the one hand it had calmed the men, on the other had also weakened their capacity to suffer; soon they began to complain about this useless stay in the trench, to blame each other and not to put up with each other any longer. Johnny moved up a dozen of positions to take his place at the side of Regis, the most civil and four-square. With Regis he looked down at the Germans about a kilometre away as the crow flies. The mist was dancing in a dishevelled and sensuous way round the motionless white headlights which corresponded to the red lights – they had counted seventy-four of them – and every so often the body of a German soldier would materialise in the beams of light to disappear at once in the dark of the hillside. Germans reconnoitring within a short distance were going over the ground on either side of the road, the lights of their electric torches wandered among the dark gullies. The sense of safety became inflated to the point where Némega ordered them to take turns for the evening meal; it was almost nine, a cobweb of blackish cloud which up to now had wandered through the sky seemed to have impaled itself on the bell-tower.

But at half past nine in the heart of the darkness and peace there shot up into the sky a red rocket which for a moment bulged out into a large ball and then evaporated. It was the signal from a German officer to a colleague that the items on the programme had been carried out as agreed but Johnny felt he was seeing the balance of Jove hanging there. In fact a moment later the shout of encirclement rose to the sky, one of the most terrible in the human scale of cries. Johnny, enclosed in a dense body of men that flowed across, rushed to the other side of the village only to see down in the Belbo valley the same concatenation of white and red lights. Only towards Murazzano did the lights seem more scattered. The dogs of the barns on the hilltop and halfway down the slope were all barking together.

He returned with the rest to the centre of the village. From within the houses there was an explosion of despair that raised the roofs. The women were weeping in the doorways, the children from their little beds and cradles, the men were carrying away blindly everything that could betray contact with the partisans, use by them. The partisans meanwhile were gathering by instinct, by a fellow-feeling, in groups and clans, for flight. Johnny was waiting for a summons from the lieutenant – he was now consulting closely with Némega, the latter assenting with a continuous pecking motion of the head. They agreed on escape, squads were already leaving almost furtively to take their chance, as if they wanted to conceal from the others their selected route in order not to make it – because of the numbers – too worthwhile blocking.

Johnny sat on the steps of the church and waited smoking. The parish priest came to throw open the doors of the place of worship so that the women could rush in to pray and beseech God, exceptionally, as in a time of plague. The men, having finished the task of getting rid of things contaminated and contaminating, lingered in the doorways sighing or cursing. The squads that were leaving went off with heads low, blindly rushing. Némega expended his breath giving to each of them a rendezvous at the secret, remote, safe hill at Lovera, which was like a place for convalescence, but they paid no attention to him almost sweeping him away first of all. The commander in purple was nowhere to be seen having already left for the bare naked woods of the Bormida, the red and white lights being at one and the same time pole star and death.

Biondo counselled calm and coolness, spoke of time galore, the Germans would certainly not attack at night. 'It's true,' said Antonio, the saboteur, 'The Germans never attack at night – in this they are like the Redskins.' He was refined, ice-cold, didactic. 'Antonio, you're a saboteur, you arrived at the right time. Sabotage anything that can be sabotaged.' And Antonio went off to sabotage the lorries.

Johnny climbed up to the look-out post to look down at the village which was becoming deserted, up there his steps had a new echo, an odd one, and at the surrounding precipitous slopes down which invisible series of black ants were descending to cross the illuminated line of red ants. Then Biondo shouted to him that he would be part of his squad but not to come down now, there was any amount of time. It was almost eleven by the watch bathed in the red of his cigarette. Then he raised his eyes to the moon, it was gliding inexorably towards the clear patch of sky, in half an hour it would shine without veils so as to coat with platinum the desert of snow down towards Murazzano.

Towards midnight the last two squads were ready to leave. 'Have we a chance, Biondo?' asked one man. 'That depends whether we make it,' said Biondo simply but with sinister seriousness. Then Johnny thought that in a couple of hours on that particular earth, under that universal moon, he would be ninety per cent certain to be dead or a prisoner and thought '*how sorry he ought to be*'. Némega interrupted him by coming to hand over to Biondo part of the brigade's funds. The lieutenant undid his boots and stuffed the bank-notes into the interstices between the leather and his thin calves. During the operation Johnny stared at Némega with the sole thought that however things turned out he would never see him again. Then the commissar went back down to the command post to invoke the word of honour of the German prisoners who would testify to their comrades as to the correct, humane treatment received and would do their best to induce their commanders to spare the innocent population. Sergeant-Major Mario was taking down the red flag, breathing heavily because of its weight and size.

The lieutenant drew up his squad on the little square which was deserted and littered with rubbish. Each man received an extra load of ammunition to meet the needs of what would soon be their future base on the Lovera, it was to be abandoned only in extremis. They would plough their way through the desert of snow and would come out on to the road where the German trucks were, for some reason or other, further apart. If within range of the Germans a man was to cough his nearest comrade had to knock him out at once. The second last to leave was Némega's squad; it set out along the ridge to Costalunga, with their heads down like dogs smelling something hidden under the snow. Now the dogs were silent, out of breath. The women in the church were intoning almost in a whisper. From the whole circle of Germans, which by this time must have been reached by the first squads to leave, there was no explosion, no alarm signal.

Biondo waited till the moon sailed anew into a cloudy patch, then clicked the heels of his boots stuffed with money. All the fires of their long bivouac had been put out.

They were descending; the concrete nature and the size of the danger that they were going towards had the effect that they began that mortal journey light-heartedly as if they placed a maximum of trust in the intervening space. Someone behind the lieutenant giggled from pure tension. They were travelling towards death, without a vow, without a prayer. They lowered themselves into the deepest snow as if into a sea. Snow, snow, as far as their goal and beyond, snow that was compact although already old, giving a slight squeak under their careful steps. The snow-clad landscape stretched between them and the Germans in their positions vast, in motionless waves, hatefully impartial. Across that motionless swell of the earth the line of white and red lights appeared and disappeared so as to produce a feeling of nausea. They were soon deadly tired of their progress, the snow was femininely yielding to their sinking feet and masculinely hostile to their extraction. They took advantage of certain depression to rest for a few minutes, rigorously silent, without seeking reciprocal relief and courage, in a circle round the reliable figure of Biondo. Johnny sighed noisily in the deadly silence: he was thinking of Tito who had managed it, who was out of the encirclement although he lay in its very heart . . . Was it really so difficult?

Further on someone at Biondo's back began to get rid of the magazines for the machine-gun, half-empty in any case, which slid out of his complicit fingers and sank like knives into the snow with an imperceptible 'zick'. The lieutenant never turned round and no one said anything. The safety of the others lay in luck and surprise – with the Germans on the alert and ready, what did a magazine more or a magazine less matter. Some of them began to turn round, upsetting the rhythm of the march, blocking the column, they turned to the moon and their companions' ancient faces, in which one read a mimed, hysterical desire to speak: it seemed absolutely unacceptable to have to die in half an hour with their last words those spoken in the village. But no one spoke, not even in the halts in the hollows, what rendered them mute was the silence of Biondo who was so honest even in the way he abstained from encouragement.

There was the line of white and red lights, the white ones making with the red a system of male and female because of a physical linkage of the monstrous column, but without a German soldier to be seen, not even a sentry, not so much out of hate for the partisans as of love of the Germans. It was a nightmare of desert nakedness, a fleet of stranded phantom vessels, and as in a dream Johnny clambered up the shore, passed between the last two trucks, thinking that the white beam of the headlights must strike him down photoflashlike, and slid down the other bank, he like all the others light and incorporeal, absolutely silent and seemingly inoperative, somnambular.

Beyond the circle no one spoke yet, neither of exultation nor of amazement, but marched on a little further, then Biondo ordered them to take refuge in a farm building which to Johnny seemed too suicidally close to the road and the early-morning Germans. But he did not protest, no one protested, everyone including himself was still lingering in that limbo of amazement and dreaming. The door of the stable had no chain, one had merely to touch it to throw it open. The stable was narrow and miserable, without a cow in it, only three or four sheep, whose breathing in the barn was like the breath of a man at sea. His comrades collapsed in that tiny space, forming a heap on it without any further movement. Johnny who had not taken part in that synchronous collapse, was left with a mere sliver of room, so he lay half on the bare tiled floor and half on the dry and thorny brushwood and with his arms embraced the rebellious and fearful flanks of an amazed sheep.

What wakened them was a first, ragged burst of fire in the paling sky. It roused them, but did not make them arch their backs – they lay in a wide-eyed but passive heap, fatigue and misery papering their dazed faces colloidally. Until at a second burst of fire which impregnated the whole sky Biondo dragged himself to the peephole of the stable and then ordered them all on to their feet.

They had to get out like lightning and crouching, the barnyard was exposed to both hills. The peasant of the house, skeletal and jaundiced, was spying out the situation at dawn from behind his sparse stack of straw and he was shivering loudly from cold in his flapping clothes. He turned round suddenly and almost died on discovering the partisans debouching from his stable and shut his eyes faced by his death and reduction to cinders. The lieutenant ran zigzagging up to him and asked for grappa for his limp and numbed men but the peasant shook his head violently, his misery equalled by his terror.

The scene was all movement. The last German detachments were reaching the last hillsides to Mombarcaro with a pace that was not particularly concentrated but energetically touristic. One had to ask oneself who and for what reason was firing these shots that burst in the neutral and amorphous sky, rare unfocused shots but lively and enlivening. No column of smoke yet rose from the village. The bulk of the Germans had already entered it and now were certainly bending over to examine the relics and excrement of the partisans. In the nearest sector, on the pearly main road, amid extremely long puffs of dust pursued by the wind, all the German trucks, towering, lurching and sinuous, as if driven by children, were moving towards a rendezvous.

Johnny looked towards Murazzano on the edge of the infected zone. The village seemed to have multiplied its volume like someone swelling up out of terror but for the opposite reason to visibility and attraction, but it seemed no more inhabited and lively than a necropolis. But there was no other choice and somone said: 'Let's go to Murazzano' – in a calm voice, deadly certain of self-evident assent. But Biondo's eye flashed a metallic No – Johnny could see his brain behind the marble-hard brow juggling with the probabilities, the imponderables, the pros and cons, the margins of safety. Until he darted off without giving any reason or turning round again, towards the top, in the wake of the trucks, certain that all the men were following him and first among them the giant Pinco who bore on his shoulder a whole machine-gun, defenceless and tremendous like a standard bearer. Johnny, all intent on not losing step, thought in a rudimentary way that Biondo might have an idea given (and not granted) certain assumptions: the lieutenant took for granted the German encirclement of Murazzano and its surroundings and thought of getting away rapidly and finally from the whole condemned area by marching behind the Germans who were at present interested in and absorbed by Mombarcaro and of then turning off like lightning to safety at the first opportunity.

They were moving along the bank at the side of the road, now they were at the bend where the scabrous and bushy plateau opened out. Biondo and Pinco were already walking on the level ground while the others were hacking at the last slope. A whole body of the enemy rose from the bushes like woodland centaurs. They were wearing brand-new German uniforms but they were dainty and got up in accordance with an Italian taste, and their hair which came out from under their helmets was Italian, Italian the way they showed their teeth, they hurled insults in Italian and demanded surrender. But they had already opened fire and Pinco had already fallen head over heels with his weapon which pressed down on his enormous back after it had arched for his last sigh. The lieutenant swearing *loudly* to himself, had knelt on one knee and was aiming his sub-machine-gun. But a volley hit him, upsetting him; he recovered his balance and fired a burst; all the Fascists redoubled their fire at him and this time they laid him out, his long, thin *banked* legs giving a last double beat. Biondo was so dazzlingly the leader that his end hypnotised the Fascists who stood there for a second with their weapons silent and laid aside as if to improve their view of their success. But then they began to fire volleys and Fred who was advancing with his hands up almost as if to give authority to his surrender received the bulk of the fire and fell to the ground.

Johnny fell back, extremely slowly, taking great care, his face calm and biting his lips, step after step out of the line of fire which was entirely Fascist. Then his back, as it grazed it, recognised the friable earth to the ridge of the bend in the road, at which point two Fascists set their eyes and weapons on him. But Johnny dodged just in time to still hear the bullets, muffled and malignant plunge into the thawed limestone.

Now he was aware that all the fire and still more all the trampling and the explosions were for him. He dived with his eyes shut and began to roll down the immense, humped, nauseating slope towards the far-off ravine south of Murazzano. The rolling motion was such as to suspend any faculty of perception or thought, and yet he was certain that they were not following him nor even firing at him, they had given up with him. The rolling descent was lacerating and interminable, it made him retch. But then a thick-skinned lack of feeling came over him, it covered his whole body, he no longer felt the terrible impacts of the metal and wood of his rifle pressing against his side. He rolled, light and anaesthetised, as if he were swimming suspended in the ionosphere. Then he came to himself and woke up a little, then began to think of braking, he remembered that the slope fell straight into the tufa cliff that crowned the ravine. But the grass was frozen and slippery, the snow where there was any had lost all power to act as a brake. 'Did I escape up there only to smash myself to pieces in the gorge?' he thought with slow fear. But he braked and stood up in time with an extraordinary headache as if his head were urinating his liquefied brain from some orifice. Then he pulled himself together, traversed the edge of the ravine slowly, almost indolently looking to see where and how he could get down it. The slope he had rolled down was completely bare and inanimate, the traces of his mad rolling fall were invisible, its high crest prevented him from seeing Biondo, Pinco, Fred and all the others. Further up the Germans in a compact body were scaling the quarry at Costalunga, they looked like a swarm of green ants clambering up a blanched vegetable. Further up still, at the highest point of the ground their trucks were standing, rendered black and dwarflike by the distance, in the very mouth of the grey grey sky. And still no smoke towering up from the village. All the campaniles around were striking the hours, lofty, cellophaned.

He turned round and lowered himself down into the gorge. Shivering in its cold and watery dark he walked on avoiding the patches of snow and the puddles of thaw-water, he pushed aside the tangles of branches, his steps and mind intent on Murazzano. It was not important when he would reach it. He was growing a thick skin against the state of after-mortal-danger, he no longer was aware – as always previously – of that extremely long electrical wave rising in his spine. And he could think of Biondo in terms of perfect, placid naturalness. 'That was his end sooner or later. I too have my end. Otherwise what should I think of myself? It is only a question of dates.'

Now the gorge was levelling out on to the woods above Murazzano, clearings among chestnut trees, and now it was time to leave it to plunge into the fields belonging to the village. He gave a start just as another man sprang up at the sight of him in the clearing. It was Regis, stripped of any weapon, clutching one arm with the other, *disabled*, bleeding from a torn sleeve. Regis' escape excited Johnny infinitely more than his own, it galvanised him, made him run through the clearing like a kangaroo. 'Take me to the hospital in Murazzano, will you?' He was weeping. 'Of course I'll take you.' 'It's not serious, is it? You don't think it's serious?' 'It doesn't look like it to me. No, it's not serious. But let's hurry to the hospital.'

They dragged themselves towards the village that loomed ahead. Regis was weeping easily and smoothly but it was something that had no particular implication for Johnny – it was something purely physiological just like the gush of blood from his arm. 'I had to make a big effort to escape, you know. What an effort! You've no idea how the sight of your own blood stops you, blocks your vision. You've no idea and I hope you never have to experience it.' 'I only hope for one thing,' said Johnny. 'If that is fate, then a bullet in the forehead or a burst at the heart like with Biondo. But don't talk any more now, Regis.'

Johnny made him stop in the shelter of the last chestnut tree and went ahead to find out if the village was occupied. Men posted on the tower of the sanctuary assured him with brief gestures of their angry sympathy, then they stood and watched them climb up together. They were on the alert spastically *grim*, many of them ready for speedy flight and for hiding in the thick woods, with blankets rolled bandolierwise and parcels of food. The women peeped out of the windows with the drawn shutters, from time to time they whispered advice and prayers to their men down below. One man stepped out from the rigid line to ask for news of Biondo. 'We were his men.' 'And where is he? Did you lose him?' 'He died up there.' 'It's not possible? Biondo?' 'He died an hour ago before our eyes.' The man rejoined the line. 'It was written.' The news and the comment were passed right along the line then the civilians turned their eyes up to the plateau where Johnny had said Biondo had fallen. The plateau was so naked and *bleak* that it reflected the colour of the sky. Regis shouted: 'I am losing my arm,' and then they ran to the hospital preceded by a team of young men with Regis repeating quietly, like a child, that his arm was lost by now.

In the hospital there were no nuns to be found, they had all been sent off to the next-door poorhouse. Johnny and Regis dragged themselves through an entrance hall decked with old chronic cases who made faces as they passed with the *grin* of idiocy, puffing over them their corrupted breath, looking at Regis' blood with wide open eyes. Regis screamed with despair and then a nun appeared. She was the kind that Cottolengo* would have taken on as a paradigm of his order: thin and strong, extremely Nordic, bespectacled. There were no doctors, she was acting as doctor. She went ahead of them into a small room, half sick-bay and half convent sitting-room. Johnny took up position in the window to keep an eye on the surroundings and movements. Regis prepared himself for the injection. The nun carried it out, now Regis hesitated to put on his clothes again, he seemed to be saying: 'Is that all? do you think, you mad old woman, that that's all that's needed to save my arm? My a-a-a-rm!'

Johnny drew back from the window. And now? Regis looked disappointed and offended, then he swore quietly but drily and with Johnny moved towards the door. The nun stopped him with her bony hand. Where was he going? Had he gone mad? Didn't he feel that he had a raging temperature? She spoke sharply, without sympathy and all in technical terms. Regis disengaged himself. Be admitted, go to bed, at once, here, with the Germans spreading out all over the place. He raised his voice. 'Not me. I prefer – I want to die in the open air, I'm not going to bed, I'm . . .' but fatigue, an attack of faintness seized him, bent him like a willow that had lost its pith.

Johnny carried him in his arms, the nun led the way, barely turning round to point out that naturally they were not taking him to a hospital which was so open to enemy inspection, they were sheltering him in the cellars, there were already a lot of partisans

* Giuseppe Cottolengo (1786–1842), priest, later beatified, famous for philanthropic works.

lying there as patients. It seemed that all the smell of all the carbolic acid in the hospital had been concentrated, caught up in the nun's stiff skirt. Johnny shut his mouth tight and puffed out his cheeks to stop vomiting. Regis was weeping easily with his eyes shut. So he did not see the cellar, low and medieval, icy-cold and suffocating, with the hint of a carbide lamp which allowed Johnny to see the three victims of the burst from the Skoda; they were lying motionless and haggard with lumps of black mould below their eyes.

He undressed him, then he put him to bed, he was still weeping liquidly and did not reopen his eyes because of the unbearable pain of seeing something intolerable. 'You'll be all right there, perfectly safe. I'd stay here myself but I would be ashamed. In half an hour's time you'll feel better and certainly won't envy me. You will think that I am once more exposed, at risk, and won't envy me. Did you hear me, Regis? I am going.'

He went out, once again through the evil-smelling entrance hall past the chronically ill decaying old men. A nun trotted alongside him; old, podgy, no more aware of anything than her chronic sick, with a pig's face in her tightly drawn wimple. She grinned and babbled, speaking of the Germans in inarticulate terms which were undoubtedly admiring ones, she grinned and babbled.

He was out – the houses cut off the view of Mombarcaro and of its enormous bare and tormented hill. He did not know what time it was, his own grim numbness made the whole day anonymous. He walked towards the tower among lines and groups of people ready for flight, cross, recriminatory, hostile. A few partisans had mingled with the crowd, survivors from other formations, they had taken shelter in Murazzano as the result of another adventure, familiar with other dead men. They greeted each other with a barely noticeable wink, they formed a thicker mass as they walked together towards the look-out tower but they did not give any particulars about themselves – not even an adventure not even something about their itinerary, the day was entirely jealously and mysteriously each one's own property. Together they smoked their last cigarettes – those had not been ruined in the tribulations of escape.

Some Germans were visible on the twin breasts of the mountain of Mombarcaro, but they were solitary and aimless, as they had made an individual truce. Then on the crest of the road their trucks reappeared, still towering and lurching, they braked with their radiators pointing towards Murazzano. Then the civilians *bolted away*, definitely, some who hesitated with one foot in the air, were swept away by the shouts of the women at the window. The partisans too set out in retreat. Johnny sat at the foot of the tower on the cold grass, which still remembered the snow. 'I don't want to run, I don't want to run just because a German is maybe going to one side to have a pee.'

The action at Mombarcaro was coming to an end, was ended, without towers of concrete smoke. Everything appeared senseless under the sad grimace of the timeless sky. A curtain of evening slipped down from the heights of the village, the streets became blurred, the German trucks became *flou* but their frightening nature, the fascination of their aimed immobility, was still the same and had perhaps increased. Yet the day was over, the air, the sky assured him it was so.

He got up and saw that all the partisans had disappeared, had gone down into the village and passed on. But he did not follow them. Only one partisan remained who seemed to be waiting for him with silent and tenacious tact. He moved off with Johnny only a few steps later than him. Johnny soon stopped on the grey road, out of the growing shadow of the houses under the first gusts of the evening wind. And he looked fixedly at the other man. Now he remembered, he belonged to the days of ages ago which were the yesterdays of Mombarcaro. He carried arms and ammunition, he was precise and boring, dependable, 'What do you want?' 'For you to tell me the direction of La Lovera.' 'Couldn't you ask right away?' 'I thought you were going there and I only wanted to follow you.' 'No . . . I'm not going there.' 'And the rendezvous with Némega?' 'Has nothing to do with me. That is the way,' and he turned to point it out to him, halfway up the wild crest which from Murazzano takes a trampoline leap on the brief plain of Dogliani. The other impressed it on his sight: 'You're not coming because you are going home?' There was no offence in his tone of voice, which was neither polemical nor insulting, only a vibration of prayer: for Johnny to tell him his programme, so that he could know what to do. 'You know I often watched you at Mombarcaro. I understood, I knew that you were the best educated of them all.' 'No. I am not going home. I won't go

home till the end. I'm going back to the partisans but other partisans.'
'Where?' 'Still in the hills but other hills.' They were far beyond the
curtain of the dark but Johnny felt them there invisible, as
inaccessible as the other side of the moon. The other sucked in his
lip in perplexity and reflection, then he made up his mind. He went
off towards La Lovera with his disciplined and clumsy stride. Johnny
followed him with his eyes as long as he could, reading in his curved
back all Némega's tonic efforts, all he would see, live through and
suffer in the future and how he would die in some particular partisan
clash in which Johnny would not die.

He set off in the opposite direction, passing swiftly through the
village alive only because of the women with their babbling inside
the houses which whistled through the windows and the barred
doors.

XI

It was tremendously exciting and significant to walk along downhill in this state of suspended partisanship. Johnny felt the way a Catholic priest in ordinary clothes or a soldier in civilian clothes can feel: his weapons rationally concealed under his clothes he was still marked – partisan *in aeternum*. '*I've stood, and fired, and killed.*'

He was terribly different from all the people going along the wide road on the crest: scattered, *sullen*, wrinkled people who walked on the hill because of supreme needs and passions: the demon of the black market, the beggarly search for firewood, the summons to the priest for extreme unction. The majority, the lazy ones, stood within sight of but away from the road, motionless and tense on the familiar fields, so untrusting that they did not give in and reply to a hail, a whistle from the road.

The day was twin to that last day in Mombarcaro, *timeless* for lack of any solar gradations; today it was worse, it *looked* as if the sun had never shone on the earth. And long frozen gusts ran the length of the road like a malignant boring joke. Johnny walked down chewing, along with the bread that came from armed mendicity, the chocolate bought at the *wayside* inn in Pedaggera which was for Johnny the eqivalent of that dreamt up by Synge for his inn in the *Playboy of the Western World.* The innkeeper, a woman, was stony, oily and spoke in monosyllables like an old Red Indian; she looked askance at Johnny fearing a requisition, in desperate mute defence of ancient lucre, she could neither bear the thought of nor allow herself the gift of a small bar of chocolate. When Johnny paid, the day was saved as far as she was concerned and, relieved, she became talkative. And she described the battle of Mombarcaro from a panoramic point of view that had naturally been denied to Johnny. It was extraordinary the way pieces of news circulated among the hills; they all linked and merged on the hill-top beyond the road through the valleys and the steep hillside gorges. The old woman was particularly well informed on the results over towards Bormida, Johnny having been in danger and then escaped over towards Belbo.

The Fascists had captured a score of partisans; most were shot that evening in the parade ground in Ceva, the rest – either because too young or successful in their entreaties – had been deported to Germany. But the episode that had most struck the old woman was that of the partisan immobilised by a bullet in one knee.

His comrades had laid him down and hidden him, halfway down the hill, in one of those half-walled huts in which the peasants dry the chestnuts in the autumn. A German patrol had arrived, had gently half-opened the door, had seen the motionless man and greeted him. Then they shut the door again and burnt the whole place down. 'You should have seen the smoke,' said the old woman: how they say it changed colour, how from being thin it thickened, when it engulfed the man as well as everything else. But the rumour was that he was not Italian but a Slav and there was nothing so continentally distant as the word 'Slav' as pronounced by her. And Johnny searched his memory for whom the Slav from the bodyguard of the commander in purple could have been to come to this end.

'And what do you know about Alba? Is it free or occupied?' She knew nothing about Alba. Johnny was astonished to hear that in all her life she had never gone down to Alba, the geographical capital of the Langhe, she had always lived between the arms of this crossroads. Her sons, those rabbits of sons of hers, had themselves not been there since 8 September, although there was business to be done in Alba in the black market with a pinch of male courage. But she had to admit she had given birth to rabbits, their contemporaries by taking the tiny risk of going in to Alba had amassed so much money that the wine casks no longer sufficed to stow it all away.

Johnny went out on to the road again – it was gloomy and *weatherbeaten* but it was the last influence of the great high hill, further down the air would be less fierce, that one could guess from the general aspect of the landscape below. The chocolate unwrapped from its rusty tinfoil seemed to be a hair's breadth from being worm-eaten but the bread was good, wholemeal, the product of peace-loving humanity.

Some kilometres lower down – the deep valleys and ravines were *as bleak* as up there but the crests of the hills were more tender, more maternal, and the houses and farmsteads had a more Christian and colourful look – then through a saddle he caught the first *glimpse* of his town. And he felt his exile horribly. He ran down to where he could see it better as if from behind a theatre curtain more markedly drawn back, he sat down on the ridge and with his weapons beside him and a cigarette in his mouth he looked at Alba.

The episcopal town lay on its ancient site with its red roofs, its diffused green, all rendered pale and degraded by the light that was no light pouring down from the sky, tenacious and unmoving and pale like some malignant radiation. And its river – its big important river, perhaps more important than the town perhaps *beyond its worth* – appeared behind it, *not fullbodied, unimpressive and dull* like a childish drawing of a river in a Christmas crib. And the mutilation of the bridge which crossed it, the gap from the English bombs, had the effect of making crystal clear the way the dirty sky and the dirty bridge corresponded to each other. Johnny could almost see the coming and going of the ferry downstream from the bridge – a hasty, *nasty* coming and going made necessary by hated needs, infected by fear. And the surrounding countryside participated in that debased state for it completely lacked the first coat of paint of the imminent spring. Beyond the river in the model countryside, the dark and sinister trees formed imposing but mysterious punctuation on the dull green leaden expanse.

Johnny was a prey to nostalgia. He stared over to where his house was – it lay buried under the reddish buttresses of the cathedral. Johnny performed the miracle of enucleating and elevating it: there was his house with its dear contents, suspended in the air, in the space next to the airy buttresses of the cathedral . . . Then the house plunged down when Johnny for a moment failed to hold it suspended by means of his inner powers.

Nostalgic feelings for the town racked him fiercely. He had been away for little more than three months, distant from it perhaps thirty kilometres as the crow flies, but in that absence and that distance he had fought and killed, had seen killing but killing that was direct and personal and had run at least three risks of dying and being buried far away from it. And now he was on his way to leaving it again in the opposite direction.

The feeling of exile was oppressive, suffocating, to the point of making him leap to his feet as if to escape from an asphyxiating level. He absolutely must make sure if it were still free or if the Fascists had already made it one of their garrisons. The idea of entering it by night smiled to him to the point of being agonising – to reach his house through the shadowy and familiar lanes, to wake his parents, to smother in an embrace their alarm and recriminations, to change his things, to tell them where he had been and where he was going and to disappear again towards the foothills at first light.

He walked on striding as never before, to the point of being impressed by his own motor power, along the absolutely deserted road, passing in front of houses which were carefully bolted and barred with the odd animal in the courtyard.

His first encounter was in the valley – a woman with a child was standing by a well at the roadside trying the chain. When she caught sight of him she let go of the pulley and *got hold* of her daughter. 'Do you know if Alba is free?' From fear and *self-constraint* the woman assumed a plausible air of stupidity. 'Are they in Alba, I am asking? The Fascists?' Her voice was sharp and break-neckedly hurried, her clasp of her daughter like a spasm. 'I don't know, we don't know. We don't go into town any more even if we really needed to go.' She had at last guessed at Johnny's condition and embraced him with a glance of universal entreaty.

He passed on, angry and wounded – was it possible that in these months his appearance had been transformed to the point where it magnetised a young woman and her child with terror on a daylight road, engaged in the age-old work of drawing water? I ought to see myself in the mirror, he said to himself, especially my eyes.

He reached the slopes of the last hill behind which one heard the heartbeat of Alba. He climbed up and was on the crest on which the little villas of the local bourgeoisie rise.

He went along a path looking at the town immediately below him with the affection and pain of a person who watches someone close to him stretched out on the operating table with the surgical intervention imminent. From that minimal distance the city acquired its colour once more but it was still, Johnny thought, considerably below its normal standard. And, in the early afternoon, a noise that was already crepuscular.

The traffic was thin and exclusively pedestrian. The asphalt of the ribbon of the ring road was corrugated, holed and dull, with no one using it. The uncertainty was such that Johnny would have paid to see a whole Fascist regiment parade along that asphalt.

Johnny who was kneeling to observe it more comfortably and more closely leapt to his feet. A man was behind him – an old peasant, rough-hewn and the result of decades of sharecropping for a wealthy family in the town – rough but unembarrassed and the kind who champions young people. In fact he said: 'Keep your eyes open, partisan.' So the town had a Fascist garrison. The old man nodded without extinguishing that knowing smile of his. 'The Muti is in town.' Johnny shouted 'The Muti!' They had actually sent in this notorious, indefensible rabble in arms. 'Since when?' he asked as if he wanted to learn the date of a death.

They had been there as a permanent garrison for two weeks but up to today hadn't done any particular harm to people. 'If you mean to hang about here keep your eyes open because every so often patrols climb up here.' 'Well armed?' 'One in every three had these things that are the fashion today – what they call tommy-guns.' 'Hm, so they are well armed.'

So Alba was garrisoned, Johnny exploded at the thought, cursed at the thought, suffered for it. He went on along the path among the scattered villas of the landowners, apparently deserted and sealed up. But at a gate a man *jerked and staggered*. It was the wine manufacturer B, something more than an acquaintance, a fellow-member of the Social Club. He had grown bald and grey, he was wearing a very worn city suit, his eyes were more wandering and watery and *lurching* than ever, his natural moroseness increased by a power of x. He recognised him, cast an animal-like glance over the whole hill, then called to him trembling: 'Where have you been all this time? Tell me – are you a partisan?' His glance ran with repugnance over the whole of Johnny's clothed surface, halting at the bulges. 'So you're a partisan too,' he said shaking his head. Johnny smiled at him. He asked him about the others, all the others, about the absentees. The young people were all away – half of them merely in hiding, but the other half were certainly partisans, and Johnny smiled at that great, silent, separate gathering. B shook his head again. 'All I know is that between you and the others you will be the ruin of Italy.'

The others were the Muti. 'By the way, what are they like, the Muti?'

'Up to now they haven't done anything really nasty but watch out after the first explosion, the first pretext.' The industrialist could predict it: the great majority were rabble from the dregs of Milan. Johnny might not know Milan as he did, in normal times he went to Milan every week to the big wine auction, in normal times . . . 'The officers are no better than the other ranks . . . they walk about with riding crops. To think how much I used to like the Milanese dialect, I had a real weakness for it – now it makes my hair stand on end to hear it in the mouths of these good-for-nothings armed to the teeth.' And what increased, set its stamp on the feat was the variation in age in their ranks – either very young, wretched *besprizorni**who had come rushing out of excommunicated children's homes or white-haired scoundrels. 'So long as none of you take it into your heads to do something in town.'

Johnny said he imagined his wife would be with him in the hills. Yes, but at the moment she was out, visiting, in the next villa. 'They all looked shut up,' said Johnny. 'Not at all, we all live in the hills – it's just that we show as little sign of life as possible. It really isn't a life.' *He ranged for a moment and very dejectedly* on the muddy path. 'So you are all partisans. Even Professor Monti has given up the *liceo* to get mixed up in this adventure. A philosopher! The philosopher!' Johnny smiled while B cast a brief and disgusted glance at the enslaved town.

Then Johnny asked after his son – he took pleasure at this moment in that routine and frivolous convention as if his new irregular, *unprecedented* character would stand out more clearly against it. 'Thank God my son is still at school in the normal way, in his usual college with the Fathers. I have never patted myself on the back so much as today at having put him in a religious boarding-school. You know nowadays the men of religion are the only ones who can make themselves respected and impose their wills. On you or on the others.'

* *besprizorni* (Russian) – children abandoned in the streets.

From the villa buried in a circle of soaking and dripping laurel there came the rustle of a gramophone record, caressing in its *scraping*, and Johnny felt himself overcome by languor.

As for B, he had for some time been struggling between terror of complications and his rigid sense of hospitality. At last he made up his mind – he led Johnny by an arm into the untended path saying that in his house there were his daughter, Signora G, an evacuee, and her daughter. 'Please don't show your weapons.' He introduced him into a *darkish* drawing-room in which three women stood out from the depths of the divan like three islands of dusk in a dark ocean. B introduced Johnny in a roundabout way in a vague manner as long-winded as it was clumsy. The three women understood in a flash with a cruel smile at B. Johnny found himself sinking into an old armchair, which was slightly damp, *right* opposite Signora G, a statuesque *icy* Scandinavian type, who struck an attitude on the divan like a sculpture by Canova.* The two girls, immature and prickly, were messing about with the gramophone. Johnny produced his cigarettes, little excited cries broke out: 'You have cigarettes! Real, manufactured cigarettes! it's a shame to pinch them from you but we simply cannot resist. We have to put up with those impossible ones, ridiculous paper and some sort of mixture of herbs that is supposed to replace tobacco but you simply can't smoke the stuff.'

Johnny was ill at ease in the nice old-fashioned comfort of the armchair with ladies young and old opposite; he struggled to rediscover his old ease and *homeliness*. 'If you will be good enough to wait we shall shortly serve tea. B has luckily a little reserve of genuine Italian tea but we can only sugar it a very little – that's the problem. Do you like tea?' Johnny said he wasn't mad about it – it was the first thing he could do without if necessary. 'What, what? An English fan like you?' said B but only to raise the tone, to re-establish his presence which had been deleted.

The two girls, their cigarettes firmly between their lips, were messing about among the record albums. They had the whole series of Natalino Otto,** did he feel like hearing *Down the avenue*? they thought it was really lovely. Signorina G was slightly younger than B's

---

* Canova (1757–1822), major representative of Italian neo-classicism.
** Natalino Otto, light music singer – *Down the Avenue* was one of his hits.

daughter and immeasurably more grown up – she radiated the calm arrogance which marks the offspring of the eminent professional classes of Turin. B was irritated by the record. 'Would you like *Forbidden Music*, papa?' his daughter said aggressively. 'I don't want anything at all. These aren't times for music, that's what I think.' 'Do you know what your daughter would do if she didn't have records to listen to, papa? Throw herself into the well.' 'Just because men have gone mad,' Signorina G interjected. B told his daughter that she would do better to spend her time studying English as Minnie, Signora G's daughter did. Signora G joined in to stress sighingly her daughter's scanty progress. 'Let's see how far you've got. They say this gentleman speaks English wonderfully. But how on earth did he manage it?' Only a feline 'Mammy' from her daughter spared Johnny a scholastic interrogation.

All this was so absurd, as if he had plunged into an unreal bath – he simply could not communicate with that kind of human being any more – no further way of relating to them except a mute, sphinxlike smile. He felt himself to be irresistibly impelled to shut his eyes in a comfortable *numbness* which only the memory of the Muti patrols mentioned by the old sharecropper were capable of punctuating with tiny *agues*.

'Besides I am reading English,' said B's daughter. 'In an Italian translation but it is an English book. I am reading Woodhouse.* *Goodbye Jeeves*.' She pronounced the 'j' in the French manner. B scowled: 'If they search the house we'll end up in trouble because of that English book.'

Johnny *gaped peristaltically*. No, there was no longer any possible relationship between these people and himself, his short and enormous past, Tito and Blondie, the nocturnal sentry duties, the *corvée* of supplies, the killings. Suddenly, sunk in the armchair, confronted by these beautiful and young women, giving off a civilised air like the kind of perfume one normally sprays on in the morning, Johnny called to mind, lamented the gloomy, dirty monotony of Mombarcaro in its poverty. But what place did these people occupy in the world? in this situation? what do they think? where do their feelings – in *défaut* of their intellects – tend? *Were I*

---

* *sic!*

now up there again, he prayed. He could very easily put up with Némega, as for Sergeant-Major Mario he was a bosom friend. What had B been thinking of to bring him into this house and certainly he had dithered deeply worried and he himself to accept the invitation, to be here who knew for how long, leaving the lonely armed road he loved. If only they had learned the merest scrap of what he had behind him the three women would have lost all their indolent composure and B would have panicked outright.

Signorina Minnie was changing the record – now she was putting on Chopin's *Tristesses.* 'Although poor Natalino is not up to the melody.' G's daughter began to defend Otto. 'On the contrary he sings it marvellously.' 'You think so? He doesn't have a strong enough voice. Listen how he falls flat when it comes to 'while the song'.

The tea came, Signora G had the ability to make her cup seem to be part of the statuary she was.

'Am I really very nasty, Johnny, if I ask for another cigarette?'

'By the way,' said B, opaque and tealess, 'that is not by the way, I wonder why I said "by the way". Johnny, do you know Nord?'

'Nord? Who is he?'

'He is the leader of all the partisans from here to the Langhe.' 'Then I will know him.' 'You know him?' 'I am going to get to know him the moment I leave your house.' 'I was asking because this Nord has already applied to me as to others for funds. Let me say right away that I find it natural, absolutely natural. And I have paid out a fair little sum in two instalments. I am not shedding tears over it but I should like to know where it goes and what it is used for. The person who makes the request and takes the money is Sicco. Sicco is an absolutely trustworthy boy but I'd like to know . . .' Johnny gave a weary wave of the hand as a sign of ignorance and impatience. B sighed and turned to Signora G. 'Is everything all right, Lalla?' he asked touching her knee. She shook her head imperceptibly. 'It's a time to have men around. I am worried about my husband. With that job of his at Fiat. If it were any old job but you know Dante's position at Fiat. If he deserts the Fascists would look for him to the ends of the earth; if he stays on the air is unbreathable. The strike last March was horrible enough but now – now!' 'Stop it with these records for a little,' B ordered the girls. Then he *shuffled his feet* and excused himself. 'I am going to see if the peasant's sons are keeping a good look-out.' Johnny pricked up his ears from the depths of the torpor in which he was sunk. 'I'm off,' he said with such determination as his somnolence allowed. 'I'm not sending you away,' said B. 'You see I thought of posting the peasant to watch the road and the paths. You know – those damned patrols.' Johnny noticed now that *dusk* had fallen, through the window panes the trees were already drowning. B came in again signalling that the coast was clear with a *flurried* pathetic air of territorial collaboration.

The moment he was outside – 'Well, keep fit and take care of your pen,' he said in a pathetic attempt to rediscover the brisk comradeship of his distant military service. 'I really wouldn't like to hear some day that . . .' 'We're here for that too,' Johnny yawned. B shook his arm. 'No don't be stupid and get killed. It will be interesting to be alive – after this. I have good hopes for later on. Which way are you going?' 'I am going to Nord. Please, when you go down into town –' 'Tomorrow morning – I can't keep away from my business. Wages run up just the same, you know.' 'Let my parents know – or have someone do it – that you saw me . . . that I am well and that from now on I am nearer and will keep them informed.' 'I'll send my manager tomorrow morning. Don't worry – a man born silent.' In the villa behind the dripping laurels the gramophone had started up again.

Far from the villa Johnny stopped and once more gazed at the town which was melting in the dusk, constellated here and there by some yellowish lights which the blackout would soon extinguish: the deep-rooted obscurity of the trees of the town walls now appeared concrete and rocky, almost like ancient ramparts. He sighed over his town thinking that the best course was to turn up at once into the hills with his back to it and his face towards the windy shadows of the high hills. But his feet kept moving towards the plain without any volition on his part, heedless of any caution. He found himself quite unconsciously at the foot of the hill, stretching out over the *outskirts* of the town on the bank of the sewer-stream smelling of mephitic vapours which suffocated the last gleam of light on the tracks of the nearby railway line.

He decided to circle round the outskirts of the town – the risk, which was absolutely gratuitous and superfluous, would do him good, would remove that patina he had acquired in B's drawing-room: yes, he had to take a risk and precisely in this very gratuitous way and precisely to be able to leave his violated town with his soul at peace.

He went on along the bank of the stream – he even loved its disgusting stench, adored the ugly architecture of the railway bridge least near to him. No one came into sight on this extreme limit of the outer circle, not even an animal, a dog – half town dog and half country one – on its evening free stroll: but from the first houses, above the impure murmur of the stream, there rose the usual evening noises but lower in volume than usual.

It was horrible to be deprived of this town through the fault of his position and of the Fascists. Suddenly in the falling shadow he had the chilling dream of finding 'himself alone' in that position, a solitary outlaw, self-banished for motives unclear even to himself, which had taken precise shape in a nightmare, and that now he was alone faced by a whole world that had become ferocious and vindictive, a world of *lawsticking* and armed guards all unleashed on him.

He stood towering over the flat bank with before him the other side which was equally flat and only slightly broken in the distance by the arch of the bridge. When in that flat expanse he saw a soldier of the Muti advancing Johnny quietly withdrew into the blackest shadow of the vegetation and watched. He was armed with a rifle and was carrying it with that indolence that could be *sullenness at armbearing* or else the terrible indolence of someone quick on the draw.

He was coming along the other bank, loose-limbed and dreamy, dragging through the mud boots that were ill-fitting, clownish. Closer to Johnny saw that he was wearing the blackguardly uniform of the Legion as if he had been born in it with perfect, insolent *looseness*; the enormous trousers flared down to the ankles *flopped noisily* against his robust legs in the unmoving air. Johnny half-raised his pistol in the heart of the shadow. The boy – he was a boy – stopped just in front of Johnny without ever raising his eyes – he was gazing at the filthy slow-flowing water of the stream as if it were a crystalline mirror for his dream that was so far away. When he was twenty metres from Johnny at the perfect *hauteur* his mouth obscured by shadow *heaved* a long and heavy sigh which very clearly moved his broad chest – the chest of a well-fed beggar – under his blouse.

Johnny lowered his pistol. The soldier from the Muti had walked on, Johnny leapt out of his hiding-place of darkness, stamping his feet loudly on the ground, standing as tall as he could. He wanted something to happen on the part of the Muti boy so that the sentimental interdict which had stopped him from firing would no longer hold.

The other had heard and guessed, he had turned round and seemed to be measuring the distance of that nocturnal duel, *shuffling his large feet* in the mud. They were forty metres apart; the Muti soldier stared into the thick-bodied dark, he slowly, *dreamily* brought his hand up to the sling of his rifle . . . and that was all. Still keeping an eye on the spectre of Johnny he retreated slowly, cautiously, along the malodorous bank until he disappeared as if swallowed up by a whirlpool of darkness.

Johnny regained the hill, the high hills.

XII

In that *early* spring the headquarters of the partisans loyal to Badoglio* – the 'Blues' – was at a spot – it was changed daily – in the wide valley below the village of Mango. Compared to the high hills the landscape here was slightly more gentle but it was like a degree of gentleness on the snout of a wild boar. It was by way of a hard chalky path between tough woods resistant to the late spring that Johnny climbed up to the headquarters to place himself at their disposal and take orders.

As he had been able to note during his approach journey the Blues too were perpetrating the same violation as the Garibaldini of the theory of guerrilla warfare which was Tito's and which Johnny entirely shared. The Lower Langhe was not yet an armed island but was making a clumsy and haughty effort to become one; in its basin the Blues were establishing a system of garrisons and – what was worse – each one punctiliously independent of the rest, each one ready to defend itself, perhaps even by pitched battle, on its own and only on its own.

In everything that concerned establishment, distribution and command structures, it was almost excessively evident that they *ranked* with the Royal Army, whereas the Garibaldini did their bitter best to distance themselves radically from it. The fact was that the Badogliani commanders, elegant, *gentlemanlike*, vaguely anachronistic, considered guerrilla warfare nothing other than the continuation of that anti-German war for which the disastrous hate of 8 September

* Marshal Pietro Badoglio, the right-wing general who headed the first government set up by the Allies after the Armistice of September 1943. 'Blues' as opposed to the left-wing 'Reds'.

had not permitted detailed planning, but which was to all intents and purposes planned and declared. The officers were, in large part, authentic army officers and this *flattered* the men, the other ranks. As little space as possible was given to natural hierarchies and that little with a *supercilious* grin. Even the non-commissioned officers, those who in the partisan forces could consider themselves non-commissioned officers and act as such, were overwhelmingly ex-Army non-commissioned officers. All this the troops were happy with, flattered and reassured; and as Johnny chanced to hear during one of the not infrequent, not too friendly conferences between Garibaldini and Blues, the latter maintained and vaunted their officer status, their level of education and their social antecedents, implicitly decrying and criticising the simple Reds who trusted blindly to mere workers and other sorts so unprepared and *déracinés* as to appear absolutely the products of a mysterious process of spontaneous generation.

As for their political badge, the Badoglian commanders were vaguely liberal and decidedly conservative, but their political confession of faith was, one had to recognise, null, it came perilously close to the limbo of agnosticism, and in some of them took the form of simple *esprit de bataille*. Their anti-Fascism however, more than ever thought of as above all an armed, potent reassertion of taste and restraint as opposed to Fascism's tragic carnival, was integral, absolutely indubitable. Yet, Johnny noted, almost all the Blue commanders, at least those who, not being regulars, had some historical culture and had at least read and digested a certain amount, would all have declared for Charles in 1681* and two centuries later would have enrolled under the banners of Dixieland. And yet what was visible was a clean, consoling *base of fair play* in the way they fought within limits without professing a political ideal with ferocious decision, in this unspoken desire to sweep away Fascism so that in a space that had been swept clean everyone could try to gain the upper hand – naturally with taste and if possible with style.

Johnny was naturally a bird of a different feather in this flock but he found in the new surroundings at last a common language, a common affinity of relations and unspoken understandings, an

---

* He presumably means the Restoration of Charles II in 1660.

ability to be together not only in the not inevitable battle, but moreover and chiefly in the long periods of waiting and rest. They were brilliant, attractive, but superficially so. And in all of them there reigned a painful nostalgia and tendency to do things according to the book, a painful acceptance of that irremediable lack of adherence to the book which brought it about that one could not form up and fight within the dear old honoured scheme of things. For this reason perhaps they tended to make of the Lower Langhe a huge armed island, like a piece of sacred soil where everything had to be done properly, according to their dear and sacred ideas of propriety. When in the High Langhe, precisely on the scene of Johnny's first experiences with the Garibaldini, the 1st Autonomous Military Division of the Langhe emerged, which was then to give birth to and take over the 2nd Division, commanded by Nord, Johnny being one of his men, the dream was almost made concrete, apart from those few but *aggressive and self-affirming Communist enclaves* which to the Blue commanders constituted almost as great a contamination of the sacred and reserved soil as the probing Nazi-Fascist forces.

As Johnny noted on his arrival at the surroundings of the headquarters women were by no means rare in the Blue ranks, thus increasing that general impression of anachronism which those high ranks inspired, a female abundance conceivable only in a late seventeenth-century army* still out of reach of Cromwell's new broom. Johnny's latent yearning for military puritanism was precisely what made him shake his head at the sight of them, but in fact at that very moment the women were working hard, cleaning, doing the washing, one of them typing . . . The mere fact that they each had a *nom de guerre* like the men might suggest to some malicious wretch an association with other women who used pseudonyms. They did indeed practise free love – but they were young women, their exact season for love coinciding with a season for death, they loved *doomed* men and love was very often the penultimate gesture of their fated existence. They made themselves useful, fought, fled for their lives, were acquainted with sufferings and horrors and terrors and bore them like the men. One of them fell and her body laid out *worked up the men to salute them militarily*. And if they were

* Another problem with English history.

captured and got away they returned infallibly, faithfully, to the base, to renewed risk, to the well-known consequences they suffered, after having seen and endured things because of which other men or women would have buried themselves in a convent.

In his pilgrimage towards him Johnny had naturally heard a great deal of talk about Nord, the big chief of the Lower Langhe. Without major details he had been able to gather that the man owed his indisputed primacy to his indubitable physical ascendancy so that Johnny was prepared for a notable impression – a physical one. But when having passed through a line of sullen, vulgar and arrogant bodyguards (their nucleus being called in accordance with the dear old indispensable vocabulary 'divisional headquarters platoon') Johnny arrived face to face with Nord, he was *struck still and speechless.*

Nord then was barely thirty, that is to say he was at the age where to a barely developed boy like Johnny the maturity of a thirty-year-old seems resplendent and distant but splendidly concrete like an Alpine peak. The man was so beautiful that no degree of beauty had ever graced virility thus and so masculine that beauty had never before tolerated being so masculine. His aquiline profile had that exact degree of softness that did not render it aquiline and it was this profile that when he suddenly appeared, *later on*, against a dark background and faced a trio of Fascist prisoners all three collapsed at his feet in a paroxysm of terror and admiration. The golden proportion of his physique manifested itself even under his splendid uniform, in his structural perfection which was clad in the exactly right flesh and muscle. His eyes were blue (the incredible fulfilment of all desiderata), penetrating but also light, revealing how Nord never prevaricated about his physical intentions, his mouth ready for the most disarmed and least hermetic of smiles and laughs; he spoke with a pleasant voice that was decisively masculine, never forced. And he moved with sober elasticity on his feet in trainers.

The Fascist prisoners would recognise him right away, when he appeared in the distance, quite apart from the individual splendour of his uniform. *He always wore the very uniform of the chief.* At the moment when Johnny was shown in he was wearing a splendid uniform composed of English cloth, jersey and leather; and other uniforms, numerous, all formidable and elegant, unique in their invention, cut, composition and general appearance, hung from the wall of the headquarters.

Johnny was recovering slowly from the shock of Nord and *braced himself* so as not to succumb to the immediate, complete, *coup de foudre** of indiscriminate devotion. By way of reaction he tried to convince himself that that absolutely exceptional physique enclosed a normal mind and spirit. And so it was but for Johnny and also the other men (thousands of them) who served under Nord, the discovery did not lead to disparagement of Nord but paradoxically to exaggerated esteem. In fact his physique was so admirable and impressive that everyone expected – ready to forgive – an exaggeratedly low spiritual level. The fact that, inside, Nord was perfectly normal and *average-standing* caused everyone to think it a miracle, an amazing fusion.

Nord frowned perceptibly at Johnny's Garibaldi antecedents: 'How on earth?' he asked in a pleasant voice as if underlining in amazement a breach of good taste. 'I had not met any others. You are speaking of the situation last November –' 'And after that?' 'They chewed us up. At Mombarcaro.' 'I know, everyone knows.' And in him the irresistible *unquenchable* partisan solidarity – although under attack and internally violated – produced a note of sadness. A Red defeat was a shared defeat even though the Garibaldini and the Badogliani hardly ever collaborated, each fighting the Fascist enemy on their own, each considering the Fascists their own and exclusive enemy.

'And now?' asked Nord. 'Now I think I am . . . centred.'

Nord said he was pleased that his ranks should be enriched by boys from Alba. Alba was the immediate direct objective of his division, his men gravitated to him from Alba. 'And I am happy to have so many men from Alba as the flower of my militia, almost a pledge of responsibility towards the town, which is our town. I am very satisfied indeed with those of your fellow-citizens already here with me. You are sure to know them . . . Ettore** – Frankie – Luciano.'

* Thunderstroke – normally used to describe sexual attraction.
** Ettore – Hector is a *nom de guerre* assumed for security purposes like most partisan names.

'Luciano is my cousin,' said Johnny. 'I know. At present he is second-in-command at Neviglie. Luciano and all the others spoke very highly to me of you, so highly that for a long time I have been here – practically waiting for you. If you live up to fifty per cent of the promises which your comrades from the town took pains to express you are destined to stay very close to me to the end, to share my food and sleeping quarters with me. Is it all true what they say about your English? Very good, it will be extremely useful to us.' 'Very willingly, commander.'

A scraping of feet was heard in the antechamber. One of the bodyguard was peeping in to find out if the new arrival was going to become important or was to remain a foot rag, so as to know how to behave accordingly. Nord's bodyguard was hated and held in contempt by the whole division, for being so disgustingly slovenly and cowardly and arrogant, so well equipped and heavily armed, so laden with Fascist and German badges which partisans – poor guys – had captured on the boundaries of the division's wide territory and presented to the big boss, Nord, who had *lavishly profused them upon his undeserving bodyguard.*

Nord appointed him second-in-command of the Mango garrison (the Garibaldini would have called it a detachment), under Lieutenant Pierre who for long had *pleaded for support.* From the window of the headquarters Johnny could see all the village he was destined for, losing the outlines of its houses and making its darkness solid at the hour of vespers, standing tall and well defended to the north and west, the two cardinal points where the Fascists from Alba and Asti – the specific enemy of the division – lay.

'Then you will tell me about Lieutenant Pierre,' Nord added cryptically at the moment of dismissal. And Johnny quickly learned Nord's unspoken meaning for Pierre quickly became the best lad and companion of the war. An air-force lieutenant who had fought the English fighters over Malta and Naples. On a minute, thin body, slightly twitchy, he had grafted an inimitable face worthy of a Gascon musketeer* restored to normality by two blue, mild, civilised eyes. His hair tended to red and was all curly, which Johnny had always had problems with but which he loved on Pierre's head. He dressed in a

---

* A reference to Dumas' *The Three Musketeers* who were Gascons.

way that was absolutely *clean and tidy* but without a hint of that vigilant display which distinguished the other Badoglian commanders. He was phenomenally knowledgeable about weapons and their use, an excellent shot, a sober and cool fighter, completely relaxed.

XIII

It was an easy-going camp. Although Pierre had a certain querulous nagging manner which ended up as *pulse* and his effective right arm was a Sicilian sergeant, Michele, a sergeant from the regular army, with a Bedouin's body at once poor and strong, a certain *blinkness* of eye and mouth, hissing his irresistible orders in the old ferocious manner of the typical army sergeants. Every other day the men did close order drill under the orders of Sergeant Michele on the bits of open ground outside the village already enlivened by a sun which was now *steady* under the approving eye of the populace, who were pleased by this spectacle of intensely busy quiet. But the men – the adolescents – had the *sullenness,* the offensive somnolence and the loose-lipped irony from the times of premilitary training.* And it was anachronistic and counterproductive to be present at the manoeuvres and patterns of the units, the men marching past with shouldered arms or presenting them, all these different, askew, unfriendly, uncollective and extremely personal arms. But Pierre approved unconditionally and the sergeant *rejoiced grimly* at the approval accorded to him by a 'real' officer. Here too, in spite of Michele, the nightime guard left much to be desired in terms of *effectiveness* and at first Johnny's principal task was to inspect the guard at night with Michele, the insomniac, the inexhaustible Michele, between the black earth and the windy darkness. Then Pierre had an airman's ability to do without sleep and in the breaks told stories about Malta and about the fighter defences and the radar and '*Tally-ho*'.

The inaction was so depressing, rusty, as to inspire the youngest

* Training in the Fascist youth movement.

men to the most desperate *raids* which Pierre and Michele stifled harshly, wisely, as if they were keeping children away from *crushing machinery.*

The best man under Pierre's order was Kyra. He was a first generation Piedmontese but his blood went far back. He had a complex and direct beauty, though with an ardour that was decidedly Sardinian that seemed to be tempered and *blended* into a Latin softness. He was short, but seemed to be made taller by the golden proportions of his limbs, with a voice at once veiled and virile. He dressed, like Pierre, with a sobriety and a functionality that bordered on the puritan, although his very physical elegance made him seem more brilliant and colourful than them all. Kyra was the favourite of the population of Mango, who greeted him, called out to him and invited him home with very much more warmth than any other partisan. And Kyra was a simple partisan without being at all simple, but no one would raise him to the rank of officer for fear of upsetting an innate equilibrium, of altering a figure born perfect exactly as it presented itself. He spent almost all his free time in a workshop in the village because he had a knack with and a passion for mechanics. He had been one of the artificers of the extension of the electrical cable and telephone line which the population owed to the partisan occupation. And he was a wonderful hand at repairing weapons and his daily occupation, almost his discipline, was filing the cartridge cases of the rounds for the Stens so as to adapt them to the calibre of the Breda sub-machine-gun. But the boy had something within him – a sadness at times cast a blue tinge over his cheeks concealing itself in the shadow of his youthful beard. Johnny liked Kyra infinitely but his courtesy was of the kind that excludes familiarity – he was a real adult with the need for, not the sensuous taste for familiarity. And Johnny was curious to get to the bottom of it – all the remaining human material interesting him little or not at all except for Pierre and Michele. Until Pierre cautiously solved the enigma for him – it was a secret known to the officers, the men knew nothing of it, and Johnny was to keep it to himself: a discourtesy to Kyra was absolutely inconceivable.

Kyra had an elder brother and he was an officer in the Fascist garrison in Asti. And, said Kyra, he was as lucky for the Fascists as Kyra was for them. 'Try to catch sight of Kyra when they bring a captured

Fascist to the headquarters or one about to be shot. You will see him agonising and following from afar from the side of the procession that always accompanies him. And should it be a case of his brother you can be certain, Johnny, that Kyra will not intercede for him although we would never execute him simply because he is Kyra's brother. But we know that in Asti his brother has similar thoughts, has stated publicly that his brother will not be spared for being his brother but that he himself will see to it that Fascist justice takes its course. These are things Nord knows at firsthand.'

Tragically for Kyra, brotherhood, which is always something formidable, was *upmost and utmost* for him. As if it were not enough that he nourished for his brother the reverential love that was both classical and ancient, the other was his hero, his model – unreachable because of respect and yet always present out of love: he was his inspiration, his commander, the one who had fashioned him for whom Kyra was simply delighted to be the workman who religiously carried out his plans. The other had planned, invented, constructed in every detail Kyra's enthralling, amazing adolescence. Pierre said: 'Those who have seen him say the Fascist brother is even more handsome than Kyra, much taller . . .' And Johnny could very well imagine him slim in his dark uniform, a monument, against the cobbled background of the barracks in Asti, of martial bearing and Fascist *sex-appeal.* While the war lasted the two brothers had no occasion to come into collision but first of all on 25 July and more so on 8 September they wounded each other deeply. The other had not been particularly enthusiastic during the whole of the war and Kyra was too young. But after 8 September the elder one changed, he was ablaze, he erupted, he was among the first and most determined and most bloodthirsty Fascists. He tyrannised Kyra, who was deeply upset, making him the butt of his fanaticism until Kyra climbed up to the partisans weeping, leaving his parents with anguish of these two counters, the one on the red the other on the black, in the tingling game of roulette that was now in progress.

'We are lucky,' said Pierre, 'and are undeserving, it seems to me. It seemed a great step to come up into the hills in our way – but think of those like Kyra how they climbed up and how they stay here. And think of his father and mother. The victory of one son is the perdition of the other. One has almost to hope for their sake that neither of them reaches the end, the moment of judgment. And for the old people as well.'

They went out to listen to Radio London in the house of some important local figures. Country bourgeois, very well disposed to partisan officers of that kind. The head of the house remarked once again what a hell the village would have been in the Red Star zone. Pierre chuckled and gently pointed out that Johnny stemmed from there. He apologised begging pardon with elaborate prolixity, then the house was blacked out and the owner turned on the set and tuned it: with practised ritual, lips pursed and eyes half-shut, as if driving a car in heavy traffic. The Allies were still tramping about in the mud on the borders of Campania and Lazio. '*Dough feet,*' said Johnny. 'What?' asked Pierre in his desperate inability to understand English which he had nevertheless studied. 'Flat feet, I called them.'

Inaction was becoming obsessive and so it must have been for the Fascists on the outskirts of their garrison town, staring from afar at the frightening hills. Then they learned that an Alpini battalion* had taken over from the Muti in Alba, half rounded up and forced into service, only dangerous, if at all, because of their toxic accumulation of fear and sense of having been coerced. Asti remained a stronghold but now the Garibaldini were spreading round the stronghold like a red belt which guaranteed, consolidated even more the security of the Blue centre on its lofty plateau.

The partisans swarmed over the hills, spring as it passed into summer excited and guaranteed their long intoxicated wanderings, being completely and naturally clothed with a thousand riches which had succeeded to the sullen, unsparing, often death-dealing nakedness of winter. In the evening the partisans *sang and fested* trying to tempt out the village girls. The dry soft roads, made everyone mad to possess motorcars and drive them drunkenly. With spring and summer they were unable – could no longer put up with going on foot, which was the weapon and discipline of the partisans. A battle with its ice-cold lesson was becoming an impelling necessity but the garrison in Alba confined itself to making two unconvincing thrusts towards the north. Of the four outposts deployed in front of Mango the first two *hindered and bothered them back home* without

---

* Famous mountain troops.

causing any trouble to the third. Not much as asked of the first, thinly held, outposts except to fire the minimum necessary to give the alarm to the whole system.

The situation was stagnating and for this very reason not likely to last. The partisans were too strong, or appeared to be so, to be attacked in their hills and at the same time too inferior and technically unsuited for the task of attacking and ejecting the Fascist garrisons entrenched in the towns of the plain. And to the programmatic difficulty of their conquest was added the material impossibility and the enormous danger of holding them against the Fascists' recovery as a fighting force. When this was attempted and carried out with the town of Alba in October '44 the experiment proved disastrous and the date marked the reversal of the situation and the earthquake which shook the whole partisan system which was restored only in January 1945.

Meanwhile security had reached a boring level to the point where the partisans' relatives from town arrived with Sunday punctuality on regular formal visits making the units like the vestibules of respectable colleges. To this end an efficient and very civilised service of transport, checking and reception was instituted. It was something that naturally also weakened the anxieties of the parents, induced them to believe that their boys, in the last analysis, being well and intelligently looked after, reasonably protected thanks to their intelligent initiative, were perhaps safer than were certain of their contemporaries biding their time and hidden away in the well-stocked cities of the plain. What happened thereafter destroyed those impressions and happy illusions in a disastrous way, when that unnatural period of almost bourgeois safety was followed by a very much longer period of horrible and desperate *exertion*, innumerable dead and unthinkable atrocities.

At all events that is how things were in May with the partisans peacefully visiting villages with markets and coming together in hundreds and by every possible means of transport in the town of Santo Stefano Belbo, the biggest and most developed of all the towns in the Lower Langhe. It was touched by the refining reflection from the prosperous plain close by, its *leading feature* consisted of its big central piazza, absolutely unmatched in size by the other piazzas of the Langhe, full of pretty girls with a bearing and ways of behaving and dressing that were clearly of the town. Alba being ruled out, Santo Stefano was the festive mecca of thousands upon thousands of partisans, Blue and Red, from the Lower Langhe. Johnny and Ettore went down there too almost every Sunday, *grudging against impeachment* on the few other Sundays, they too breathing that mild, restorative air of a way of life that was almost civilian, they too taking their *chances* with those *hills-over famous* girls, they too finding for that afternoon the sweet old demands of *savoir faire* in terms both of gallant conversation and behaviour, made more acute and re-inforced by the fascination of their brand-new status as partisans, and returning at last to the evening hills with a feeling of satisfaction and a *fling.*

This large village, being the geographical centre of the confluence of the Red and Blue zones was consequently, on holidays, the reef on which the two waves broke. The girls had a fair hand in it, they welcomed and defined and sharpened the divisions, wearing in their hats and buttonholes blue ribbons if they preferred and kept company with Blue partisans or vice versa flaming red ribbons if with Garibaldini. But often they changed ribbons with the sudden switch of liking and it could happen to an anxious Blue partisan to spot in the scabby piazza his girl with with a brand-new red ribbon in her hair. So quarrels were frequent, the men all armed and almost all with arms not rendered safe, frequent and indeed systematic the sarcasm aimed at the non-aligned local boys who tried to defend their place with their girls. Esprit de corps produced frictions and provocations, duels, and the two headquarters, being unable to permit themselves to even think of putting Santo Stefano *off limits*, organised on Sundays a special and mixed military police.

And this faction-torn, troubled mecca of Santo Stefano Belbo lasted until the course of the war was reversed and the by now irresistible advance of the Allies from the south was matched by complete autumnal disintegration in the partisan camp. The Fascists, at the peak of their counterattacking wave, did not occupy Santo Stefano on a permanent basis, but garrisoned the neighbouring town of Canelli with one of their strongest and most specialised anti-partisan units, which at any hour of the day or night carried out lightning motorised raids which made of the partisans' joyous summer mecca a dark place of nightmares and death by ambush.

To excite the partisans even more in their intoxicated state, amazing news came down from the high hills about the 1st Division, their twin which held positions on the steep wintry hillsides trodden by the solitary footsteps of Tito and Biondo. An English officer was with them – a major, described with one voice as a calm gentleman getting on in years with a healthy ruddy face squashed under a little Tyrolean cap and the whole anachronistic garb of a globetrotter in a *Punch* drawing, shot through by a tremendous directness of thought and action. 'I bet he's a Scot,' said Johnny, gazing at the misty, distant high hills which sheltered the Englishman. And Pierre: 'If you're interested I give you permission to go up there and see him.' 'I'll see,' said Johnny, 'one day is as good as another . . . after all he means to stay, doesn't he?'

The arrival of the Englishman and his mysterious transmitter guarded by triple sentries had poured on to 2nd Blue Division a Golconda of arms, uniforms etc. etc.; the nearby Red formations seemed exhausted, outclassed, vanished into thin air. Out of bounden duty and with the announcement that the very same Golconda would soon be emptied over 2nd Division, headquarters command sent into the Lower Langhe a brand-new truck packed with men armed and fitted out after the drop. It *swept* through the low hills like a fascinating publicity van with its rigid and haughty men, inevitably looking like mannequins, buttoned up in ultra-proper English uniforms and since it suddenly rained (in the intimitable manner of rain in the hills in a variety of sheets differing in the way they fell, spectroscopically different in density and colour) as if at a command they put on their camouflaged groundsheets, giving due prominence to the bulge at the back to hold the knapsack. They were all armed with Stens or Enfields,* a couple were showing off a Thompson,** the aristocratic weapon of partisan dreams. At the sight the partisans went wild with joy and *suspense*: the urgent desire for the automatic weapon and the consequent dislike of the ordinary hand-loaded weapon were becoming a general problem for the commanders. From the height of their truck as if it were a publicity campaign the mannequins threw down handfuls of English

---

* The Lee Enfield, the standard .303 British army rifle.
** The more robust form of sub-machine-gun.

cigarettes with a cork tip and packets of K rations* which the partisans threw away after having nibbled at them and tasted them. 'This is really the beginning,' said Pierre ironically, *fullheartedly.* And 'I really must go up and see this Englishman,' said Johnny. But a few days later the rumour spread through the hills – it was impossible to deny it – that the major was dead, crushed by a partisan truck with defective brakes in one of the stony lanes of Mombarcaro so well known to Johnny. Even the civilians were stricken with grief at the news.

* American army rations disliked by all soldiers.

XIV

The day Rome was liberated* the Fascists carried out a strong thrust at the heart of the Badoglian system. It was quickly discovered that these were soldiers from the Asti garrison, bold and tough units, very different from the clumsy Hamletish garrison in Alba, which invariably cut a poor figure against the partisans' night raids.

The first shots exploded in the plain of Castagnole, which was drowned in mists of heat, and had about them something festive, enlivening, a suggestion of Sunday bells. The birds, disturbed and frightened in the low ground were making for the heights, flapping their wings over Pierre and Johnny's intent heads. The garrison of Castagnole put up a short formal resistance at the first contact, then opened the way for the Fascists towards the adjacent garrison at Coazzolo, of which, so Johnny had learned, Ettore, his fellow-citizen and friend and ex-colleague as air-raid warden was part. Coazzolo held out a little longer favoured by the steepness of the foothills, and the Fascists lost time setting fire to a house and enjoying this very ordinary spectacle. From Mango the fire, although close by, was scarcely visible because the sky being drained of colour thinned the column of fire into fairylike unsubstantiality.

Pierre wanted to take up a position in front of the village and fight and die for its virginity. But Johnny pointed out that the round-topped hill to the right of the village crowned with thick and useful vegetation and with a slope that was appreciably steep was much better. But Pierre pointed out in his turn that that plan opened the way for the Fascists to penetrate into the village with the foreseeable consequences of fire and sword. 'They will burn,' said Johnny, 'if we

* 4 June 1944.

fight from inside the village and we won't hold it. That we won't hold it is a fact becaue at this moment we are not in a state to fight the Fascists in battle. If you asked the people of the village you'd see that they think like me.' But Pierre was chivalrously upset at the idea of the raped village and Johnny began to get worked up at this vast difference between them. 'Pierre, if we kill one of their men and they make a clean sweep of Mango and another village as well the day is ours. Our job isn't to hold positions, our job is to kill Facists. And if we are more successful in retreat I am ready to retreat from here to the sea.'

The civilians from the lowest hills were climbing up in flight, visible in the gullies like flocks of rabbits.

Finally Pierre sent his men to the round-topped hill, they were careless and amateurish, lingering in wide open spaces, with few arms and very little ammunition. They took up position on the top of the hill facing the road to Valdivilla, with the sergeant going to and fro to get them in place and stay there. Then he took his place in the centre behind the Breda machine-gun. Johnny cast a glance at the few reserve magazines and was furious at those theories which would make them melt away uselessly, platonically.

While waiting he lay there lazily, with a hint of intoxicated voluptuous pleasure at the imminent *exertion*, in the soft and extremely warm grass, with his rifle beside him, at once near and far from his relaxed hand, looking in the grass like a snake that had been straightened and turned into wood by a marvellous taxidermist. From all along the line there came little waves and fragments of conversation at once restrained and wide-ranging, personal and general, fantastic and hysterical, until from the centre Pierre ordered silence and Michele repeated the order with his voice which was heavy with catarrh in high summer. Then one could catch the tiny alarmed movements of the birds in their provisional refuge in the highest branches. Nothing was yet visible on the hill opposite at Valdivilla, which was harmonious and functional as a human limb. All over it the deserted space was green and the silence hummed electrically. Nothing and no one except a dog – even from up there one could see its erratic happiness – walking along the road to the village which was drawn as if with chalk on the solid hillside. Then Johnny looked sideways at the village which seemed to be aware of its excessive nudity and dazzling quality in the full noonday light. People were barring and bolting everywhere like a fortress or a submarine, the closing of the shutters and doors was like shots from a firearm. Even the noise of the electric drill had fallen silent. Its owner, the carpenter, a puritan, had worked up to the reasonable limit, austerely imposing the rights of work on the war and its opposing parties.

At eleven the Fascists came into view; they already wore camouflage uniforms, but they did not escape even for a second or in any detail the partisans' young eyes. There were a lot of them, a battalion, the last bend on the road was belching them out in continual waves. Then they left the road, leaping agilely over the ditches and climbed up the slope, slowly and crouching. Over their heads Johnny caught sight – very far away – of a group of trucks, probably with the reserves of ammunition, a first aid unit amid a few men of the rearguard. And his heart flew down there – here was the solution – disappear from in front of them as if by magic, get round the hill at breakneck speed, fall on the rear of the trucks, kill the men, loot the trucks and then set them on fire. With this burning nostalgia, with this despair over future times perhaps not likely to be witnessed, with his eyes on the figure of Pierre standing tall and about to give the signal to fire, Johnny raised his rifle to his shoulder in the direction of the Fascists.

But they kept them waiting, they were climbing up very slowly, taking every precaution, capable of forming a front and watching intently for five very long minutes the most motionless and empty and innocent bush, searching the rows of vines minutely, as if time did not matter to them.

It was understood that firing should be by command but some adolescents could not hold out and fired on their own the moment they thought they had the deceptive Fascist flesh in their sights. Then they all fired and from a *gasp* from Michele it was clear that the Breda had already jammed. The sergeant was working away to clear it with fingers that were already bleeding.

After the burst of fire the Fascists had completely and perfectly blotted themselves out on the ground and from their vague line, for the time being, came nothing more than a trill of whistles. Then they fired a big salvo which bit into the parapet of earth in front of the partisans. Michele had mended the Breda and fired back at the bank of the road from behind which the Fascists were firing as if from a trench. 'You're too high, Michele.' The sergeant said Sorry and immediately afterwards noticed that the Breda had jammed again. A new burst of fire from the Fascists shaved the tops of the trees overhead. The partisans replied with instinctive fire. It was clear that the Fascists were not suffering more losses than they were inflicting on the partisans but all the men were possessed by the lust for fire, by its moral support. It was certainly already past midday, with the Fascists pinned down below, Pierre clung to his short French police pistol and to the certain joy of keeping the village inviolate. Johnny was suffering atrociously from thirst. The Fascists, without advancing a step, kept up that fire of theirs which was as heavy and controlled as it was ineffective. Some hundreds of rifles and a few machine-guns were in operation but the bowl in the hills produced a din worthy of a great battle. The Fascist fire, being too high, cut back the branches over their heads with a *crack* at once terrifying and festive.

The mistaken nature of the system and the lack of esprit de corps were painfully clear. Now it only needed some partisan formation to deploy very visibly on any one of the lateral heights ready to plunge down excitedly on the Fascist mass and force it to withdraw but not a single man stood out on the crests which were as clear as if cut out against the sky. Instead one of their trucks moved very slowly towards their line almost as if it had trouble with its motor or feared the ground to be mined. 'Let's hope they're not bringing up mortars,' said Pierre. The airman had a damnable fear of that quintessentially earthly weapon.

Johnny noticed then that the sun was no longer filtering through the branches and the green had become a kind of liquid blackout. He looked up at the sky, which was vertiginously putting the last touches to its change. Compact masses of black clouds crowded together in the centre of the sky where a pool of pale light marked the point where the sun had shipwrecked, Johnny hoped for a storm but the storm was aborted although the sun writhed in labour pains.

At that moment the first double salvo from the mortars was heard leaving the edge of the valley – that homely but tremendous noise of huge pot-lids. Pierre's skin became as grey as the pupil of his eye. The round fell short, as was foreseeable, it smashed the bushes in front, raising a wave of pulverised earth. But the whole partisan line was in commotion, most of the men wriggled away on their knees like animals, seeking, searching for a better place. The second round was fired and this, also foreseeably, was over, and scraped dully against the steep hill behind them. Then the third round came down, still inaccurate but *ranging* inexorably. The fourth landed almost exactly at the corner on the left; the crash of vegetation mingled with the shouting of the men. But as the cloud of dust cleared one man remained erect, athletic-looking, and shouted with the high, firm note of an approaching siren. A fragment of shrapnel had taken out an eye and the little ball, like a ball of butter, was running down his cheek. Then he fell to the ground and among the trampling of the retreating men Michele collected the eye and wrapped it in his blue battle scarf. The wounded man, with his hands pressed to his face, was carried into the village from where some civilian would transport him to the hospital in Santo Stefano. The sergeant had shoved the package into his pocket.

They were retreating to another hill, sprinkled by the broken light of the struggling sun. Johnny and Michele in the rear turned round often but the camouflaged uniforms still did not break out of the abandoned green. Then as they climbed the hill which was ribbed with stone they had a wide view of the Fascists swarming up towards the village. They sat down on the naked crest and watched in detail and at their leisure. Immensely slowly they were eating away at the last slope, feeling every square centimetre of ground, only a few imperious trills from a whistle broke the motionless atmosphere. Then the forward scouts must have signalled that the village was empty because they all accelerated and rapidly disappeared from the view, the village now harbouring them along with its fate. 'What will they do to the village?' asked Pierre. 'Nothing.' 'What do you mean "nothing"?' 'Nothing. They'll requisition bread and salami, they'll eat in the square, they'll read a sermon to the civilians . . .' And the sergeant added: 'They'll smear the walls with their usual slogans in black paint.'

They waited for a long time for some sign of harm in the village but not a single shot echoed and not a curl of smoke spiralled up. Then Johnny saw a farm cart going downhill by a little side road. The man on the driving seat, all jacket and hat like a scarecrow, was driving the animal calmly, only hinting at whipping it; the body of the wounded man lay between the sides on one of which, bending over as if preaching, there sat the young curate of Mango. The air was so still and thin in its sunless transparency that one could catch or deduce the real friction of those distant wheels on the white stones that emerged from that road of escape and peace.

Then some Fascists emerged from the enclosed space of the walls and appeared on the road and the hill but not with the air of resuming the battle, no, they were *careless and strolling* as if taking an after-battle walk. You might have thought them tourists exploring the place not even very interested in the daily surroundings of their mortal enemies, asking themselves at each step and spot what they could be doing at some moment or other in the day in this war. But the sergeant became furious, he said with that sinister voice of his that he could not bear the sight and now he was going to take a handful of volunteers and go down to counter them on the little road and cut short in blood that offensive walk of theirs. But an ambush on the outskirts meant authorising the Fascists to put the village to fire and sword and Michele fell on the ground again with that strong and poor Bedouin body of his. Johnny touched him on the back. 'Sergeant, let's do it this evening when they are leaving. They don't have much transport and the trucks will be so full that they won't even be able to move an arm. We'll surprise them like a lot of men getting punched when their jackets are half-off.' The sergeant understood, 'They'll maybe just put up with it and go away. If we kill one of them the day is ours. For anyone who knows what's what. And the one among them who knows what's what will understand too. And he'll eat his heart out all the way back and all night.'

Pierre accepted but stayed with the main body. The sergeant leapt up, collecting the few remaining magazines and four other men. Those who stayed showed their plundered cartridge pouches or their tired and sceptical faces.

They plunged down the reverse slope then at a sustained pace along a small road, sunk in the hollow, parallel to the main road, towards the point of the matinal appearance of the trucks. The shape of the hill was such that the little road acquired a length more than thrice that of the main road. Johnny however had plenty of time and led on at a normal pace. Peasants appeared, sudden and unmoving, like the kind of statue you discover in the interstices of a garden as you walk along. Only further on did a young and critical peasant climb up to the side of the road to ask if they were running away and as he passed Michele punched him. It was an underarm blow, swift to the point of invisibility, the man collapsed on his back in his field.

Johnny went on ahead, he himself was amazed at the way his sprint was progressing. One man complained of a stitch, the noise of the trucks was still not travelling through the greying air, but there was no time to lose in the search for a good place for the ambush. Did the sergeant know the ground and the surroundings well? Yes, but for the moment it seemed everything had gone from his mind. At that moment the noise of departure rose across the hills, but so distant still as to sound thin and pleasing.

They climbed up on to the tufa and took up positions there on their stomachs. After their burst of fire they would let themselves slide down and so away through the gully but taking enough care not to dislocate anything or break a leg. Anyone immobilised would be the greatest martyr of the war – he would have to die a thousand times as a sacrifice for the dead Fascist. Behind them, on the other lip of the gully, among the mists of the dew and the dark of the scrub a solitary house showed white and smoked in the evening, the voices of the unwitting inhabitants were like the peeping of birds in the nest already burdened by the dark.

Their view of the road was horribly direct although only their sweating foreheads emerged from the tufa. The sergeant said: 'I'm sorry but I have to –' and he turned on his side and urinated. The liquid hissed on the chalk. The others were country boys, stolid and resolved, they clutched their rifles as if to bend them out of shape.

They were still far off but the noise was already so great and such that all Johnny's hair was standing on end at the thought of the sheer volume of traffic in transit. He said with a forced voice: 'At the last truck, eh?' 'The last one.' It was difficult, the last truck, either the column immobilises you with terror to the point where all the trucks, including the last one, pass under your nose or excitement makes you fire at the very first one in the column. Michele said of the Breda anxiously: 'It will jam after three rounds.'

The noise was coming closer and it was terrible as if rather than a noise of motors it was a din of weapons. Everyone's hair was bristling on their heads with an icy vitality at the tips and the roots. From the mad rumbling noise there also emerged the sound of a soldier's song, shouted, recalling Dopolavoro.* 'Idiots,' thought Johnny and remained reasonably calm.

They came out of the bend with lights turned off, spectral attackers in the incredulous evening. The five men were there on the tufa looking almost straight at the very sides of the trucks, feeling themselves naked and exposed to being transfixed. The whole column had emerged, the machines and the men spectral, from the sides there also emerged whitish patches that looked like re-quisitioned livestock. The men were singing at the top of their voices and the disjointed well-known words – even more than the motors – flew up on lethal wings into the faces of the men in ambush.

That was certainly the last truck. They fired with all their weapons into the line of spectres who had appeared at the sides. Two – three twisted, one fell into the road, as if the blow were a prodigious fist of wind which had seized and thrown him away. The truck gave a lurch, made a dash forward and then checked as if the driver had braked and then the officer in the cab had shouted to him to accelerate, in a death-throe ground out by wheels and earth.

While they were rolling along the spectral tufa towards the gully which was already shadowy, they heard the din of the whole column stopping, the trilling of the whistles which punctuated the universal clamour of hate and fear, a few rifle shots and the boom of a few hand-grenades thrown at random.

The five went off light-hearted and calm through the dark gully, Johnny and the sergeant lighting a cigarette after a while. They had heard the start of the general move towards the plain, the motors themselves in harmony with the men's hate and thirst for revenge. Only after covering a long distance did they climb up on to the main road and keep to it into the village. The Breda had jammed but in a holiday mood Michele would repair it until tomorrow.

They could hear the village, which Pierre had reoccupied and it shone with many lights in the late evening as if after confronting the Fascists they felt like defying the nocturnal planes as well. Very probably at that moment all the surrounding, conscientiously

* Dopolavoro – literally 'after work' – the culture and leisure organisation created by the Fascist régime.

159

blacked-out villages were asking what on earth Mango was doing. Closer at hand they heard an excited and anxious murmur of voices, critical and proud, which told Johnny that absolutely nothing had happened to the village. All the people had poured out on to the street which cuts the village from top to bottom and had mixed with the returning partisans in the coarse and homely aura of the lights inside the houses, in a comforting kind of public festive conversation. Johnny sent the sergeant to report to Pierre and made his way through the hybrid crowd. People were extraordinarily loquacious and euphoric like someone who has come through an ineluctable and feared test magnificently and can now hope for a long period of *untiredness*.

The Fascists had stayed there for hours but had not got up to anything. Certainly they had requisitioned a lot of stuff, referring them for payment to Marshal Badoglio (by the way would the government that came later on also recognise this kind of loss?), had eaten a rich and comfortable meal in the square in front of the Commune, then rather than terrorising had mocked and made fun of the stiff, reserved people for having wagered – and still wagering – on the defeat of invincible Mussolini and Hitler and finally had set about dirtying the walls for the edification of the partisans: Long live the Duce, long live Graziani, long live their battalion commander; death to the partisans, a formal promise to Nord to come back and capture him and skin him alive. Pierre had already sent a runner off to Nord and he was expected to arrive at any time, to see for himself the writing that referred to him. Johnny went to look at it, the letters gleamed in the unsteady halo of light, black, lacquered and thick.

The sergeant was shouting to him to come and eat but he did not go at once. Having lit a cigarette he went to the edge of the village: he had laid an ambush and had certainly killed – that was a big step forward and a recompense and reward for his own death.

Deaf to Michele's repeated summons, he sat on a wall, high above the abyss of the valley, which was already brimful of night. Where he sat was the last patch of immobile air, the threshold of a zone where winds were forged, from which there rose an oceanic constant whistling of whirlwinds. He trembled abundantly and for long.

XV

The partisans were all in camouflaged uniforms now – where had they found so much of that stuff? – cut and sewn up again by the dressmakers of the village and in the heat they went about in shorts, their weapons slung on chests that were browning visibly. And the rumour was going the rounds that the partisans of 1st Division were walking about in shorts recovered from the khaki silk of the immense parachutes used for drops. It was time the English did something for 2nd Division. Was it really possible that Nord, that star, could not get his way? A few little drops did arrive but like samples and consolation prizes: cigarettes with cork tips and an assortment of weapons. The garrison at Mango had a Browning machine gun,* sturdy and *unjamming*, with abundant ammunition, and four Stens, of which one went to Johnny. So Johnny gave away his old carabiniere rifle and took to going about with the Sten, rapidly getting used to its toy-like lightness and apparent unreliability. But regretting the old rifle when the alarm had him lying along with the others on a crest and firing down and at long range.

The Fascists – those of Asti – did not show up again; as for the garrison at Alba, it was so shaky and jelly-like that it had become an exquisite pastime to turn up one after another on the nearest hills and fire indiscriminately at night to force them into insomnia and gradually into nervous exhaustion. As for the Germans, they were no more present and real than the Hyksos.** But the Allies one saw in the sky: sometimes, as if stuck to the ceiling of the sky, huge silvery formations of Flying Fortresses went gliding along *en route* to who

---

* The Browning had a very high rate of fire.
** The Hyksos, a warrior people in ancient Egypt.

knew where; they glided along grandiosely, like galleons, leaving behind them thick, unobliterable white wakes to which the partisans lost their hearts. Then their eyes fell back to earth, looking in perplexity and depression at the Lilliputian patch of the world they had to occupy and defend as their final objective in that global war. The last to lie back on the ground was always Pierre, although he said he did not feel like committing follies to get on board a bomber. 'You know, Johnny, in our airforce to be posted to the bombers is equivalent to being failed?'

The heatwave was dense and tightening its grip, the earth exploding in all directions like a chestnut in the fire. Nothing was less cool than these high hills at the height of summer in the intervals between the winds. On such days everyone scattered without permission, looking for private ponds or the distant bank of the Belbo or even the shore of the Tanaro river, which marked the frontier of the partisan realm, and in the Belbo there was a drowning.

Johnny was crossing a field between ricks of wheat like totem poles when Pierre called to him from the crest of the hill to come at once, they had had an important invitation. Several hundred deserters from a Fascist Alpine division were about to arrive at Nord's headquarters, entirely German in equipment and training, and Nord had invited a party of his junior officers to be present at their arrival.

As they walked towards Nord Pierre, stumbling along (he was a very willing airman but a little short in the legs), looked radiant, saying that it was a great acquisition for the partisans and a great loss for the Fascists. They were all from the Veneto – and that was stock that he liked. Johnny *grinned*. 'I hope Nord has thought of putting a couple of machine-guns round about – partly as a joke, partly so as not to die.' Pierre not only did not agree but glanced at Johnny with a particular melancholy like a true believer at a hopeless agnostic.

From that point they looked down on the valley with the headquarters; the new site was a big rustic house, newly painted and in a yellow rare in these parts. The space in front of the house was swarming with people but the deserters had not arrived yet. They made for the bottom, straight down the slope, through grass that put no brake on them.

Nord was encamped among his guard and the invited officers. He was wearing overalls but his beauty and physical splendour were such that even in overalls he seemed to be in full dress. Around him were his bodyguard, magnificiently fed and muscled, armed to the teeth, clad in English khaki with German accessories. The bowl was full of sun, in an uproar like a station platform swept by the tinkle of the bells that say a train is arriving. They got close to Nord, who was talking to an English officer, so English that Johnny was flabber-gasted. Now Nord went off and the English officer stood in statuesque immobility directing at the road the deserters would arrive by his frozen blue eyes and the pale blue smoke of his *cork-tipped* cigarette. His uniform fell everywhere in a slim cut that had nothing Latin about it, with an indefinable rich sobriety. The triangle open at the neck was filled by a perfect puffed cravat of honey-coloured silk. Round his waist he wore a white belt – the real *army white* – from which hung a holster of similar shining whiteness with a big Colt .45 and on the coarse stuff of the holster was written in blue ink and with such lettering as the roughness of the texture allowed: LADY REB. From his pocket a tiny corner of a blue Badoglian handkerchief emerged which the Englishman wore with a smug touch of irregularity and affiliation.

Nord turned and laughed to Johnny: 'You're blinking and taking a deep breath. He's just as Italian as you or me. From Turin, if I'm not mistaken!'

The other confirmed his Turinness and smiled with measured pleasure at the complete success of his fancy dress. Then he introduced himself as Lieutenant Robin of 2nd Division. And he led them to understand that his joke almost always worked. Nord explained that Lieutenant Robin had been sent by Lampus to take over a certain number of the deserters. 'This 1st Division of yours,' said Johnny, 'if they're all like you is better than the Coldstreams.' Robin smiled; said that Major Temple, the late Major Temple, had involved him in a kind of fantasy, had wished to have him as his aide and allowed him to get his hands into the containers reserved for the English mission. And Nord said to Johnny: 'This is what will happen to you when the English drop to us.' At that moment a sudden and joyous alert rose from the entire bowl.

They had caught sight of the deserters, in a compact body and gesticulating, flanked by fraternising partisan scouts. Nord's eyes shone, then he turned round and gave a sharp negative sign to the little hill behind which the two machine-guns were sited so obvious was the sincerity of the arrivals, at once joyous and tearful.

They arrived in compact platoons and with hardly an interval between them, preceded and enveloped by their own applause and that of others. They were loaded with German arms and made it apparent that they knew how to use them in the German manner. There were perhaps three hundred of them and they marched past towards the top of the bowl where Nord stood. Their eyes – searching eyes that could tell a leader – were immediately fixed on him and now they were shouting to him out of gratitude and dedication.

They had no officers and were led by sergeants like their elder brothers. The sergeants wanted to draw them up in formation and present arms but there was an immediate fusion and embrace. Johnny and Pierre dived into the whirlpool and were embraced, kissed and slapped on the back *in whole reciprocation*. In that maelstrom they compared arms and uniforms, the deserters offering everything in exchange for something to change into at once in place of their detested and unlucky Fascist uniforms, offering, say, for a pair of trousers that were not grey-green their stupendous German semi-automatic rifles in place of the wretched weapons of the majority of the partisans. They talked and shouted in the dialect of the Veneto, the sweetness of their accent being done violence to by the pitch of their shouts, and a yell of indignation and shame burst out when they learned that Alpine troops from the Veneto like themselves were acting as garrison for the Fascists in the nearest town. They begged to be sent at once to fall on them and kill them, kill them all. 'Filthy Germans and a republic* that is filthier still!' yelled an incredibly young and massive blond, airing his uniform as if to rid it of the greasy and animal smell that had built up in the German barracks. 'We're brothers, damn it! How could we fight you, brothers?' They had a strange way of insulting; they didn't seem to be insulting but merely uttering recriminations, and would kill recriminating.

Johnny and Pierre disengaged themselves at last from that love because of a pure and overwhelming feeling of not being worthy of it. They sat halfway down the slope, Pierre plucking blades of grass

---

* The Italian Social Republic, ruled by Mussolini as a German puppet.

and Johnny, to give vent to his emotion, lighting a cigarette with a *scratch* of disproportionate loudness. 'Can you believe it – I was on the brink of tears,' said Pierre. 'They're really great boys' 'I hope they won't have a nasty wakening tomorrow, Pierre. But it will happen as it has happened with all the other great boys. I'm not saying idealists – merely great boys. Tomorrow they'll see that everything doesn't fit into their dream of love and they'll get hardened to it like you and me.' 'We must be better,' said Pierre. 'Are you unhappy, Johnny? Are you in some sort of crisis?' 'No,' said Johnny, 'I am exactly where I would like to be.' 'You're not sorry about being a partisan?' 'Unhappy! If I think – if imagine I might have lost this chance from fear or an easy life or for any other reason, I begin to shiver.'

The boys from the Veneto were dispersing slowly as if exhausted by their outburst in the arena-bowl, the late night striking them so that they now appeared only in a sort of fractured unreality. The share-out had been made between Nord and Robin and the Veneto sergeants. A good half were loading up again for the long evening and night march to the high hills of 1st Division. 'What will Nord do with his share?' Johnny inquired. 'Will he split them up between the various units or will he make them one command?' 'I know Nord,' said Pierre. 'He has already seen what they are like and he'll keep them close to him as a second bodyguard.'

The divisional treasurer came and handed over funds to Pierre. 'How are the finances?' 'Never richer. Everyone pays up. Millions.'

The first Sunday in August Pierre dedicated to his fiancée. He had found time to get himself a girl with the directness and goodwill he put into everything. The girl lived in Neive, the big village at the bottom of the Mango valley; it was divided into two neighbour-hoods, the upper one dominating the grim crags that fell down to the river, the lower one spreading from the foothills to the railway tracks, which were deserted and inactive since the day of the Armistice.

When Pierre had left, Johnny immediately saw a car draw up at the deserted checkpoint. He cocked his Sten and went over. But it was Ettore, his precocious masculinity enhanced by his being a partisan, his adult moustaches *flourishing*. 'You knew where I was,' he said right away, 'but it never entered your head to pay me a visit. Don't tell me you were too busy. These are great holidays for everyone.' It was true, Johnny admitted, but idleness when it is too complete pins you down even more than the most intensive work. Ettore did not go on and opened the door for Johnny. 'Have you still got anything left over from last payday? Right, then let's go down and get rid of it in Santo Stefano.'

The lure of civilisation *toppled* on top of Johnny and buried him. In a second there was no madness he would not commit to enjoy town girls, a walk in a square without dust or mud, soft drinks, ices and the cinema. And then Santo Stefano offered all these. 'How come that you have a car?' 'A military secret,' said Ettore putting it into gear. 'Does it look to you like an intact, healthy machine? Well, let me tell you that at least two essential pieces are missing and in the tank I have scarcely a drop of petrol that is not petrol. But we'll get to Santo Stefano. On the way back we'll have to sweat but if we get fed up with it we'll throw it into a ditch.'

It was exactly like the old trips, with in addition the pleasure derived from long abstinence, and the weapons between their knees were stridently out of tune and useless. Ettore trembled with a frightening charge of physical energy; he drove dashingly. On a steeper stretch of road, he said between his teeth, 'I don't know what it is that keeps me from seeing what a *crash* is like. I feel like running the car at that tufa. I'm going to do it now.' 'Go on then,' said Johnny coldly. But Ettore thought better of it and took the corner with double prudence.

They were at the top of the last hill, high up above the town, lying behind the thin sparkling ribbon of the river. From up there they could catch the colour and the crowds in the main square. Ettore went into neutral for the last part of the descent. 'There are bound to be two girls who feel like a car and have a weakness for the Blues. I'm worried about the petrol but I'll pinch it from some partisan vehicle. Preferably from a Communist one. Will you give me a hand?' Johnny agreed even though the theft of that most precious stuff was one of the most fatal of *casus belli*, which merited point-blank fire. 'About the two girls, Johnny, leave that to me. You are a chap with all that it takes but – no offence meant – you don't get off with girls right away. Let me do the talking – I'm more straightforward. Too much grammar puts the girls off.'

Johnny laughed and watched all Ettore's preparations for a great entry into the town. But it was scarcely on the level before the motor let them down; immediately after the bridge it sneezed and jerked and came to a halt, irremediably. They had to go into the square pushing in the most embarrassing and depressed manner, amid immense gusts of laughter from the Communists.

Ettore made for a mechanic, who came over to them with ill-dissimulated exasperation. He said: 'I've got to see to a score of your machines already,' pointing an oil-stained hand at a cemetery of carcasses. 'We will pay,' said Ettore drily. Then the man devoted himself entirely to their vehicle, calling on the help of a small boy of his. Ettore said loudly that he was afraid the non-existent petrol would be stolen; the mechanic said he could vouch for himself and his people, but he declined any responsibility for the other partisans, especially the 'Reds', whom he could not gainsay.

They left the mechanic's and went to have a look at the square. They went to the top of a little flight of steps and looked back. It was a swarm of blue and red, with a *striking*, significant balanced quality. The Blues were more elegant and supple, amazingly inclined to indulge in poses and long moments of leisurely self-examination. Their *toughness* was the Communists' chief physical characteristic – they looked to be cut out for a long grey campaign, for a prolonged and planned effort; above all they had an impressive look of being able to go on when for the Blues everything was long over. A few Communist commanders, Johnny noted, indulged in a certain showiness and decadence in their uniforms that was quite 'Blue' and all the more striking because embryonic. They had – the Reds – almost a weakness for skin and leather; leather abounded on them in every way, cut and detail. Most wore red scarves, very long, which sat on their broad backs like collapsed windsocks, some even went so far as to wear red shirts, of a poppy colour that was breathtaking and dazzling.

Esprit de corps and rivalry were there in the embers but that day, at that time, Badogliani and Communists seemed to enjoy the best of relations.

There were crowds of women; the girls were elegant, with a city touch, knowingly flirtatious and actually drenched with perfumes that were still acceptable. They seemed to be madly in love with the partisans, with those of unequivocal city extraction, they mixed with them, clung to their arms, listened to their whispers with lowered heads and half-shut mouths, some of them carrying on their shoulders the weapon lent them by their man.

A report struck the square mute and motionless, then had it swarming away centrifugally. A partisan showing his girl of the day his weapon had fired a shot, miraculously without spilling blood in that crush, which then went and splattered against the metal sign of the hotel, with everyone pointing to that hole in the metal and imagining it in their own flesh. There was a move to lynch the guilty man; the middle-class citizens evacuated the square, pale and swift; from the windows, balconies and terraces the mothers were calling their intoxicated daughters home with torn from them cries, half of authority, half of helplessness.

Johnny had turned pale at the shot. Now he was watching how the promenade re-formed, calm, forgetful, as if drugged. 'We are laughing now, Ettore. But the moment will inevitably come when we will weep. Then naturally we'll laugh again, the great final laugh. But will we be the ones who go through the great lamentation to make landfall in the great laughter?'

Ettore went off and after a little Johnny saw him again in the centre of the piazza, making towards a couple of girls who seemed to be unattached. Johnny hurried up not to miss the spectacle, which was always an attraction, but when he arrived the game was already over and the match lost. Ettore said they both had bad breath. 'But didn't you see they were already fixed up,' Johnny observed. 'Garibaldini girls?' Ettore denied it. 'No, they didn't have the red ribbon in their hair.' 'No, not in their hair but they had a little ribbon in their buttonholes.' Ettore was dumbfounded. Nothing annoyed him more than to be found lacking in his attempts on the other sex. 'How is the car?' said Johnny. 'It's a dead loss. The clutch is gone and there are no spares to be had. We'll go back on foot or get a lift.' 'Who did you requisition the car from?' 'In Neive.' 'Who from?' 'I don't know the name – but it's the family of the girl that Pierre is making a play for.' '*Great God!*' gasped Johnny.

The square seemed to produce a bigger and bigger crowd. Women who had got over their shock and new partisans were coming into it like a spate. Johnny, withdrawing to one side, said there were too many of them. 'There are too many of us. If it doesn't end this winter – and it won't – even if we assure the peasants who keep us going of the opposite you'll see how many of us will be left. But now the weather is good, the others are in a state of crisis. Our kingdom is unbounded and untouchable and you can see how many of us there are.' 'And then,' said Ettore, 'this place doesn't even count. This is a funfair – that's the word, isn't it?'

The main current of the crowd brought them towards an assembly of Reds; they had hoisted a comrade on to a kind of platform and were inviting him, forcing him, to sing with fierce pressure. The boy nodded, a proud, thickset and *grinning* figure. All around and from below the demands increased and then he struck up 'The wind is whistling, the storm is raging' in the Russian version* with a splendid bass voice. Everyone was drawn towards that platform, even the Blues, even the civilians, in spite of obscure, instinctive repugnance for that song which was so genuinely, tremendously Russian. Now the Red chorus took it up with a physical and vocal challenge that rang out like what it was meant to be and meant to say – the challenge to and humiliation of the followers of Badoglio. The antagonism was at its pitch under the sun; the sweat dripped from the square necks of the singers. Then the chorus died away to rise up again immediately in a burst of fierce applause mixed with fierce whistling from the Blues, but as a pure contribution to the intoxicating clamour. Some Badogliani proposed counter-attacking with their own song but the Blues, even the other ranks, were too *nonchalants* and then what song could they oppose with anything like equal power to that overwhelming, Russian song? Said Johnny to Ettore, whom he had found again on the edge of the Red belt, 'They have one song – that's all. We have too many and none. That song of theirs is tremendous. It is a real weapon against the Fascists which, we have to admit, we don't have in our armoury. It drives the Fascists mad, I'm told, just to hear it. If a new-born child sang it they would shoot it dead.' 'I have a constant itch, a constant itch,' said Ettore solemnly.

Then a car made its way into the square from the right, slowly and stubbornly, through the encrusted crowd, and from the car a voice began to shout indecipherably over the megaphone. But round the car the Reds swarmed and the civilians disappeared. Now you could understand what it was saying: a neutral and deliberate voice like that

* This Russian song became a kind of signature tune of the Communist partisans.

169

of an announcer in a big railway station gave notice of the threat of a Fascist attack on the Red line and ordered the Reds *at stations*. Trucks for transport just outside the town. Ettore gave a *jerk* of revenge, 'It's their turn. They've always wanted it.' The megaphone repeated its message and the Reds withdrew out of the town. 'Garibaldini to their own lines. Mount the truck outside the town. Fascist attack on the positions Isola – Montegrosso – Loazzolo' – and then the war-cry: 'Death to the Fascists!'

The car slid forward and stopped alongside Johnny and Ettore. The megaphone uttered the warning once again right in the faces of the impassive Blues. Then from the back seat a Red officer got up. In his lap, Johnny saw, he had a parabellum and a box of candied fruit which he nibbled uninterruptedly. The man was a perfect dark type, his skin ambered and magnificently polished by his sweat. 'It's our turn. Satisfied, you Blues?' Johnny said: 'The same as you are when the Fascists prefer us.' The man laughed, showing all his pointed teeth. 'Wish us good luck.' 'Naturally.' 'Then,' said the commander, 'have a candy,' and fishing it out he held the little grey mummy of a pear. 'Would you mind giving me that mandarin instead?' 'Not at all – but it's red!' and he laughed childishly as if at an unintended coincidence. Johnny took the mandarin and then pointed to Ettore. 'I have a comrade here.' 'Forgive me,' said the man, 'we mustn't ever fall short – ever be forgetful – when it comes to comrades.' He laughed once more and handed Ettore the pear. Then he gave a sign to the driver to go, saying goodbye with his thin bronzed hand. Now entirely superfluously but because of an irresistible urge for the epic and for publicity the megaphone kept on in the indifferent and half-emptied square: 'Garibaldini, back to your posts, all of you! Fascist attack on your line . . .'

'What do you say to that type?' asked Ettore. 'I say he is a good type and won't go far with them.'

They went towards the eastern exit of the square from which there came the snorts and sneezes of the lorries leaving to the wild *bracing-cheering* of the men already on board or boarding. Then the noise went into the distance and vanished and Johnny listened intently to the distant horizon of Monferrato as if to catch the beginning of the symphony. But nothing pebbledashed the compact immobile sky. They turned back to the square – the Blues too were getting fewer, the civilians had all withdrawn already. 'I've had enough of this place,' said Johnny, firmly and aggressively. 'So have I,' said Ettore with decided simplicity. 'But we'll have to make it on foot.'

They were making their way along the long road towards the distant hills with the sad determination of someone who already has the staying power and experience for roads when a van overtook them to brake catastrophically a few yards ahead. It was a van of Nord's sapper unit. Since there was no room in the cabin they settled down in the van with two other partisans, massive, solid peasants who had got into the partisan movement as if it were a kind of adventurous, legionary body of manual labourers. Much of the van was taken up with boxes of ammunition and a corner was covered with a layer of dozens upon dozens of strange bombs, full-bellied, clad in a little black skirt. Johnny and Ettore picked up one each and lifted up the skirt with a prurient sense of shamelessness. They discovered a bottle of thick, veined reddish-brown stuff, giving off in all directions a sense of death and destruction. One of the sappers felt he had been elevated to professorial status simply by the way they were intrigued. 'Plastic bombs. English. Formidable. Good against men, houses, tanks, anything. Nord gave us them – he begged the 1st Division for them. But how long are we going to have to depend on 1st Division? When will the English drop to us?' With a touching expression of skill and *surprise-making* one of the two peasants had extracted a bomb from under his foot which was still shod for winter and now with a knife was cutting a slice from the resinous belly. The two uninitiated were expecting some sort of demonstration but the man confined himself to putting it in his mouth and chewing it carefully. With a *snap* Ettore asked if it was good. The man *grimaced contentedly* and the sapper explained that the plastic was edible with a nice almondy taste.

They put them down at the Mango crossroads – the village with its usual look bearing witness to the total calm of the day. In the evening hum there rose from the plains, skimming the gilded hills, distant rifle fire, *ragged* and merely hinting. Johnny turned his back on the horizon with its battle and listened carefully to the sapper who was talking to Ettore. 'Naturally,' he was saying, 'our work will mostly be at night. So when you hear a fine bang at night think of your sapper

171

friends who are throwing everything upside down and then turn over and sleep on the straw. A pity that all the work inside the town has already been done – and done damnably badly.'

Ettore went off. Johnny watched him on his way – at the bottom of the hill he attacked the first slope of the pass with a smiling step. For Johnny there was an unfading magic about a man walking alone through the deserted hills on the topmost peak with his shoulders straight against the enormous sky. Then he disappeared from sight and Johnny looked far down through the bluish haze of distance to the plain of Monferrato. In the distance it looked like a summer shore scarcely *bubbling* under the pinpricks of the continuous firing. He remained there till he was tired of that senseless noise and set out for the road Pierre would return by. He sat on the cool bank and lit a cigarette with the desire to really do something by smoking that cigarette. He removed his pistol which, as he sat down, had stuck into his thigh and stifled a burst of dislike for the gun and for all weapons. The wide sunset valley from Mango to Nieve was clad in a chiaroscuro which was completely autumnal; and the wind, now rising, struck all its leaves with a watery sound which brought with it immense melancholy. Then from the village there came arcane, incredible, the voice of Michele, who was posting the guard for the night.

Pierre arrived at eight. Johnny waited for him to climb up in a kind of friendly ambush, directing him at the end with the red tip of his cigarette. 'Everything OK in Nieve, Pierre?' 'Everything OK. But today in Nieve there was that first driver of Nord – the one from Turin – the nastiest of all that nasty bodyguard. He came down to Nieve to show off. He is a shit but is shamefully better informed than the best of us. Well, he was going about saying, maybe just to show off, that soon we'll go down and occupy the town.' 'Have we all gone mad then?'

XVI

One morning in September a car from headquarters picked Johnny up from the village. They were driving along the road to Castino – three bodyguards and a warrior he had not seen before, tiny, with a half-caste complexion, in complete German uniform from his helmet to his little boots, always silent, only stretching out an oily hand every time Johnny reached for his cigarettes.

That trip was the most spine-chilling Johnny had ever made in the daily *suspense* of partisan life. The descent to Belbo – unforgettable; the corners on the vertiginous gullies beyond low walls were confronted with never a change of speed, with the most violent applications of the brakes *in extremis*. The rear mirror reflected back to Johnny the excited driver's ugly mug; the half-caste at his side had stopped smoking, his cigarette was visibly dwindling to virginal ash which the jolts cut off short every so often and from apprehension his skin in the shade of the uncongenial German helmet took on the hues of certain soft skins of over-ripe fruit. Of the two other guards one urged on and the other swore.

It happened at the parapet of the bridge over the Belbo; either there was too much brake or the brakes did not work, the vehicle skidded and went right into the low wall, knocked a hole in it like cardboard and hung suspended over the void with its rear wheels above the shingle twenty metres below. No one moved or spoke or breathed. Johnny started at the narrow *glitter* of the shallow water and the wide expanse of the jagged shingle. In the immaculate silence the chatter of the half-caste's teeth could be heard. Everyone knew that the mere hint of a movement to escape would break the miraculous equilibrium and the vehicle would fall headlong. With enormous caution Johnny looked sideways but the road was perfectly and lastingly deserted. And the edge of the breach in the wall could not be reached without a sudden, fateful sideways movement and grab. Johnny hungered for life, life was the tepid *hush* in the air and the tepid profile of the high hills, so firm and solid with their roots in the earth. No one any longer stared at the shingle below, all were looking at the firm, solid, impassive sky and the guard who before had been urging on was now chewing away at prayers like an inspired child. The car was swaying perceptibly and the half-caste shrieked then *scrambled off*, his short German boots bashing into Johnny's shoulder. The car ws swaying, out of the tail of his eye Johnny caught sight of the half-caste already in safety, motionless now, and forgetful of everything, concentrating on *recovering*. He whispered to him to hold the car back by the rear bumper with all his strength. The half-caste *braced toadlike, crouched* and held fast. They all filed off on tiptoe and holding their breath. On the road the driver began to laugh coarsely. Johnny felt the rough road under his feet lovingly, then the two guards exchanged a look of understanding, went over to the vehicle and hurled it into the void. And everyone held his breath waiting for the *crash* that should have been theirs.

Johnny voided the tide of saliva due to nausea. Then he said quietly: 'Pigs, ruin and shame, pigs! All three of you. What it needs is a burst of Fascist fire to knock you off – all three of you.' The half-caste was crazily miming innocence and congeniality; an insulting expression that said we don't give a damn for your insults flitted across the ugly faces of the two guards, then a flash of the possibility of acting the bully, then fierce emphasis on their superior muscularity, and the one who had been praying a little earlier slipped away with his hand on the monumental pistol in his belt. But they were already covered by the to-and-froing of Johnny's Sten like the head and shoulders of a snake, all three of them. The half-caste fell on his knees, the other two retreated towards the breach in the wall, halting with a start in front of the chasm. 'What are you going to do now? Is this a joke? We understand – you're playing the strong man just because we gave you a fright without meaning to.' 'I won't shoot you. I can only hope the Fascists do soon.' 'We'll tell Nord you aimed at us with your Sten.' 'And that you hoped the Fascists would kill us.' 'You can tell Badoglio if you like.' 'And we'll tell him that you sent him up saying '"Tell Badoglio if you like".' 'I'll get to Nord first. Now we're all going to walk, all four of us and you don't know how to walk any more, you plebs who aren't – forget about driving around at all hours – even worthy of creeping along where the other partisans march.'

He backed to the edge of the wood and then turned round and walked off. When he turned round again the three were still there on the bridge with a little country crowd interviewing them.

He climbed up in the cool heart of the wood along paths that were slippery at first but with a pleasant sportive slipperiness, his rage evaporating in the cool, damp breeze of the wood. Then he reached a clearing from which, by turning round, he could just catch sight of the powerful mass of the hill at Mango and thought of it as so much a *place* of battle and revolt and of the men, his comrades there, Pierre first of all, his discretion so massive; he thought of these things fleetingly but with all his heart. With him and behind him all the noises of the carpeted hill, all the *brisk* noises of life before autumn. Only at one moment did he catch sight of the headlong flight of a partisan vehicle launched downhill towards who knew what goal.

Now from the outer edge of the great wood, from above, there came a chattering of men, but almost infantile, as if the branches and the ferns by filtering it robbed it of adult power, and climbing a little further, Johnny at length came upon a squad of men *perched* on trees and poles, running up a telephone line. He slowed down as much as he decently could so as to go on enjoying the spectacle of orderly and joyful activity, which looked to him like the encouraging physiognomy of a regular army going about things well.

Nord's new headquarters rose on the watershed between the Bormida and the Belbo with opposite it the last hill before the Tanaro river and behind it the last hill before the plain of Alessandria: a motionless buoy – that watershed – in a whole, in an agitated sea of hills which had petrified at a signal. And the headquarters was in a huge completely rustic house as if it had been constructed by a patriarch for his family whose generations went back for centuries, the monument of monuments of peasant life, and it stood in a wide clearing, in a circle of old strong trees, which at every hour of the day cast the shadows – now short now long – of the branches, moved by the eternal wind, on to the white grainy walls,

In the clearing bodyguards were idling or going to and fro,

rendered unnatural by the muted silence as they stood or moved about on the grassy carpet, and in a corner splintered by shade and light were women, squads of them, doing the general laundry with an active and happy air and the joyous sense of doing their real, natural work. The smell of the soapsuds struck Johnny in the face across the rarified air, carrying with it the comforting sense of domesticity in the open air. Some of the bodyguards were teasing the washerwomen with an irony that was healthy and straightforward and had the effect of joyfully urging them on with their work. Everywhere a sense of intense and peaceful activity which had absolutely no connection with the war, and then Johnny with a natural switch wondered what they were doing, what they could be doing, in that same enchanted moment – the Fascists, all the Fascists in the world.

He walked over to the romantically imposing, sun-beaten entrance which was not under direct surveillance. But from behind the house there came, catlike, the noise of approaching motors and then a heartbreaking, distant, unintelligible cry which floated away like thinning smoke over the vast abyss of the Bormida valley and a moment later came the sound of a volley, short and almost casual, rather like a weapon being tested or an experimental shot at an immortal target.

The entrance in the penumbrated hallway robbed Johnny of any ability to discern things; then a questioning voice urged him to come forward and he did so following that beacon. It was a bureaucratic type, dressed entirely like a civilian, and with an air that had nothing to do with a free life freed from its clerkly *pattern*, sitting naturally behind a very proper desk. He asked him who he was and what he wanted but always with a clerkly tone of voice which had absolutely no hint of partisan colouring. Then he replied that Nord was busy and that he should wait there. It was funny for Johnny to be instructed with such bourgeois naturalness and to comply with the same and as much naturalness. 'Can I see the paymaster meantime?' No, he was busy for the same reason as Nord was busy, they were dishing out cash to people invited from the units in the upper Bormida valley. At that moment a new burst of fire barked outside, but lightly and as if refined, and a quicker than lightning tremor ran through the employee and his chair creaked beneath him but in a moment his face had resumed all the deeply bored impassiveness of the *routinier* . . . At the echo of the shots another face rose up from another desk only now coming into view. He was scarcely a boy but pale and with hair already thinning and when he rose up he appeared in a complete and perfect uniform – that of a junior German officer. He was extraordinarily slim and the uniform was naturally too big for him but without having a comic effect – indeed with an incredible added element of romanticism. He went with an old man's step to the peg where his German knapsack hung, extracted a cigarette and lit it, then he went back to his desk and immersed himself once more in his work which, even from a distance Johnny judged to be that of translation. The *routinier* seemed to resent his mate but essentially because of the total, undisguisable sadness which spread around him.

Then the paymaster appeared and was not surprised by Johnny, he knew the conference had been summoned. He confirmed to Johnny that it was for the plan about Alba and that Nord had already cross-questioned other people from Alba, Frankie and citizens who had come up from the city by any transport they could find. 'But it is purely academic – it has already been decided.' They went out on to the clearing into the delicious pool of patchy light. 'Who is the little German officer and what does he do?' 'Austrian. Second Lieutenant Schimmel. He deserted about a month ago. The first partisans he met wouldn't believe him, they tied him up and interrogated him in their own way, terrorising him. Fortunately our adjutant was passing nearby . . . but he's just begun to recover. Nord wanted him at HQ at once but for the moment they don't know precisely what to get him to do and so that he won't get dispirited we are making him translate German proclamations and circulars the text of which we have known for months.'

Johnny *relented almost to melting point.* He wanted the Austrian to feel all right and not to have regrets . . . The paymaster said it was impossible even to guess – his sadness was so general and all-embracing – from every other point of view an excellent comrade, with a kind of good manners, a sort of respect that almost made you feel uncomfortable. As for the town, whatever you come up with it has already been decided. Just imagine – Nord is already putting together a special uniform for his entry.' 'A shout, I imagine, a roar.' 'It is a blouse of black rubber with a whole chain-mail of silver-coated zips.'

From the high bank above the Bormida a priest emerged – one of the type common in the mountain parishes, the political crudity of their minds corresponding to their hard, massive, aggressive physiques. He was flanked by an officer from the headquarters, icily deferential, and they were carrying on a lively but subdued discussion. 'I'm not the only priest in the zone,' he was saying, 'and I should like to be relieved a little of these duties. I mean I should like a certain alternation – a system of rotation, that's what I mean.' 'Because of your conscience, reverend father?' asked the officer with casual but feline directness. The priest *waved* a big negating hand in a disjointed way. 'I am not discussing your sentences. It is not up to me to make their peace with men but I would really like to be relieved somewhat of the task of putting them right with God. You are my witness that in this present week I have discharged this task at least four times and on three different days.' 'It is simply because, reverend father, you are the priest in the zone in which the headquarters is at present situated and it is at the headquarters and only at the headquarters that all the justice in our area is carried out. You will admit that this rigorous centralisation of justice constitutes a solid guarantee for what can be . . . a load on the conscience.' The priest nodded with that uncoordinated and massive depth of feeling of his. 'I request you, however, to explain to your commander my desire – for an alternative – without naming names headquarters would have a good idea of where to turn for this – alternative . . . No, no thank you, I shall go back on foot, it will be good for me, better in fact,' he said hastily to the officer when he saw him signalling to a bodyguard for a vehicle. The officer recovered his composure and said: 'May I suggest to you, reverend father, that you limit your – contribution to confession – I mean your presence at the execution may not be strictly necessary.' But the priest raised a hand, firm and threatening this time, which cut clean across a filtered ray of sunlight. 'No, no,' he said loudly, 'if I begin I wish to and must finish, one of these unfortunates might – at the last moment – need me – perhaps only a glance from me.' The priest went off towards the thickest part of the wood while as he passed, stooping and strong, the bodyguards stood lazily to attention.

'A day of firing-squads,' sighed the paymaster. 'Frequent?' 'Only someone who is permanently at a headquarters has an idea how heavy the losses are in this kind of war. Some of us are already having nightmares – myself I find that it is really difficult to sleep and I am only the paymaster.' 'Who were the ones today?' 'An officer from the Littorio Division* and a Republican from Asti who was wandering about. Yesterday they shot one of our men flagrantly guilty of rape and theft.' 'Good,' said Johnny.

Nord came out into the clearing. His beauty was radiant. He halted in a brightly lit square of sunlight in what was still a perfect summer uniform: a shirt of khaki silk cut from the rich expanse of a parachute, shorts of khaki gaberdine sent to him as a present by the commander of 1st Division which fell with perfect *aplomb* to his sandalled feet. He was trying comically to detach himself from another partisan in glorious contrast to him. Now at the beginning of September he was hairy, bearded and wrapped up, extremely clumsy because of his very small stature and sturdy build, with such an armoury distributed all over his large surface as to awaken laughter rather than *awe*. But Johnny could not smile as everyone else did because it was his first sight of this man of ferocity and blood. As the paymaster said it was Blondie, the commander of the garrison at R the highest and most uncomfortable of the many villages held by the Division. 'I have treated you far too well, Blondie,' Nord was saying, glad to cheer his bodyguard with *comics*. And the other with a *hoarse* voice replied: 'Don't say that, Nord, don't say it, if you want to avoid mortal sin. You are damning yourself with these words. If you were not already damned for the injustices you have meted out to me. And I am not talking about funds but about weapons and ammunition.' He had a timbre in his voice and a rhapsodic flow of colloquial speech that put the finishing touches to his primitiveness. And yet his difference from his surroundings – a difference which was deeply felt, intentional and defended – raised him on to a higher plane than the surroundings of the headquarters which were somewhat *stilé* and certainly opulent.

With amused patience Nord explained that he had given him enough and more than enough for two normal garrisons. 'Normal

* One of the divisions in Mussolini's Republican Army.

garrisons – quite right – but not R. Nord, you have no real idea of what R is like – Why do you never come up?' 'I've been there, Blondie, in the spring.' 'Once – but you have to come oftener. You came once like a bishop. Are you a bishop, Nord?' The clearing roared with laughter with Nord giving the signal for it. Blondie laughed too but in *full-voiced* polemic and shouted: 'If you won't change the way you are with me I'll change the way I am with you. I'll drop you and go over to the Red Star Division.' The bodyguard quivered but Nord smiled and said in his most relaxed manner: 'Drop me then.' Blondie *staggered. Gaped, shuffed* his feet, breathed noisily, but he was under Nord's spell, it was clear he would think of himself as one of Nord's men even when it was all over: he was under a spell, bound hand and foot. He would slaughter the entire Red Star Division if it so much as wrinkled its nose at the name of Nord. And he left in his desperate enamoured state and to escort him half a dozen of his men, from the same shrunken stock, emerged from the roadside.

And Nord came to *sprawl lengthwise* on the warm grass, revealing an unconcealed, soft feline voluptuousness. What could be seen of his flesh was honey-coloured and it was not sunburn because he was a man of the shadows and must be the reflection of the rich khaki. Nord remarked on the abnormally dusty state of Johnny's shoes and that he had sent a car for him. 'Your bodyguard had other ideas,' said Johnny and related the story of the bridge. 'I ought to whip those people,' said Nord. 'Yes, you ought,' said Johnny but Nord resented his words with an immediate glower. And as a reaction he cast a benevolent glance round the guards who silently came and went on the grassy carpet. Then he said: 'Now about Alba. Out with it.' 'Can we listen?' asked the paymaster and the officer. Nord signalled to them to come forward and sat in their midst, throwing down for general use a half-packet of English cigarettes.

Smoking slow mouthfuls of that flat, thick and deceptive tobacco, Johnny set out to the best of his ability the various and different possibilities.

Military: the Fascists wanted nothing better than an engagement in the field which offered them the means to crush in a day more than they could eliminate in a century of raids into the hills. To retake the place the Fascists would certainly put into the field their best and most expert units against which the partisans did not have – in terms of pitched battle – one chance in a thousand.

Factors leading to psychological passivity: given that there had been neither the wish nor the means to evaluate those who had enlisted the partisans were what they were – the flower and the dregs – as always happens in all volunteer units. What was extremely interesting and important was opinion in the towns, whether large or small. Since they did not see them but only heard them on the heights the citizens considered them to be archangels – but that way the citizens will be able to see us – and like good citizens if they have to praise nine of us they will stigmatise us ferociously because of a single one. Why not – if we can – appear to be archangels until the final *smash*?

Factors leading to political passivity in the narrow sense of the word: there were still Fascists in the towns all the more insidious for being disguised. Unlimited opportunities for spying. 'Nord, you will have your fine lists drawn up by our people who are both competent and keen and immediately we are in the town we will have round-ups and they will all be sent to camps but you know all those who are within etc. etc. as the Apostle said. And then what will happen to many of your men in Alba, or better – or worse – to their families after the place has been retaken?' 'I've thought of that,' said Nord, 'we'll keep them all in the hills.' 'Just for once they won't agree with you. They will rush into the town ahead of all the others even if they have to walk over you.' 'Then I'll post them on the periphery guarding the approaches, visible only to the country people among whom spies don't take root.'

Last and not least – passivity due to propaganda or other psychological reasons. They would lose the city again – inevitably – and what would the repercussion be on the people in the hills? The people who fed and supported them but who had to be always sure of their final victory. What sort of autumn and winter was being projected for the defeated survivors from the town?

Nord paled. 'Are you saying it won't all be over by October or November?' 'By a miracle, perhaps, yes, but not by a process of logical deduction. The Allies seem to be more flat-footed than they are.'

Nord leapt to his feet. He said he had taken careful note of everything and would bring it forward again at the next meeting of the commanders and the leading members of the CNL.* 'Naturally,' he said, as he moved off, 'you have spoken just as you would if Asti and not your own town were our objective.' 'More than naturally. If the garrison in my town was too tough a nut and if the taking of Alba was a question of life and death for us I would put my English at your disposal to call in the bombers of the RAF.'

Then Nord invited him to dine with him – a slice of meat and a roll of bread – and Johnny felt an internal tremor because he had never heard the names of simple items of food pronounced the way Nord did with that Biblical weight. But it broke off immediately when Nord added: 'And we'll pass round the wine from the Cinque-terre** sent me by an admirer. It is adorably potent and has an edge after which I will hate any sweet wine.'

In the mist of the meal the telephone rang in the other room and the operator *peeped hurriedly in* to announce the headquarters of 1st Division. Nord *jerked* one of his officers to the set – he went but then returned to urge him personally to come to the set where Mauri, the commander of the group of Divisions, was personally on the line. Nord went out and there was a good ten mintes of *rattling inquiry* and excitement and incredulity of which none of the guests could make head or tail. Then as he came back Nord was glowering and looking sour. 'Do you know where last night's drop to 1st Division ended up?' Ah, Johnny said to himself, that solid noise overhead that had persecuted his sleep. 'I'll give you odds of a thousand to one.' One of the bodyguards *sneered for cessation of tantalisation.* 'All into the hands of a Communist brigade. The one at Monforte.' There was a burst of swearing and disgust with the bodyguards *leading* it. Johnny smiled *very humorously.* 'What are you laughing at, Johnny?' 'I'm thinking of the faces of the English mission. It is always delightful to imagine the English in these cases.' 'Delightful? They are furious, says Mauri. They wanted to get 1st Division over to Monforte to attack the Reds and to make up for the bad luck. They're seeing red, says Mauri.' 'They should take it out on their idiots of pilots.' 'What idiots of pilots!' shouted Nord with real passion. 'The

* CNL – Committee of National Liberation – a multi-party organisation which organised the Resistance at national and local levels.
** A (in those days) remote district on the Ligurian coast.

pilots made no mistake. They were guided on to Monforte!'
Incredulity and mystery. 'It is a mystery – but a mystery about
knowledge. The Communist headquarters knew the message,[*]
knew it was positive and referred to 1st Division, knew the layout of
the signal fires because they copied them, and the pilots were happy
with them. In short the planes were guided by threads from
Monforte.' 'A big drop?' Johnny inquired. 'A medium drop – enough
to clothe and arm Mauri's latest brigade.' 'So it will clothe and arm
them pretty well,' said Johnny. It was grotesque and acutely painful to
imagine the insignia and accessories of the Garibaldini on the
classical imperial khaki, sewn on to it with a diabolical signature of
mocking and victorious polemic.

Confused and disappointed, they all went out into the clearing.
Johnny had had enough of the headquarters and craved for the
healthy outpost at Mango, he longed for Pierre and Kyra. And Nord
had had enough of Johnny and of everybody like him who held him
back from throwing himself, as if of his own volition and natural
inspiration, into the *full plays* with his bodyguard. Yet he app-
roached him once more. The failure of the drop had forced his
lineaments into a *grim* beauty worthy of a medallion, into the right
posture to stamp him on the memory. He asked whether he wanted a
car – but after the accident that morning . . . 'You would spoil my
pleasure for it will be a holiday to go back on foot.' 'As for the town
que sera sera. Meantime I am keeping up the pressure at night. They
are hysterical children and they'll very soon go mad. And perhaps we
shall take the town without striking a blow. One of these evenings I
shall send you people from Mango to kick up a noise. And I shall tell
Pierre to put you in command because you are practical.'

Nord went off towards the embrace his waiting bodyguard was
preparing for him and Johnny for a last time looked at him in
admiration and said to himself that he could no more deal with his
fascination nor was he any better equipped to do so than the fierce,
primeval Roman *fighter*.

He was walking downhill. The team of sappers had finished their
work and the wires, which now functioned, had already their own
autonomous and sylvan life and in the thinning light they shone

---

[*] The BBC broadcast coded messages to announce arms drops.

disdainfully. After the volleys of the morning the wood had a new *haunting* quality for him, as if it were a real workshop of nature, in the vibrant silence, and with an observant eye and a light step he avoided the abnormally raised spots, which seemed to be inflated, with on them the tallest grass and white flowers which seemed incredulous and terrified at their disproportionate exuberance.

Down below the stream appeared: from its shallow waters – insufficient even to drown a child – there emerged a fierce glare, sharp and aggressive, like a play of swords. He did not cross the bridge – not to avoid the poisonous sight of the carcass of the car – but because the idea of the ford put him into a state of childish excitement. So he climbed down the bank between the road and the water and took off his boots at a point where the crossing emerged at a narrow cleft in one of the white chalky rocks running up towards the high hills.

He waded in: the water was cold and massaged his calves energetically, beneficially. But when he reached the other side and was preparing reluctantly to put on his boots again he noticed at the edge of the current a little basin of water naturally shaped and happy. Johnny did not resist it, he freed himself of his clothes and weapons and immersed himself vertically, monolithically in that motionless whirlpool, up to the shoulders, with a long-drawn shudder, the perfect equivalent, more than perfect, of an ejaculation. In fact when he rose up and then slipped in again to the same depth and with the same care as before the water this time was completely destitute of sensuality. He got to the dry ground – there was thick, hard vegetation in the extremely narrow strip between the shore and the overhanging rock – dried his hands not to damage the cigarette he was now lighting. Then everything was perfect except for the cigarette – he simply could not bear that English tobacco so sticky and soft. A partisan truck passed in a hell of noise and dust; since it did not turn off to Castino but went on towards Bosia Johnny thought it had something to do with Frankie and the sappers.

In the perfection of his leisure he began to *trim* with the burning end of his cigarette those hairs on his arm which had grown beyond *standard* but soon the white *glow* of his skin plunged him into the depths of meditation. Never as at that moment had he been drawn, forced to think, to see his own physical reality, his carnal substance and form. It was even miraculous to confirm, to realise fully, for the first time the faculties, the uses and forms which were specific and unrepeatable in every part. His hands, for instance, had suffered from his being a partisan – not their backs still thin and slender, with the distinct and powerful embroidery of the *elated* veins; but on his hands war had weighed heavily to the point of making an incision. '*Dr Jekill* and Mr Hyde*,' Johnny could think comparing back and palm.

All over his skin the long unwashed patina was rich, silky and absolutely without odour, or at most stupendously enriched his male smell. He felt he could say that he could at that moment smell with a woman's nostrils. The thought of the war descended on him like a grey wing – not a black one – on to the golden whiteness of his skin, which was silky and absolutely smooth, without down to distract, to intercept the hand. It was enormously, perhaps sacrilegiously exciting to forecast, to fantasticate over the target and the opening which had opened up in that intact integrity. He shrugged his shoulders, having had enough of immobility, of fantasies and refreshment and dressed himself in haste.

He reached the ravine and clambered up over its muddy track and was on the slopes of the gigantic, mammoth hill of Mango. The black woods which seemed to be carbonised, leant over him undulatingly, and the open, fleetingly glimpsed grassy slopes on some of which herds were grazing, appeared as high and motionless as a pile of wandering boulders stopped by a miraculous hand in the midst of the vertiginous hillsides.

He got to the crest in an hour, feeling nauseous from the climb, offering his *grim* sweat to the gracious, feminine ventilating air of the crest. And on the path along the crest he set himself to walk at his ease, rewardingly, passing a lonely house which he vaguely knew by the name of Cascina** di Langa, completely without a thought of the part it would play later. At its ancient gates which were in constant peril from the great winds, an old, magnificent magnetic wolfhound bitch mounted guard with ferocious perplexity and a stupendous sharpness in its pupils and ears. In the dusty courtyard half a dozen

* Jekill – *sic.*
** Cascina – farmhouse.

very young and *grim* partisans were wickedly kicking a worn football while from under an invisible doorway there came the sullen groan of a recalcitrant and sorely tried car engine. From behind the far corner of the house – it was compact and smooth like the brow of a blind beggar seated on the hilltop road – a partisan lowered the weapon he had levelled at him without understanding the mad gesture Johnny had tried to make to him.

Johnny hastened along the soft grass-grown path and in a twinkling was at his pitch of happiness at walking in a free flutter of wind and looking down at the distant landscapes. The mechanism of walking had been completely obliterated and there remained only the overwhelming feeling of pure movement forward. He quickly came upon a trio of partisans whom a long stretch of cover had hidden from him. They were certainly of peasant origin to judge by the clumsiness of their gait, their uniforms and the way they bore their arms. As he passed them Johnny asked where they were going.

'We're going to Mango to see the explosion and the people who died.'

Johnny stopped. 'What explosion and what people who died?'

'At Mango they were trying out a mortar this morning about midday. It exploded. Four were killed on the spot and two are at death's door.'

'Their names?'

'We don't know yet but Kyra must be one of them because he was the inventor of the thing.'

'Did you know Kyra?' asked Johnny as if probing an impossible confusion.

'Great god, he's asking if I knew Kyra!'

Johnny set off at a mad run as long as he had breath, shouting the name of Kyra.

Mango, even when unentered, was visibly under a cloud: a poisonous patina clung to the walls although they were bathed in the *mellow* afternoon sun. The guards at the entrance were silent and gloomy – even the youngest of them; they signed to Johnny to come in and at his query confirmed the catastrophe. 'The dead are already in the church – the dying are with the doctor.' 'What happened?' 'All hell was let loose.' 'And Kyra?' 'Kyra was the first to go – if anyone was first in that group.' 'Where is Pierre?' 'At the doctor's.'

He made for the doctor's house looking with veiled eyes at the crowd of partisans and villagers who garnished the crest of the hollow where the terrible experiment had been carried out. Pierre was coming out of the doctor's door, bent, his vest stained with blood from carrying the dead and dying. He became aware of Johnny with a *ghastly* glance as if he had drunk too much. 'Did you hear it even in Castino?' 'I heard nothing.' 'Amazing – an explosion like that? His brother in the barracks in Asti must have heard it.' 'What was it?' 'Nothing – an absolutely unforeseeable piece of bad luck. I'm no fool about weapons and shooting. Well, it was bad luck and nothing else. The bomb exploded along with the propellant charge in the base of the mortar.' Then Pierre enumerated and named the dead – the two in their death throes were dead as well now. 'Go and see Kyra, Johnny. He still has a marvellous face – his face. The . . . damage is in the belly but now you can't see it any more, they have covered it with flowers. Then tell me if you too feel that he is smiling because I don't trust my own eyes today.'

Johnny climbed up to the church, drawn by the echo of the chanting and by the halo of the candles beyond the door. The dead were *neatly* lined up not yet in coffins but on hay-sleds: five unknown by name to Johnny in spite of partisan acquaintanceship and Kyra. He looked at him over the bowed foreheads of the sisters from the sanctuary. He was smiling with a shadowy smile. And then Johnny smiled at him. Michele *urged* at his side, whispered to him with his voice that was both tired and so adult: 'Are you smilling. Johnny? Aren't you a disgrace smiling in front of a dead man?' 'He died when I wasn't there. Am I supposed to make a long face now that I see him again?' The sergeant said: 'Right. I think he is pleased with us but it's his brother he wants to come.'

They walked out pursued by grief and suddenly drowned in the turbulent sadness of the sunset, a pale and stormy seal set on the golden day. The unstable, gloomy sky was pregnant with a nocturnal storm. Very lazily, lancing very deep, Johnny tried to remember what he had been doing at Castino when the mortar exploded. In the fluid twilight the women came and went – those who had stayed at home to deal with the evening tasks so as to have time later for sorrow and prayers met those going home exhausted to cook supper which had taken second place to immediate sorrow and prayers.

Johnny found Pierre in the mess. He had not eaten and was supervising the men's meal. Johnny ate nothing and smoked. The *stalking* footsteps of the men sounded heavy as they went to and through the church on sentry-go under Michele's inspired metronome.

'Pierre? Kyra really is smiling.'

At that moment the vigorous, windy passing of Nord's car made a breeze outside. Before they *scrambled to their feet* Nord had entered wrapped in a black raincoat. He said to accompany him to the priest's house, outside he pushed aside the prompt bodyguards and as they walked asked what sort of a chap the priest in Mango was. 'A good chap,' said Pierre with his invincibly querulous tone. 'A young priest – anxious to be of use.'

They arrived at the moss-covered priest's house. Johnny knocked at the door, Pierre introduced them but the housekeeper almost fainted taken by storm by the black wind that was Nord. The two priests were supping on leeks and bread under a feeble lamp. The parish priest was old, fleshy and morose, the curate a lad, skinny with eyes popping out of his head. Faced by Nord's assault he leapt to his feet wafer-thin. And he replied to Nord with the same monosyllabic conviction as when he took his vows. Nord had a marvellous voice for basic occasions.

'Will you go down to Asti this evening at once?'

'Yes.'

'Go to the barracks and ask for Lieutenant X?'

'Yes. Lieutenant X. Yes.'

The old priest had abandoned himself to senile, indecipherable muttering with wearied shakings of the head.

'Tell him, tell him without mincing your words, because he is a man of iron that his brother, the partisan Kyra died today in an accident with a weapon and we shall bury him tomorrow at Mango.'

'Yes.'

'Tell him that Nord, the commander of the 2nd Autonomous Military Division offers him a safe conduct for the journey to Mango, his attendance at the funeral and his return.'

The old priest smacked his lips loudly as if to warn the curate of possible hidden dangers and complications. Nord smiled in a lordly way. 'Curate, do you believe in my safe conduct?' 'I do and so will Lieutenant X . . . I think.'

'Tell him too that a truck from my headquarters' platoon will pick him up on the borders of the area under my command.'

'I shall tell him all that.'

'How will you get to Asti? My trucks can take you to a certain point.'

'I have an old motorcycle of my brother's who didn't come back from Russia. If you give me petrol.' 'Pump it out of my petrol tank.' Then the parish priest with his ill-omened voice asked when he expected to be back – perhaps in the middle of the night? 'No, at dawn tomorrow. Having delivered my message I shall go to the seminary in Asti to get forty winks.' 'Then give my regards to Canon Y.'

Outside the sky was darkening in great waves and the wind was growing into a whirling storm. Nothing was more lively than the efforts of the living for a dead man. The petrol was pumped out and poured in, the old motorcycle put to rights by Nord's driver and man and machine dived trembling and *raging* into the whirling darkness. When the sound died away Michele, the sergeant, said neither affirming nor questioning 'He will accept.'

But Lietuenant X did not come. The curate, thinner and more sharply outlined than ever, reported that something snapped in him when he declined but decline he did. The other five had their families who had been summoned around them but Kyra went into the earth without anyone from his kith and kin. On his return in the much trodden dust the curate whispered to Johnny that he had never seen a man like Nord but that next to him certainly came Lieutenant X.

XVII

The psychological warfare operation entrusted to the garrison at Mango was fixed for the middle of September and Johnny felt much better about it than he could ever have dreamt. Pierre entrusted to him all the lads armed with long-barrelled rifles as the best adapted for long-range fire and a machine-gunner to confront any possible offensive thrust by the exasperated garrison. *Last but not least* Pierre gave him Sergeant Michele with his absolute hoarse command over his youngsters.

Johnny had his orders – to get as close as safety allowed and to batter, as long as possible and as hysterically as possible, the façade of the Minor Seminary where the bulk of the Fascist garrison was quartered. To keep his distance, to resist absolutely the magnetic attraction of the road blocks.

Johnny lucidly imagined – and did so with a sort of martial pleasure – his and his men's objective: he saw the grey, compact mass of the Minor Seminary dominating the most neglected and sad, the most wintry section of the road that ran round the walls of the town. But on the immediately preceding evening his pleasure was considerably reduced by a new instruction which altered things: in principle Johnny had to escort to a suitable position a couple of recently dropped English mortars under the command of two officers from 1st Division who said they were deadly sure of landing four good shots on the Seminary-barracks. Johnny lamented loudly about the risk to the adjacent and not so adjacent houses. Pierre said: 'I am assured that they are two artillery officers, one of them a regular. Don't be a pessimist a priori.' But Johnny was not enough of a 'Blue' to believe so wholeheartedly in regular officers.

The mortar crew from 1st Division was waiting at Neive in a truck with the weapons, ammunition and rangefinders. The truck was big enough to carry Johnny's riflemen as well as far as Treiso from which they would proceed on foot to the last overhanging hill.

Johnny and his men went down to Neive on a calm September evening which with its *mellowy* breezy freshness invited a walk rather than a march. The men walked down eating their rations, stale bread and first-class belly of pork, continually urged on, hastened, scolded by the sergeant.

At Neive they did not find the truck from 1st Division right away: it had parked, unintentionally concealed, in the maze of streets in front of the railway station which was rusting and mouldering from long disuse. There were not more than three minutes of search but they sufficed for the youths to get lost. Neive was the biggest village near Mango and much better endowed with the fruits of civilisation and the youths went in irresistibly attracted even for pure contemplation. Johnny set Michele on their heels *sniffing and roaring.*

The two officers from 1st Division were smoking beside the truck. The one who in terms of physique and attitude looked like the regular was instead the engineer from the reserve; the regular was the excitable little man who was shuffling his nervous feet in the thick dust. In the shadow of the tarpaulin the tubes of the Stokes* among *grim, set-in pride* faces of the men from 1st Division. Now the officers and men from up there were looking *superciliously* at Johnny's boys whom the sergeant had netted and sent on ahead. 'They are bigger than our 81 millimetres,'** said Johnny for something to say. Well, the engineer plunged deep into an impenetrable highly technical secret but the regular officer agreed with him in a nervous, comical and almost pleasant voice, 'Yes, 86 instead of 81.' 'And better?' 'You can never tell with mortars.' 'With a rangefinder?' 'No with sticks. Using the good old way.' 'I'm from Alba, you know,' said Johnny with the slightest hint and perhaps a touch of humour. The little officer understood, chuckled and said not to worry.

Now the loading was done and the truck set off for the hills to the south-west, Johnny's boys beginning to talk tough and the men from 1st Division in an unfriendly and polemical silence playing the

---

* An English mortar so-called after its inventor.
** Italian army mortars were 81mm in diameter.

veterans. Tobacco flowed profusely – at 1st Division they were swimming in Navycut.

They ended up in the little square in Treiso, the last Blue garrison before the town and the truck's last stop. The road to Alba with the weapons and the ammunition in an enormous unmanageable box which would cause problems had to be covered on foot. But it was still early; if they left at once they would arrive above the town while evening was still imperfect whereas their programme indicated, prescribed deepest darkness. So they lazed all over the square while the local partisans stared anxiously, ashamed of themselves, at their colleagues from 1st Division with their incredible, prestigious weaponry and equipment.

Johnny withdrew to the outer wall of the square to smoke in solitude and *absentmindness* almost as if attempting an exercise in *souplesse*. Just when he had attained mental vacuity his eyes fell on the village cemetery. Ghostly in the twilight, watched over by concrete cypresses in austere affection so enormously superior to the corresponding nearby village of the living. '*Each in his narrow cell for ever laid – the rude forefathers of the hamlet sleep.*'* Then the commander of the local troops arrived to disturb him.

As far as the dusk allowed one to see he was a delicate slim boy although clearly of peasant stock; ten to one that he was the local teacher on whom education had conferred primacy and rank. He approached fingering his poor uniform and hazarded the opinion that this time this was something more than a normal tiring nocturnal raid.

'Something more, we hope,' said Johnny. 'You have mortars,' said the other open-mouthed and with different admiration. 'They have mortars,' Johnny corrected. 'The ones from 1st Division.' 'When will they clothe and arm us like that as well?' 'Just as soon as an English officer decides to come down a couple of hills and find out that we aren't worse than them. How are things here?'

He said that now things were going well – too well in fact – a real holiday. But it had been hell with the previous garrisons, it had been hell. And that colonel of theirs he would be a big commander – perhaps bigger than Nord – if he were on their side. 'Now we are all

* From Gray's *Elegy in a Country Churchyard.*

192

right,' he said, 'I have most trouble with the Matteotti Brigade* who are pushing into my territory towards the river. There aren't many real partisans for the moment but there is a civilian among them whom they call the commissar who goes about recruiting, app-roaching and tempting my men, and then he is carrying on real political propanganda among the farms. Next time I'll take this measure with my rifle. Not that I have anything against Socialism – in fact I'd like a kind of Socialism of my own but these are not the right times for propaganda. I'd chase off anyone who came to my group talking about monarchy or the Liberal party. That's for after, for after.'

Night was falling fast; *right* on to the village there was an unusual dark veil but down below where you could imagine it was exactly over the town ragged cracks and rings and whirlpools of light broke that veil. Johnny whistled, Michele whistled back and they set off.

It took an hour to get to the hill overlooking the town after a blind march unravelled through paths and ditches to the low explosion of curses at its difficulty. And the sergeant developed a hardness that was extremely Prussian, once he burst out to Johnny at his side: 'And our great commanders want us to take and hold Alba with these snotty-nosed creatures?' The engineer from the reserve, who was clearly extremely short-sighted, dragged himself along miserably behind and alongside Johnny his helper.

At last they were on the ample crest of the hill and sat or stood on the cold, soaking, itchy grass. And Johnny contemplated his town, his *ghastly, forsaken town.* A boy near him whispered to another that the town had a curfew from six in the evening. Certain the blackout was applied with extreme, fierce rigour; and yet from the pitch-black houses there rose a kind of ghost of light, a kind of malignantly feverish, dirty exudation of the light within, which was projected vertically towards the downpouring of an identical, miserable light from the shattered sky. Johnny trembled and coughed. The river, a snake of black marble, giving off horrible gleams each time it received its miserable share of that light from heaven and hell was '*outlething Lethes*' to Johnny's eyes. And it sent up as far as the hill the idea of its special flowing sound. Now Michele was savagely hitting a youth who was trying to *strike a match* to light a cigarette stub.

* Presumably a Socialist formation named after the murdered MP.

On the southern outskirts of the town ragged gunfire and the *thudding* of hand-grenades echoed but they made clear even up on the hill the demonstrative *teasing* nature of the partisan attack and the formal defence by the Fascists in their outposts. Only noises arrived unaccompanied by phenomenology. One of the officers gave Johnny a dig with his elbow asking for information. 'Partisans tiring them out at the south gate of Alba. Certain to be Garibaldini. Now I'll show you your objective.' And Johnny pointed him physically at the blind, polyphemic mass of the Minor Seminary on the near edge of the town. 'Then spread your men out on the slope in front as a defence against possible patrols.' The men spread out like a monstrance round the weapons which were getting ready, watching with night-blinded curiosity, the men of 1st Divison who were busy with the aiming sticks. By half past ten the weapon was loaded and sited, metaphysically directed at the unchanging sky.

The first shot was like a single *knell* which violated, exterminated the entire immobility of the night. Then everyone stared down as if there were only a twinkling in which to catch the instantaneous blaze on the roof of the building. But a minute passed and nothing flashed out in the unresponsive darkness. 'Dud. Defective detonator,' the engineer cursed. But at the moment a silent flash showed red to the north-west of the town on the banks of the river. There was an error of more than a kilometre and Johnny blushed in the darkness in front of his gaping-mouthed but unquestioning men. The two officers produced a dense, unblushing argument about data, charges, tables – the regular turned to Johnny to ask him if he knew the area where the shot has landed. 'Yes, on the naked banks, thus saving our souls. Are you going to try again?'

In agony Johnny was there at the corrections, the remeasurements, now the engineer was weighing the explosive charges in his hand. 'Take my word for it,' he was saying, 'now they simply aren't big enough. You were too impressed by the length of the first shot.' But the regular stuck to his idea.

In the grim greying night Johnny saw the bomb come out with a spin on it, slow and drunken, like a heavy compact fish emerging drunkenly. He shouted 'On the ground' and flattened himself out, seeing with the last blink of his eye the men diving headlong into the dips in the ground. The explosion, the rustling *sweep* of the fragmented clods, the posthumous groan of a mortally wounded sapling. But none of the men groaned or was too silent and so Johnny was quickly freed from his terror, the sergeant was passing criticism by smacking his lips drily, the two officers stood absently passive and totally disarmed, not only not offended, but grateful to Johnny for the orders which he was giving out flatly. The hill was to be evacuated immediately to avoid a reaction with a mortar from the awakened garrison, the squad from 1st Division were to go back to Treiso with their weapons and baggage, he and his men would do down to the town for the final action. Provided that all that useless din had not wakened and activated the Fascists, had led them to let loose a company halfway up the road.

They made their way down to the *very* black shore of the petrified lake which was the town through places and ways familiar to Johnny. The men were silent now, tense and elastic, fairly reliable. In twenty minutes they *sailed* into the thick grasslands by the river, crazily soaked, but equally pleased after the steep paths on the hill, which were phenomenally uneven, blotted out by the dark and requiring too much tension. Their swishing through the high grass sounded enormously loud, *sweeping*, not yet obliterated by the rushing noise (although near) of the waterfall at the power station. Johnny turned round to look back at the line of men in the hoary light: '*yea, we were a ghastly crew*'*. Michele came up alongside him. 'This is your town. And you still have your father and mother here. Maybe they know that you are so close by. But perhaps the Lord will send them an inspiration.' Johnny whispered that he preferred it not to be so – soon they would start firing and they would at once begin to be anguished.

From the tide of grass they passed on to the terra firma of a lane and then out on to the little bridge over the channel by the power station, the men splashed by the waterfall which deliciously sprinkled Johnny's face bringing to a perfect level his coolness and equilibrium. After the little bridge the squad split up – half with the sergeant to take up positions on the side of the power station aqueduct, the others with Johnny and the stuttering support of the light machine-gun which had been Kyra's to take up positions between the tennis court and the *yard* of the sawmill to stop any encircling trick from the nearby roadblock and even more an

* Almost correct quotation from Coleridge's *The Rime of the Ancient Mariner*.

ambitious sortie from the carriage gate of the Seminary-barracks. Finally Johnny said: 'If they don't react and we manage to control our fire we will set up a din for a good half-hour. The attack is to be at midnight exactly at the very heart of the sleep they long for.'

In the new *endroit* nothing had changed since peacetime for Johnny; apart from the enormous *decaying* tennis court nothing had changed except the piles of wood to be worked on, as if the sawmill had just finished its day then and nothng – no one had touched the deserted piles. Which neatly and smelling not unpleasantly of dampness concealed the positions of this men.

They took up their positions immediately spasmodically turning their ears towards the blind walls of the building not more than forty metres away. Soon the men lying there began to cough to the blasphemous whispered rebukes of rigorously silent comrades; but they rebuked them from a pure impulse to be tough, otherwise they were afraid of nothing. Even if the Fascists were nearer than ever before with only a minimal diaphragm interposed between the uncomfortable breathing of their miserable sleep. Johnny was *absent-minded* and physically *cosy* in spite of the damp, only a deep-rooted desire for a smoke churned his innards like a pin probing everywhere.

The silence of the town was perfect and immanent, that silence in which his father and mother shared. What else could they do, the two old people, except be silent and wait, wait for his own living body running up and smiling and *waving* as if nothing or little (and that for a short time) had happened, or else for news of him, the final news. Already they could be silent and wait till the end, nothing to falsely half-break the silence and the waiting. 'These madmen want to take Alba!' he shouted inwardly. Someone was spasmodically throttling a cough, others asked what time it was under their breath, the dew sweated on the metal of their weapons with an infinitesimal clicking noise.

In the immense wave of the first stroke of midnight Michele opened fire and all the men followed him. And a second later behind the high walls the hoarse Fascist trumpets blared in a paroxysm of impatience.

The partisans redoubled their fire, the trumpets went mad, and as if in a state of mad excitement Johnny's boys came out from behind the heaps of wood and went towards the blind walls of the barracks, but madly, blindly, as if they wanted to knock their heads against them. Some had reached the *défilés* nearby but the others were actually behind the trunks of the trees in the avenue, sticking their heads out at the *gleaming* asphalt ten metres from the barracks. In a second a shot, ten challenges and twenty insults were hurled at the sealed windows. Johnny had at once stopped shouting for attention and a withdrawal, now he had mingled with them at this front of fronts. From the other side Michele's men, caught up in the din, had intensified their fire and were mixing with it savage shouts. Johnny from behind a sweating and repellent plane tree on the edge of the asphalt was covering the carriage door and the lowest windows with his Sten. They were so close that every so often he could catch through the walls of the barracks what was going on inside, what they were trying to do and what they were saying in there. Of the soldiers some were weeping freely, without pretence, others were clearly inspired to reaction and rebellion by a paroxysm of fear and exhaustion; but the latter did not open the windows to reply to the fire but at the top of their voices threw back the insults and added to them a certain exasperated prayer to give over. One of them with a louder and firmer voice than the rest, was asking – certainly an officer – to lead them out to fight like men, just for once, head on.

Johnny *was sickened* – they had been there for five minutes and the men were not withdrawing, they were drawing deeply on their voices and on their ammunition pouches. He himself had he given in to that general madness and blindly fired bursts at the windows would certainly have felt better but he had, as always a sacrosanct idea about ammunition and did not manage to jettison it even now. From the sergeant's side too they were firing unsparingly. He turned round suddenly and covered himself with the trunk and his weapon at the flickering arrival of a shadow. But it was only a messenger from the sergeant, a young boy who dragged himself along on his elbows and looked round so correctly and according to the rules that by himself he made up for all those other madmen. The sergeant was asking what to do. Given that they had almost finished their ammunition, fall back and rendezvous at the place arranged? Certainly if the aim was merely to create a hubbub no one could return more glorious and triumphant than they. The boy crawled back with the same unalterable prudence.

Johnny shouted to withdraw; at the second shout they obeyed, turning round to fire a last shot, they were no longer on the asphalt nor in the avenue, now they were treading the grass of the very nearest countryside. They had withdrawn into themselves and Johnny sighed on the verge of dizziness. But the boy with the light machine-gun went mad. He leapt on to the asphalt again, facing the barracks and the whole town, brandishing the light machine-gun he shouted challenges, definitions and solitary triumph. And now he was off erect and certain on the *gleaming* asphalt towards the centre of the town. Johnny and some others shouted after him in the *sickeningness* of their own madness, but all that could stop him now was a burst of enemy fire. Johnny felt on his neck the torrid breath of Michele who had come up to find out what was happening.

The man was going to be lost and with him the light machine-gun. Johnny leapt on the wet leaves of the avenue, crossed the ditch, landed on the gleaming asphalt behind the man *grinning* at his back as if at a mortal enemy but when he was within reach a shot, tremendous and all-embracing in its singleness, rang out along the avenue and the boy bent over, raised himself again, fell rigid. And at the same time you could hear the pounding on the asphalt of the feet of the man who had fired the shot and was regaining the cover of the roadblock.

Johnny dragged the wounded man by the feet along the asphalt, which aided his task, towards the ditch. The roadblock had closed down again like a tortoise and in any case the sergeant was covering it sufficiently. But if the men lodged in the barracks took courage from the *exploit* by the roadblock they would annihilate them with a laugh. But they made their way soberly but not light-footedly, hastening but not too much, past the barracks without its losing a *nuance* of its sepulchral nature.

Now they were in the open country in the direction of the river – four men were carrying the wounded man; he was not gasping but breathing almost normally. No one knew where and how he had been hit, until one of the bearers who had been feeling his chest announced that the man was bleeding copiously over one of his hands. Michele lit his clumsy cigar-lighter with its huge foul-smelling flame and with it bathed the wounded man's chest. He was certainly unconscious and had begun to gasp for breath and the men took turns at carrying him. A trumpet sounded out from the barracks. Johnny *jerked direction* towards the ghost of a farmhouse in open country before the river. They had to lay the wounded man down for a few minutes and think things out and decide what to do about him. The grass was soaking, extremely thick and resistant to their feet. The outside of the house seemed to *warp and shrink* simply in terror at their arrival and to the background of the *sweeping*, rushing sound of the river the guard dog burst out with a bark. The timbre betrayed it to be some sort of cur, soberly and grimly faithful, with nervous and inexhaustible vocal power, it rapidly went mad and everyone felt it had reached the limits of rage. The sergeant went forward, calling to it by smacking his lips, he stopped on the edge of the courtyard calling it with sweet names, calming it, but the dog grew louder and madder, and then Michele sighed and fired at it, this too a shot horrible in its solitude, and the animal collapsed in the misery of the soaked-up dust.

Johnny lined the men up facing the indecipherable town on a bank planted with willows, the men too motionless and vibrating like the saplings. Johnny knocked at the door neither a breath nor a *shuffle* replied. He knocked again and they could hear hearts beating on the other side. Johnny put his mouth to a crack in the old solid door and whispered into it with the irresistible quality of fatigue. 'Open the door. You are awake and up. Don't pretend. You heard you dog being killed. Open the door, I need your house for five minutes. Then I'll leave and maybe you'll have to give me a cart and a beast. I'm talking to you frankly. Open the door.' Then the man replied, fear and uncertainty making his voice oscillate to a pitch of most tremendous anger. 'What sort of people are you?' Johnny uttered the word soothingly at which the other said: 'Maybe you are partisans but what if you are criminals?' He meant Fascists. 'We are partisans,' said the sergeant with such an island* accent that on the other side of the door Johnny could see the man, prickle in return, his uncertainty and suspicion multiplied. Then Johnny said in dialect: 'We are partisans and one of our men is badly wounded and all the rest are a bit jumpy.

* The sergeant is Sicilian.

They will beat you up and I won't be able to stop them.'

Then the man sighed and unbarred the door. The darkness continued as they all entered, then a match was scratched and a petrol lamp lit. The man said: 'You are –' 'Yes, I am –' Years before they had known each other by sight when he went to bathe down-river and each time he met the man at work in his field which was threatened by the river. With mortal fear he asked if the Fascists were at their heels and when Johnny said No, he begged them not to make excessive noise so as not to give his mother up there a heart attack.

The wounded man was laid gently on the tiled floor and the lamp lowered over his head so that he looked horribly as if he were beheaded. He was certainly in a very grave condition but he was breathing irregularly and gently. Probably he was already gone. The men took turns to have a look at him which in each case was of no avail and final. Michele was plugging the wound and asking around for handkerchiefs for the job. It was certainly a case for surgery and the nearest adequately equipped hospital was at Neive. 'You have a cart and an ox. Harness it and put them in the courtyard.' 'I have everything you say and I shall give to you them because you would take them anyway but don't count on me to be your guide.'

Johnny's men of peasant stock ran to the stables with a dash and a competence that were absolutely professional. And in a minute the beast was out, *harnessed* and attached to the farm cart – a mule which in an intrigued fashion sniffed at the dog stretched out in the dust. The man asked at what headquarters he had to ask for his things. Johnny said there was no need – in a hour he would find them just before the entrance to the *tunnel* in a pasture. The peasant beamed with unexpected happiness and wanted nothing for the petrol lamp which Johnny took away to light their passage through the tunnel. And the man did not notice the sergeant who carried off a little hayloft ladder precisely to help with the transport. They skirted the river, its paucity of water acquiring a threatening quality in the dark, crossed the last little bridge over the canal to the power station where it flowed into the river, and began to climb. The man was groaning tearfully but his body which was reasonably comfortable on the layer of forage laid out for his comfort was motionless. The mule worked away, calmed and stroked by the men who felt touched; Johnny had gone on up ahead as the only person with knowledge of the deceptive road to safety. He was the first to reach the summit so far ahead that he had to wait several minutes for them, spurring them on from up there with a voice that was muffled and even more effective. And he was left alone a second more for a last undisturbed look at his town – from up there it seemed to be long and compact, fabulous, like a black iron cruiser on a black sea, that was here flat and there apocalyptically wavy.

The mouth of the tunnel *gaped* in the dark, darker and more visible. The first rusted rails gleamed here and there in the darkness of the mouth. The cart was unloaded and put to one side so that the beast could graze peacefully until the arrival of its master. Johnny took the wounded man and six men, the sergeant and the others continued up the mountain making for Mango so that Pierre would not get ideas into his head and act on them. The wounded man was to be carried to Neive by the tunnel and gaining a couple of hours.

The tunnel swallowed them, Johnny first with the lamp, the wounded man and the four bearers with the little ladder and the two reserves last. At first they made good progress, it was even interesting, without too much stumbling, in a not unpleasant coaly atmosphere, but further on one of the bearers stammered with a parched mouth: 'How long is it?' 'Kilometres.' 'How many?' 'I don't remember – but kilometres.' A comrade mocked him – was he afraid a train would come? 'No, of course I know that the line has been interrupted for months but it isn't the train I'm afraid of – something quite different.' Johnny *checked* the conversation, at that moment nothing was more counterproductive than conversation and of that fantasticating kind. But further on (how far had they advanced? two thousand or two hundred metres?) the talk began again like an irresponsible vital necessity to which Johnny himself was now subject. And the one who had mocked previously started it up: 'Tell us what you were afraid of – besides the train.' 'I still am,' said the other with an effervescent smack of the lips. 'Mines. Mines – that's what I'm afraid of.' 'What mines?' said Johnny harshly. 'Who told you the tunnel was mined? When and by whom?' 'Who knows, boss, the partisans may have mined it for the Fascists or the Fascists for us. Who knows?' 'We'd know if the partisans had mined it.' 'Who knows? So many people do things on their own, out of their own heads, in this war.'

He stopped there but it was an agony to put a foot down as it was a poisoned relief to raise it again. Now the bearers were asking to change over with sharp, *imperative* voices and the reserves submitted *sullenly*, heatedly contradicting those who made the request. The wounded man was making a whistling sound through lips that were dry, half-open and deformed. Johnny took his share of the carrying and that was good because he felt himself to be once more fully a part of the aim, the reality of the job. But when was the tunnel going to end? It was like love and war.

He went up ahead again as the bearer of the light. A headache had him in its grasp and perhaps something mysteriously more like a vague illness that would never be shaken off. And the exchange of fire at the Seminary-barracks was something that happened a week ago and the testing of the mortars an event in his childhood or had it ever happened? At that moment he stumbled and in his attempt to keep his balance rolled halfway across the tunnel *flashing* with horrible lightning speed over the sides and roof, then he stopped *crashingly* against the side. The soot was still greasy and as repugnant to him as the skin of a serpent. And by the lamp he saw the enormous, thick, leprous patch. The wounded man was groaning – he must be suffering horribly if he must and could express it with that reedy, ridiculous, unavailing groaning.

But there was the mouth of the tunnel, half-closed yet open to the bluish, turbulent light of just before dawn. There was a sigh of liberation and a concerted *rush* to the open.

They climbed acrobatically up the embankment and arrived at the foot of a swollen, interminable slope with a certain deserted look but a different one from the natural, foreseeable absence of man; nature itself appeared at that extraordinary hour to have deserted itself. On the ridge stood a farmhouse, phantomlike among the tall, solid, guardian trees. They laid the burning-hot wounded man on the dewy grass and Johnny sent the lightest and speediest of them up to the sleeping house. They were to come down with a cart and a beast to go on immediately to Neive. They followed him with their eyes till he plunged into the rising mists.

The wounded man *reeled* now and the moaning had become thicker and louder. 'Couldn't you have studied medicine, boss, at some university or other?' said the boy simply. They sat round him, coughing coarsely, and so as not to look at him looked at the sky in the birth-pangs of the light. The boy did not reappear on the denuded ridge to make the expected signals. Johnny sent off one second to him in lightness and speed. But when he had started out the first messenger appeared on the ridge which was beginning to clear; neither cart nor beast appeared behind him but he was slicing the air with cordial and comforting signals and now the shutters of the house were opening energetically to the reality of the day. And in that reality the wounded man gave a little cough and Johnny turning round like lightning saw on his face the lightning stamp of death. He was no longer the madman of midnight but the man touched and burnt by a sacreligious Fascist bullet. He confirmed with his head the steady yet interrogative glances of the others.

The cart was coming down, pulled by a *sportive* cow with two peasants, one old and the other a boy. The boy gazed at the dead man shrinkingly but the old man lingered behind him. 'He's dead. I was in the war of '15. I saw a lot of them.' They laid him out on a layer of sacking. A boy asked if they were all absolutely sure that he was dead. The old man looked at him ironically then said: 'They'll soon confirm it for you. We have a doctor in the house – evacuated from the town,' and he took a step forward to goad the beast. In the light, which was by now confirmed, a boy saw the damage by the soot on much of Johnny's skin and clothing and *goggled.* But another came and whispered to him: 'I've learned something, Johnny. His mother and mine are one and the same person.'

It was a huge farmhouse in an excellent state *everywhere*, sufficient to guarantee the rich life of a big city family and able to employ half the tribe of Abraham. The doctor came out on to the threshing floor in his pyjamas, slim and feathery with the build of a bird. He had a tic of impatience when he established how long he had been dead. The numerous women of the house peeped from the well-curtained windows. They withdrew the dead man into the porch, the beast remaining harnessed to the hearse. Johnny went to the pump to strip to the waist and wash himself. The old man (was he the patriarch?) came and observed him as he washed with a keen but avuncular eye. 'You're thin, patriot. And yet we peasants don't look after you that badly.' Johnny puffed in the dripping water. 'I left a house where they looked after me infinitely better but I wasn't any less thin than this. Have you any soap?' The old man *beamed* in perplexity – he was cunning and tried to be even more so. 'You really must be of a good family to ask for soap these days. These are times when there is no more soap. We could make it for ourselves with animal fat but –' 'So I'll ruin your towel.' 'Ruin it, lad, the women will wash it.'

They went back to the porch where the urchins of the houses were drawing near on trembling feet and the old man chased them away like chickens. 'Keep him under the porch for me till the truck comes up from Neive,' said Johnny. The patriarch trembled. 'I'm neither weak nor frightened, if I were to tell you all I have seen with my own eyes but – if the Fascists arrived up here and found him in my house. Look, patriot, look at the size of my roofs and the number of my people.' 'Don't worry about the Fascists. They won't climb up here. It's us who are going to go down to take the town – in ten days' time.' The simple announcement cut through and silenced the noise of the immense threshing-floor. The old man opened his eyes wide, then he took off his hat and scratched loudly at his skull which was covered with the age-old scabs. 'Ah, yes. And what will Mussolini say to that?

XVIII

Late in the morning of 10 October they were above Alba. A thousand of Nord's partisans blocked the last *gorge* before the city in the shadow of the last hill barring their way. A group of partisan officers stood on the crest, their binoculars trained on the surrendering city. From among them motorcycle dispatch riders slipped in and out – having a good time, unnecessary and haughty, frowned on by the massed partisans on foot, surly and resigned and *knowing* like all infantry.

The negotiations, the last, were dragging on. At that time two partisans officers, one from 1st Division and the other from 2nd Division in a room in the Bishop's place were insisting on the immediate evacuation of the *groggy* Fascist garrison under the supervision of the Vicar General of the Curia. But it was taking a long time – a suspiciously long time. And the partisans had been tramping about on the unresponsive fields for a long time. Pierre said: 'A dispatch rider has reported that the ferry seems ready for an extrordinary amount of traffic but nothing has crossed yet. Johnny, what's wrong with you?' What was wrong with him! he had to smoke because of his horrible excitement but the smoke had poisoned him. '*I'm in rotten shape* and at the very moment of re-entering my own town.' He had turned round a thousand times to look in the faces of the hundreds of partisans detailed and waiting for the occupation of the town had caught himself judging them as if he were looking at an attractive but dangerous suitor for his sister. Now the partisans were on edge, all the more silent because on edge, and were noticeably pressing towards the mouth of the last hollow in the hills. Said Pierre: 'By this time they should all be out according to the last agreements. What do they want? to stay on in the town in their own blood?'

The windy, massive rustling noise of Nord's car arrived. It and its occupants were ready for the gala entrance. Two drivers, rigid from now on, and in the back seat, alone Nord sheathed in his black rubber top with the chromed zips – dominant, alone, monolithic and as arcane as an Assyrian commander. The empty place at his right was literally covered with packets of cigarettes. Nord signed to him to come over, signed to him to help himself to tobacco. 'What do you think, Johnny? Late, I think?' 'The business was never a very nice one but now it isn't decent any more. Just imagine for a moment the moaning Fascists who don't want to leave and us giving them a shove up their filthy backsides.' 'What do you think of the Vicar General? Do you know him?' 'He's very much all there – in his own way. I know that the young priests in the seminary call him a donkey of genius.' And when Nord giggled: 'Don't laugh,' he added, 'that was how they described Victor Hugo too.'

A dispatch rider framed himself in the car window acting out an advanced state of nervous exhaustion and even greater dustiness. 'They still aren't withdrawing. Are they playing party games in the Bishop's Palace?'

Then Nord ordered all the men to line the naked crest that dominated the city as a distant and eloquent vision for the undecided Fascists. The men rushed up and stood there like a line of pillars. Johnny looked down with this heart in his mouth. He looked at the reddish fortress-like walls of the Bishop's Palace surrounding the last negotiations. And the town on balance seemed empty but alive with a secret heartbeat. Now a more lively movement appeared round the ferry. If only he had binoculars! The divisional paymaster came up in full gear for the first time – he had binoculars and passed them to Johnny – but he did not look first at the ferry, he looked at the south gate. Johnny pointed the field glasses at it and caught sight of a neurotic swarm of some three hundred Garibaldini already clamouring at the first houses of the town, ready to break the truce and be the first to enter. 'You'll see – they'll be the first in. And I don't want that if only because I am disgusted by their disgusting *proneness to propaganda*.' He had spoken with tight lips and with mortal enmity and added: 'I am going to tell Nord that he should send us as far forward – to the north gate naturally.'

But at that moment they were overtaken by a dispatch rider, shot up straight from the Bishop's Palace, over whom Nord leant from his dominant perch. The partisans gave vent to their impatience by surrounding him to the point of suffocation but the dispatch rider spoke in Nord's ear. Nord stood up – deadly fury seeking to distort his marble looks. He shouted so that everyone could hear: 'Tell them that I am coming down with all my men and that if they have not cleaned out the town by eleven I shall use every weapon to see that not one leaves alive.'

And the partisans descended, their mere footsteps detonating like shots. With no eyes for the flags which were appearing on the first houses, deaf to the cheers of the first people liberated, the surge died down only on the edge of the asphalt of the ringroad. They almost groaned at contact with the warm asphalt – after months of mountainous wastes the occupation of a real town was intoxicating, overwhelming. As for the men from Mango, Pierre had to jump on to the asphalt and confront them all, shouting not to take another step forward, that there was a truce to respect. Curiosity saved him, for all were distracted to watch the car in which the two commanders of the 1st and 2nd Divisions were preparing to enter the town – an enormous yellow, martial machine, gleaming spoil of war taken from the Germans with on the mudguards bodyguards armed with tommy-guns and behind, over the motionless heads of the two chiefs, a man – *pillarlike* – brandishing a Bren* on a revolving mount.

A few minutes later the partisan envoys came out of the Bishop's Palace, unrecognisable, sweating and pale and after a moment to recuperate gave a smiling confident signal to advance. The wave *toppled and shot forward*, jostling, drowning motionless Johnny who was at an emotional pitch *realising now the true glory* of it all in spite of the grey premises and the black future eventualities. His was the first town in North Italy, of the one, fighting Italy. In the air there was the exciting and oppressive *boom* of the citizens' cheers and the din of all the many bells of the town. Shutters opened like shots, people rushed to the balustrades as if they wanted to dive down for a total and immediate embrace. The urchins were already going in and out of the legs of the advancing partisans overcoming with the love of younger brothers the panic sense of weapons, uniforms and faces.

---

* A Bren gun – the standard British light machine-gun.

Johnny, exhausted with happiness and the sense of being a new man, was making his way with a sigh towards the centre but Pierre said, 'An officer and a detail to the riverbanks to oversee the Fascist exodus. None of us must fire or lay hands on their baggage. Johnny, what about you?' Johnny beamed – yes, this was a stroke of genius, a source of liberation and happiness; he had entered his own town and yet he was continuing his duty as a partisan without interruption just as if he were stationed in the Alps. The sergeant came with him along with the American machine-gun and thirty men. They went along the avenue of that night of confusion – past the Seminary that had been a barracks but was now deserted and wide open and stinking of residual smells in the welcoming air. Most of the boys were bad-tempered and critical – why should they be denied the trip to the town centre, the crowds, the girls? – so they walked along with a gait that was decided and fractious and made them all the more adult . . .

The avenue was entirely deserted and resounding only to the echoes of the immense outburst of joy at the centre and the echo of the *bourdillon* of the bells landed on the unresponsive asphalt like padded lead. Then they left the asphalt and through the grass made for the ferry which was coming into view.

A shiver that seemed to speak of posthumous summer happiness ran over the water but the shingle and the banks were desolate as if sterilised by the crowded, miserable presence of the depart-ing Fascists. Johnny posted his men at a certain distance, the machine-gun discreetly sited and ready, and then kept an eye on his men to make sure that, embittered and incited by the roars which came from the town as if from a football ground where a goal is being scored every minute, they did not take it out on the evacuating troops. They kept passing along the banks, they and their miserable baggage train, at a smart pace, but at the narrow mooring they had to mark time or halt, giving uncomfortable glances at the paradise of the other bank and the hell on this side, looking at the watchful partisans – some with embarrassment, some with shame, some with fear or bitterness – and with a general effect of dejection. The officers passed – too many of them in proportion to the other ranks – and went through the Caudine forks* with downcast eyes, only an occasional one giving vent to his shame with unhindered weeping. The partisans mocked them loudly and an officer stopped short in a fury to give at least a verbal reaction, then Johnny jumped on to the path and hissed at him 'Don't be a fool!' and the officer continued towards the ferry bent and limp. The Fascists who had been ferried over were resting on the other bank not at the edge of the water but beyond a poplared clearing and a little bank from which they emerged waist high as if wishing to follow the process of the exodus and at the same time on the alert to take shelter at a sudden burst of automatic fire from the partisans. The civilian ferrymen did their job tight-lipped and with inscrutable faces talking to the Fascist officers only when they could not avoid it, about the distribution of the men and the stowing of the baggage. They had a considerable supply of arms and extremely abundant ammunition, all of which the partisans observed with malign, beaming cupidity. And certain suggestions began to circulate, quiet and whispered – some rather more nasty – so that Johnny had to remind them all that the agreement spoke of 'including arms and baggage'.

It was a matter of hours – to let a thousand pass with perhaps three hundred already through. And now the men were kicking the ground, because of their hand-tied boredom, a fed-up feeling at the miserable sight of the enemy, hunger (it was half past one) and longing for the town which still re-echoed with cheers and peals of bells. Even the sergeant came to Johnny to protest but out of pure hunger. He said: 'You see, Johnny, what makes partisan formations different from a regular army is this – in a real army when you are a long way out they always remember you in every possible way – for your pay, your rations and even the post. But not with the partisans – with the partisans a man a long way out even on a decisive mission is a dead man – isn't that right?'

At two o'clock the sun dimmed and disappeared, from the other side of the street leading to the ferry a Garibaldini unit arrived doing the rounds. A small but picked unit to judge by the look of them and the particular cleanliness and imposing nature of their uniforms and

* Furcae Caudinae – the Caudine forks – was a narrow pass in which the Roman army was trapped by their enemies the Samnites in 821 BC.

weapons. They sketched a salute to Johnny and his men, very briefly and soberly, then stared down fixedly into the low, static river of Fascists.

These were the men who had misrouted the English drop – all had Stens or Enfields and were perfectly dressed in English uniform although in order to distance themselves more – almost to make a mocking distinction – they had loaded that antinomic battledress as much as possible with their antinomic badges: red stars and red scarf, with a resulting 'militia-man' effect which alarmed and struck even Johnny. And even kitted out so Englishly, they imparted to the evacuating Fascists a greater shudder along with a longer feeling of unease and *strain*. Some stumbled and some turned aside to stare at the Reds in excitement and fearful admiration.

Then their leader rose up – he set himself to rights with his elegant loose-limbed way and came down the road with a firm and taunting step, crossing without expression the slow sewer overflowing with embarking Fascists. He came down on his knees in front of Johnny. 'Are you going to offer me one of your English cigarettes?' 'How do you know I have English cigarettes?' 'By the blueness of the smoke.' Johnny chuckled and gave him a Craven. 'I like them a lot. Damn those bells!' The *boom* of the crowd had died away but the roar of the bells *rolled on*. Then Johnny said he thought they had any amount of English cigarettes – even more than the 'Blues'. The other glanced at him with *askant humour*. 'Are you going to take us to court?' 'No, I am asking out of pure admiration. How did you manage it? Who is the genius who –' *He grinned*. 'The genius is dead. That is all he did – But he died a few days later in a clash with their cavalry at Verduno that began well for us but ended very badly precisely because we lost Gabilondo. No one has any illusions – we will all have to end up like that – to make way for the springtime boys – the ones who will win – but really Gabilondo had to be the last of us to die.' 'A Communist?' 'Gabilondo? From head to foot. Perfect.' 'And you?' 'Ugh,' he said, but the contempt was for himself not the idea. 'Besides look at my comrades on the other side of the road. Look at them, there are fifteen of them. And they are the cream of our brigade. Well, only one of them is a Communist: the thickset one with the freckles and glasses. And I am the least Communist of the fourteen non-

Communists. And yet I am ready to eat the heart of anyone who gives the slighest smile at my red star.'

Now his comrades were signalling to him and whistling for him to return. 'I'm off – my men are getting annoyed because they are late in getting to the brothels.' Johnny *nodded*, that was now the dominant topic in the subdued talk of his men. But the man went on: 'According to you – my friend – how many days will the Fascists leave us in possesion of the town?' And he paid no attention to the pricked-up ears of the passing Fascists. 'Two weeks,' said Johnny and when the other *grimaced* 'Am I an optimist?' 'A super optimist.' And he made his way across the flow again.

It was three o'clock – the embarking serpent began to show the rings of its tail. And Pierre arrived not to take over or for any other service reason but from inexorable need to be nostalgic. He had red eyes, shamelessly. And when a conversation of general interest emerged the men gathered round forgetful of the Fascists filing past. 'The people, Johnny, the people, boys, the people,' said Pierre referring to his red eyes. 'You will see, you must all see it. People taking partisans home for dinner or into the cafés for a drink. The people! Johnny, this had to be done just to understand the people. I sincerly believe, lads, that with these people we will hold the town to the end.' The boys *hurraed* and Johnny smiled and then coughed over a mouthful of smoke. 'And you will learn in any case that I have been designated third in command.' And the men *cheered him* madly causing the fearful Fascists to start. Pierre blushed and said: 'Thank you but I feel horribly incompetent.' 'Lieutenant, you are the best of them as far as being conscientious goes.' 'But I am talking about competence,' said Pierre. 'Michele is right,' said Johnny. 'You are conscientious and don't worry too much about the competence. Think of those commanders who have neither one nor the other.'

Pierre signed to him to go off and see the town and his family. 'I want to see them all on the other bank,' *grinned* Johnny. It was not true, he was sick of that amorphous, impure river, but he wanted to put off as long as possible his meeting with his town and his family, did not want to put ashore so quickly on the interoceanic island. Besides it was almost all over – all that remained was a small group of officers, the higher ranks, with an abundance of followers and baggage. Here was the colonel in command who awoke in Pierre and

Johnny the whole sickening sense of the wretched state of a class and in Michele an irrepressible feeling for rank. He was old, paunchy, an obesity that spoiled the tolerable discreetness of his uniform, with the wizened face of a bureaucrat more worried than ashamed, completely unarmed among his super-armed *attendants.* He looked like nothing more than the liquidator of the bankrupt military-Fascist administration of the town. In contrast his retinue surrounded him with the most martial and prompt attention. They got on board the vessel and then Pierre and Johnny went forward as if to set a seal on things. Then the colonel with a sign invited them closer and at the same time signalled to the ferrymen to wait before casting off. But it was another officer who spoke – an officer in his forties with a hard face and trembling lips, perhaps the senior staff officer of the regiment. With piercing eyes he looked fixedly at the blue scarves and asked or rather *stated* whether they were supporters of Badoglio. 'That doesn't make any difference, sir,' said Pierre. But the officer took this for granted and said: 'And you are officers.' 'In your particular sense – only he is,' said Johnny, referring to Pierre. 'You look like an officer, too,' said the other, 'in the only true and important sense of the word. Right – now you occupy the town. In fact I want to go further. I can imagine that you occupy the whole of Italy, this town like the whole of Italy. Right – what will you do with Italy, my boys?' 'Something quite small but entirely serious,' Johnny responded and Pierre assented after him with his *inimitable earnestness.* The other pressed the point: 'But will there still be an Italy with you people?' 'Certainly – a different Italy, an Italy on our lines but always Italy. Please don't worry.'

The colonel sighed heavily, the officer saluted *tautly* imitated by part of their escort and the ferrymen gave a hefty tug at the cable towards the other bank which was packed with troops half-concealed but clearly very anxious. And as if someone had given a signal from the ramparts suddenly the town resounded with cheers and bells. And a light flashed through Johnny's mind. It was done – that was what lay behind the long depressing process of evacuation – the liberation of the town from Fascism and supremacy in an Italy that was fighting. And Johnny and Pierre embraced crazily above the waters which lapped their feet while on the naked bank, the men danced to the rhythm of the bells and hurrahed at the top of their voices.

'You are free,' said Pierre to the men. 'Go and enjoy the liberated city. I see the relief patrols coming this way. And tomorrow we'll start to fortify the banks.'

They were *leisurely* climbing the banks towards the city when a ragged incomprehensible tumult of voices on the other bank made them stop and turn round. Some people – certainly officers – not accepting things, must have harangued and inflamed the Fascist soldiers in the half-concealed clearing, and those they harangued now replied with a roar of voices rising to a savage diapason caused by burning shame and the biting feeling of revenge.

The men returned to the nearest mole and crouched there and the sergeant sited the machine-gun. The patrol who were coming up also ran for cover forming a cohesive defence and showing readiness to fire. Meantime the ferry boat was coming back on its last trip, slowly and almost in a Sunday mood, but now the crew, although exhausted, became aware of the preparations on either bank and clutched at the cable to accelerate wildly. But from the other bank the *gong* of the mortars rose up over the freed town and a second later the sergeant's machine-gun crackled. Amid the curses of the men one could hear the *scrambling and screaming* of the population surprised by the firing. The sergeant let off another burst voluptuously while over the town the sirens wailed a general alarm while the mortars redoubled their funeral *gong* and more and more units ran up to the bank so that in no time four machine-guns took up position alongside Michele's. As they fired the partisans cursed, begging to have a flotilla of boats at their disposal to cross the river and engage hand to hand with the filthy Fascists. But shortly under the fire of all the machine-guns the Fascists disappeared after a last simultaneous volley not aimed at the banks but at the unmissable town.

And Johnny took off after Pierre had told him what to do. Headquarters (under the command of an officer from 1st Division, rumoured to be a military genius, a master of tactics) was in the Municipal Boarding School; the partisans in part quartered in the School itself and the majority in the barracks – those from Mango in the barracks.

Johnny entered the town, alone and slow, through the lanes of the medieval quarter which was now reassuming a certain animation after the great and prolonged draining away towards the centre under a sky that was steel-grey and wretched. The population had visibly sobered up, struck like lightning by the thought of consequences, reprisals and punishments. Inevitably, thought Johnny, and he asked the first persons he met what damage the treacherous mortar fire had done. None – except some damage to the roofs, *easy to mend.* Now the partisans came into view in groups, off duty, asking the way to the brothels, the tailors' shops and the photographic studios, *shamelessly beggaring for* petrol and cars that had been hidden away. But patrols were also going about, serious and tense, extremely committed to their task, in true austerity.

Johnny strolled towards the centre and his part of the town. What prevented him from breathing normally was the raped look of his town – happily and consentingly raped, in wedlock, but raped. At a crossroads he stopped to allow a partisan unit to pass, reasonably orderly and in step, reliable, and Johnny's heart preceded them with huge grateful bounds towards their tour of duty on the increasingly grey riverbank.

At another crossroads where the crowd was still thick, lively and optimistic, a voice called to him loudly: a well-known, basically disagreeable voice, totally bourgeois. He turned round and it was Alessandro as always in shining shoes, as always with his hands in his pockets and on his shoulders his envied original Burberry and his usual avid, searching, sad eyes. Hiding, seclusion had aged and corrupted him. He came up with an impassioned, almost aggressive stride which made him hold the waterproof on his shoulders so that it did not slip off because of the way he thrust himself forward. He gripped Johnny's hand with a ferocious *clutch* which at once became limp and his voice was rasping, hysterical. 'But you are always in the midst of everything.' 'And you go on being nowhere.' 'Let me take you for a coffee – buy you a drink.' 'Thank you but I must go home without losing any more time.' 'Take a cigarette at least.' 'I can offer you English ones.' Alessandro accepted the absolute novelty of Capstans. And Johnny took advantage of his first reflective mouthful to force him to walk with him towards his house. Alessandro's walk was at once uncertain and angry. 'You are in amazing form, Johnny. I look a bit consumptive in comparison. The mountains suit you.' 'Yes.

A sporting life, you know.' 'Yes, I've heard people whispering about that kind of life.'

But fifty steps further on he could no longer continue fencing. He destroyed his cigarettes in his *clutching* fingers and confronted Johnny with a burning furrowed face. 'Johnny, how long do you think you can hold the place?' 'A fortnight. Long enough for the others to organise a counter-expedition of a certain seriousness. But don't go about saying so.' *His face distracted.* 'And you tell me like that! And you'll leave us in the lurch! You'll leave us in the lurch.' 'Inevitably. All the partisans naturally who don't die in the defence.' 'Great, great!' he whispered in desperation, 'so why did you do it?' 'Something we couldn't resist.' 'Ah, you didn't resist temptation. Alba – like Mecca in short. 'Maybe – but for many of us in the religious sense of the comparison.' 'Religious! the partisans, I don't like your partisans. At last I have seen them face to face and I don't like them. If this is a case of saying "we couldn't resist" I don't like them.' They fell silent because a group passed them still celebratory but not excessively so, but still radiant with optimism, hope and faith.

'Tell me, Sander.* Did you like the Fascists? Will you like the people who retake our town?'

'No I didn't like them – I never will.'

Johnny sighed with sadness and fatigue. 'You have to choose, Sander. You have to choose which side you dislike least.' He nodded but in black despair. Then he enfiladed Johnny with a series of questions about their command structure, their reserves of fire, defence plans, relations with the Communist partisans (these he obviously disliked to the point of *intolerance*, of madness!). Johnny merely replied: 'In your hiding place you must have done a good deal of thinking!' 'Not a good deal but enough. You know – seclusion! You have to think to drive any deadly boredom but if you think you go mad. Listen to this – do you know who I saw on the balcony of the town hall with your leaders? Sicco, Sicco the lawyer!' he pronounced the name and the description with sobbing contempt and incredulity. 'Sicco on the balcony among the leaders – him too!' 'It's natural – he's part of the CLN** – he has worked and

---

* Dialect diminutive of Alessandro.
** CLN – the Committee of National Liberation which organised the Resistance in most towns or localities.

taken risks,' 'Who? Sicco?' and he laughed and sobbed.

Johnny cast a glance at the shadow of the houses neighbouring his own. 'We'll see each other again, Sander.' 'Yes,' he replied, 'one day this fortnight.'

The sky was dimming and the people uncomfortably, with reluctance, but irresistibly looked up at it as if to chase back into the mysterious places of birth and progress the dark and the night, the deeply worrying first night of liberation. In a different way but for the same reason Johnny looked at the sky as if to hasten the dark and anticipate the night and find out what that first night – the prototype of fifteen nights – would be like.

An old woman, almost a next-door neighbour, crossed the street *stridingly and purposedly to meet him, waving severe, legitimately reproaching hand.* 'Johnny! What sort of boy have you become, Johnny? who hasn't been home yet since this morning and your parents in despair because you should have been with the partisans who entered Alba. Yet you've been away almost a year without warning' – *and she renewed the reproached waving.* 'For hours your poor mother has been on the balcony calling down to the partisans to ask about you – if they knew you – if you were there – if you were dead or wounded.'

'I'm going home, signora. I have been on duty on the banks all this time.'

He climbed the already dark stairs attempting to recapture his old peacetime step, the one from those days, but in vain, the narrow staircase and the stairs themselves seemed to re-echo with a stranger's footstep. On the landing outside his house there was a yellowish patch of light and the light and dejected bubbling noise of a supper that had been waited for an extraordinary time. *Breathless Johnny strode in as for* a burglary. They smiled and embraced him blindly, his father's reading glasses fell and shattered on the floor. From a corner a puppy leapt and barked, but once only and then retreated and sat, recognising the blood. And the puppy plunged a dagger into Johnny's heart – that living, *plushy* toy to replace him and in some way to fill, to warm the long desolate evenings of so much . . .

He was afraid his mother would die from choking, he felt against his body the terrifying sobbing, the ferocious breathlessness. He freed her, held her firmly and upright at arm's length – she was a blind statue of reproach and love, of pride and terror. That was what her strong *restless* fingers said on Johnny's sober, coarse partisan material. At the first break his father's mouth opened to express male reproaches for the secret decision and his sudden, secret joining up with the partisans but his mother shut it again with a *flat lovely command*.

'Sit down, you are so tall I can't see you all any more.' 'I've never felt better, mamma. It is – this new life.' She nodded thoughtfully. 'And – the danger?' 'Up to now I haven't run any really. Really. You know I think the boys who stayed in town live much worse with the fear of round-ups, the searches, the deception –' She nodded even more thoughtfully, then had a sudden decisive tremor of determination and joy. 'But now you are here for good.' Johnny *gaped*. 'For good? You're not saying you want me to leave the partisans?' 'No, never.' Johnny smiled. 'You know I have seen more than one mother climb up to take back her son. We laughed so much at them. And you, *dear old lass*, are very much that kind of mother.' He cast a glance at his father who was fingering the weapons he had laid aside with the apparent casualness of the old soldier. 'That's what they call a Sten?' 'Yes, but don't touch it because it fires the whole lot.' 'I was saying,' his mother resumed, 'that you will be in town for good now that you have taken it – until the end of the war.' Johnny smiled. 'But we won't hold it for long, mamma.' She stopped and *gaped* and his father wheeled round. 'What? But then –?' And his father: 'But I heard the opposite. I heard you will hold it always, that they won't chase you out again. This morning when I was going about looking for you I heard two of your officers who were telling a whole lot of people that the Fascists can do nothing now because every day we will have English planes overhead forming an aerial umbrella, that was what they were saying.'

'Don't spread it about. But I shall be satisfied if we are still here in a fortnight. How long have you had the dog?' For four months they said. 'It looks nice. What's it called?' 'It's so nice. Mickie.' 'Is he good company?' 'Very. And did you see – he only barked once – he recognises the blood.'

A sudden *rippling* down his back *reminded him*. With embarrassed gaiety he said he wanted – indeed had to change. His mother *scolded* herself for her forgetfulness and absent-mindedness and led him to his old room. Now everything seemed to him to be happening not only *out of necessity* but *out of his choice*. Even the dear books in the bookcase opposite the bed. *Fingering* in the trunk his mother asked him if he was going to take a bath. 'I don't have time – I'll wash tomorrow in the showers at the barracks.' Then he *patted* his bed as if it were a big domestic animal. 'You'll sleep really well there tonight, Johnny,' she said. 'I won't sleep there at all. I shall be out tonight on duty. We shall be patrolling the banks of the rivers. And besides do you know how long it is since I slept in a real bed? Ever since then. Always in stables or in the open.' 'That's why – just for one night.' 'I can't, mamma, besides it would be a very bad return to old habits.'

They sat at supper while the precocious October evening beat fluidly on the old window. Johnny wanted to master the new dog but the animal was still shy and diffident, he had to go to a lot of trouble to be approved and make it accept *morsels*. 'Did you have problems with the Fascists?' They took hostages more than once but his father had always been out and now seemed offended and annoyed at having been excluded. 'Of course there are spies,' said Johnny, 'that is why I didn't want to come home for a moment.' 'But you took them all. I saw them leave in columns up the hills to your prison-camps. I was sorry for them.' 'But who can tell who and where the spies are. And how were things otherwise?' They said they were hard up. 'Will you hold out for a few more months? because it is a question of months. Then I'll come back and throw myself into work.' 'We are counting on you, Johnny. I'm still there,' said his father with an energy that was uniquely touching. 'But don't worry, Johnny. We're not down and out – in fact this evening I can give you a thousand – two thousand lire even.' 'Thank you, we have a kind of weekly pay. But you can't always count on it. Maybe now with the muncipal taxes that we'll take from the Treasury.' 'You'll do that?' his father burst out highly excited and unable to understand. 'But it's natural – above all it's legal. They are national income – and we are the national government in the town now.'

The dog was becoming increasingly familiar – now it was asking for pats even with electric *wiring*. It would become a splendid companion – afterwards.

His mother said she had seen Ettore in the crowd of partisans but he had not seen her. 'Is he in your unit?' 'No – but he lives near me.' 'You mean to say you aren't together?' she insisted, chiding him. 'Did you have words – so that you split up.' 'No – on the contrary but in the partisans we see things very differently, we live very differently from before. But we will get together, Ettore and I, before long.' Her eyes darted. 'Johnny, you're not a Garibaldino?' Johnny laughed a No. 'Who is your commander?' 'Nord.' 'Good. They talk about him a lot.' 'Did you see what a very handsome man he is?' 'No, but I hear all the other women saying he is.'

Supper was over – very oddly even the food tasted middle-class. Then Johnny offered his father an English cigarette. He examined the blonde tobacco closely and said he thought he recognised the taste. 'I must have smoked them before – the very same – in that other war. We had an English battalion alongside us. They never fired a shot naturally.' 'That was an honest war, very different from this one – much cleaner,' said his mother.

The night – a peculiar, odd night, *propped* at the window pregnant with treachery and safety. Johnny indicated the radio to his mother – she should turn it on. Radio Turin, naturally, not the English radio. 'I want to hear what they are saying about us – about the town they have lost. I bet they won't say a thing.' His father made to turn it on but she anticipated him, she was after all still the priestess of the radio. After a final flourish of light music they read the communiqué. The Russians were advancing like a tide, the Allies were having problems with patrols in Northern Tuscany. Then they plunged back into light music again. His mother looked to see if Johnny wanted the music then turned the knob.

'Give me a pullover – one of the old worn ones. It's for the night on the banks. Soon we'll have pullovers and leather doublets – English stuff.' His mother gave a start. Some sort of noise in the street but she jumped, it would inevitably be like this, agonisingly like this, for the whole town for the whole of these two weeks. 'When you hear heavy firing or the noise of planes go down into the cellars. Tell all the rest. Specially you, mother, the same old inquisitive, brave and imprudent woman.' He got up with an ease that intentionally combined determination and leisure. 'Will you be here for dinner tomorrow?' 'But I'm a partisan, mamma – I don't think I'll come home again.' It was too much. 'All right, I'll try to get leave for Sunday midday.

Meantime don't go looking for me in town because I shall get myself posted outside on the banks – permanently.'

He was searching in vain in his mind and memory for something to take away from home and insert in his new life but he found nothing necessary or even suitable for it. His mother was at the door, her anguish tempered by the certainty that she would see him again, perhaps by chance. 'Take care, Johnny. There's nothing as valuable as your life. And, if you can – don't kill.' The stammering that came from his father's lips was intolerable, but it was he who had to say the quietest and most hopeful words. 'I'm sure to see you again because I am about a lot.' 'Yes, but but don't go out too much, papa.'

He was outside in the supernatural immobility and desertedness of the town. Everyone had gone back in, locked away, buried away from the others. The blackout had never been enforced with such ferocity, he was sure that if he had turned aside to push at any door he would have been answered by locked resistance. The first beam of light in the dark shone out from the municipal guardroom, the former cubbyhole of the air wardens, and the gap allowed him to glimpse partisans and police watching and waiting side by side.

His steps exploded on the silvery pavements and echoed vastly, merged from time to time in the greater and heavier *thud* of the patrols on their rounds or on their way to the banks. He walked close to the houses as if the better to catch their unimmurable breath of fear, fear at the undertaking and at the punishment, fear at having given too much expression to joy and approval by the light of day under the *owl*'s glances of the spies. Johnny walked on, feeling sadness for his liberated town. Other blades of light and faint emissions of noise from the doors of the bars – frequented only by partisans as he could tell from their voices. He passed a Garibaldini patrol, feline and tense, splendidly isolated in its redness.

He made for the enormous, long, evil-smelling spectre of the barracks. And from the new unimpeded vast space Johnny looked up at the sky, mattressed with white clouds and wondered which of those round shapes to the north-east was directly over Turin, the place where the Fascists had taken official note of the loss of Alba and already in a bitter feverish state were planning its reconquest.

The enormous, sinister gateway of the barracks swallowed him. An under-age guard was standing there perhaps frightened by the very smell of the barracks. Besides nervousness was running through Johnny too. He went on through courtyards and doorways in a dim light poisoned by distant disinfections, in the acrid presence of the ghosts of the late Royal Army. Soon it was all merely a labyrinth with a single outlet – that of madness. Where were the men quartered? And were they sleeping already or had they been overcome by, drugged by the *spell* of the barracks? He called for Michele through the dusty filters of the deserted and *haunted* rooms. At last the sergeant *cried back*. And he appeared, ghost-like, at the door of the exact room.

All was unhealthy darkness, tortured by an extraordinary number of red cigarette tips, some of them rotating and madly making patterns because of the odd behaviour and restlessness of the smoker. Pierre had not turned up again. Johnny looked around for a free bed. 'I think there are some cynics,' said the sergeant humorously, apparently not displeased. Johnny lay down. The men were shut off and morose, *humming* at most, time passed in a nervous *hush*, an uncomfortable change of sides and uncontrolled smoking. Johnny, his nerves growing doubly within him, understood. The men were afraid of the town, of being shut up, of coordination. They lay on their narrow camp beds with the same sense of entrapment, of defencelessness with which the Fascist soldiers had passed the night in the woods on the hills. Maybe all men dreamt only of the moment for going on duty, on sentry-go or better on patrol, to get rid of the enchantment of the trap.

Pierre came in at ten, most relieved to see his men even in that neurotic *diseased* shape. He lay down on the bed next to Johnny. 'How are things at headquarters?' 'I have to go back, I'm afraid. I don't like it there, you know. My head is bursting. Talking, suggesting, deciding. Civil government, food rationing, the proclmation about spontaneous handing in of all gunpowder, the plans for a mobile defence. I feel incompetent, Johnny, incompetent and ashamed and *sick*.' 'What do you think of the commander in chief?' Pierre, perhaps encouraged by the perfect darkness, protrayed him with an *allure* and a freedom which was entirely unusual in him: a good-looking man, about thirty-five, a military look but with a splendid smile and taciturn and when he spoke he used only well-chosen and technical terms. A remarkable type, that was it, but as for the rest: 'Pooh, as we used to say at the Academy.' Then he gave orders for the spell on the banks. 'The sector is upstream of the bridge as far as the second rotunda. Send the sergeant.' 'I'll go. If you send the sergeant you are no friend of mine.' Johnny called the sergeant to pick the men for the patrol by the river. 'See you pick those who are suffering most from being shut up, the ones who are sick of the town and the barracks.' 'Then take them all,' said Michele simply. So it was a very substantial patrol that Johnny led to the banks, in a new state of freshness, with a revival of martial bearing, in the dripping night, along the soft paths, towards the deep-flowing river.

The men began to patrol the naked banks, lively, with light hearts but intent on their work. The waters were black and from so close at hand practically silent, the impact of the other bank on the more distant waters indiscernible. From behind there came at intervals what seemed the rattle of the town's nightmare sleep on the razor's edge. Later a high night wind began and continued to play on the summit of the innumerable poplars with a noise that was more continuous and more watery than that of the fleeting river. The air was extremely damp, striking to the bone, and the sergeant said that for further sorties they ought to take blankets and to hang about muffled up like so many nuns. Johnny was sitting on the incised granite of the second mole, his head vertically over the black and amorphous water. In the dark which was now complete (gleams of white, more imagined than perceived, on the spectral sector of the other bank) the waters were no longer silent; but a lapping and eddying and whistling as if around the prows of the counterattacking Fascists or at least of riverborne reconnaissance parties, of disembarking spies. Johnny smiled at the thought but imagined what it would be like on those other nights, nearer to H hour, what *strain* and *distraction* and *exhaustion*, to become aware of, to enucleate and interpret the thousands of noises, large and small, of a night full of treachery and fading glimmers of light. Even now if you kept your eyes staring in the darkness absurd visions of light, confusion and magnesium . . .*

The belfries of the town were striking midnight. The cold and damp had had its effect on the men, on that *briskness* of theirs which had made them come out and all patrol together. Now a deputation

* From flares fired to illuminate the area.

222

came trembling to Johnny's granite stones to get permission to take turns. Did Johnny not know a hut or a mere shed for agricultural implements in the neighbourhood to light a little necessary fire or smoke an invisible cigarette? Johnny pointed out in the fibrillating dark a hut he knew of old in the midst of the soaking fields – the only building in that area and often endangered by floods. The men *s'enfonçaient* towards the spectral hut trembling at the sudden assault of the dew on their calves. But very soon they were back coughing and cursing. Their little fire had spread to a pile of dry maize leaves and an irresistible, toxic smoke had driven them out.

Johnny had walked along the whole length of the sector he was guarding up to the lee of the bombed bridge and had exchanged matches and anodyne talk with the Blue commander of the other unit. The sergeant was still at the second mole, still squatting like an Indian on the granite which was growing colder and colder. There was something about Michele that spoke of colonial service with native troops and of masochistic pleasure in it. For hours he had looked and thought and only now uttered his long, honest thoughts. He scanned the flat expanse of the opposite bank and the width and faecal nature of the river once more and said: 'Well, I don't think they'll ever make it. They'll never cross.' Johnny did not reply, then, 'We'll hold the town at will, I say. The Fascists will never manage to cross this river. And, Johnny, does it rain much in these parts in autumn?' 'Normally.' 'And does the river get really big?' 'Yes.' The sergeant was delighted at this phenomenon so outside his Sicilian experience.

Johnny squatted beside him. 'I'm amazed that an old sergeant has forgotten pontoon bridges.' 'I'd like to see them launch one under our eyes and under our machine-guns. I'd really like to see them launch one.' And he pointed in the turbulent dark to the wide and level sandy beach just below the bridge in full view of the town. Johnny said: 'You surely don't expect the Fascists to land right in front of the town?' The men were gathering round now *sullenly concerned* at Johnny's arguments. 'The river goes on for kilometres and kilometres and our line is only at certain points and it's fairly thin. To cross anywhere down there is nothing special.' The darkness itself could not eclipse the ray of the sergeant's *grinning eye-closed* perceptiveness. 'Let's just hope they attack across the river because, if we're beaten, we will be able to escape towards our hills. But if they encircle us by land, well then, Michele, they will crush us and we will all drown in the river which will be really big because of the rains.' And there was no objection while the wind and the river swelled their *unbarriered sounds* and the cold increased and the empty mystery of the night.

XIX

Johnny went to Town HQ as slowly and dreamily as possible. There were few citizens about, hurried and minding their own business. On the other hand the influx of partisans continued and became even more marked. Johnny was often passed by trucks which unloaded whole units in the main squares. At first he thought they were intended to reinforce the garrison but he quickly saw that these were prize-trips: after shopping, café, cinema and brothel, these men were going back in the same transports to the twilight hills. And the men did not seem to mind.

The Town College, now the Town HQ, stood in the old quarter round the Bishop's Palace, like an ocean-going tanker still surrounded by a wood of sailing-boats and coasters. Its side was long, elliptical and metal-clad, with a whole series of miserly openings like portholes and the propylaeum stuck out like a prow. Under the propylaeum stood two sentries from 1st Division, very tall, armed with tommy-guns.

Johnny went halfway along the very long glassed entrance hall which looked out on to the courtyard. The Fascist and partisan occupations had not succeeded in blotting out the old, clinging scent of kitchen and laundry and the sweat of young students. If anything they had raised it to the level of the acridity natural in military communities.

The outer office was full of smoke, shuffling of feet, the squeaking of benches. From the adjoining room there came willing but inexpert *typewriting*. The waiting men were low-ranking partisan commanders facing a line of civilians, suppliers and entrepreneurs: the latter seemed to be overflowing with goodwill but uncontainably anxious and tic-ing, excitedly ready when summoned. The partisans

225

were for the most part Reds and they seemed nervous and annoyed, as if the Blues were taking advantage of their preponderance at the HQ to force them to sit in the outer office.

'What do you want?' a voice that was a web of bureaucratic shrillness and ill-will said behind Johnny. Johnny turned right round and saw the familiar *routinier* of 2nd Division, still in civilian clothes, still entirely at his ease with the partisans (who perhaps were not his bosses nor yet his brothers); he looked exhausted, irritated and asthmatic.

'Have you come to see Captain Marini?'

'Who's he?'

'Town Commandant – just imagine,' he said more mocking than scandalised.

'Not so high up,' Johnny replied. 'I'm looking for Lieutenant Pierre.'

'Officially summoned?'

'Yes, under orders.'

His feeling of weariness and ill-temper were not such as to stop him from rushing to keep an eye on what a guard was up to who, apparently on his own initiative, was bringing two civilians into the sanctum of the HQ.

Another guard, a boy with a bright lively face, came to tell Johnny to wait for Pierre in the courtyard and Johnny *sick* of waiting ran out to enjoy the grey vastness of the college courtyard.

Every air duct in the immense entrance was blocked off by a truck from the partisan car-park. In the farthest corner Johnny caught sight of a little group of ex-army officers, immaculate in their well-preserved uniforms, come together and presenting themselves to offer their services to the partisan command. The group and the individual stared at each other for a moment in pure *puzzlement* and distrust.

Pierre arrived after a few minutes with his usual stripling's gait, but seeming weighed down and aged by life at the headquarters. He suffered from acute nostalgia for his men and wherever they were stationed and asked about the other ranks and the sergeant. 'We are ordering a quantity of waterproof blouses because heavy rain is expected. I'll see that our men have the first share. 1st Division and even the Red brigade already have English groundsheets.'

Said Johnny: 'You people here are bound to follow the Fascist radio minute by minute. Have they talked about us at last?'

'Not a word. Perhaps they mean to have a single communiqué when the town is retaken. If they manage it.'

'You're changing your mind, Pierre?'

'In here I see certain things that puzzle me in short.'

They went and squatted uninhibitedly on the cold stairs leading to the inner door and the officers down below looked critically at the pair, especially at the man with the braided cap of the air force. Pierre sighed. 'I and these people there should be brothers by vocation. Yet I don't give a cent for them. They have thought everything out and we – nothing. They begin with the city and we have to begin with the hills. If we lose the town we shall go back to the hills without batting an eyelid, following the grain of our luck. But they won't leave the town. They'll hastily take off their uniforms, they'll pray that anyone who saw them won't give them away, they'll curse their naïveté, their sentimentality, their patriotism, they'll curse us for forcing them to button on their uniforms again and for not being real soldiers. Believe me, Johnny, I don't feel like exchanging a single word with them. It's just as well for me that Marini has decided to speak to them personally.'

'Where are Nord and Lampus?' asked Johnny.

'They have gone back to the hills. Don't be wide-eyed. The hills are infinitely more important than the town. Naturally they'll come flying back at the first alarm.'

A bunch of drivers was crossing the courtyard to get into their *wanted* trucks. Passing in front of the embarrassed, rigid group of waiting officers, they cast a glance at them with a gleam of disgust, with deliberate disrespect. Pierre's pale face flushed then settled into sadness. Now they were starting the motors, asking the maximum from them, as if their roar were a sequel to their disrespect for the officers who were now more nervous and *self-contained* than ever.

Pierre took his eyes off that scene which wounded him and began to produce written orders and bank notes. 'I envy you, Johnny,' he said. 'You're going out of town, just outside it, to keep watch over a stretch of river. You will be between a Red detachment and a unit

227

from the Canale Brigade. You'll be based on the farmhouse called Gambadilegno.'*

Johnny took a deep breath and Pierre envied him. 'Here's your billeting chit and fifty thousand lire for the cost of the billet. The people are with us body and soul and they will help us even more if we pay reasonably for the disturbance. Besides we've never had so much money.'

Johnny pocketed it all, the money forming an unusual protuberance in the pocket of his blouse. 'The men will be happy,' he said. 'They were suffocating in the barracks and they are suffocating in town. It affects them too much, they don't trust it and end up by hating it. That is perhaps the main footnote to the behaviour of the average partisan in town.'

'Excellent,' said a voice behind them. 'That is really a tip-top remark. One of your men, Pierre?'

It was the garrison commander, tall, brown and *staid*. He wore an army officer's uniform unadorned by any rank or ornament and to increase that puritanical sobriety he did not wear boots but simply long trousers with the turn-ups immaculately brushed free of dust. He had a magnificent smile but a fixed one that never faded, the smile that can be born of the greatest ability and faith in one's self just as it can be a cover for the most tremendous incompetence and irresponsibility. At his side was his adjutant and he for Johnny was the '*queer bird*'. A camouflaged uniform, very thin and wide, the cut more that of a Fascist legionary than of a partisan, enwrapped his fakirlike body which was surmounted by a tiny and compact head, with very close-fitting grey hair and wearing glasses, the head of a cultured monk. What struck one at once in him with shameless clarity was that he seemed desperately in love with Captain Marini and would always be his man anywhere whether Marini was a Fascist or a partisan commander or some captain adventurer.

'So you are going to the river?' said Marini with his immortal smile. 'Have you got fishing tackle by any chance?'

'Would I have a chance to use it, captain?'

'You would be sure to have day after day before you for pure sport,'

---

* Literally 'wooden leg'.

said Marini and moved over towards the officers with his fixed smile and a fine walk.

Pierre accompanied Johnny to the entrance between the two sentries who looked askance at them. 'One of these days,' said Pierre, 'I shall dig out a motor bike and come and spend a whole afternoon with our people. Let me find the men in their good old form.'

Johnny slipped into a barber's. The owner was resting out of breath on one of the two deserted armchairs. He started, took note of the cut and the shampoo and began to cut and chat. 'I had just finished. I was literally exhausted. You can't imagine the work yesterday and this morning – up to a few minutes ago. All partisans – an invasion.'

'They all needed it badly,' *growled* Johnny.

'Ah yes, they needed it badly and I never worked more willingly. But the trouble is I was alone. They left me high and dry. I had an assistant and a helper for market days. Well, both of them enrolled with the partisans yesterday, right away. Of course I'd have done the same if I were a young man instead of the father of a family. They have left me in the lurch and there's nothing so hard to find today as young workers.'

An hour later Johnny left the barracks for the banks outside the town, weapons and ammunition loaded on a requisitioned cart, his men relieved, breathing deeply, magnificently eager for their new destination by country road, soft and melting in autumnal tepidness, towards that constant fascinating objective of bank and river with a delightful feeling of a truce in the iron frame of war, Johnny at the hand and the sergeant in the rear, completely relaxed.

The farmhouse called Gambadilegno was exactly halfway between the shining main road and the curtains of mist rising from the river. And it was so far from the town that none of its noise reached it except – and that very blurred – the soundwave of the sirens each time they tested the general alarm in town.

It was a medium sort of farmhouse but the stable and the hayloft were adequate to take the thirty men. The mistress of the house (well prepared to have partisans assigned to her and blessing heaven that they had assigned Badogliani to her and not Red Stars) was a real heroine and fell for Johnny, going so far as to praise him in his presence, to his great confusion, and to order his men firmly to love, respect and obey him, and even managing to overcome her innate aversion to the Southernness of the sergeant once she saw that he was faithful and indispensable to Johnny. Besides this she proved a real genius at preparing food in great quantities, simple and rich, and always strove to reject at least half the money Johnny obliged her to accept. The husband, to whom she was wife and sister and mother, doctor, lawyer and ambassador, was a little man, all white and wrinkly, of infrequent and bitter words. At first Johnny was convinced that the billeting chit was the most unexpected and intolerable of disgraces for the old man but later on had to revise his opinion – that monosyllabic and evasive behaviour derived not only from his natural acidity but from his almost total inability to be effusive. In reality the old man was more pro-partisan than the majority of their sympathisers. Their two sons – both of an age to be called up and both dodging the draft – were of the common type of youth that is chained to the earth with all the sweetness and edginess of their kind – both were entirely unable to relate to the partisans, to their world, ideals, needs and habits, but they took part in their work and games with a bitter, undissimulable sense of inferiority, as if they saw them committing themselves totally and recognised the intoxicating nature of that act of commitment and their own inability to commit themselves. And as Johnny noticed, they always gave expression to keen-eyed sarcasm at the expense of those of Johnny's men who were of obvious peasant extraction as if they were convinced that the partisan adventure was the exclusive business of town boys.

The bank, its nature helping, was dealt with in less than a day. An emplacement was made for the Buffalo* and a site for the Breda and, for the rest, the riflemen scratched and dug according to their taste or superstition. There remained guard duty. By day it was a pleasantly strange duty with a good deal of a boyish game about it; but at night it was a hard and burdensome duty, the extreme task for a fully developed and adult man in the viscid coils of the treacherous unhealthy cold from the river. Days and nights of sentry-go passed and Johnny and Michele had to react to the way the men became used to it and their tendency to slack and underrate the importance of their guard, by combating their instinctive conviction that that

* The American machine-gun.

stretch of river of theirs was precisely the one where nothing would ever happen, that the Fascists might appear and cross at any other point except theirs.

The river and the other shore seemed to encourage, to justify their slackening off. The shore had such a secluded and mythically wild look that it made one think that it could not and must not appear on any map, being scarcely known and that at best to someone watering his animals or a searcher for the flotsam of the river, and remote from both Fascists and partisans. The only sign of a constant presence and human activity was the blackish skeleton of a distant stone-crusher long abandoned. As for the river, it ran past with a wide and smooth current, concealing, according to Johnny, a subaqueous life infinitely richer than that which lay beneath the tumbled, energetic currents opposite the town. The stretch assigned to them overlooked half-a-dozen still, deep ponds which made the men regret they had not occupied the town in midsummer.

For all these days not one man or beast was sighted on the other shore.

The early afternoon hours were still warm, good for basking in the sun, and it was during these hours that the English fighters made their appearance in the still, stable sky. The sun beat on their sides like a mute explosion and that echo was the only and immediate way to recognise them in the desert of the sky. Partisans and citizens shouted with joy at their vertiginous appearance. Johnny thought it was the usual pilot in search of a prey but there really was something friendly and protective in their constant slow circling (*hovering*). Their eyes would have liked to follow them beyond the limits of the horizon and when they disappeared the men in great excitement discussed the question of air cover and the terrible effect of machine-gun fire cutting down infantry on the move.

At the end of ten days the men had had the river; some began to shout *mutinously* to be relieved with renewed longing for the pavements, cinema and cafés; others for whom the town was a position like any other fell ill with longing for the high hills whose nearest ramparts loomed behind them in majestic clarity at favourable times in contrast to the lightly rising mists of the river. Johnny himself felt he was tired of the river or rather of that stretch of river and would have rejoiced at a change of sector, preferably downstream of the town bridge. To whet his desire Ettore arrived on a requisitioned trap, having come on a private visit from precisely that other pole of the river. Ettore and the rest of the men from Mango were mounting guard on the airy, in themselves adventurous cliffs over the river at Barbaresco. There, Johnny remembered, the river was narrow and very deep, slow like a flow of lead, and the immanent mystery of the dense groves of poplars on the other bank, which was as near, contributed to the pleasure and liveliness of the guard. Then there was a little ferry-boat, close by and working, which they used every day to cross the river and go here and there on the flat, rich land beyond the river which was free of fighters, where they were applauded and fêted by the inexperienced people and presented with fruit and vegetables for the whole unit.

Of all of them only the sergeant in his southern rootlessness was happy, firm, impassive, like an erratic boulder.

The Fascists saw to a resolution of the psychological problem by attacking the town – attacking it frontally, head on, at eight precisely, almost as if it were a factory shift.

It was a delicious morning, little patches of mist dancerlike on the river soon destined to vanish in the sun, the last irresistible sun of the year. Johnny was washing himself in solitude in a nook of the bank and perhaps it was the water dripping away that prevented him from hearing the din of the trucks and armour on the main road beyond the river. The first Fascists to debus and to take up position on the banks opposite the town exchanged the first shots across the electrified water with the partisan sentries alert on the opposite bank. And soon the wail of the sirens split the clear sky. Now the Fascists were firing massively and from the volume of the partisans' reply it was clear that a good part of the garrison had come down to the banks in question.

The men crowded round half-naked Johnny and ordered him to lead them to the bridge where the battle was.

'No way,' said Johnny. 'Suppose that is a diversion, suppose the main body were to cross just here?'

The men shrugged, they were visibly galvanised by the magnificent din of the unfolding battle.

'Did the Fascists tell you in a dream last night where they were going to cross?'

The men were trembling in rebellion because of the physical need for exercise and display.

'I have my orders. Then they could shoot me.'

One man answered that it had never happened.

'Do you want me to be the first?'

Michele stood motionless and silent, strangely, unprecedentedly neutral, and Johnny felt irritation at that neutrality much more than at any other form of insubordination.

He stiffened. 'Take up your positions. Smoking forbidden too.'

They went off, depressed and incredulous, withdrawing their hearing from the intoxicating din which crushed the unsuppressible distant stretch of river. One man threatened to fire at the first stone that stood out a little from the other bank. Michele gave him a cuff on the neck. But the last to pass, a boy with a sad and mature face, said: 'You're right, Johnny. We behave like the kids at football who run wherever the ball bounces.'

Then a rapid noise from the road to Gallo made them all turn suddenly and before the truck could turn off into the little road to the farmhouse they were certain it was coming for them to carry them to the epicentre of the battle. On the threshing-floor they leapt on to the truck with the mistress of the house blessing them one by one and the old man weeping. Madly they pestered the driver, who was already a champion at reckless partisan driving. He deposited them in front of the clothmill, at once a monument to and scaffold for the industrial revolution, now rising out on the naked banks, dark and martial like an *alcázar*.

It was immediately behind the front line, the bank on which the fierce wave of battle was breaking. But Johnny *fell in abstraction*. In the colour of the earth and of the air there was such warmth and delicacy, a golden moderation and maturity, that Johnny was enchanted and lost himself in the search for the end of one of his very first summer vacations.

He was jolted back by the loud applause of the citizens from a group of houses on the outskirts, among them a woman who scattered an apronful of sweets on the partisans. They gathered them up voraciously and then got up again with slow, ponderous reassuring gestures about the Fascists. An officer from 1st Division appeared like an elf in front of Johnny in perfect battledress and perfectly gloved. He indicated a stretch of the bank and gave him the general and very specific order to fire at any Fascist who raised his head on the other stony shore.

'Nothing particularly serious,' he said, 'we'll hold them there easily.'

'Have they opened up with the mortars?'

'Not yet. Perhaps they haven't even brought them. Do you have an aversion to them?'

The men ran to their positions, unworried, but well scattered on the wide grassland and soon tingling, malignant bullets came from the shingle opposite which was apparently deserted, frying slowly in the liquid and receptive atmosphere. The running men turned towards the shelter of the lateral bank but one of them stopped short in the grass saying 'I'm wounded, I'm wounded,' ecstatic in voice and gesture. His ecstasy caught hold of everyone, it made them all take root around him in the warm *crisp* grass. The sergeant took the wounded man in his arms and carried him into the long shadow of the high bank, with his service knife he ripped his trousers. It was a small broad-shouldered boy, one of those who take a good share of all the food, and the hole seemed more tiny and slight in the vast flab of his thick thigh. Two men raised him up to deposit him at the mill where others – civilians – would accompany and support him to the hospital.

They spread out on the warm slope of the last bank and could detect the soft-sounding way the Fascist bullets sank into the pneumatic belly of the bank. The highest bullets, the best-aimed ones, flew a good couple of hands above the highest and most exposed partisan cap and Johnny felt the fierce ricochet of the Fascist bullets, the lowest ones, against the granite of the platform.

He was seized by a frenzied desire to fire even knowing that after a first magazine he would be satiated to the point of nausea, but just now he was in a real frenzy for that magazine. He was carrying the Sten, the most useless weapon in the field, and at that moment the last thing he could do was order one of them to lend him a rifle. He took a better look ahead. In spite of the constant firing at the dyke no Fascist was to be seen on the open naked shingle nor on the bare untilled ground beyond. They must be firing heavily from behind the railway embankment some three hundred metres away. Looking about more carefully Johnny surprised a Fascist truck at five hundred metres which had come to a halt in a lane under the railway and was shaking all over as if it found itself facing an unexpected obstacle or was preparing to surmount a blockage that was already giving way. Johnny could guess at the excitement of the driver and so encouraged Michele who took hasty aim and fired. The burst went high and the massive vehicle slithered into cover like a snake.

Now the men seemed perplexed and detached behind the butts of their idle rifles. In the centre, with the Fascists presumably strung out along the edge of the vast stretch of sand that belonged to the Sanatorium, the din was enormous and continuous as if the side that first slowed its rate of fire was destined to lose, but for Johnny and his men there was nothing to see for they were blocked by the promontory of the first platform and by the two remaining arches of the bombed bridge.

At last, towards half past ten the Fascists came into sight in Johnny's sector too, they slid down the railway embankment and crawled forwards through the thin bushes towards the shingle which was rutted by carts, towards a rustic hut, a fisherman's, abandoned, which was reflected in the nearest water. Then all Johnny's rifles exploded from the bank and at the sudden fire the Fascists dashed back towards *very scanty* cover. But they did not withdraw to the embankment they had left but stopped and fired, malignantly but without effect, from the clayey shingle with its hollows and from the precarious bushes. To forbid them the hut all that was needed was light but timely rifle fire.

Bored and disappointed Johnny slid on his back down the slope of the bank, turning his back to the Fascists, as if in a comfortable sofa. He was basking like this in the unseasonable sun, looking first at the lofty spiralled sky then at the houses on the outskirts which were trembling imperceptibly as if in high summer, in the abnormal *haze*.

Then he glanced at Michele, idle in the Buffalo's fortification. 'Fire a few rounds, Michele, have some fun.' He shook his head. 'It would be a mortal sin to waste like that. What is the nub of the battle? They don't even have mortars. They won't manage, I swear, to dip their little toes in the water – in no way are they going to cross the river and retake the town.'

'I'd say a madman thought up this engagement. I could eat, Michele.'

'I could eat too. Do you think they'll have dealt with the nuisance by midday?'

'You never can tell with a madman.'

At eleven they had a flying inspection from the town commandant and he was followed by his adjutant, his wide camouflaged uniform fluttering in the breeze from the river. With them was the officer from the mill and all three had their holsters unbuttoned.

Said Captain Marini: 'I bet you'd sign on for a battle like this every day for the duration.'

Michele said: 'It's deadly boring to be on the left flank.'

The din at the centre was louder and long-drawn as if everything depended on pressure on an electrical device. Johnny *frowned* and said, 'Is there really any reason to fire so much in the centre? Don't let us give the Fascists credit for being geniuses, but suppose all they were after today was to bleed our ammunition with a view to the more real attack tomorrow or the day after.'

Marini turned off his smile like a light and *stalked* towards the centre.

At half past eleven a runner came to summon Johnny and his men to the centre to replace a squad which had exhausted its ammunition. Magnificently protected by the natural labyrinth of the banks, they crossed the bastion of the railway and slid down to the centre opposite the Sanatorium. They were held up for a moment near a group from the Canale Brigade. They were older and more robust than the average boy-partisans who were inclined to *abuse them* just because of their age and preponderance in weight, an imposing and fractious body of heavy infantry. These men were in a damp depression and siting two English mortars which headquarters had just acquired and had entrusted to the older men as the only ones who could make good use of them.

The men of the Canale Brigade had now set up the mortars and their dull parting explosions began to echo behind them. It was impossible for the Fascists to hold out long under that fire. In fact they reduced their fire considerably as did the partisans so that a vast and ambiguous silence spread over the water. In that silence there emerged what became an enormous din of friction as a tank came out of the greenery and advanced towards the shore grinding the sand with monumental clumsiness. From there it let fly with all it had. The monster advanced till it bathed its first tracks in the boiling water. Johnny could clearly see the savage ricochets of the partisan bullets against the steel plating, then he plunged his face in the ground under the broadside from the tank. A mortar round arrived just on its left wing. In instant truimph the partisans emerged exposed from the waist up. The tank's machine-guns were silent, it backed away with clumsy haste, while the partisans shouted to the mortar crew to do it again and finish it off. They doubled their rate of fire but the centre did not so that the tank regained the stretch of sand and then the wood.

The Fascists were withdrawing with the engines of their departing vehicles at full pitch. The sirens wailed the end of the alarm into the faded sky and the town walls seemed to leap from the uproar within.

They decamped comfortably, kicking the little heaps of cartridge cases, towards the embracing applause of the town they had saved. Johnny, *uneasy* and withdrawn, was caught in the whirlpool of a Red unit which was leaving energetically for the town and disentangled himself with a considerable effort and much lurching about. The men advanced under Michele's orders. Pierre had obtained a ticket for them for a collective dinner in a restaurant in town, for the afternoon he suggested the cinema at his expense.

The walls were black with an exultant and gesticulating crowd. With Pierre's permission Michele gave in to his military instinct and ordered the men to march at attention. The men rebelled and criticised him mockingly but in the tumult of the triumph they ended up by taking up and maintaining the rhythm. The bells boomed.

Johnny and Pierre went on into the town. The cheers because of the wear and tear on the vocal cords were dwindling into hoarse passionate talk and comments, into greetings that crackled from pavement to pavement. The bells continued like mad. A man came up to them and said: 'We were expecting the English planes – everyone was waiting for them. Why didn't they come as arranged to give you a hand from the air?' 'But who said it was arranged?' said Pierre.

They had to draw aside when faced by a silent black saloon car with two men armed with Lugers* sitting on the mudguards. Nord's profile gleamed at the windows and his hand waved in a somewhat pontifical sign of greeting. In the wake of the vehicle two partisans, a Badogliano and a Communist, were fighting in the gutter in the middle of the road. With difficulty Johnny and Pierre separated them amid a circle of citizens who kept backing away.

'What has got into you?' Johnny asked the Badogliano.

He panted, 'I wanted to shut his dirty red mouth for good. He saw Nord's car and said, "Is that your big chief arriving?"'

---

* This was a well known make of German pistol.

XX

The sun no longer shone – what followed was a time of downpours. The heaviest rain in Johnny's memory fell – rain that was born big and heavy, that drenched the ground, swelled the river to a frightening volume (people stopped being afraid of the Fascists and began to be afraid of the river) and soaked the very stones of the town.

Johnny looked up at its incessant beating on the windows of a room in the college. He was sitting at a proper desk. His work, which Pierre had implored him to do, consisted in collecting, sifting and transmitting the information and rumours among the people about the forthcoming Fascist attack. The day after the defeat Radio Turin had discussed the question of the town. Without mentioning the attack the announcer spoke about the forthcoming, inevitable recapture of the town which was temporarily fouled by the rebel occupation. In spite of the rotten rhetoric everyone – partisans and civilians – took the announcement entirely seriously. The people who came across by the ferry and went to the markets on the other bank asked to be heard on re-entering the town since they had information of vital importance. Pierre, affable, patient, selective Pierre, was soon overwhelmed by the work and called Johnny to his aid. The men had already gone back to the farmhouse called Gambadilegno under the orders of Michele who was more than capable.

Pierre and Johnny heard of Fascist movements, light signals, concentrations of flotillas of landing craft in some remote bend of the river, of long-range guns already sited on the hills beyond the river. They listened, raised objections, investigated, went into things, scribbled, thanked and dismissed. Then Johnny smoked and watched the beating rain and Pierre was mad with longing for a real coffee. A mania for coffee was the only vice Pierre had inherited from the sybaritic Air Force. A good many of the informants were boys, urchins, who for the fun and the adventure went all over the other bank of the river, and Johnny was convinced that all in all they were the most worth listening to: they had a very acute and selective eye, familiarity with the equipment and the main features of modern war and had the possibility of getting close with impunity to any possible Fascist concentrations. Apart from the priests, of course, priests were the most cautious and most precise source – the ordinary little priests of the villages beyond the river. Pierre and Johnny knew that before coming to them they had given a similar and perhaps more detailed report to the Curia. At the end Pierre was shown in to Captain Marini for the final account.

At dusk Johnny walked about in an English raincoat and weighed down and disgusted by the rain went on to the crumbling banks. At the town gates the roar of the waters welcomed him. The river had wiped out October's banks. The sentries had fallen right back to the embankment of the main road. The bubbling mud looked even more terrible and lethal than the maddened waters. The highest surges, swift and apparently cast in cement, just touched the remaining arches of the bridge. In the tune of the river however you could hear the coughing of the invisible sentries. The chaotic sky, where this deluge was forged, was hateful, and drew down curses.

He slid down to that cosmogonic chaos of water and went up to the sentry.

'How are things?'

'I'm getting TB. Have you got a cigarette rolled? I have tobacco and paper but this damned rain makes it impossible to roll. Give me a rolled cigarette.' But even smoking was impossible, the ferocity, the implacable nature and the *restlessness* of the water forced open fingers cupped to protect the cigarette and in a flash made it disintegrate.

He went over to the other sentry, huddled in a tongue of land holding out against the turbulent current. He had had enough, he said, of the water and the town. 'I have been in town since the day we entered it. I can't wait to leave it. I wish God would calm the waters so that the Fascists can land and we can have this big battle. I am fed up of living so wretchedly, of feeling like a mouse in a trap. This isn't a life, it's not the proper life for us. You are on the staff? Great – that's good – tell them at headquarters what I am thinking in this rain.'

Johnny climbed up again to the road and threw a last glance at the river. In this case nature was carrying off an exceptional triumph: for once nature was having the upper hand over men in the competition about who could be the more frightening; for everyone it was infinitely better to advance alone against an army of SS rather than to have to deal with a single one of these muddy surges. He looked at the river again almost as if to provide himself with material for his nightmares.

He hastened to headquarters under the downpour and amid the first evening patrols; the men were coughing and dragging their feet on the submerged asphalt, some wore sacks on their heads.

Johnny had had enough of headquarters, enough of the work he did there, and enough too of Pierre. In a couple of days he would see that he was sent back to the farm amid ignorant, out of joint but invigorating men.

Pierre said no rather bureaucratically – he needed Johnny for another three or perhaps four days. 'The captain has decided to put up barricades at the four town gates. We have very little labour.'

'How do you mean "very little"? there are two thousand of us in the town.'

'I'd say Yes to that if there were half as many of us left to defend as took it.'

'I know.'

'So for the barricades we will need civilian labour to be provided by the young people. You will help to draw up the lists. Another couple of days then you will go back to the river.'

They were in the Social Club in a reading-room sunk in two armchairs the red *pelouche* of which *glowed agonisingly* in the low flame of the autarchic* candles. They had opposite them, half hidden by the shadow, a partisan, certainly asleep. Noise came from the billiard room along with puffs of smoke. Although there was now in

---

* Mussolini had pursued an economy policy of 'autarchy' – self-sufficiency – which became a shorthand for poor quality.

prospect a scarcity of tobacco after the great feast they made of the cigarettes dropped by the English.

'Everyone tells me I should go and look at the river,' said Pierre.

'It's terrible,' said Johnny but Pierre did not seem to be relieved. The partisan who had dropped off stirred as if in a nightmare. The bartender arrived with a tray with two glasses of astragalo* and a candle. Taking his drink, Pierre asked him if he was serving in the Club in Fascist times.

'Yes, sir. The last of them – the ones you chased away were poor things. But the earlier ones were bastards, tremendous bastards. I was scared out of my wits by them – even just bringing their orders. Sometimes I served them when they were talking about round-ups, how they killed and tortured you people.' His uniform was worn and crumpled, he had a mousy face. 'But I got some satisfaction out of it too. You see I learned my job in Montecarlo and then in Switzerland so I can't not be a democrat. One great satisfaction was when the radio announced the surrender of Finland last May.** They looked each other in the face and shook their heads without comment. And I went off behind the bar so as not to make rude gestures in front of them. But I made plenty of them behind the bar.'

Then Pierre said to Johnny that a check of the ammunition had given them not more than five hours of heavy firing.

'Lampus,' said Johnny, 'can Lampus who is the recipient and repository of the supplies the English drop not supply us?'

'Marini says that Lampus is afraid that he won't have enough left afterwards.'

'Ah, afterwards. And the English can't oblige us?'

'Apparently they have their own difficulties. Not to mention the atmospheric conditions.'

The unknown man awoke, stretched himself bringing his face and hands into the half-light. His hands were plump and very pale, his face round and unhealthy, bearing the stamp of a precocious moral corruption which was already incarnate in him. 'Ah, is that so?' he said to the two with a colded voice. He got up – a strange, repellent

---

* A species of leguminous plant, one variety of which was used as a substitute for coffee.

** Finland had been fighting against the Soviet Union on the side of Nazi Germany. It concluded a separate peace.

figure, with a simple roomy blouse on his narrow chest and at the other end very tight leather trousers on his thick thighs. 'Ah, is that the case? Then I'm off to enjoy the delights of the town. Can you show me where the brothel is?'

'Get the bartender to tell you,' hissed Pierre.

The next day something was certainly hatching. Coming into the headquarters Johnny saw the two official cars of Lampus and Nord carefully sheltering under the portico with around them an abundance of bodyguards, all splendidly equipped and armed, who looked with repugnance at the swamp the rain had made of the courtyard. The rain had slackened out of pure physical necessity and the sky began to look like the sky again after day upon day of *distortion* caused by birth-pangs. Johnny looked away from the guards and turned his eyes on to the wrinkled *routinier* who had got up on the wrong side of the bed.

'What's happening? Where's Pierre?'

The *routinier* was slightly more courteous than usual perhaps feeling close to Johnny because of shared repugnance at the bodyguards. 'The Fascists have asked to parley. The priests are right in there naturally. Pierre is there but he's absolutely invisible. He's in there with Lampus and Nord and the top brass and the Vicar General of the diocese.'

Johnny rushed through a succession of headquarters rooms where the attachés were sitting, idle and anxious, as if no work was worth doing given the uncertainty whether the request would be accepted or rejected. No sound came from the sanctum of the headquarters. Johnny sat down and waited like all the others, enjoying the empty comfort of blissful ignorance.

The commanders came out half an hour later, relaxed and smiling, surrounding the Vicar General who seemed the most pleased and optimistic of all. 'If we priests have – as I firmly believe we have –' said the prelate in his robust and cordial voice, 'to represent the population, I am and will be witness to the reasonableness and thoughtfulness of this headquarters concerning the fate of our dear town.'

Lampus was massive and feline as always, supremely elegant and martial as always, exquiste as always, the career officer *par excellence*, the commander of a group of divisions who addressed the smallest of the boy-orderlies with studied politeness. 'I am certainly not,' he said, 'the kind of fanatic who rejects a parley but certainly ours is not to be dismissed.' Then he produced a metal box of fifty Craven. 'May I take the liberty, monsignor? for your guests and visitors naturally.'

The Vicar waved a hand to say a no, so short and abrupt, that everyone thought it had been a gaffe by Lampus. But the priest hastened to say: 'Haven't you any cigars instead? For my own use and consumption?' Everyone laughed politely while Lampus apologised exquisitely for not having cigars.

Johnny has withdrawn into the glass-covered entrance hall lying in wait for Pierre. And it was him that Pierre was looking for in the confusion of the various bodyguards. The meeting would take place that very afternoon, naturally on this side of the river, the Fascists would have to run the risk and accept the implicit inferiority in crossing the river. 'You will be one of the party,' he said. 'Nord has ordered me to choose men with some presence, who can put on a show.' 'What's the use?' said Johnny. 'We'll arrive at the place like so many mud statues.'

Pierre went off to shave and Johnny and the guards waited in silence looking with blasphemous eyes at the sky which was reinforcing the rain. This is what being a partisan was all about – to sit, mostly on the earth or a stone, to smoke (if you had any), then to see a few Fascists, to get up without brushing one's backside and make a move to kill or be killed, to inflict or receive a grave that was half-revered, half-loved. The rain was falling with an overpowering continuity, as concrete as something to build with. Pierre came back shaved and along with him the Vicar General with mountain boots and his robe carefully rolled back.

The Vicar got into the second car with Lampus and Nord, the latter wearing the same striking uniform as for his triumphal entry into the town. Johnny found a place in the last car with Pierre, Captain Marini's adjutant and the Communist commissar attached to the headquarters. Each vehicle had clusters of men on its mudguards. So they left the town which was at the heart of the question.

They were going to climb halfway up the slope then they would take a country road to the river as the Barbaresco ferry. At every bend in the hill (the drivers were driving in a restrained way) the town appeared in its entirety but fully given the multiple films of rain between it and the hills. To Johnny's eyes it had not a stony but a fleshy substance, extremely alive and wriggling like a huge cornered animal which thrust out its inadequate but still firm paws against a yellowish flood of danger and death. All the rest was an expanse of incredibly swollen but compact sheets of water which all of a sudden were suddenly transformed into enormous whirlpools while on the farthest shore the flood buried the countryside under a foul yellowish sauce on which, because of an optical illusion, the groves of poplars seemed to float like enormous rafts made up of huge numbers of trees. Everyone looked in that direction and the Communist commissar, a surly and taciturn man, said ironically: 'I'd really like to see them try to cross. Forget about a division – I'd just like to see the boat with the flag of truce cross.' And everyone laughed nervously at the prospect of seeing a whole boatload of big Fascist bosses drown.

The cortège of vehicles halted halfway up the hill where the road to the summit forked towards one of the paths running down to the river at the entrance to which there stood a line of partisans headed by Ettore. They were muddied from head to foot and when they came to attention for the new arrivals they splashed mud for metres. With the bodyguards ahead as path-finders they began to walk down splashing, the mud they whipped up quickly spattering everyone's uniforms like an agile leprosy – in particular the Vicar's habit and Nord's uniform of black rubber. From the farmhouses high upon the hill or deep down in the valleys the peasants watched that stumbling but majestic pilgrimage from their doors or from under the archways. One could already hear the roar of the river even through the downpour of rain, two bodyguards went back to support the Vicar by the elbows, Ettore fell, Pierre fell twice in a row literally disfiguring himself.

From where they halted at the farmhouse designated to receive those taking part in the parley the river was partially visible and it seemed as if the partial nature of the sight made it even more tremendous. The commanders went into the farmhouse, the body-guards, Johnny and Ettore spread out on the bank or at the tip of the promontories keeping their eyes and ears fixed on the other bank which was battered by the mud and blackened by the rain. The river was swollen to the point where it came within a hair's breadth of its highest and steepest banks but with a marvellous compactness and smoothness like that of molten ore, the heavy rain sinking without eddies into its polished metallic surface like the souls of the new-born in limbo. Every so often in the haunting setting with nothing but the noise of water the cry of some bird robbed of its nest, driven mad by the rain.

Every so often an officer from 1st Division – once it was Pierre – came out of the farmhouse to ask if nothing was yet to be seen or heard.

Johnny lowered himself to Ettore's precipitous look-out and they were the first to see them. From a backwater a broad flat-bottomed boat emerged rowing with derisory ease and sureness across the over-swollen waters. In the middle there was a tight blob of black and grey-green between the two poles of the two powerful rowers. Johnny and Ettore *gaped* at this ironical sort of dress rehearsal while the bodyguards went down to the presumed point of disembarkment.

The Fascist officers got out and immediately sank in the mud up to their knees especially a particularly obese one who had already attracted the grimaces and sarcastic remarks of the bodyguards. The drier officers were already busy enough freeing themselves so that the fat man held out his hands to the partisan guards. They formed a chain and pulled him roughly out of the clutches of the mud uttering liberal comments about their effort about the officer's fat and the abundance of his diet.

They were all on firm earth. They scattered around them the widest of smiles and the most cordial of thanks, noted with heavy *humour* their massive accumulations of mud, then they offered German cigarettes. At length they regrouped, taking as their pole of attraction the most good-looking of their number, fortyish, raven black, Sardinian-looking, who tried to dissimulate his contempt for the partisans no less than for his companions. Pierre appeared at the door of the farmhouse and showed them in.

'Well,' said Ettore, 'I'm glad to have looked them in the face. After all getting to know people personally is always a critical point. Well, I am managing to hate them.' There was nothing left but to withdraw under the gateway for the rain was continuing ferociously and the sight of the river was now sickening. The gateway was narrow and packed with antipathetic bodyguards, the last available spot was the actual gutter of the entrance with all the stinks of the confined space raised to a pitch by the great damp. An hour passed, flesh revolted at the harmful damp and disgusting smells. Sometimes they seemed to hear through the wall agitated voices and then absurd comments and inferences ran through the gloomy porch.

Half an hour later it was all over. Pierre was the first to come out to prepare their passage and he was black in the face. Johnny and Ettore accompanied him to the riverside to warn the rowers to have the boat ready. 'We'll let them have it,' whispered Pierre. Said Johnny: 'It's better that way. It must have been a comedy of reticences. Us keeping quiet about having ammunition for five hours, them keeping quiet about the fact that to take a town by force is a nasty business. What right, for example, does that dirty fat pig have to the town?'

The Fascist officers re-embarked somewhat riskily. They were not smiling but their faces were not particularly tense either; the result of the discussion had been taken for granted. The most vigorous of them sat down last, then he turned to the bank in general and Pierre in particular. He said clearly: 'We'll meet again on the field of battle.' 'Most certainly,' Pierre replied quietly for everybody.

The rowers pushed and left the bank. 'Let's wait,' said Ettore. 'There's every chance that they'll shipwreck.' But it did not happen, the boat crossed over again ironically as it had come and ten minutes later, the Fascists having disappeared into the poplar grove, a dozen motors were heard starting up on the main road.

They climbed up again to the road. *Sweeping* rumours had certainly astonished the neighbourhood so that in spite of the mud the peasants lined up along the road, paying particular homage to the Vicar among all those armed men so that for Johnny the scene took on a taste of the old medieval order of things . . .

The road was streaming with rain, the cars dripped enormously, in the plain the disputed town seemed to have dissolved, to be lower and flatter, as if its foundations were slowly giving way to the erosion of the flood. The indifference which might have been born of *routine* vanished suddenly and in that setting of mud the town was once more as precious as on the first day of the occupation.

Next day Johnny left the headquarters to return to the little *marooned* island of the farmhouse called Gambadilegno. In the morning while the rain beat so proudly on the windows of his office he had seen the bodyguards trampling in the mud in the courtyard waiting for the detail for the aqueduct to escort them by truck to open the cocks and so make the flood more complete. Later still from that window he had seen the sappers leave under the command of Franco to lay the last mines.

He left. The town seemed to be absent from itself, the traffic and the coming and going minimum, the shops open but no less inaccessible. Johnny tried a well-known door in order to stock up with black market cigarettes.

'Don't you know what happened to me?' asked the black marketeer, an old bald man, helpless and sly, almost in tears. 'I was robbed of my cigarettes. Robbed, pardon the expression, since it was your comrades. One evening a partisan arrives, takes some and pays, ditto the next evening, but he advises me to stock up as much as possible because next evening he would bring me, he says, any number of buyers. I restock mostly from my little capital – very anxious as you know to please the partisans – well they arrive punctually, four of them take all the tobacco without paying me, giving the alternative of being arrested because, they say, the black market is just as much a crime for us as for the Fascists.' He sobbed. 'You know I deal in the black market from pure necessity. Either the black market or I starve to death. I am a violinist but these days there's no more demand for violinists. I don't want to go to the headquarters. It was a blow but never mind. Try someone in the café. Not the bartender – the waiter.'

Johnny tried and came away with his demands met by the young, lively waiter who could turn his hand to anything. Ten packets of Nazionali and the waiter was so pleased at the importance of the deal and the promptness of the payment that he felt he could not get enough information about Johnny's job and destination. 'On the banks. Bad – very bad.' 'Not at all,' said Johnny curtly and was off to the banks with ten packets of cigarettes, the Sten and three and a half magazines.

Out of town the soaking wetness of the countryside was incredible; the gelatinous earth could no longer hold up a man or even the simple weight of a machine-gun tripod. The river made a noise louder than the pouring rain; it was very wide, swollen and gorged like a wild animal after swallowing its prey and yet it seemed to have lost as much in virulence as it had gained in muddy hyptertension. To Johnny's left the hills were already blotted out by multiple curtains of rain scarcely tinted by the shadows of the heights, while to his right the so much lower hills beyond the river seemed nearer and looming more than was natural over the flooded plain: those low hills of the other bank on which the Fascist guns were already *brooding*, aimed at the heart of the rebel town.

Nothing human was to be seen on the ground: the partisan patrols, if there were any, swam about blindly in the riverine mists, the peasants were bottled up in their byres tied down by time and mysterious apprehension. Some dog barked but the sound came across muffled.

Johnny reached or rather waded to Gambadilengo in the evening amid the thunder of the river and the wavelike motion of the mists. The animals were lowing in the byres, the men, still invisible, were coughing inside.

'Thank goodness,' said the housewife, her face worn with the depressing weather. Johnny at once asked how the lads had behaved.

'They are lads, logically,' said she shrugging, 'but they really ought not to have done what they did to my poor husband.'

'Did they lay hands on him?' asked Johnny freezing.

'Oh no, no that. But the ones that sleep in the hayloft have pissed all over the forage out of sheer laziness and incompetence. So half the hay was fermented and we've had a severe loss. They are lads naturally. But every day your sergeant has had to use his hands and I assure you he has a hard and heavy hand.'

He went out. Michele materialised as he turned the corner of the house. He seemed to have aged and when he spoke exhaustion had given him the beginning of a stammer. He coughed a lot, spitting, shutting his eyes each time because of the violence of the expectoration. He was wearing the waterproof jacket provided by Pierre – being of inferior material it had turned under the interminable rain into something like a box of soaking but solid cardboard. There had been nothing else, said Michele, but mounting guard and getting wet – but too much mounting guard and too much rain. And the men . . . Well, he didn't feel like blaming them any more . . . Someone else was to blame, he added.

Johnny understood and said hurriedly: 'I was under orders. I longed to come back here but they kept me on. I had a very bad time at headquarters.'

They were sitting on stones which were dry and sheltered, but their feet sank in the mud. Michele drummed with his fingers on his jacket which gave off a wooden sound. 'I am the only one left who wears it. The lads soon threw theirs into the river. But I am one of the old school and it seemed to me . . . Have you noticed my cough, Johnny? Listen to it – that cough. Every time I cough and I cough every thirty seconds, my eyes shut tight and in the dark inside them I see artificial lights. We have no change of clothes, we get soaked to the skin and we dry ourselves to the skin. We'll all end up consumptive.'

'It's almost over, Michele. As it was bound to – the parley failed . . .'

'Was there a parley?' asked the sergeant casually.

'Yes, yesterday, downriver but it came to nothing so the Fascists will attack in strength. One of these days.'

'I wish it would be tomorrow. But I wish there was a little bit of sun overhead when we are fighting, for Christ's sake.'

The battle was not next day but next day there was a little bit of sun. Immediately after midday it made a timid but triumphal appearance in the still amorphous sky while simultaneously the rain drizzled. This miserable state of affairs was enough to give the men back some poise – they laughed, sang, stretched their spirits and their bodies. There was heavy traffic on the main road – a whole succession, clean cut in the clarified air, of trucks, vans and motorcycles. All that was a serious preparation for the impending engagement but it ended up by being cheering and comforting. The men who were off duty went with the sergeant to the main road as if to a fair while Johnny stopped to watch Frankie's men bury the last mines in a stretch of mud and gravel on the left of Johnny's sector. All the sappers handled those black toys but only one placed and covered them with slow tenderness. When he had finished he set up at the end of the stretch a notice with written on it: 'Hands off' as a transparent warning to the partisans. Then Johnny felt free to join the others on the thronged, extraordinarily resonant road.

He made his way towards where the sergeant directed him with a great deal of hand-waving and found himself alongside a truck loaded with men, weapons and ammunition. The weapons were rare and precious mortars, the men the Venetian Alpini who had deserted in May. The miraculous spell of sunshine continued and even the drizzle was pleasant with its gentle, sporadic slaps. It was pleasant too to feel under one's feet the solid road after some much of soaking fields and meadows.

A hundred or so Blues with a few Reds mingling with them, surrounded the truck enjoying the sun, the firm earth and the spectacle of the unloading. At a certain moment the pulse – rather bumbling and peaceful – of a plane reached them from the dilated sky. Then the two insects came into view disturbing the centre of the sky and aiming at the town. But the sirens were silent and they pulled up – one darted towards the north and the other came along the main road at two hundred metres as if for a joyous friendly inspection. It was certainly an Allied plane and the men waved in greeting.

The plane dived and machine-gunned the men and the truck with catastrophic suddeness. His ears deafened by human cries, the howl of the engine and the burst of fire, Johnny dived into the ditch and a man followed him *crashingly*. As the noise of the roar of the plane went into the distance he could make out the sly crackle of a fire. Johnny lifted his face from the mud, clambered out waist-high and saw the plane swoop over the hills and take aim for the second pass.

'*Idiot and pig!*' he shouted and buried his face in the mud once more. He felt enormous, huge and naked, more tender than a new-born babe, the ditch not a shelter but a conduit for the unfailing burst of machine-gun fire. The brief initial burst scraped the road, then the second struck tremendously at the metal and wood of the truck which staggered like a bear under the impact. Then the plane disappeared.

The men came to life again on the street, astonished at first, then cursing.

One hazarded the guess that it had been a German plane. They almost lynched him.

'What planes do the Germans still have?'

'It's a bloody Ally. An English one, I bet.'

'Only the English are such shits, the Americans much less.'

'They play these tricks too often and we have had enough of them.'

'Calm down, lads,' shouted an officer of 1st Division. 'Calm down, I am off to report to headquarters.'

'How the Fascists would laugh!'

Then they found the dead man – at the moment of the attack one of the Alpini was standing on the truck unloading. At that moment the boxes of ammunition began to leap and explode on the truck which was flickering sparsely with flames. They carried the dead man some distance away and turned him on his back which was horribly holed by two rounds from the machine-gun, the rags of his blue shirt nailed to the lips of the crater-like wounds.

The ammunition was exploding mechanically with slow but punctual sympathy setting in motion a *ghastly* metronome in that *ghastly* suspended moment. On the main road the headquarters cars whistled as they arrived to find what had happened. The peasants, who had reappeared, ranged themselves on the edges of their fields, shaking their heavy clumsy heads. The rain started again.

XXI

Next day – 1 November – was a day without rain but with a wind with an edge to it that was already wintry. The men, still soaking wet, could not bear the new cruelty of the wind and almost all of them went back into the stables they had left. Very few stayed outside on the bank of the river or as much of it as the mistiness of the day allowed one to see, so that to Johnny the bank looked bare and abandoned as if the battle had already been fought and the two armies destroyed, pulverised by their very hatred.

Going over to the main road he saw more clearly every detail of the three big villas spread out on the hill opposite: 20 mm machine-guns thrust their stumpy barrels from the ogives of the little turrets and on the lawns one could see a movement of men but scanty and numbed by the cold.

Then the wind fell and all the men came into the open and it was at the moment when they were almost fully assembled that there arrived from the town, by all possible means, the announcement and confirmation of the general Fascist attack next day. They were doing things seriously, it was learned, with an abundance of men and materials, with generals in command etc. The only uncertainty concerned, obviously, their crossing point.

'Right, it's exactly what everyone wanted,' said Johnny to his men but now they seemed to enjoy the certainty considerably less than they had previously poured scorn on the useless, stinking time of waiting. 'Tomorrow is 2 November,' one boy said out loud as if to himself. 'It is the day of the dead, tomorrow.'*

Michele climbed up on to a higher point of the bank, considered

---

* Ognisanti – All Saints' Day or Hallowmass.

the river and the opposite bank carefully, then came down again saying with heavy irony that in spite of the way it looked and its hypertension the river now looked as gentle as a lamb. On the main road the traffic continued: motorised dispatch riders darted in all directions carrying and confirming news until the men in the front line became irritated by them and invited them to go back to the safety of headquarters and to spare them news heard over and over again. The men were beginning to pay for the high state of intoxication of 10 October with a strong tremor and funereal reflections.

In the afternoon – a dull but not raw afternoon – all the men assigned to the southern defence collected on the immense courtyard of the farmhouse at San Casciano, located in the centre of the partisan positions. They collected and counted themselves and found they were not more than two hundred. Then they exclaimed: 'How come? Three thousand of us took the town. Will there be two hundred of us to defend it? Where are the other two thousand eight hundred?' and they were not placated by an officer from head-quarters who assured them that hundreds of partisans were gathered in the town as a mass of manoeuvre and hundreds more were in positions lower down the river. The man next to Johnny – over thirty and with sad eyes and a hoarse voice – shrugged his shoulders, said they would be beaten just the same.

'Us or them?' a boy inquired of Johnny.

'Us,' the man made clear.

Johnny wandered about the courtyard in a state of bizarre satisfaction, the pleasant energy he rediscovered in himself when-ever the others were drifting in distrust and depression. He walked the whole length of the farmhouse, which was huge and had about it some of the antiquity, the imposing character and functionality of the ancient rural buildings of the Cistercians. Then he went back to his teenagers: like good lads they had put everything behind them and forgotten it and now were watching intently and excitedly target practice by a couple of Polish deserters from 1st Division, formidable marksmen even if both were remarkably drunk. The target practice over they were still excited and lively – indeed they seemed to be exultant now at being only two hundred and began to joke and *badiner* pitilessly about the next day being the day of the dead. In the end they came together in a general, powerful chorus of extreme gaiety and defiance.

The officers were invited in, the proprietor of the farmhouse having a weakness for officers. On a chain a large cauldron of hot wine was hanging with a ladle to draw from it. The proprietor had a certain air that could not be dissimulated of a *star receptioning* the losing side. The person who preceded Johnny in the queue for the cauldron was an officer of perhaps forty, tall and strong with a foreign face. 'Captain Asther,' one of his companions from 1st Division asked him, 'what will your German brothers do to you tomorrow?' Asther – a German therefore with a massive head and a retreating profile – smiled and with the help of the ladle very summarily mimed a throat being cut. But no one believed that the Germans would take part in the business next day: they would at most intervene in the event of an enormous rout of the Fascists, which it seemed could legitimately be excluded.

When he had drunk Johnny went to a little horizontal window cut in the naked wall and through it saw the shadows of the town walls in the low dancing mists, the towers and belfries were disappearing in the ashen sky. He had never realised until that moment how attached he was to the city and how little he could do for it. Behind him he had the buzz of the officers' anodyne conversation, outside the men were continuing their chorus with a piercing effect, their mouths wide open to the spectral sky.

He turned to a group of officers of 1st Division grouped round the cauldron, which was now drained but still gave off a pleasant smell and heat. One of them was complaining about something with a drawing-room air. He was an odd man, young but half bald, about twenty-five, clumsily wrapped in an English uniform which he could wear with distinction. His voice was heavily colded.

'All my handkerchiefs are finished. Believe me, handkerchiefs have represented the greatest problem of my partisan existence. Someone who gets one cold after another like me. Oh, the battle for the town will find me in my worst form. My only handkerchief is filthy and I have a cold that is killing me. How can I be expected to fight like a lion for the town tomorrow?' A general slight smile of understanding and justification broke out. And yet it seemed to Johnny that the man had a basic seriousness, a melancholy determination glowing in the depths of his lively, intelligent eyes. And he continued frivolously:

'I confess I'd like to be in my brother's place. My brother has been a genius. Not like me who am waiting here to fall dead tomorrow in my blood and the mud of the flood-water . . . and my brother warm and safe in a Swiss sanatorium – a first-class one too.'

Someone started to condole with him for his unfortunate brother but he went on quickly: 'For goodness' sake, don't be sorry for my brother. He's a big lad, a real athlete, with splendid lungs. But right after 8 September he said to me: "Giorgio, let's be honest, let's make intelligent use of papa's money. Here things such as people have never seen are going to happen and at the end not many will be left to tell the tale. Let's both go off to Switzerland while there's time and shut ourselves up in a nice sanatorium. We'll stay there till the end, a matter of months, lying in deckchairs and taking walks until everything is over in Italy and occasionally laying traps for the nurses." Well, I couldn't make up my mind but my brother could. And now allow me to envy him with all the energy my cold leaves me.'

He sniffed, making much of the gesture, and continued: 'You all have an idea of our present situation. Well, allow me to sketch for you his present situation up there in Switzerland. I had word of him to begin with and am in a position to put you in the picture. He has a whole apartment to himself, cut off from the outside and the cold by a window, which is very thin and very pure, absolutely unbreakable, armoured. In his dressing-gown in an armchair he reads all the most exciting and ferocious war stories which are for sale in the pacific Swiss bookshops. When he stops he watches through the window the spectacle we are forbidden and have forgotten, of the little Swiss towns down in the valley, all lit up with clusters of lights.'

'Helvetia felix!' sighed an office of 1st Division, very blond and draped in a naval cape.

Giorgio got up, attracting all the remaining light on to his precocious baldness. 'A kingdom for a handkerchief – even a used one,' he cried with a blocked nose. As no one made an offer he untied his blue scarf, his unit and battle badge, with a sigh and blew his nose on it.

At the farmhouse the housewife had prepared a special supper –

she too seemed unable to conceal her conviction of being a star preparing a meal for them for the last time. 'Signor Johnny,' she said, 'what will I do tomorrow when you are fighting all round here? how will I take shelter from the bullets?'

'Stay calmly in the stable, sitting in a corner, with doors and windows bolted.'

'Keep quiet and comfortable in the warmth of the beasts,' said Michele.

'Yes, and I shall pray for you all the time.'

'Many thanks.'

Pierre arrive at Gambadilegno in the precipitous dusk in a sidecar. He had been assigned to the northern defences between the railway tunnel and the ferry at Barbaresco, so they would be separated tomorrow. Johnny shook his head. 'It's here they will attack, that they will cross. I feel it.'

Pierre said: 'That's odd – everyone feels they will cross where we are.'

They went into the house and Pierre addressed the men with a flat series of facts and figures and dates. More particularly he announced that citizens with degrees in medicine, surgery and pharmacy had voluntarily set up a medical service, the wounded would be sheltered by the massive and relatively near walls of the cemetery. This was a nasty shock however necessary. The partisan lads were often amazingly ready for immediate risks, for instant death or wounds or mutilation, but most drew back when faced by the arrangements, the programming of all these horrendous things.

Outside in the black night Pierre's sidecar had to be dug out with the aid of the electric torch, Johnny watched him mount the bike then said: 'In the best of cases we'll see each other tomorrow night on the hills.' Pierre wriggled on the saddle and then – perhaps allegorically – turned on the headlight, 'We are pessimists, all of us, too pessimistic, so tired that – you'll see – things will go very well.' And so as to confirm his faith he dashed off without a farewell.

Johnny lingered a little in the courtyard although it had started to rain again, normal rain, but a rain that promised duration and constancy. Michele came out, stared with repugnance at the formless sky and for tomorrow foresaw cold rain and fermenting mud.

The men had crowded the stable stealing space from the passive beasts. They seemed relieved, heedlessly they were playing a game that involved slapping each other's hands. Michele joined in the game.

At the detonation of the slaps the housewife began to weep in a subdued way.

There was nothing particular wrong with her – she merely felt the absence of her husband and sons whom she had sent off into the safe hills far from the Fascists who were going to come. And then she could not stop thinking that tomorrow was the day of the dead. 'And this terrible rain that falls like a punishment from God,' she said, raising her chin towards the roof which was whipped by the rain.

The lads were still playing their game but it was clear that they had had enough and were carrying on from sheer lack of an alternative and so as not to fall prey to thoughtful stillness. Then Johnny signalled the *overdue* end of the game and sent them all to sleep except for the first round of the double guard on the bank.

The housewife came close to his ear. 'Wouldn't you like to sleep in my sons' bed?'

'No thank you.'

'Not even this last night?' she added unwittingly.

'No, signora, thanks all the same. I shall sleep very well in the manger as usual.'

'Have you never had a chance to sleep in a bed?'

'Yes, sometimes – but I didn't want to get the habit again. Afterwards it's too hard.' The sergeant came up with his bony hands reddened by the game. Johnny told him to go and lie down but the other refused absolutely. He didn't feel like shutting his eyes and besides he didn't trust the guard: would Johnny take a bet that more than one of them would go to sleep on duty?

'You think you'll be able to sleep, Johnny?'

'Yes, I do.'

'Lucky you. All right off you go.'

'I'm off. Wake me at four.'

He went to the manger and began to undress, that is to say taking off his jacket and boots and loosening a fastening here and there. Then he moved away the heavy muzzles of the beasts and rolled into the manger pulling the fodder up to his neck. He turned with his face to the wall to get away from the breath and licking of the beasts. His head was completely empty, he was merely enjoying that damp warmth and the freeing of his ankles from the sawing weight of his boots. The darkness was absolute, square, something marine in the breathing of the oxen and increasingly *sleepily* he listened to the noises: the scratch of a match, the full roar of the river, the drumming – now so pleasant – of the rain on the roof and outside the hoarse voices of Michele and the sentries. He had time to think, very precariously, of how used he had got to Gambadilegno and how uncomfortable he felt at the thought of leaving it. Sedentary life – as a partisan? he could still feel – already in the well of narcosis – the wide, rough, extremely hot way the oxen licked his abandoned arm.

Michele shook him and Johnny was conscious of heavy rain beating down before he was of the imminence and inevitability of the battle. He looked down at his wrist and read half past four.

'Your watch is keeping very good time, Johnny. It was me that decided to wake you half an hour later. What's the use? I have a distinct feeling that they won't come. Do they have to come just because we are waiting for them and we have been told to wait for them? They won't come, Johnny. Everything tells me so – the river, the banks and the air.'

The night had not added a wrinkle to the thousands on his face but the sergeant's voice was sinking into the abyss of muteness.

The mistress of the house, already up and about, wrapped in her dressing-gown of darned wool, was absolutely determined that they should take a spoonful of honey melted in a glass of warm water. It helped, fighting and defeating that rough, corrugated rusty feeling of total inner emptiness. But now the old woman was weeping and wringing her hands. She had held out, held out, but now she was giving in. They made her put on an overcoat, they wrapped her in shawls, they made her sit in the most comfortable shielded spot in the stable among her affectionate animals. And Michele flooded her with assurances and oaths that today there would be no battle, it was all nonsense, nonsense and bad dreams, and today would be the quietest and most boring day of the year. But the old woman noticed that the dogs were barking in a way she didn't like, the two men said it was because of their men all being awake and moving about.

'No – the dogs are barking in a special way.'

They went out under the heavy rain amid their men who were

nervous but in good heart, staring into the countryside which was still indecipherable. They went to their mole and took up their positions there. What could be seen was ten steps away and in these ten steps were the livid waters and the even more livid shore. Johnny looked back at the hills – from the chaos of night the turrets with the machine-guns were emerging whitishly but the courtyards seemed deserted and bewitched. The men shivered, the water as it became clearer had an icy breath, the men shifted their feet in the grip of the mud. Then the opposite shore came into the light shamefast, virginal in its morning wildness, seeming not only not to include men but actually to exclude the idea of their arrival.

In spite of his loss of voice Michele said there would be no battle, the men argued pro and contra and soon were betting hard, cigarettes, their next pay or else ammunition. Meanwhile Johnny looked towards the town: it was waking from its morning mists, rising up only with the gables of its building and seeming to have no foundation, fabulous.

Five struck in the belfry as they emerged and at the fifth stroke a great din broke out.

'You've lost, sergeant,' said Johnny coldly and Michele nodded with a mute little smile.

The machine-gun in the first villa was already at work with a very low elevation and Johnny opened his eyes wide because it was aiming at this bank. So they had crossed already, secretly and without hindrance. From the town the sirens howled frantically.

The machine-gun fired a very long burst and more and more *slanting*. Its tracer bullets ploughed furrows in the curtains of cast-iron rain and plunged into the wooded cover packed with Fascists. They were now replying with mortar fire, steady, orderly and patient fire, which fell on the hill with the first villa raising on it one step after another of *crash*, smoke and dust. In the heavy rain which diminished everything, blotted it out.

Johnny felt fine as always in the din and complexity of battle. He was only burning with impatience at being tied down on this useless, stupid, absolutely vacant bank when it was only too obvious that the Fascists were attacking from the landward side – from the direction of the highway. But he had to stick to his orders and await a counter-order, which would arrive who knew when and how given the impassable state of the fields and the absurd partisan faith in individual initiative and fantasy. Two hours passed thus in empty and exciting theatre-*seeing* among the machine-guns and mortars and their great noise which seemed to have nothing to do with anyone else. The agonising wait was meagrely compensated for by the absolutely unforgettable capture of the Fascist boat which had lost its way, which came sailing down the swollen river to land by chance on the bank which bristled with rocks and briars and rifles. On board an officer and a soldier. The boat had obviously come adrift from the Fascist landing fleet because of the violence of the water or the clumsiness of the men. The two got out with their hands already raised and by shouts Johnny guided them so that they did not fall into the minefield. The men stripped them of pistol and rifle but did nothing else to them. The officer was very young with a general look of a badly fed, argumentative bureaucrat who had, against nature, put on battle dress. He had had enough of the river and would soon have had enough of the battle had the river not tricked him. The moment he was on dry land and disarmed he looked uncomfortably at the exchange of fire between the villa and the riverbank and said in a Southern accent:

'You are the officer in command. I see you are taking due notice of my misfortune, I wish you to know that on our side we have orders not to touch a hair on the heads of partisan prisoners.'

'You will have some,' said Johnny and detached a man to escort them to the rear with orders not even to touch them with fists or feet.

The machine-gun in the first villa was still firing bursts but now they were short and had pauses in between, as if from overwork or economy, while the Fascists were letting them have it with their mortars as before. The last bomb had exploded in the middle of the courtyard. Suddenly the machine-gun let off a last, interminable, frantic burst of fire, aimed so low as to fall on the slopes of its own hill, then it fell silent for ever.

'We won't stay here a minute longer,' said Johnny, wiping the streaming water from his face. 'The banks aren't important any more. It's all going on up on the main road. Michele, we'll collect the men and the weapons and move at right angles to the road.' But at that moment a runner appeared from the high walls of the farmhouse at San Casciano, making his way through the mud that was a foot deep and the moment he was within hailing distance shouted the orders which Johnny was carrying out on his own.

It was a very slow, painful move across fields which seemed to have no end, in the entrapping mud, under a furious rain, in which the weapons rusted visibly, the men suffering under the weight of the ammunition boxes. Michele, loaded with the Browning machine-gun, urged them on from behind with the hoarse shouts of a horse-dealer. The machine-gun in the second villa was already powerfully pumping fire down on to the countryside, which was lined with groves of poplars, and volleys of rifle fire were being returned from the first lines to come under attack. Now both sides added mortar fire but somewhat parsimoniously. It seemed as if the trilling sound of a whistle was flying about but it could be a mistake on the part of Johnny's *strained* sense of hearing. They arrived out of breath, with kilos more mud, at the immense courtyard of San Casciano, which although deformed by the mud seemed like a celestial port of call.

Johnny went to the porch to knock the mud off his boots against a pillar and then he caught sight of a partisan, an older man, *chieftain-like*, with eyes sunken in his greyish skin, who was passing like a monk through the twilight, conventual porch. He raised his wrist from his soaking cape, read the time and said to himself: 'Half past eight. It will be a miracle if we hold them up till nine.' Johnny asked him for instructions and with a gesture the other indicated the central turret.

He entered and stopped at the foot of a metal corkscrew staircase. Three officers were standing on the three levels all with their field glasses, all in a navy-blue cloaks. The officer on the second floor was the half-bald one with the brother in a sanatorium in Switzerland. Given the height of the tower and the flooding in the plains in front everything had the air of a naval battle seen from the bridge.

'It's the man with the teenagers,' said the officer on the highest floor in a friendly way, the blond who had said Helvetia felix. 'What weapons have you?'

'A Browning and twenty rifles.'

'Who has the Browning?'

'A first-class long-service soldier.'

'Good. How many rounds has the Browning?'

'Fifteen hundred.'

'Excellent. Take up position on the right along the irrigation canal.'
Johnny turned to go out and the bald one said at his back: 'You don't
have any illusions, do you? They are breaking through as they like.'

They got into the irrigation canal and Michele sited himself with
the machine-gun at a join in the cement. The knee-high watery mud
was freezing and the immediate coughing of the men exploded like
shots. But cheered, fortified by the din of battle fusing around them
they *rose excellently to trenchership* and gazed with the eyes of rapists
at the mysterious, feminine flat space in front of them. But where
were the Fascists? Now the second heavy machine-gun, its barrel
coming lower and lower, fired bursts unsparingly, the rifle fire was
total and the Fascist mortars were working at full pitch. The trills of
the whistle were now more easily heard and unmistakable. But the
countryside in front of Johnny remained virginal, sacred to Pan,
totemic. He turned round but did not manage to see the town, which
was caught between the vapours of the earth and the sky which was
growing lower and lower. Only the walls of the cemetery appeared at
the farthest edge of the earth, phantomlike. He gave a last glance at
the banks which had been abandoned to the river: it was flowing
along swollen, completely extraneous. The men were very busy
shifting their feet in the mud, someone was humming, others were
commenting on the battle which was proceeding without phen-
omenalising. From time to time Michele looked at him out of the
corner of his eye over the machine-gun emplacement, the rain found
a labyrinth on his wrinkled face and he constantly saw to the rain-
soaked belt of ammunition.

At half past nine the first partisan line broke and Johnny saw clearly
that the machine-gun in the second villa had been removed from the
ogive. The Fascists too had reduced their fire, a runner crawled
through the mud to warn them not to fire on the first men to come
into sight for they were the men from the first line retreating. But they
did not retreat in Johnny's direction, they appeared beyond San
Casciano and took off for their favourite hill. They were in a plaster of
mud and rain, symbiosed with their weapons by the mud, they
dragged themselves towards the slopes of the hill, roller-skating
madly in the treacherous mud, constantly slipping, falling, balancing.
The still invisible Fascists were taking aim at them but only

occasionally, and in fact they seemed more worried by the mud than by the rifle fire.

Then a sacred silence fell and lasted as if the very Fascists had abandoned the open country and sought shelter against the anger of the rain. But the machine-gun in the third villa, exactly in line with Johnny, was taking aim, slowly and calmly, and from the angle of the barrel Johnny calculated that the first Fascists were five hundred metres away. The mortar crews on the left and to the rear of Johnny were getting their tubes ready and the ammunition boxes laid out around them were few indeed. From the central turret of San Casciano nothing – only a silence that seemed to come from a megaphone – and that for quarter of an hour. The lads strained eyes and ears, in vain, towards the dripping greenery until one of the youngest turned round anxiously. Johnny asked him brusquely what he was looking at.

'Nothing. But see if by any chance they are at our backs.'

'Do me a favour – look in front of you.'

At that moment the third machine-gun opened fire, suddenly heavy and accurate, at a frighteningly pronounced elevation, into the green curtains; it fired without excitement but with a kind of pompous dignity. And the mortars were firing too, in dribs and drabs, but Johnny saw nothing except their sparse explosions in the deep mud.

Until one of Johnny's adolescents went mad and fired a volley to the front at the height of no one's green knees and some others imitated him. Johnny did not have time to reprove and restrain them because from two hundred metres away the Fascists replied with a powerful, compact volley which skimmed Johnny's trench and flew past to splatter against the walls of the cemetery.

The whole line was on fire while on the Fascist front dozens of whistles trilled. And there they were, never seen in such numbers and never so well, all in abundant equipment with gleaming helmets, green as lizards, their dashes forward gravely imperilled but also exaggerated by their instability on the ground as they jumped. Michele let them have it with the Browning, the firing of all the others as nothing to it. The first Fascist officer upright and holding himself like a green bronze statue took enough for six men and fell. Immediately a single sharp whistle sounded and the Fascists withdrew clinging to the mud, withdrew to the curtains of green from which they returned the fire. The men had ducked their heads, more than one did not raise his again but Michele's Browning was enough to make them withdraw further and keep them there. Now they were no longer firing – but they had certainly passed the word to their mortars to intervene. They brought down heavy fire, not accurate enough to kill, not far enough off target to be dismissed. Meantime the partisan mortar crews had risen from their holes and were packing up their weapons calmly but irresistibly. They indicated that they had used up their rounds.

An hour passed like this, Michele working for everybody, most of the boys had wasted in half an hour the rounds saved up for months. A boy on the right called Johnny's attention, calmly, politely, then showed him a wound in his left arm; with great calm, almost with gratitude. Johnny signalled to him to go back and the boy left the ditch, crawled on all fours in the mud towards the banks; there he would get up and walk with ease to the cemetery.

The Fascists resumed with all their weapons and under the close, hot roof of fire another boy fell sitting in the mud and perhaps on his own ordure, with his back to the bank and to the Fascists, trembling with panic and stammering epileptically. Johnny hit him, those next to him shook him, but the boy no longer moved, he did not roll his eyes or emit a sound, all his centres were blocked by terror. Johnny and another took hold of him by his filthy garment and dropped him in the field behind and shouted to him to crawl away. But he remained like a transfixed firefly then he came to a little and began to swim away, millimetre by millimetre in the mud.

Johnny turned round, he began to fire with the boy's rifle at those flashes of green lacquer which were the Fascists. The third machine-gun had stopped firing, but the Fascists were not winning a metre, pinned down by the line of fire of the machine-guns.

He scratched the mud away from his watch and read ten past eleven and once more lost himself completely in the brevity and interminable nature of time in war. He could very well have begun to fire a moment ago having just started on a magazine or, equally well, have been firing since the beginning of the world using all the ammunition produced for him by all the other men. A boy came alongside him and spoke to him with his mouth almost in the mud:

'Take a look at Michele.'

He had spoken with such calm and lack of allusiveness that Johnny looked to his left almost absent-mindedly. The sergeant was lying face down with his head level with the tripod, the barrel of the Browning seemed to be drinking from the mud. A child could tell he was dead but to go and discover that fatal hole – that made Johnny freeze. He said to the boy with the news that he would follow him to take care of the machine-gun – not any particular boy up to now but now he was standing out because he had told him about Michele with that calm. He dived into the mud and swam towards Michele. He pulled him down into the ditch by the feet, turned him over, he was light and docile. He laid him out, holding him by one hand under his wood-like neck. The bullet had gone in at the forehead, above the left eye, a little clean hole, but enormous if you looked at it in the centre of the closed *sealedness* of the face. The spurting blood had, like the water, a difficult and varied course, blood and water fought with alternating success to turn his face red and then white again. Johnny leaned over him, cold and silent, feeling mutilated. From the walls of San Casciano there came the terrifying signal to withdraw. Panic seized the adolescents in the trench. Johnny shoved Michele's dead body by the feet into the cement tube so that his noblest part was sheltered from the verminous rain.

The third machine-gun had started to fire again, it was firing its last rounds to cover the withdrawal as much as possible, the youths were already crawling in the mud and did not stand up until the high walls of San Casciano, which seen from the ground seemed Babylonian. Johnny had loaded himself with the Browning and had to shout for someone to look after the ammunition. The Fascists' harassing fire was sporadic and inaccurate, it was a torture to reach the cover of the farmhouse which was mockingly near, out of breath because of the effort and the spasm at hearing the gasp of one of their number who had been hit. Behind Johnny the boys let two or three belts of ammunition fall. Round the corner of the house was a partisan, clad and shod in mud. Did Johnny see the big farmhouse on the top of the last crest before the town? That was the last line with abundant reinforcements, fresh men, intact weapons and mountains of ammunition. And the headquarters staff at full strength.

No crack of a passing bullet, no distant explosion – the countryside went back to being empty and bewitched under the magic power of the rain. During their withdrawal they met the men from San Casciano – they were withdrawing calmly, some with their hands in their pockets, all erect. They very blond officer came alongside Johnny for a moment, his cloak immaculate, armed only with a pistol, treading the mud with light feet as if it were a *plaything*.

'Your teenagers have had more than enough,' he said.

'Yes, the long-service soldier is dead. I don't see the bald one with the brother in Switzerland.'

'Dead. I left him behind in the turret. Did you like him too? A bullet through the window.'

They were pinned upright in the mud as some bullets, very few of them but malignant, buzzed among them on a trajectory between the hills and the banks. And one of Johnny's boys, shouting showed his two arms pierced by a single bullet. From the hills they redoubled their fire and everyone threw themselves face down in the mud. Had the Fascists already got ahead of them on the right and up ahead? Then a partisan's savage shout at the hills warned them that the ones who were firing were the partisans positioned on the hills who took them for the advancing Fascist forward troops. Another burst of curses and threats and the firing stopped, deeply mortified, and nothing was heard other than the sound of the falling rain.

The unit had reached the foot of the last slope and Johnny sighed at the agony it entailed; it was so plastered with fermenting mud that the whole surface pulsated. The seething clay had a very few, almost ironical clumps of soaking grass. Johnny began to scramble up on his knees, anchoring himself in the mud with his free hand; he scrambled up and fell back. So too did the men, their distress drawing from them curses and insults. With one downward slip they lost in a flash what had cost minutes of painful ascent. The one who was falling down knocked down another who was climbing hopefully and both collapsed to the bottom in an embrace of despair and insults. Another lot of ammunition for the Browning got lost and half the men, despairing of reaching the crest, began to go off across the plain and so were lost for the last stand.

Johnny was lying halfway up the hill, panting and madly thirsty in that orgy of water; through his sleeves the mud had made its way in up to his armpits. He turned to look towards the enemy; through a belt of mists he saw the Fascist forward troops half a kilometre away sniffing round the perimeter walls of San Casciano. The rain was so heavy that each drop now dented skin that had been beaten too long. Then he threw the machine-gun further up to be a goal *embedded* in the mud, reached it climbing on his stomach, threw it further again, and again reached it, until he emerged on the crest, a statue in mud.

There was no one, neither sight nor sound of defenders. Then one of the men who had stayed with him pointed to the courtyard of the farmhouse. There there stood a frightened, perplexed group, many adolescents, probably the ones who had fired in error a little while ago. This was the hundreds of fresh men, the intact weapons and the piles of ammunition tree-high. But he did not rebel nor did any one of his men, the desperateness of the situation almost flattered them. Then the strong older men who had evacuated San Casciano arrived and they too stood there without grumbling, and at once set about preparing whatever was necessary to put a roof over the great edifice of defeat.

Johnny looked down at the town lying beneath them, doomed; it stood there, surrounded by the waters, in naked, trembling flesh. He coughed, handed the Browning to the new machine-gunner and went to the farmhouse to drink. Captain Marini was standing in the doorway and his adjutant showed himself from round a corner attacking a field telephone in vain.

'Nice to see you again,' said Marini. 'A lost match. I can't blame either Lampus or Nord who don't intend to throw other men, other weapons, more ammunition into the battle. If the Fascists came up the hills, the way things are going today we'd have nothing but stones left to throw at them. We'll try to do our best alone. Do you want a drink? Take your time, I think they'll give us quarter of an hour's breathing space.'

Johnny did not reply, he found his bitterness too great, too extraordinary to diminish it by recriminations. And then the adjutant was such a devoted and compassionate figure – still in camouflaged clothing, he trembled and dripped as if they had just extricated him from the bottom of a well. He was furious – still in vain – with the telephone.

Inside the family of peasants, terrified, stumbling, stammering, mechanically drew buckets of water from the internal pump and offered them mechanically. Waiting for his turn Johnny looked out of the window and approved at a glance the way the boys he had left had taken up position between two dripping elms. From the next window Marini was asking in a sharp voice someone down below something about a machine-gun. One of the unit who had evacuated the third villa said it was out of order, it had lost an essential piece. Johnny asked Marini for a cigarette, oddly enjoying this accumulation of misfortunes; the captain offered in a twisted handful the remains of a packet of cigarettes.

Shortly afterwards the Fascists, invisible, opened up again with mortar fire, very fast and with a maximum of precision. Just as Johnny was raising the dipper to his lips, a shell crashed on to the roof and over the edge of the dipper he saw he disintegrating chimney pass in a flash, framed in the window, while a woman of the house fainted on the tiled floor. He ran down to take up position between the two elms, he lay down behind the Browning which was disfigured by mud, its sight blinded, and stared with swollen eyes at the misty plain through dozens of films of rain. There were a hundred of them left, he calculated; it would take a miracle to stop their first bound. But time passed and the Fascists did not come into sight not even as a joke or a taunt. A man from 1st Division said somewhat morosely that they should stop staring at the plain and pay attention to the hill opposite; in the Fascists' place he would keep to the hills protected by the vegetation and very much less boggy than the low ground. And as an experiment and piece of research, he went forward alone and erect through the skeletal vineyard. He was only too right because a big burst of fire exploded from the hill opposite and left him dead on the spot between the rows of vines. They opened fire with all their weapons at the crest and the Fascists who had appeared disappeared again. Except for one who was now skilfully trying to take cover and hide in a clump of cane halfway up. But Johnny saw him and so did a machine-gunner of 1st Division and they both fired a long burst together into the clump of cane. Canes and man *croaked and cracked* together, the canes twisting over him as if to take revenge for the damage the riddled man had provoked.

It took more than an hour for the Fascists who were fighting with all possible care and caution to dislodge them from that last position.

From the house a red Very* light went up into the cast-iron sky. The signal for the general withdrawal and it seemed that the Fascists too knew about it because they reduced their fire almost entirely. But they had advanced very far and made progress on the left with encirclement in their grasp. Captain Marini was bawling to order immediate, rapid withdrawal.

Johnny rose to his full height out of the cover of the elms with a dazed feeling which was that of defeat; a real defeat in battle, personally worked at and endured. For the last time he looked at the plain, to the field of their defeat, from the most remote riverbanks to that muddy hillside, in the afternoon rain which gave it twilight shadows. And it all seemed to him like a swirling dream and not anything truly real, the reality being to be touched and fingered by a *new go at it.* But it was not a dream, not for the Fascists, not for Michele, his corpse somewhere down there under the dancing mists, half-buried *in a very shallow grave.*

The men, the lads, were as dazed and reluctant as he was, they moved about in a withdrawn way under the occasional Fascist fire, lazily but luminously thinking that the town was indeed lost but that there was a world of difference between losing it at three instead of at quarter past two. Until Captain Marini became furious and pistol in hand got them together and forced them to withdraw.

Johnny along with the others descended the peaceful little valley which sloped down to the first houses of the town, no Fascists yet appearing on the crest. A few steps behind Captain Marini invited everyone to keep in mind where the dead were: 'Remember the places, tomorrow we shall parley about the dead, right away tomorrow.' The men heard him but did not answer, walking down clumsily, disjointedly, the easy descent already *too much* for their exhausted knees.

They arrived opposite the first houses, which stood for all the other houses of the town: sealed, bolted and barred at every point, not going to open up for prayers or threats. They went on towards the avenue which led to the real stone heart of the town. In order to shorten, to minimise his pain, Johnny jumped down on to the tar and with a leap crossed to the other side, having thus a single fleeting *glimpse* of the town.

*A flare fired from a pistol named after its inventor.

Many of them sighed with relief at setting foot on the first hill but for Johnny it did not seem protective and even less maternal; it had instead a grim, sinister look, *giving token* of a punishment to come and that only too soon.

Climbing up that first slope they were level with the roofs of the town, the roof-tiles crackling under the rain like firewood, seemed algae-clad and bubonic, those roofs which were so *red and mellow*. An officer of 1st Division said: 'Ask me in fifty years where I was and what I was doing on 2 November . . .' but he was interrupted sharply by the sudden, crushing, absurd sound of the guns from the distant plain. The shells were not flying in their direction, on the route of the partisan retreat, they fell on that hill road which had been used for the descent of 10 October. It was now *crammed* at its middle and last bends by a multitude of civilians who were laboriously escaping from the Fascist reoccupation and reprisals. The partisans swore and shook their fists at the plain, the crowd up there halted rigid and with bated breath under the unexpected direct shelling. The Fascists redoubled their effort and the crowd up there *pivoted and squirmed* as if in a trap, then collapsed on the streaming road, caught between impassable steep slopes and precipices. Fortunately the shells were *ill-fused* and after a last broadside the guns fell silent and the uninjured crowd hastened to stream down into safer valleys and dells.

The partisans began to climb again but Johnny stopped and turned round with the Browning at this feet, allowing the last men to overtake him with a thousand splashes.

'Why did you stop?' asked Marini who now sounded more like a junior master in a boarding school than a commander in the field.

'I want to see the end.'

Then the captain stopped, grasping his field-glasses. They had before their eyes the modern part of the town in squalid *rain-battered* geometry, the only living thing appearing to be the long hair of the avenue planes whipped by the wind.

'Where is your adjutant?' asked Johnny.

'I sent him back into town to rescue certain documents we had forgotten. I wouldn't like him to be trapped.'

'Oh, he has any amount of time,' Johnny observed. 'They are entering at a damnably leisurely pace.'

At that moment a petulant little noise came up the hill from the greasy tar of the second avenue and after a little two light tanks appeared zigzagging in the water with their brave helmeted heads sticking right out. 'Just look, they had tanks as well and didn't use them. Did your plan of defence, captain, also foresee a tank attack?' Marini did not reply – he merely looked at Johnny askance with a kind of disarmed indifference.

Then a body of infantry came into view, deployed in two lines down both sides of the avenue, their rifles pointing up at the barred windows of the houses. Then two big semi-armoured vehicles advancing at a walking pace. And Marini said he was as sure as death that they were carrying the commander-in-chief and his staff. 'Sure – and in his head he is writing and rewriting the text of his imminent dispatch to Salò.'*

The rain was furious.

Captain Marini shrugged, the weight of the rain and of defeat . . . 'Let's go. Come on. Let's say goodbye to the town until the day of victory.'

Having reached the centre the Fascists went personally to peal the bells.

* Mussolini's seat of government.

XXII

The nights were polar, the dawns and evenings raw, but noons and afternoons had the soft warmth of the Indian summer, in that first November, in the plain at Castagnole. On such an afternoon, with a primordial peace and perfection, Johnny was on guard on the straight stretch of road from Neive to Castagnole with Ettore who had left his unit, which had been cut to pieces in the town, and had joined up with Pierre. They were watching the boring stretch right down to its curtain of gilded haze but the principal reason for their guard was the big mine buried at the last bend before the village. It had been laid long before the operation in the town but no Fascists had come upon it so that the mine had been kept here as had the guard to go with it. Johnny wondered if the partisan guards were there to warn the civilians and so save their lives or to keep the civilians from wasting that precious mine by jumping on it. However the people in the village were perfectly informed, so much so that their prudent diversion had imprinted a well-defined path in the adjoining meadow, which was now so clearly visible and enticing that even the Fascists, should they pass that way, would perhaps instinctively take that path rather than the mined road.

Ettore, with his rifle on his knees, was sitting on the kerbstone nearest the mine perhaps to put some life into the banality of their task by such exciting proximity. He spoke and his voice grated, both of them bore the after-effects of the great *soaking* in town.

'I feel like death if I think of tonight's sentry duty.'

And at the very idea Johnny shivered in the sun and dreamt of his old fur coat at Mombarcaro so martial and warm. Without regret he had thrown it away on one of those forgotten hilltops because the spring and summer to come seemed so eternal to him, so entirely sufficient to defeat a couple of Fascist régimes. Besides he had lost the habit of being on sentry duty; in town he was an officer and therefore exempt from the daily sentry-go but after the defeat almost everyone had been put on the same level for duties; only Pierre of those around them retained a superior and meaningless command *feature*. Their lads had grown unnaturally (the immense power of defeat to make people old) in stubbornness and criticism and the lack of Michele made itself bitterly felt. Pierre had hoped that Johnny could replace him at least in spirit but how could Johnny – not a born sergeant – replace a dead sergeant? So guard duties had been noticeably less frequent because the squads had dwindled after the defeat in the town. A group of people, the very youngest, had gone back to the town, to their houses, to their people, insisting that the town had proved only too exhaustively that the times were not yet ripe. Worse still, the partisans had left the town enormously impoverished in terms of ammunition to the point where they could not commit themselves to more than a shadow of *engagement* with the *pushing* Fascist unless the English hurried up and made a mammoth arms drop at some place in the hills.

Ettore shook a fist towards that curtain of gilded haze at the end of the long stretch of road and asked himself when they would come.

'They will come far too soon,' said Johnny. 'Retaking the town isn't a goal for them, it's a starting-point. They will come all too soon and they'll crush us on all the hills.'

'I heard this morning from people in the market that the Fascists in town are behaving very well. They've had practically no reprisals and continue not to do any harm. They have put out a proclamation which promises indemnity to all partisans who give themselves up, assuring them that they won't enlist them but will put them down for labour service. Naturally only the ones who are not accused of war crimes. And it seems the proclamation is having its effect – the season we are entering is a great help to them in this.'

'And I have it from Pierre,' said Johnny, 'that the new garrison is in very good shape, all chosen elements from the Republican army and not the old moaning type of Alpino. *They are going to give us a damned bad time.*'

'What?'

Johnny repeated it in Italian.

The bustle of the village reached them on the gilded rays but Ettore cast an unsympathetic glance behind him and wondered why the devil Nord had put them down for garrison in that village instead of in Mango or else in another village right in the hills. He was fed up to here with the plain and longed for the old hills; bad professional attitude, thought Johnny. He too detested this village of Castagnole, an uncongenial village, ambiguous, amphibious, split into two hamlets: the one with the railway and market in the plain and the old feudal part fortified on a bare and corrugated hill. They were quartered in the hamlet down below. And Johnny did not like its situation, its people, the way the houses were distributed, the road and the side roads, the fact that it had a railway, and not even the nocturnal sound of its bells. And he hoped to leave it very soon, maybe under the Fascist attack.

Ettore signalled that Pierre had arrived. On the surface of it he had come for a simple inspection but more plausibly to enjoy the rather melancholy heat of the old, tried countryside. He too was a fish out of water in that new village among new men whom he only half knew, who were untested.

'Pierre, why the devil did Nord put us down for this horrible village?' The previous garrison of Badogliani had dwindled greatly after the disaster in town and they had come down to reinforce it so that the Communists didn't feel tempted and encouraged to come down in force and pinch the garrison from the Badogliani. The Red line on Lower Monferrato was deep and solid, practically intact.

'Do you understand now?' asked Pierre.

'I've understood,' said Johnny, 'but you'll see how we end up with this strategy of garrisons. And the end will come only too soon. They will beat us and disperse us one by one, garrison after garrison, with our consent and it has to be said with our help. It only remains to be seen who will be beaten and dispersed first – the Badogliani or the Communists.'

'And these bloody Allies are amusing themselves with patrols,' said Ettore.

'By the bye, where have they got to now?'

'I don't know,' said Ettore,' I haven't listened to their radio for ages. I don't go into people's houses to listen, I simply don't like the people in the damned village.'

It wasn't just the population of Castagnole. Everyone was changing, gradually, everywhere. The partisan defeat in town had had its effect on them too, on their hopes of a reasonably near end to the war. For months and months they had given and helped and taken risks solely in return for reassurances of progress towards victory, for the sake of their crops and herds and peaceful journeys to fairs and markets, with this nasty business of Germans and Fascists buried for good. Now, after the hard lesson of the town, they had to continue to give, help and risk their heads and their roofs, with victory and liberation in the foggy distance. For months they had given and helped and risked, smiling and laughing and asking a whole lot of trusting questions, now they had to begin to give in silence, then almost *sullenly*, and finally in mute and then no longer mute protest.

'Only yesterday morning,' said Ettore, 'yesterday morning I got up from that damned straw with a hollow inside me, with a damnable need to have breakfast and feel the heat of the oven. So I go to the pizzeria in the square. Ring and the young housewife appears. I ask for a sandwich and indicate that I can pay. She makes me a roll, hands it to me and when I offer the money she refuses with a sigh.'

'Is that all?' said Pierre mysteriously *dulled by sadness.*

'Is that all? You should have seen the fatigue, the repugnance and the offensiveness of that sigh! I lost my head – I had got up on the wrong side. I saw red! At that moment nothing seemed easier to me – more natural and logical than to shoot her at the counter. I don't know what held me back but I did nothing, only a little later I sighed myself. But I don't know what I may do next time I hear people sigh at me like that as if I were a frightening armed beggar.'

'Calm down, boys, calm down,' said Pierre in a voice that was not calm.

Their relief arrived – two sullen and decided boys, never seen before, who on arriving hurled curses at the mine and the minelayers. The three went back into the village into the grey semi-deserted square with its chilling air of being provisional – a mere staging point, unfaithful and unsupportive, before defeat and rout. Pierre made for the telephone exchange but before parting from them said that that evening he would be thirty. The other two gave him their good wishes. Pierre smiled gaily, the real gaiety of people who have a normal basic melancholy and said that in all conscience he couldn't complain if tomorrow they were to kill him, he was so tremendously, so shamefully better off than the average.

As for Ettore *he stalked* off to firm up his major plan. He had put into it savage determination, not even for Fascists were his eyes as ferocious and staring as for women. Very probably he looked on women as something hostile, ridiculous, to be conquered and transfixed and to leave transfixed with a *grim jeer.* He had planned it and was working it out alone, Johnny having confined himself to giving a kind of carte-blanche, being so irredeemably unable to work *in team* in that sector. But before leaving him he asked somewhat ironically how far on he was. And Ettore said harshly: 'On the eve. It has to be. The girls are longing for it and we are dying of it. It's got to happen.' And with a martial stride he made for the upper village amid people who were few and either sullen or indifferent. He was off to arrange the evening of dancing, definitely, in strict privacy, because it seemed impossible that it could be confined to the two of them alone.

An hour later he was back masking his triumph in his usual way under the most bitter of masks. The evening had been arranged for the following evening in a little villa outside the village – four girls and four partisans, gramophone records and drinks. The guest booked for Johnny must be an intellectual. 'She must have a lot of odd ideas in her head,' said Ettore, 'as thick as grasshoppers in a field on a summer night.' And none of the three men dreamt of contradicting him. Pretty, though, the thin kind, snaky.

'What did you tell her about me?'

'I said you were ace at singing English and American songs,' said Ettore and Johnny blushed at the enormity of the price.

Next afternoon they climbed the hill to take a shower in the local school, Ettore having hinted that, God willing, there might be a chance to show one's skin. On the way back Ettore explained that Johnny's girl was called Elda and that he was worried in the case of his own conquest by the jealousy and interference of a partisan, someone who said he was a partisan in civilian clothes. He too was invited at the precise request of Ettore's girl who seemed to be afraid of him.

In the evening they knocked at the little villa, high up on the sinister rolling country just before the sinister river which still showed the after-effects of the great October rain. When they knocked adjacent shutters squeaked and banged, the girls shouted to come up and come in, music came from the blacked-out windows.

In the dark corridor Johnny recognised Elda by her gliding rustle and her strange bitter perfume, which were immediately distinctive of her personality. They laid aside their weapons (their nasty weapons, said Elda) and made towards the light, the warmth and the music. The comfort assailed Johnny and left him breathless. And so the mass-produced furnishings of the drawing-room seemed to him to have an oriental sumptuousness. And how complete it was from the divans to the ashtrays of massive glass. Two red-hot electric stoves radiated a sensuous and boiling heat, enervating, while on every little table, *hob and knob*, lay packets of cigarettes, which had Elda's touch about them. The other three girls were rural heiresses who, in peace-time or when the war was still reasonable, used to go into town once a week to shop in the main street; now desperately and *compromisingly* attached to Elda, the evacuee, and intoxicated past all remedy and grown accustomed to her daily lessons and exhibitions of caprice and fantasy and style. The prettiest, a fine example of pleasing animality, was certainly the girl on whom Ettore had designs and Elda's favourite. She was called Thea. The other two men were already at their posts. One a partisan from the previous garrison who usually kept as far away as possible from Pierre and his men, a village boy with some sort of office in town wearing a kind of natural indolence which his experience of town life helped him to express more effectively. The other, Ettore's rival, was a well-built youth with almost albino hair and deep blue eyes, a solid face vaguely authoritarian and punctilious, which certainly did not go with all that blond and blue. He was in civilian clothes this one, and had the *nom de guerre* of Paul. According to Ettore's description during their anticipatory insomnia in the stables in the lower village, he was a partisan but wore civilian clothing because he belonged to the partisan Secret Police. 'The other evening,' said Ettore, 'when I was bringing all my guns to bear get Elda and Thea, I learned that he hates us, hates us. He told the girls that we are partisans of course but the common kind, disgusting soldiery, and advised them – Thea above all – not to fall in love with our uniforms. He really is a real partisan and a high-class one, even if he is in civvies, because he belongs to the Secret Police and as proof has shown the girls a little pistol he carries on his belt inside his trousers next to the skin.'

Elda guided them to the drinks – home-distilled but richly and competently – and they flooded their half-empty stomachs with *sweeping* beneficial effects. Elda had that bitter perfume and in her voice there was something bitter which was sharp, birdlike, thin like all of her.

They turned to the gramophone: 'Shall we go on with the slow tempo ones or shall we change to something livelier?'

'Please go on with the slow tempo ones,' said Ettore.

The record was put on, Paul appropriated Thea and Ettore fell back, impassively, on another girl who was only too conscious of his falling back.

Elda clung close, it was fantastic that something so slender could be so welcoming. And she smelt so good and all-conqueringly, that perfume was not a sprinkling of something artificial, it was, he told himself, the most noble distillation of her real and true chemical composition.

'Are you all right, Johnny?'

He could not answer being reduced by the *comfort* to a point of idiocy.

'I like you, Johnny. I can say that I liked you even before this and you are just the kind of person to understand my thoughts. I like you because you have mad eyes. Do you know, Johnny, that you have mad eyes? You're mad, Johnny.'

He did not object, being too grateful and attached to the perfume and her clinging.

'You are mad. Johnny. Perhaps you don't know?'

'Yes, in a normal way.'

Then she said she was eighteen, leaving Johnny astonished: it was the pure truth but it was also a most atrocious slap in the face to truth. They danced, the indolent man in the armchair took the records off and put them on again with an eternal cigarette in the corner of his mouth, with a constant ironic glance at his three fellow villagers with their urge to get to know new men. Thea was dancing one dance with Ettore and the next with Paul – rigorously. But when dancing with Ettore the girl was on her guard, she never lost sight of Paul. Then

Elda whispered to Johnny that the evening might end badly, she seemed happy about it, and clapped her hands at that possibility with her special, eager sincerity.

'But isn't what is going on around us these days enough for you?' Johnny commented.

'It hasn't much to do with me,' she said with a childish pout. 'You see, Johnny, the girls are so much less important than the boys these days. You boys have so much to do and get so much inspiration from these times. And we girls feel we are less important than you, in such an inferior sphere –'

'Some of us die, Elda . . .'

'We die too, all of us, of boredom.'

'Yes,' said Johnny . . . feeling he was replying to someone who had asked him if he had by any chance ever dreamt of fighting in town.

'You have been beaten.'

'That's right,' and he put his neck on her fragile shoulder. 'You can feel the bruise of defeat on my neck.'

Then Elda's fingers, the *clue* to her galvanic slimness, wandered over his neck, sweet and painful, forcing him to shout and at the same time stripping him of any power of vocal utterance.

'Beaten. I adore beaten men.'

The gramophone was stopped, the dance interrupted, drinks and conversation were started up as a truce, the initiative coming obviously from Paul, who was so authoritative and open, so much a boy and *man-shamming*.

It was *shocking* to find Elda in a conversational posture and mood.

Paul got up like a chairman to give direction to the conversation.

'You ought to know, girls, that we won't stay much longer in this place. It is basically an evening of farewells.'

'Oh, don't talk about your business! After all men are still men – even in the unofficial version,' *squaffed* Elda.

'I'm sorry,' Paul went on, 'but I know the Fascists will carry out a big operation as soon as possible . . .'

Johnny took his eyes off him, bored and annoyed, but Ettore, his rival, gave him encouragement and attention.

'What do you know precisely?' asked Ettore.

'The town garrison will make a move very quickly and in strength.

They're already pushing their cavalry forward into the hills round about.'

He spoke like a real man from Intelligence.

'Do they have cavalry?' asked Ettore astonished.

Paul savoured his triumph and went on: 'Yes, up to today they've used it for little recces and round-ups of limited range. A few partisans taken by surprise have already fallen under the horses' hooves. A burst of fire and then they gallop over him. Earlier the Fascist officers used the horses to give riding lessons to certain married and unmarried ladies in town.'

'Oh,' said Elda, 'I'd love to have riding lessons!'

'Elda!' Thea rebuked her.

'I'll kill you,' Johnny whispered.

'Go on then but there's nothing I wouldn't do to have riding lessons from the devil himself.'

At that moment an adolescent voice, shrill and impassioned, called to Elda from the street, two three four desperate times, and the girls and the two local men glanced at her and whispered the boy's name. Elda frowned, smiled and hastened to the window which gave on to the street and quietly, maternally *called back*.

'I'm here. Chico, can you see me, Chico?'

All that could be heard was the inarticulate whispering of the young boy, an imploring repetition of her name.

'But what do you want, dear impossible Chico? Be reasonable. I am here and have partisan guests. Real partisans, Chico.' Another long whisper, a barely audible 'Elda, Elda,' in the coma of a mortal love-sickness. At the window Elda became worried but then calmed again and her recovered patience restored to her voice a haloed perfection.

'Be good and reasonable, Chico. My dear little boy. No, don't get excited, I said dear little boy but it didn't mean anything. No, Chico, I am not your official fiancée. No, Chico, you dreamt it. Yes, I love you but I am not your official fiancée. Now go and have a good sleep, Chico.'

She withdrew even though the boy in the street kept on calling to her with agonised high and low notes. She came back into the room and, very much the lady of the house, reimposed dancing.

They danced. 'Tell me, Elda, did the boy tell you he could kill us? All of us, you and me, all of us.'

She breathed a yes.

'What are you getting up to in this damned unfortunate village, Elda?'

'I am bored.'

'Somebody will certainly curse your evacuation here. You who come from Turin. But you certainly come from much further away than Turin, don't you, Elda?'

'I am bored.'

'Are you too bored to do you know what?'

'No – never.'

'And . . .'

'When you like. At any moment. When you like. Oh what a horrid record. Whoever put it on?'

'Don't worry about the record. There's no need. We have a music inside us – don't you see we are dancing – internally.'

Outside there was a burst of firing, then rifle shots – then more bursts of firing, more shots. And the whirling, skidding roar of a car which still seemed to be stuck in one place.

The girls screamed. Johnny and Ettore ran to their weapons which they had laid down and forgotten and took up positions at the windows, while the indolent villager seemed more and more nailed to the armchair at every explosion, and Paul walked up and down the room with terrified eyes fixed on the windows.

'What do you think, you from the Secret Police?' said Johnny ironically. The first burst had frozen his blood but now he had completely recovered.

'The Fascists, the Fascists,' the village boy vomited from his ugly mouth, unable to jump up from the armchair.

A whole sequence of automatic rifle fire, complex and solid and functional like the blows of a pneumatic drill, exploded in the frozen air in millions of crystals, the partisans running on the echoing cobbles, the car continuing to buzz not far off like a big beetle caught in a bottle. An instant later a sub-machine-gun fired a burst and both recognised Pierre's Mas.

They burst out into the deep night, dashed towards the village with the station over the cobbles, which were hyperbolically resonant in the silence of all weapons that had followed, almost as if they were waiting for the two of them in order to start up again. On the edge of the square someone fired at them, malignantly, laying them flat on the cobbles. They slid backwards to the cover of the corner of a house. The frozen cobbles were hard and sharp. Johnny felt one of his hands bloodily warm but he was sure it wasn't a case of a bullet but of the cobbles. 'What is it? Fascists?' Ettore panted. Johnny finished licking his hand. 'If they're not firing at shadows. But it's possible.' From the other direction came the last hammering of the semi-automatic, the burst spattering against some wood and that was the end. The car was purring, already far off, with a thin and definite purr.

Then Pierre's voice, calm and clear but respecting the late-night hour, called them to assemble at the crossroads under the frozen impassivity of the burghers. The matter was explained and cleared up in spite of the mystery surrounding it. The sentry at the petrol dump on the edge of the village had opened fire at the mysterious car that was coming at him. The car had gone round in a circle and had replied with fire from its windows. The rest had followed naturally. Not Fascists but some hateful flying-picket of Communists who had come to try and steal the precious fuel from the tattered, dis- integrating Badogliano unit garrisoning Castagnole. Pierre called out the whole guard and it was a lethal experience for Johnny and Ettore to have to go from the sensuous warmth and excesses of Elda's house to the painful rigour of the night and of guard duty. Pierre had not uttered a word at the pair's unjustified absence but had looked at them *knowingly*.

The next afternoon Paul was dead. Sitting in the barber's chair his little pistol with the safety off fired and wounded him in the stomach point blank. Johnny and Ettore ran from their sentry post on the hill above the river when he had already been taken to hospital and was dying, the doctor using the last drops of mephedrine for a painless death.

The village was furious and trembled at what had happened, extending to all the partisans the gratuitous cruelty, the deadly dilettantism of what emerged. And they demanded an immediate burial (purely a question of time) as if from a chain of events – one of them Paul's death – the population was inferring a general tragedy suspended in the air. So that the funeral, although imposingly escorted, turned out to be unfeeling because of haste and condensation. While they were in the cemetery watching the coffin being lowered a young boy burst in yelling that the Fascist cavalry had come down from the hills of Treiso and was descending on Neive four kilometres from Castagnole. The priest and the sexton remained, under the cover of tasks to be done, people ran to their hiding places, the partisans to their positions. But it was useless to dig themselves in near the mined bend in the road and nothing happened until an unknown partisan of the lowest and most bestial peasant stock said he would look for the boy, put him between his knees and cut off his ears. At five in the evening in the hostility of the dusk rather than of the Fascists, Pierre broke up the line they had formed and set them at liberty in the hated village. In tacit agreement Johnny and Ettore made for Elda's little villa as if to an indispensable first aid post.

But the girl kept them waiting and when she appeared said No and then burst into tears and hysterical cries which sent them straight back to the plain.

XXIII

Towards the middle of November they were patrolling the road to Santo Stefano at their ease far from the village of Castagnole and close to the Red forward lines. The road before them was deserted and without movement except for the flights and landings of the sparrows and the air, close at hand and very distant, was a well of gilded transparency. The landscape was so clear that you could catch the slightest movement (and its purpose) by the peasant on the edge of the highest and most distant threshing floor and you could dream of touching the belly of the tower on the highest hill with a barely extended finger. When, travelling south from the highest hills, came a *throb* of planes, scarcely troubling the surface of that lake of air. There had to be a lot of them, a whole squadron, although their consolidated noise was perfectly fused into one. And in that throbbing there was a strange intriguing circularity. The third man in the patrol asked for an explanation. Ettore said, somewhat petulantly, that it was a simple overflight – they were flying over with neither eyes nor thoughts for the poor partisans, in order to unload their bellyful of bombs somewhere or other. Johnny did not declare himself; he was too caught up in the thought that that low red-hot throb was shattering the peace and the grass on the graves of Biondo and Tito. He shook himself only in order to express the certainty – heartfelt – that they were English. But they could not be passing over – in any case it was a mistake in their route – because that throb, now even more condensed, was coming lower and circling more and more. And then there was a sudden light in Johnny's mind.

'They're making a drop?' he shouted. 'They are dropping stuff into the open mouth of 1st Division!'

Ettore and the others began to dance in the road even before they had been convinced. It meant military supplies and warm things for the whole winter and now it could happily go on and be a Fascist winter.

'They are dropping it in full daylight, under the noses of the Germans and Fascists in Ceva. And they can't do anything about it – watch our manna and that's all. Lampus is strong enough to keep them pinned down in Ceva.'

In the mad splendour of that daylight drop they all started dancing again on the tattered asphalt, *hurraying*, until the people from the nearest farm burst out on to the threshing floor, gazed at their dancing and shouting, climbed on to the nearest stack for a wider and more direct sight of the *eventful sky*. When the friendly rumble vanished they rushed back to Castagnole, intriguing and frightening the rare passers-by by the impetus of their race.

Pierre grabbed the phone and savagely asked for the headquarters of 2nd Division. They made contact ten minutes later; Nord in person on the phone who, with triumphant calm, confirmed the drop, the biggest in history, no less than four four-engined planes, right into Lampus' mouth, under the noses of the strong garrison at Ceva. He had already sent over his most able officer by the swiftest means to make an inventory to see to the distribution.

The news got out, echoed all round; it intoxicated the partisans on solitary guard in valley or on peak, it flooded the village; such news that it made those *grim*, isolated and overworked people interrupt their work, smashing their hard mask of reserve and distance and bringing to light their long repressed capacity for enthusiasm and solidarity. Meantime the partisans, having exhausted their cheers for the drop and the Allies, fell prey to their usual apprehensions of being badly done by during the share-out if not entirely forgotten. 'Lampus will have to make the shares more equal this time.' 'You can be sure Lampus will do the honourable thing.' 'I don't have too much hope. Nord gives in too much to Lampus'. And they gave farewell looks at their despised rifles; now they would at last have automatic weapons, the love and sickness of those times.

But the joy turned into pain; what had looked like their salvation caused their mortal ruin. After the town the Nazi-Fascists had gathered a strong force (half German) precisely to crush Lampus, who had got too powerful, and after him the lesser commanders.

That big daylight drop under their noses merely put forward the hands to H-hour for the general attack and three hours after the drop the German artillery opened up with all its guns and the Fascist infantry clambered up towards Lampus' proud lines. Under the great, completely new hammerblows of the guns, all the hills were instantly covered with people and a moment later they were all gone. The most prepared and frightened of the men from Castagnole, which was still uncommitted, packed their things and furtively, hating any possible followers, set off for certain obscure places which they had long ago studied and selected.

Great was the luminosity of the day and greater still the thunder of the guns; at all events it was a great day – such as almost to eclipse the day of the town.

'What is going to happen if the town garrison attacks simultaneously?' Pierre shrugged and sent Johnny with all his men to keep watch on the stretch of road to Neive while he remained at the exchange with a boy to send any news to the front line.

With their eyes and the muzzles of their guns they swept the unmoving, gilded almost irridescent straight line, but the gunfire on the high hills was too absorbing, overpowering. So, thought Johnny, my life and that of those others is at stake, the dice in the bottom of the cup. Good, he was ready again.

Hours passed in empty guard-duty; every half-hour Pierre's runner arrived with the latest news: things were going magnificently up there, Fascists and Germans dying in heaps, the stuff from the enormous drop had been all secured and was being used. Later the Red brigades from the high hills had come into the Blue line and now they were fighting side by side in a union without precedent.

But if they lifted their eyes to the hills opposite, they saw them crowned in waves with fleeing peasants with equipment and reserves sufficient for a long flight and an even longer period in hiding. Every valley had its flood just like at the end of winter. Johnny stopped and questioned the fugitives. They stopped reluctantly, replied that they had not seen even one Fascist or German forward unit but they set off again with relief and speed, getting further and further from their houses, women and animals. And the blessed dusk swallowed them in no time. It was cold, with jabs of frost, their hands curled on the metal of their weapons. At dusk the enemy artillery dwindled and then stopped, leaving the world of the hills more terrified than relieved. When they returned Pierre informed them about the last telephone call: everything good, victory that day and good hopes for the next. The men received the news with an indifference that was close to incredulity. They supped hastily and badly; for recreation they walked about in the deserted, barred and bolted village, then on guard once more, in a cold and anxious state at least equal to the worst spells on guard on the river in town. But then they still had the hills to take refuge in; but now, losing the hills, how would they end up?

The night swallowed the profile of the highest hills like titbits and a rain fell in intermittent downpours which made the men shiver and curse. The exodus of peasants continued; sentries were already hoarse from the rain and too frequent challenges. The men stopped dead anxiously declaring themselves to be friends, passed on wrapped in cloaks, humpbacked, then they disappeared again into the dark, which they prayed might be without other men. Pierre, being useless on the telephone, was in the line, sad but 'a regular'. The men asked his opinion, responding once more to command and rank. But what could Pierre say? Then the men began to blame the English for the idiocy of that drop in full daylight.

Ettore, arriving for his turn, whispered to Johnny that Elda was waiting for him in the square. Johnny went there. The village was scantily and at the same time extraordinarily illuminated; the lights were dazzling red like the light of a furnace and moving to and fro on the walls made them look like fluttering folds of tents of an ephemeral bivouac of a routed army. Elda was standing at the corner, deaf to the jokes and invitations of the men going on duty. She seemed to be shaking and in the reddish reflection from the café at the corner was paler than ever, her face more than ever eaten by her eyes. But she was wearing a little coat with fur trimmings, so delicious, so metropolitan, that Johnny forgot everything.

'Something terrible is in the air, isn't it, Johnny?'

'Yes.'

'As terrible as in the town?'

'A joke by comparison.'

'This one?'

'No – the town.'

'When do you think you'll be in the midst of it?'

'The day after tomorrow at the latest. Some of us will envy Paul.'

'What do you mean?' she cried, hysteria taking hold of her again at the repetition of Paul's name.

'Yes, envy him for his unique death. They'll kiss us in dozens, they'll capture us in hundreds and the ones they take will have cause to envy those who were killed outright.'

She grasped him by the arm, but it was to drag him to the centre of the square, in the heart of the darkness and solitude.

'Johnny, make an effort to talk to me as if I were a serious and reasonable girl. You don't have mad eyes, Johnny. I was mad and drunk that other evening, Johnny. Johnny, don't you want to hide? I can hide you, you and your uniform and your weapons. For a little while, Johnny, till the storm has passed.'

He smiled and pushed a hard finger into her neck, thrusting it in towards the carotid, and a sigh that was almost swooning escaped from her.

'You're mad, Elda.'

'You are mad. And everyone like you is mad too.'

'Get off home. It's as dark as pitch and the men are excited.'

'Johnny, can't I do anything for you – this minute?'

'It's too late. Thanks all the same. Really, I don't lack anything – nothing is of any use to me,' and he turned towards his post.

'I'm sure you don't have these,' she called after him and stretched out to hand him three packets of cigarettes. Then, before he did, she fled, her little figure a trifle for the night's devouring capacity. Johnny distributed the packets in the pockets of his blouse and returned to his post. How could he know that to get him these cigarettes Elda had gone to the repugnant pizza-maker, who was a general dealer in the black market, and without speaking had lain down on the counter and pulled her skirt up over her face?

The rain started again but light and freakish. There was something up – a getting together and a whispering. Men from the garrison at Neive had come running up to ask Pierre if in the event of an attack from the town he would push towards Neive or would they have to fall back on Castagnole. Pierre said he would push towards Neive and the leader of the patrol said his men were getting fewer, he only had to turn round for a moment and a man disappeared, slipping away as quiet as mice towards the river, then they crossed it looking for refuge in the sleepy pastoral countryside over there. They were no loss, they all agreed, a case of untried and inexpert adolescents, frightened; it was better not to have them on one's conscience if they had to give battle. Besides something similar was happening in the garrison of Castagnole itself, to the supreme indifference of Johnny and Pierre.

Towards midnight the flow of country people dried up and it seemed that there would be no sign of any more passing when a strong force of partisans, obviously coming from another valley, calmly turned up in front of the position. They came, they said, from the Belbo valley and were looking for the ferry. They were in solid ranks in the grip of their commander, pretty well armed and equipped.

'Why are you trying to cross the river?' Pierre inquired.

'I know that over there there is complete calm. Oh just long enough for this hullaballoo to blow over,' and their commander motioned with his hand towards the shadowy hilly world behind them. The pitiless light of the electric torch showed him to be an extremely stocky young man with a heavy face and eyes that darted acute natural intelligence.

Said Pierre: 'What will happen to you then with Lampus and then with Nord?'

The commander shrugged. His men were pressing round and behind him to reinforce him against doubt and any contrary opinion.

'Lampus is smashed,' he said.

'Not at all. I know that today he held on magnificently and that very probably he will hold out tomorrow.'

'Pooh, if not today he'll probably be smashed tomorrow at their first assault. There's no hope for him any more nor for Nord in his turn.'

He adopted a tone and attitude that were apologetic and illuminating.

'This time they aren't joking. Half of them are Germans, you understand me. This time they are closing off all the hills like in a zoo and they'll make us be the monkeys. And we don't want to play at monkeys. We'll cross back over the river again when it's all over. If everyone thought the way you do . . .'

Pierre said: 'If you cross back again you could be treated in a way you can't even imagine just now.'

His face broadened into an enormous, mute smile. 'I understand but I'm just not afraid of your kind of court martial. It wouldn't take me much – coming back to this side – to hand myself and my men over to the first Garibaldini detachment. And then tell Lampus and Nord to come and punish me.'

The men behind him muttered massive assent and agreement. Then Johnny came up to Pierre's side and pointed out the road to the river to them; in the sudden silence and in the filtering atmosphere of the night the commander believed he heard the sound of the waters.

'It sounds very near,' he said politely.

'It just seems like it – you'll have to march for a good hour to get there.'

The squad set off in good order more compact than ever towards the river. And Pierre before putting out the torch looked at Johnny questioningly.

'I couldn't stand him a moment more,' said Johnny, 'and do you know why? Because he is insolently, unbearably right. We'll all end up at the river. So you see it is only a question of days. Then, naturally, only the luckiest of us will reach the river. But then, and this is the big difference, what measures will the Fascists have taken on both banks?'

It was contagious and not even too clandestinely contagious. An hour later five men were missing.

'I could sleep a couple of hours,' said Pierre.

'I could sleep for five or six. I am staying,' said Johnny.

'I'll relieve you in a couple of hours.'

'Don't worry. I feel I couldn't shut my eyes even for a moment.' And suddenly he trembled because he had repeated the exact words of the sergeant, and near a minefield like then, and for the first time in his life superstition seized and shook him.

'They're not going to finish us off,' said Pierre. 'We have the men from Neive in front of us.'

In his attempt to shake off superstition Johnny stammered: 'Do you trust them?'

'No, I confess I don't.'

That night was endless. In confronting it and its frightening mysteries the men exhausted precious energies for the morrow. The darkness moved to and fro as if blown by an enormous enemy mouth. The cold was sadistic, the scratch of a match was a great noise. And what was this sacrifice for? To get through the next day, to its first light with the overwhelming reveille of the artillery and early morning news of defeat and general rout, and then the Fascist flood. Johnny sat, smoking Elda's cigarettes, and kept awake and thought, light-years away from the man at his side. Every hair was standing on end with the cold and the pain of that constant bristling and needling! Only his damned mind did not grow numb.

One of the boys said to a companion in a childish whisper: 'For weeks I've been planning to take a quick trip home to get a pair of my father's long drawers. But how can I get home – it's at the head of the Belbo valley?'

XXIV

The guns preceded the sun; they opened up heavy fire accompanying and almost urging the birth and diffusion of the light, then when day was there they fell silent. And the day revealed in the plain of Castagnole the renewed flood of peasants fleeing, fleeing.

Ettore looked with an unwavering eye at that worrying and depressing spectacle. As for Johnny, after the torment of the night he felt rather good. The light of day with its realistic sizing up of country and people, the hammering of the artillery itself, had restored his balance. In the village Pierre lived clinging to the telephone body and soul but his calls either had no reply or they replied to him very vaguely: 'We don't know anything. We know as much as you do. Let's hope. Lampus is strong in spite of the artillery. You can't hear their guns any more? That doesn't mean the worst.' The village, as Johnny saw it on his periodical visits for information, seemed plague-ridden and quarantined, which was all the more striking in the soft caress of that interminable Indian summer. All the men had practically disappeared, except for a few methuselahs, sitting outside, basking in the sun out of reach of any danger and attack.

Towards midday the flood of fugitives became thicker, one of the main currents debouching straight into Johnny's arms. Emerging from the thinned and almost transparent woods, they suddenly saw those men in a line and under arms and, not recognising them at first glance, they shied like foals and scattered in terror, until Johnny waved his hands to them and went to meet them over the soft grassy fields. They were coming down from the highest hills and from further south as their *zézayant** accent proved. To the question

* *zézayant* – lisping.

where they were going they invariably answered 'Down, down' to a *lowland* without Fascists and Germans. Had they seen any? No, thanks be to God and their quick reaction they had escaped in time and were going 'Down, down'. But a lot had stayed in their places, men of peace, unskilled in arms, but they had hidden themselves, buried in certain holes and crannies prepared long ago. One said: 'I too had prepared my hole but hadn't tried it out. The thing frightened me – I preferred to escape further downhill, it was too like a grave.' And besides it didn't seem an absolutely safe expedient, the Germans seemed to have brought with them packs of unerring sniffer and hunting dogs. At this unheard of news of wolfhounds, the partisans too started to tremble and were unable to ask for further information about these damned dogs. Replying to Johnny's questions, the fugitives never stopped casting glances at the crests behind them as if a Fascist vanguard might suddenly crown them, then an engagement and death would be immediate, almost automatic. 'Yes, of course they have killed a good few of you people, and one or two of us have been taken and hanged.' Great the number of granaries and farmhouses burnt, up there the sky was covered with smoke, enormous quantities of animals carried off, they would live in abundance on them all winter. As for the grain, they had given orders to carry it out into the village square, the sacks were cut open and emptied into the mud and their huge heavy artillery trains had gone back and forwards over it till it was made one with, irremediably mixed in the mud. Even if things ended well, famine and starvation awaited the surviving hills.

In the afternoon partisans came into sight – no longer in squads but in little wandering groups, never more than four. And they didn't even stop to ask for news and directions about roads or to discuss the situation, but with definite lack of interest filed past the men in their positions towards the river as if they knew the road like the palms of their hands. In fact from the river there rose across the flat meadows such a message of peace, almost like a retreat in a nursing home, and that more than one of the Castagnole garrison could not resist was clear from a simple glance round.

At a certain point those left asked Pierre what his programme was. He did not answer; he looked at the surrounding hills, never so clear and sharp, never so *unresponsive* and indecipherable. Without answering he went back to his telephone while Ettore remarked how everything resembled – on a small scale – the day of the armistice. 'It's true,' said Johnny. '8 September was a matter of telephones – either too silent or too talkative.'

At four the great silence was formidably disintegrated by a series of salvoes as direct and hammerlike and deafening as if Castagnole were their precise and sole objective in the whole world. The partisans gave a start, in the village people screamed, but it was clear that they were still firing in the Belbo valley and not in the Feisoglio valley. But Feisoglio lay some fifteen kilometres from Lampus' main line. The women had calmed down a little externally but now they pressed round the partisans to ask them if and when they were going to evacuate the place, thus leaving the village open, empty and not liable to chastisement by the Fascist flood. It seemed as if they could and would give everything for their withdrawal, that they would retreat with gifts and benedictions provided they went off to become the fire and hangman's rope of some other village.

Pierre was hitting the phone frantically. Finally he got through, at the other end of the line an unknown officer with a weakness for humorous slang. Pierre had asked, fairly much according to the book, about Lampus and the fate of his 1st Division.

'They're wankers,' said the other.

'What?'

'They've gone all soft.'

'What are they doing?'

'Madonna!'

'They're escaping?'

'The whole length of the line.'

'What are you doing?'

'We're getting ready to defend ourselves purely out of a sense of honour – as volunteers. They can encircle us at any time. They are coming down like avalanches.'

'And what are we to do down here?

The other made a dismissive noise.

'You're a damned idiot. Yes, I said idiot. Put me on to . . .' but the other hung up.

But quarter of an hour later Nord was on the phone. His voice was deep and neutral as always, except when he was talking about love affairs or male jokes. 'Give us our orders, Nord,' said Pierre, the very tension of relief and entreaty sounding as if it were a command to Nord himself.

Nord tranquilly made it clear that this was his last telephone call; immediately after it he was going to pull out the line. 'Do you still have a lot of men with you, Pierre? We don't need many. Fifteen or twenty are enough. Will you move to Cascina della Langa and occupy the ridge tomorrow morning. You've only got to watch to see if they are attacking and are coming up from the town as well. No, no, don't put up any resistance. Just fire one volley and then it's each man for himself. We will hear your volley at Castino and will understand and act in consequence.' Pierre hung up with a smile and ordered the men to fall in at once and set off. The men all agreed. They fell in, pushing aside frantic women; what was important for morale was a decision, some sort of programme. And they set off leaving the women in tears of relief and motherliness.

They were strong, extremely fit for marching (each one of them having in their young legs a whole life's road) and, chattering and singing but careful of the steep slope at twilight, they passed Coazzolo and, when evening fell, Mango. Neither of the villages allowed an atom of light to escape, as if in an absurd effort to obliterate themselves in the dark. And there was no sound except the crackle of the frozen branches. A boy said he knew a short cut and very scrupulously described and recommended it. But it was idiotic, the others insisted to take a short cut to a clash, unequal forces, suffering and death.

Beyond Mango there was the real Sinai of the hills, a vast desert with no civilian life on the peaks and at most a few wretched huts in the folds of some valleys. The night was complete, the path invisible under their groping feet, and a sinister wind, seemingly born of a hillside cemetery, blew in gusts and when it fell the whole atmosphere crackled as if from the friction of its own layers of frost. Only the dogs on the farmhouses halfway up the hill, smelling them passing overhead, bayed briefly and irately, with their masters certainly cursing them and promising to kill them because of that unwelcome and perhaps fatal sign of life. Further on the steep hillside fell away and hung majestically over the Belbo valley. The men halted for a minute and looked reflectively down into the valley, a motionless sea of ink. Then they raised their eyes and levelled them on the grey hill of Castino opposite, its peak rigorously extinguished, half drowned in the night, and thought of Nord and the men around him, of the Germans and the guns of tomorrow.

Since they had not eaten at midday they were hungry and Pierre said that at Cascina della Langa there had always been – even tonight – haven and food for the partisans. The woman of the house was one of the strongest, most daring and greedy women in the hills and she gave food to the units on their way through; at the end of each month she presented the bill to Nord, who always paid down to the last penny. She would take them in and feed them even with a general attack imminent.

Johnny was the first to come out into the frozen courtyard, open on three sides to the sky, making for the little window on the ground floor pierced by light. He heard the rusty vibration of the wire,* the swift scraping sound on the ice and the fiery heavy breathing, scarcely managed to move aside and the shaggy, baying cannonball grazed him. The others began to call and calm the wolfhound, while the little window's light went out and a woman glided through the dark.

'Who are you?' she asked in a hard masculine voice.

'Partisans.'

'What kind?'

'Blue. Nord's.'

'What brigade or unit?'

'Pierre's – mine.'

'If you are Pierre, my dear son Pierre, tell me who you had with you the last time you were here.' 'Michele, who died in the battle in the town.'

That was enough – the door was thrown open, the light kindled. The bitch was quiet now and sexually submitted to the caresses and rubs from the men.

They all streamed into the kitchen and the woman said: 'Tonight I shall cook for you and maybe you are the last partisans for whom I shall make a stew, because tomorrow I shall cook for the Fascists and

---

* At night peasant dogs, being attached to a sliding ring on a high wire, were able to run across the courtyard.

the Germans, provided they don't kill me, when they come to learn from someone all I did for you partisans.' She must have been more than fifty but she looked much younger because of her very diminutiveness and the galvanism of her person; she had oily, still black hair and a black petticoat that stank incredibly. She proposed polenta and sauerkraut, cheese and hazelnuts, but the men shouted that they wanted meat for this very special supper. The woman looked at Pierre and Pierre assented, then the woman signed to a couple of partisans to come out with her to take and kill. And now her eyes shone when Pierre told her that the expense of that night did not go down on Nord's account (Nord was quite likely to be killed next day) but that he, Pierre, would pay in cash and liberally.

So they had chicken and rabbit and their broth, which they ate avidly, sitting crowded together on the tiled floor, in the fused glow of the chimney and the carbide lamps. All the danger and anxiety, all tomorrow, forgotten or at least set aside, with that great old woman who watched them eating, sitting with legs wide apart on her high-backed chair. Every moment the sentries came and drummed on the windows and with grimaces warned them to leave a reasonable amount over for them. Outside the wind blew continuously and the bitch went to and fro with her nose sniffing at her curdled territory. But after supper, even in the sheltered warmth, their minds perforce turned to the morrow, to that night itself, to the possibility of not being alive to wake up and eat twenty-four hours later. So the faces became tense and all talk's *stir* stopped.

'You sat up all last night, Johnny,' said Pierre. 'Go and lie down and I'll try not to wake you till tomorrow.' Johnny got up, extricated himself from the squatting crowd and asked where the stable was. 'And don't undress, Johnny,' 'I haven't undressed since I was a partisan.' Outside he did not make straight for the stable but went out of the courtyard to confront the night for a last time. The violence of the wind made him really bend double. Nothing was visible in the undulating dark, audible in the sinister, purgatorial crackling of the cold branches under the omnipotent wind.

The stable was low and narrow, overpopulated by animals, and it was very hot because the animals were not sleeping yet and their breathing was thereby reduced. He made his way through the animals and reached his favourite manger. He rolled into it, long and narrow like a rustic coffin; did not even take off his boots, hardly unlaced them.

Day broke on quiet motionless deserted hills from a sky that was quiet and promised peace. When Ettore came in to waken him his uniform creaked at every wrinkle and every movement. 'Will you believe it – my ears are no use to me any more,' said Ettore. 'It was last night – I ruined my hearing by the effort to separate out every other noise from that of the wind.'

Johnny came out on to the crest and looked towards Castino. It had never appeared so gleaming and vivisectionable in the crystalline air, but no movement of men was to be observed. Johnny sighed and went over to smash the frozen crust of the pond outside the gate with blows from his heel. He did not wash; he extracted from his inside pocket his toothbrush and barely cleaned his teeth with the burning water. Holding his breath, Ettore dipped two fingers in the water and passed them over his swollen cheeks. That was all.

'Where is Pierre?'

'He's trying to hold off the old woman and her sympathy.'

The woman had just appeared in the courtyard and was making signs to the two of them. Did they want a kind of breakfast with bacon fat, eggs and anchovies. The three refused and as if nothing had been said she went to set free all the *poultry* in the courtyard, which the sun was beginning to bathe.

Ettore said to her: 'Destiny doesn't change but if I were you I'd keep them shut up.' But the woman completed her work of liberation, always followed and escorted by the she-wolf, then came over to them again saying that nothing would happen, that if it was going to happen it would have begun already. 'So you really don't want a special breakfast. I'm saying it because I have a special liking for you and for no other reason, and you are three partisans as I always dreamt them – well-brought-up, fine citizens.'

Pierre collected the men and disposed others on the ridge looking towards the last bends in the road to Alba. It was fine and warming to sit on the tepid slabs of stone among the grass which was becoming elastic again, with one's eyes wandering at ease and untiringly over the deserted road. The bitch wandered about in their group, now avoiding and now soliciting their claps and rubs, always grateful and friendly, and the last mists of dawn, so quickly dissipated on the hills, were rising up in no time on the distant marine plain, already thin when they were spun and now phantomlike against the great naked shoulders of the Alps. And as the mists rose the men counted with longing for them the towns that revealed themselves, so peaceful and hospitable.

When all the weapons (a whole world of weapons) opened fire on the valley of the Belbo and the myriads of explosions leapt tiger-like and travelled for long across the hills, they leapt to their feet and ventured to the crest overhanging the Belbo. Nothing was visible because of the sudden drop and the enormous cliffs towards the bottom, but Pierre realised that they were smashing the dam below the bridge over the Belbo for the front attack on Castino. And at the same moment from the transparent woods round about peasants who had taken refuge there the evening before popped out and fled, escaping to the high hills. They went past in torrents without a glance or a word.

The tumult soon stopped when the partisan guard on the bridge was put to flight and then silence reigned, even more sinister. They caught the voice of the woman of the house, not too excited, calling all the animals back inside amid the frequent short, *tough* barking of the bitch.

They left the surroundings of the farmhouse and climbed the lofty hill opposite, which swept the road to Alba and the whole hill at Castino. A calm swarm of them was attacking the first slopes at Castino. Johnny lay down on the grass, which was already dry, and sank into a dreamy vision of that great attack. Roads and lanes and paths were full of them, climbing up with the proud calm of confidence and awareness: men, vehicles and supply trucks. And quickly from invisible hollows, there rose towers of smoke, rich black smoke, columnar and oscillating ever so slightly in the almost motionless air. From every tree, from every ditch men leapt out and ran madly away, *heart-pulsing* and darting off like rabbits.

Johnny looked at what was close by. Ettore, in order to see and hear better, had taken off his helmet and Pierre was wringing his hands and with them some unfortunate blade of grass between his fingers. 'Since it is written,' he said, 'I wish it were over for Castino.'

In their multitude they were now climbing without firing even more slow and relaxed, as if lasciviously enjoying the advance. On the vast slope halfway up animals that had been let out of their stalls made a savage sortie on to the still deserted meadows and, smelling the smoky and electric air, began to kick and circle madly. The air was so motionless and transparent, apart from the areas polluted by smoke, that one could pick out and count the men up there in the village who were occupying their unhappy, *shabby* positions. Ettore said that they were within mortar range but nothing exploded yet.

The spectacle before them so hypnotised them that only a peristaltic turn-around by a boy made him shout an alarm and make them all turn to the right. On the flat ground by the crossroads, now crowded as if for an exact *outsprung* of the ground, a whole procession of civilian prisoners dragged themselves forward, bent double under the bestial weight of ammunition boxes, and Germans were guiding them at the sides and back. And some of them acted as herdsmen in the very middle of that miserable mass of hostage-coolies. Behind them with a tremendous friction on the *replying* ground, came half a dozen guns and limbers. The *wheeling* of the gun trains, the groaning of the prisoners from the effort and the fear, the shouts, urging them on and terrorising them, from the Germans, with their chests flashing because of the belts of ammunition which caught the full sun, all formed a vocal cloud which suddenly darkened the Edenic sky. 'And look! There are priests among these poor creatures,' shouted a boy and his index finger wandered over the mass, pointing at and almost extracting four or five black-garbed figures from the grey crucible. Every so often a German raised his sub-machine-pistol to his arm and fired a burst into the suspended air like a whiplash.

The new spectacle hypnotised them once more, leaving with their arms and weapons dangling, their mouths half open and an icy dew on their temples, so that an unseen German forward unit suddenly appeared on their left and could fire at them from fifty metres with murderous swiftness. They were scattered far and wide. The top of the ridge over the Belbo was a spray of shots. Johnny dived over it with his eyes shut and Ettore too.

Johnny knew that Ettore was safe; both rolled madly down the slope, one of them now behind, now ahead. But the thought of Pierre tortured them, much more than the hard knocks at full speed against the bony, root-filled, bumpy ground. In a cottonwool capsule the echoes of the German shots reached and passed over them not yet on the slope but still on the tragic hill. Very few rolled down after them, the majority had fled centrifugally, almost certainly into the jaws of the Germans. Someone who had already landed at the bottom of the slope was calling on them in a tentative whisper to which *shock* gave an undesired sonority.

Johnny landed against the base of a tree. He got up with every slightest part of him groaning and saw that Ettore was raising himself up a little further over with the same difficulty.

The ground above them resounded with new rolling descent. They looked up to recognise Pierre's dear form but it was someone else, one of the youngest, groaning fiercely at each roll and bump. When he stopped and raised himself up they saw him to be tremendously bruised round the mouth with lips which bled purple. The moment he was on his feet he threw himself on the other two with outstretched arms and clutched them and begged them not to leave him alone, to take him with them wherever they were going. While they consoled him roughly, new thuds made them look up and it really was Pierre coming down in little leaps and bounds, unharmed, almost erect.

'And the others?'

'I don't know – one was still in the grass but on his face and I did not recognise him.'

The boy with the smashed mouth trembled like a leaf and said that now they must expect the wolfhounds and . . . He cried out; they had to gag that bleeding mouth by force and drag him bodily further downhill behind a clump of bracken. From down there, the weapons being silent, they heard a deep lewd laugh from the ridge and then a collective groan as if people were getting rid of an ordinary weight and the slope began to re-echo with a something new rolling down. In a minute two dead men landed at the bracken. They bent over them and turned them on their backs; they were two men from Castagnole, not very well identified. Johnny could not even be sure of their *noms de guerre* but two men with whom he had shared guard-duty on the mined road, shared the meat last evening, rubbed the bitch together, lent and borrowed matches . . .

They scattered again as the Germans once more began to fire into the wood; the most successful bullets scarcely sent a cloud of dust over their heads.

They slipped down closer to the stream. On a kind of promontory screened by sufficient vegetation, high above the first visible stretch of water, they stopped, not knowing what to do or how to get their bearings. The boy allowed his violet blood to spurt liberally and was still trembling like a leaf. His lips were swelling horribly and their *pooled* handkerchiefs were useless. The Germans on the top of the hill were still firing but just for firing's sake.

Johnny fixed his gaze on Castino. The great swarm had halted under the last hump in the hill before the village and it seemed (but all his senses were deceptive and not to be trusted) that the partisans had opened fire.

Pierre whispered: 'We had better look behind us. Perhaps the dogs are not just a story.'

Ettore didn't know anything at all about dogs and said so.

'But they are special dogs which never bark unless they have a man at bay.' The boy went mad again and clung to Pierre, sliding down to his knees, along his short, thin body. 'Help me! Hide me, hide me safely somewhere!' 'Where can we hide you?' Maybe if he had been a pebble or a grain of wheat or a songbird but he was a man. 'You are a man!'

At that moment the crest had a kind of earthquake, while the immense sky above them was torn by the thunder of the guns. They went face-down on the ground as if they had received those enormous cannonballs on their Lilliputian necks. The Germans were shelling Cestina and at the same time the attackers opened fire with the mortars. And from the first shots a great cloud of dust stained the façade of the village.

Ettore suggested getting out of there.

'Where to?' asked Pierre. 'At this time of day they are everywhere already. East, west, north and south.'

'Don't let's move,' implored the boy.

'We have to move,' said Johnny. 'Pierre, you give the direction and we won't blame you even if you send us into the jaws of the enemy.' Pierre rose on to his knees and said lightly: 'Then shall we try to walk along the Belbo and see if we manage to arrive somewhere before they do?'

They felt their way down through scrub and down steep slopes towards the peaceful stream and the more peaceful road. The shelling made a bridge very high above the stream. Almost at the bottom, almost within reach of the water the boy had another crisis. 'Don't take me any further! You're taking me straight into their jaws. Hide me, hide me!'

Pierre whispered to him not to shout, that way he was bringing them down on them. 'Do you really want to hide?' Ettore asked him. 'Well, look there,' and he pointed to a pool of water, very deep and absolutely motionless. 'There's enough there to hide you to perfection and for an eternity.' They left him there, wading in the icy water up to their calves on a bottom of treacherous moss. The sky was still straddled by shelling and the noise of the battle at Castino fell to a uniform level of noise. When they put foot on the other bank the din ceased, apart from some sporadic rifle fire, from which they concluded that the defence had been broken, the village evacuated in haste.

They were hardly on the other bank. 'I am dying to see the Bormida valley,' said Ettore. 'That's where I would like to be.'

'It's because you are in the Belbo valley,' said Johnny. 'If you were in the Bormida you'd be longing for the Belbo.'

They advanced through the scanty riverside vegetation towards the village of Rocchetta, keeping a constant eye on the road running parallel, still deserted but no less sinister for that. Now the village was very near at hand. It gave a feeling of peace and safety in the favourable air; its houses were beginning to appear white among the green when an old woman dressed in black rose up as if out of the ground and, spreading her arms, barred their way.

'Where are you going, poor things?'

'We're trying to get through.'

'The village is full of them, you poor things.'

'Germans or Fascists?'

'Both kinds.'

Pierre whispered: 'Have they killed people?'

The woman assented with a grave inclination of her *haggard* face.

'Have they been burning?'

'They're going to. Get back on to the other side of the river, get back up the hill and I shall pray for you poor people.'

Then the boy fell on the old woman and hugged her, sinking his face in her black breast. 'Hide me in your house – there must be some little safe place in your house, there is in every house.' She struggled in vain. Johnny ran to free her and she fled wildly with her blouse torn.

They waded back but so blindly that they found themselves confronting a steep, smooth rock, wide, with only one chimney to climb by, and it was as close to the village as they had ever been. And as they climbed they had the deadly feeling that they were doing so under the others' laughing eyes and pointed rifles. But they managed to climb up to the top and came out on the first round breast of the enormous hill among *scrub* and *bush*. The boy had got there first and lay down at his full length, as if struck down by sleep, exhausted by fear and anxiety. They sat round him, glancing *uneasily* at the vulnerable back he offered. Pierre, but without conviction in his word, almost as if he wanted only to test his voice after the *strain*, said they could try to see if the crest was still occupied. 'They're bound to be there like flies.' 'You couldn't put it better, Johnny,' said Ettore, 'surer than death. Oh, I'm hungry. I'd like to be able to eat one more time.' At that moment the village of Rocchetta went up in a cube of smoke, dark as the smoke of a locomotive, a real base for a majestic tower of smoke which is what it very quickly developed into. Johnny lit a cigarette. 'Are you mad, Johnny!' whispered Pierre. But with his elbow Johnny pushed down his snatching hand and said: 'Leave me alone, Pierre, leave me alone,' and to ward him off better climbed away from them. At the noise of his steps on the resonant ground the boy woke up with an outburst. Johnny kicked him gently till he lay down again. Then he started to climb again like a solitary, meditative walker in the woods, then he stopped and turned round. Then he signalled to the others to join him at the top and see what he saw.

Eighteen towers of smoke, compact, unshakeable even by a strong wind, rose from the village of Castino, making of it a dark temple for the gods of the underworld, with no people around the pillars of that gigantic fire so that it burnt in proud solitude far from little men. And down along the main road from the hill some of the attackers were already descending again in ordered platoons and companies, most without helmets out of relief and for a break, singing or joking, and there followed them an interminable procession of groups and carts of booty and captured stuff, and at the end a solid and heavier rearguard. But from the ridge and in the first depths of the Bormida valley the shots *raged and roared* in hot pursuit.

They would be upon them in less than an hour in unwearied joyful squads and patrols, and yet without ever breaking their strong line. They were giving a real lesson in how to round up and the others would take the lesson to the grave and that was the real importance of the lesson. Johnny felt himself at one and the same time marvellously good and horribly bad; looking at that ordered multitude descending to climb up again immediately, he felt all his organs perfectly, happily alive and functioning and healthy, and yet a bullet, very soon, would hit them and block them and corrupt them all. Heart and lungs, hands and feet. He remained alone for a little, apart from those three squatting there, smoking the last cigarette, concentrating on the deeds of men and the splendour of the sun. Slowly, powerfully, the knowlege invaded him that he would not see the setting of that sun. He would fall there on the edge of the scrub or at the feet of those trees, in shade or sun, or would he be hit during the ascent, his body rolling down into infinity, to the river? And would he lie there on his face or his back? And would anyone touch him again?

'Johnny?' Pierre called up opaquely. 'Are you in agreement to make an attempt towards the crest at dusk?'

Johnny assented in a very friendly and appreciative way.

The big column from Castino had by now certainly reached the plain near the invisible bridge over the river. A burst of fire echoed, another, a single shot like one full stop after another, all that followed was a *gasp* or suffocated wail from those taken prisoner. A man, perhaps two, had been shot, their bodies would lie emblematically at the big crossroads.

Day was dying away, as long as a millennium for the living and triflingly short, non-existent, for those to come after. It died away comatosely in the sky where the great smoke still ruled grimly and miserably revealed its vile carbon origins and that misery re-echoed spectrally on all the hills.

They set out towards the crest without speaking any more, hoping for time to get used to the new, special silence of the woodland world, made by a concentrated noise, as if they were hearing a distant fire fall back into its ashes.

Halfway down the slope they lay down again, each one orientated towards a cardinal point of the compass, the boy calm now from exhaustion.

'The moment it gets dark, we'll set off again. We'll go along the river,' said Pierre with his by now constant hint of not being in command but of suggesting and consulting. 'Yes, along the river,' said Ettore almost fiercely.

And all four fell silent, picturing in their minds its peaceful banks, in their peaceful pre-winter nakedness, its peaceful waters in their peaceful pre-winter severity, peaceful must be the sound of the angelus from the isolated parish churches on the other peaceful bank, and there must be far from the river and the roads a peaceful farmhouse with peaceful and slightly stupid people who would signal to them in a decent way to climb up into the hayloft and up there to wrap themselves in a peaceful sanctuary of hay with just the slightest *tunnel* for breathing.

'Shall we cross at the Barbaresco ferry or at the one further down valley from Casagnole?' asked Ettore.

Pierre and Johnny made a movement with their heads as if to indicate that the choice was as unimportant as arrival at the chosen point was to be feared.

XXV

The sun sank, and the loss of it was enormous, immeasurable. A wind replaced it, vesperal, mournful and creaking. Weaker than in the open sky where it had begun to attack and shred the majestic columns of smoke high above the punished villages, it blew in the wood as well multiplying its secret life and the reason for sudden starts. The boy started to tremble and rave again but now with murmured groans like a child under a nightmare.

They got up and took the first steps towards the heights. They were making their way through the wood between the valley, which was lacerated by sporadic firing and the perfectly silent ridge, halfway up the hill. They were walking in the wood in an area of shadow that became more and more dark, with the wind rising, and it felt as if every other feeling and instinct was annihilated in this primeval march towards the plateau of safety through the steepest of risks. And – 'We are getting through, we are getting through,' Ettore continued to whisper with a kind of ghostly voice as if as a collective suggestion.

They were faced by a clearing with a last bewitched play of light and shade and absolutely lacking in that noisy and creaking life of every other point in the wood. Johnny went into it first, with under his feet a feeling of an asphodel-covered* plain under his feet and was already fairly far in when a burst of sub-machine-gun fire and some rifle shots lacerated the surrounding world. The earth spurted up and the branches crackled under the shots, and a second later a man, a partisan flew down head first, flashing towards them, barely touching the earth, entirely weightless and airborne. As he passed he shouted to them get away, away, and all of them followed in his

---

* In Greek mythology the asphodel was the flower which grew in the Elysian fields.

vertiginous wake, while up above the firing resumed, rancorous and probing. Johnny threw himself down at a run but the boy barred his way. He had thrown away his rifle and was falling on his knees, his hands clasped on his breast, paralysed and doubled up with terror. So that Johnny ended up on top of him with his knees together and catapulted him down to roll over and over, following and kicking away at him as he rolled down, in a short-lived escape.

The two found themselves alone on a high spur above the river which in the dusk now emitted only noise and not gleams of light. Johnny stretched himself out covering the first steep drop with his Sten while his heart was breaking because of the absence of Pierre and Ettore. The boy was lying on his back and seemed moribund, then he began to wail: 'You rescued me but you have crushed my chest. I'm sure to have a lot of broken ribs.'

'Breathe deeply and see if it hurts.'

'Yes it hurts.'

'A lot?'

He tried and said No.

'Then you haven't any broken ribs and so thank me.'

The boy said: 'I've lost my rifle.'

'So I saw.'

'And now I am getting rid of the ammunition,' and Johnny heard the dull landing of the bag on the ground. 'Now I'm not a partisan any more, am I? They can't kill me any more because there's no proof. They can stop me and interrogate me and even put me in prison but they can't shoot me on the spot. What do you think?'

He sighed: 'You are wearing a grey-green blouse and camouflaged trousers. They'll kill you simply because you're dressed like that. You haven't anything to change into and you can't go about naked because they will understand and will kill you naked as you are.'

The boy was so tired that he showed only partial disappointment.

The precocious night hung heavily from the sky, with still distinguishable in it the floating chaos of crestfallen and scattered smoke, the road parallel to the river was only a phantom of itself. 'Ettore and Pierre will look for me,' he thought, 'they won't try to pass without me.' And acute jealousy seized him of the new partisan who was the couple's new companion. Then a sudden crackling made him shake with fear then with joy because it was Pierre and Ettore and the third man crawling about looking for him.

Of the third Johnny could hear only the whispering voice and obscurely guess at his stature. He had a gritty voice, rheumatic, which betrayed an age considerably above the partisan average. He was called Jackie. He rubbed his hands in a very friendly way and said he had ended up well in excellent company in that headlong flight of his.

They had to give up the idea of the river, Jackie having made it clear that it was absolutely inaccessible, the crest being thickly manned by the enemy, mostly Germans, from the crossroads at Manera to Mango. So they agreed to pass over into the valley of the Bormida with the prospect of being fixed up pretty well since Jackie knew it very well and had 'bases' there. So at dead of night with the glow of the fires giving the position of the villages and guiding them far away from them they set out making for the river and wading it. But the boy fell into panic again and began to rave and wriggle and this time without more ado they shook him off in the wood. He followed them madly and caught up with them still in the wood.

While they waded across Jackie said it would be best to leave the boy behind – all the more since he was unarmed. As he said this Jackie's voice was older than ever. The boy clung to Pierre, holding him back as as crossed, then when Pierre paid no attention he turned nasty. 'If you get rid of me,' he shouted at the top of his voice, 'I'll bring them down on you.' 'And we,' said Ettore, 'will drown you at once in these few inches of water.'

Then he ran ahead and reached the bank first. But faced by that momentary solitude, faced by the ghost of the road, the boy turned back and joined them. Pierre seized him by the collar. 'You are making a hellish noise. That's enough – find life or death on your own.'

'We're going to have to get rid of him seriously,' said Ettore.

'I'll follow you everywhere,' said the other with the petulance of extreme desperation. 'You're not going to shoot me, that's for sure with them so near.'

'We won't shoot you,' said Jackie's calm, gritty voice, 'but to do away with you . . .' and they heard the hissing unsheathing of a bayonet.

The boy ran on to the road and there suddenly had his inspiration.

When they reached the road he was kneeling down examining a conduit that ran under the road and opened out on to the slope above the river. He scarcely raised his head and whispered that he had found what he needed and from now on he would have no more need of them. They all knelt down to examine the tube. 'The Fascists won't dream of poking about in this tube and I'll be fine here until it's all over.'

He was taking the measurements to slide into it. Now that the boy had made up his mind Johnny *relented towards him.*

'Before you slip in, are you sure you can stand it?'

'But what is there to stand?'

'Nights and days can pass and maybe there are nasty beasts in there.'

'That's nothing as long as they aren't men.'

'They'll pass overhead with guns and limbers. The noise will drive you mad and maddened you'll come out and they'll shoot you down easily.'

But he was absolutely sure he could hold out and slipped in head and shoulders first and Johnny pushed him right in by the feet.

They bounded across the road and began to climb, aiming for places where their mental geography avoided and excluded habitations. They climbed on open ground and in the scrub and then in woodland and here they got their breath back. Once they turned round and saw the valley of Rocchetta partly on fire and partly dotted with their camps and billets. Other reddish clouds hung drunkenly in the total darkness over other villages throughout the rest of the Belbo valley. But there was no wind and no shots either.

Jackie asked for a rest. 'I'd dead with walking. You see I'm not your age any more.'

They sat on the clotted earth, leaning against creaking trunks and after a little Ettore asked very sleepily if the cold could harm them much if they fell asleep there. Pierre somewhat excitedly replied that they simply would not sleep there and then Ettore said: 'Don't speak to me in that tone of voice, Pierre, you ought to know what sort of a day we have on our shoulders.' Nevertheless after a little they started climbing again.

They passed a solitary farmhouse, miserable, and stopped in front of it for no more than a moment to listen to the deathly silence within and guessed at the feverish vigil of its gagged inhabitants. Until the watchdog rushed to the end of its chain. Enormous, piercing was the resonance of the barking and they fled far off while the animal continued to bay at the ghost-sound of the retreating footsteps. 'Bastard,' panted Jackie, 'I love dogs more than any other animal but these days they should all be exterminated.'

The wave of the great hill was powerful and invincible, they marched much further before Pierre expressed his conviction that now they must be at the same height as Castino, almost at the summit. So entering another large wood they halted in its most sheltered and *ventral* part, come what might. They sat on the clotted earth, leaning on the creaking trees, breathless because of the cold which was becoming more intense, feeling to the full over and within them in its entirety their human misery which had up to then been masked and drugged by their excited desire for life. Their heads drooped but their eyes did not close, to keep their hands warm they had left their weapons on the ground, they adhered to it like metal fish on dry land. Hunger tortured them with Chinese fingers. Tomorrow, tomorrow at the latest, in order to eat they would burst open barred doors and point their weapons at solitary and mortally frightened women. It was not to refuse them food but because they did not want them even to come in for a second under their roof, in case they simply left their smell. Tomorrow.

Jackie spoke and his voice sounded like a lullaby in spite of its hoarseness: 'If we reach the Bormida, if we get through, I know a farm just outside Perletto sited in a gorge which certainly won't be on their maps. There's an old couple there, generous and very brave. They'll take us in all four of us and give us food and a safe nook to sleep in. We must just take care to get there without being seen by other people and above all by their officers who are sure to be searching everywhere with their field glasses. Then we will have food and will be able to sleep thirty-six, forty-eight hours, seventy-two hours on end.'

He got up and walked in a circle as if taking exercise against the cold.

'This is a big round-up but it won't last for ever and we can last it out to the end simply eating and sleeping. Do me the favour of thinking about it with me. Home-made bread, the kind that crackles in your hand and slice after slice of pork belly, very white with that wonderful round little red streak.'

'Get lost!' said Ettore.

Then it seemed to Johnny that Pierre, from the deep aybss of narcosis, said that they had to have a sentry, they absolutely mustn't all fall asleep, with a thread of renewed excitement in his fading voice. Then they were all motionless and no longer alive, tiny frozen objects in the creaking wood.

XXVI

The dawn was like a dusk. Miserably Johnny stretched himself and unknotted himself and stirred himself to wake up the other numbed men. So he saw Jackie in the light. He was over forty and lightness was his principal characteristic from his sparse and spread-out hair to his skeletal legs, their skinniness pitilessly underlined by the abundance of the cavalry breeches and the army puttees. Then he wore a waterproof blouse, very wide compared to his poor chest, crossed only by a carabiniere's bandolier. They were all on their feet and listened hard. The silence was perfect, almost bewitching, but it ended too soon.

Voices and noises, filtering through limitless but very pure air, rose up to warn them that the Fascists were up and ready down there in the Belbo valley. They set off to come out of the night's wood in the direction of the ridge between Belbo and Bormida.

A desperate group leapt out of a thick clump of bushes on the way down and they were within a hair's breadth of firing bursts at each other. They were partisans, all in English uniforms, clearly men of 1st Division scattered northwards by Lampus' defeat and now floating about on those unfamiliar hills. One of them was carrying his Bren slung round his neck, his hands gripping the barrel, ready to fire.

Without stopping one of them asked where they were going.

'To the Bormida valley.'

The one with the Bren laughed *strainedly*. 'Go on, go on!' and they went past and downhill. Ettore turned round and said: 'And you are going to the Belbo? Go on, go on!'

They arrived on the ridge, giddily high above the enormous valley, and lay there gaping. All the roads and hills were swarming with Fascists and a big column was climbing the road to the crest seeming to be bigger, more compact and tremendous at each bend. They slipped sideways into a little wood of dry pines and settled down, each one behind a trunk and looked down into the Bormida. The marching column was eating up a stretch of level ground. Down there in the valley more than one house ended by going up in flames, the smoke condensing in lofty pillars in the *unstirred* air.

Jackie stretched out a trembling hand and pointed out Perletto, inaccessible and on fire.

At that moment a tumult broke out halfway down the hill towards the Belbo. The Bren suddenly fired a burst, heavy rifle fire followed, became more intense, the Bren gave another quick burst, then the hammering of unopposed rifle fire and nothing more.

So the columns from the Belbo were climbing up to meet the column from the Bormida. The latter was entering the penultimate bend before the crest. They had to clear out, choose whether to die in the Bormida or the Belbo. All were for the Belbo but where? They were everywhere and were closing, closing in.

'If the bloody earth would just open –' sighed Jackie.

Then Johnny saw the big gully and pointed to it. To the left of Castino the great breast of the hill fissured into a narrow but deep gully, darkly edged with entangled vegetation which fell away precipitously almost to the flat ground of the Belbo.

'They have a fantastic fear of ravines,' said Johnny, 'but let's hurry up before they spot us with their field glasses.'

No one was convinced but they all ran to the ravine, climbed down inside it like reptiles on the steep hard wall. And at the bottom Jackie showed his hands, torn and bleeding from having grasped a green blackberry shoot so as not to fall headlong.

Down there it was very cold and dark with icy dirty water which trickled grudgingly through poisonous growths of a green that was eternally sunless. They went forward a little towards a thicker green and dived into it immediately, listening so hard that it was painful. But they heard nothing and would continue to hear nothing unless the others arrived at the brink of the gully. Ettore looked hard at Johnny once but Johnny shook his head almost imperceptibly.

Hours passed (the campaniles at Castino and Rocchetta rang them regularly) in the torturing quiet, while they had sights before their eyes and noises in their ears that often made them jerk their heads up and aim their weapons at the rim with a great, enormous rustling noise. And the others tightened their lips and narrowed their eyes so as not to strike down the culprit with a word or look.

The Fascists could not be finding anything because no shots echoed. Later a low and confused murmur arrived down there as if the two columns had met and were fraternising and resting together. Pierre asked the time in a tiny whisper but everyone's watch had stopped or been damaged. Then eleven was struck on the campaniles with a sad vesperal note.

Pierre suggested going a little further down the ravine, after all it was still the ravine, and they all nodded agreement, for it seemed that that simple change of position might relieve them a little. They descended another hundred paces or so towards another green thicket and another hour passed with the rim still virgin. Then Jackie took it into his head to speak and whispered to Johnny's cheek. 'Well done, you were right. They have a terrible fear of gullies.' 'The Italians not so much but the Germans yes. They never go down into them.' 'Let's hope ours are Germans,' said Jackie.

'Don't say let's hope,' said Ettore, a prey to superstition.

A few shots exploded, neither distant nor near, and very paradoxically proved to be a relief to their suffering ears. It must be near midday and the others would have to break off and sit on the ground for their rations. They went a little further down, another hundred steps. The dirty stream had reached a certain noise-level and the wall had become more soft. There for the first time they heard the others: voices and calls, loud and sharp, but adolescent, sounding as if they were off duty, almost as if they were playing games.

They went further down still and stopped because the slope flattened out so much that it came almost level with a patch of gravel and neighbouring fields. They lay flat and without breathing on the rubbish left by the waters and the stones trying to guess where the others were and what they were doing. But the only thing they could make out was that they were all Italians.

A man came towards them holding a pail. He was a serf with an animal face and movements, he was speaking to himself with a lowing pedantic voice, merrily. He was certainly the idiot servant of that big farmhouse – the kind that more than one peasant in these parts took from the orphanages and kept for life in service. And

Johnny trembled at his approach, trembled at that idiotic face, his walk, and his incoherent muttering.

He saw them even though they flattened themselves on the ground and his brutish eyes shone. He threw his pail to the ground, snorted, then began to dance and gesticulate, while the four of them made caressing signs as if to a big dog in an awkward mood. Then his animal voice rose higher to a certain clarity and comprehensibility.

'You are partisans. Partisans. There are partisans here. Now I am going to call the iron hats. The iron hats will come and kill you where you are.'

Johnny and Ettore were crawling towards the spot to seize him by the legs and throw him by them into the ravine where they could stun and throttle him, but the madman saw them and laughing began to back away. At that moment an old peasant appeared with knotted brows, saw and understood, clutching his head. He ran to the servant and seized him, he called him gently by name and begged him and meantime *mimicked* to the four that the Fascists were in his courtyard and that there were a lot of them, they were still eating and they should run off keeping to the ravine. They left crouching, while the old man clutched the idiot even closer – he was now struggling and bellowing something about the iron hats.

They kept going down but soon fear that the idiot would get the better of the old man or would shout so much as to alarm the Fascists seized them, forced them into rushing upright along the ravine which fortunately now became deeper.

They were drawing near the mouth of the ravine, their terror at seeing it blocked by patient Fascists taking aim growing with each step. But it was perfectly open, almost sabbatical in the liquid breeze of a sylvan peace. They got their breath back and looked out ahead. The road in the valley was deserted and quiet, the river beyond gleamed sparingly in the sun through the thin screen of green on the bank. Then they raised their eyes to the enormous, motionless breast of the great hill of the day before and felt for it an agonising nostalgia.

'Let me go first,' begged Jackie, 'in consideration of the fact that I'm not your age any more.' He already felt in his chest the oppressive sense of the dash that had still to be made.

'Why didn't you stay at home with your damned age?' said Ettore but Jackie did not hear him, he was running to the road like a deer with his little skeletal legs, Ettore followed him then Johnny, without looking to their sides, making for the hollow in which the first two had disappeared.

Pierre was the last to set out but at once the road was swept by fire from a semi-automatic rifle. Pierre stopped as if nailed to the spot, then took off again and arrived with a few leaps at the little hollow. They threw themselves into the water together so impetuously that the first splash went across to the other bank while the semi-automatic began to fire again. Johnny glanced to his right and saw a patrol emerge from the corner of a house – there were three of them but only one was firing with the semi-automatic. They had taken cover behind a pile of gravel on the road and were scanning the first steep slopes of the hill as if they had already lost them from sight. At last they withdrew, perhaps fearing that the partisans would reply with fire from some unknown spot.

They climbed up a little then lay on the grass, each one pointing to a cardinal point of the compass. So long as the semi-automatic hadn't warned and recalled down the hill some patrol moving along the crest.

'What are you thinking, Ettore?'

'I am thinking of the difference between the present and the days in the town.'

'Didn't the idea ever cross your mind of something like this down there in the town? Never once?'

'No, never. I went about like a drunk man down there in the town. We were all drunk.'

They were too hungry and the one who could hold out least and was the most intractable was old Jackie. At last he exploded: 'I don't know and don't care what your programme is. As for me the moment it gets dark I'm making for Cascina della Langa. By now the Germans will have left. The artillery has done its job. I am going up there and the old woman will give me something to eat – oh, you bet she'll give me something to eat.'

'You have long-term plans, eh?' said Pierre. 'When it grows dark ...'

And yet the twilight arrived, with them gazing all that time at the big hill opposite, less and less overrun by their units, evidently they too felt tired.

Later a rumble of trucks rose from the close-by depths of the Belbo valley and later still, perhaps at Cossano a series of bursts of fire. And it was as if those bullets entered their flesh and cut it to ribbons, and they threw themselves about as they lay on the *tough* grass from pain and fear directly felt. Because these volleys sounded so measured, accurate and so officially spaced out that there could not be the least doubt that they were executions. Perhaps at Cossano.

Then they gazed at the sky and its boundless reflections on the hills and each look was a prayer, a command to the world to take on darker tints, to drain the sky and the earth of the colours of day. Until all the remaining colour in the sky faded to a few dying embers in a bed of dark ashes, then Jackie got up, mightily stretching his spidery little body and said: 'Boys, do you understand that we are alive and on our feet at the end of the second day? They won't last the Six Days of the Creation, will they?'

They set out. Because of the darkness and their caution they took more than an hour to reach where they could see the crest. With the suddenness almost of a mirage the big farmhouse on the crest appeared, massive and bewitched, with lights in the cracks of its broken blinds. They climbed up a little farther and then the voice of the bitch exploded; short and rounded and probably it had already begun to move about but no darker silhouette imprinted itself fleetingly on the black walls. Yet Jackie cursed the dog but Johnny whispered that it didn't matter in any case the Germans were still in the house. They strained to hear across the gap but they did not believe him but Johnny had heard, as if in a realm of dreams, the mingled voices of the German soldiers. 'They're there and they are celebrating.'

Ettore and Pierre said nothing but Jackie called him a 'visionary'. Maddened with hunger he was feeling his way forward for the last leap to the summit. When they distinctly heard the padding of the invisible bitch on the path on the ridge and could almost hear the air being drawn into its throat preparing to bay. It bayed, Jackie clenched his fists in the dark and said: 'I'll knock you out . . .' then they heard a window being flung open violently and the drumming of steel-shod feet at the corner of the house with repeated alarm calls in German. Then a first burst of fire. They rolled blindly down into the dark cutting void while other volleys rang out.

They came to rest, the Germans were no longer firing, the bitch gave another couple of howls. The moment they came to a halt Ettore hurled himself on Jackie: 'I'll lay you out, you old cretin,' and repeatedly struck frail Jackie who groaned under him and made an excuse about his hunger and age. Then Ettore let him go but said: 'Be clear about it – we don't want this old fool with us any more, this old fool who will have us turned into corpses at any moment.' The three walked on suddenly almost as if they wanted to lose him in the wood but Jackie ran after them, groaning that yesterday he had saved their lives, even if unintentionally. After half a kilometre of wood they were together again, in acid, scolding comradeship.

They were travelling to the right halfway down the hillside in the thickest and most crackling wood, knowing only too well where they were going to end up and yet not knowing what point there was in making their way *thither*. Before them lay the great wood of the Madonna della Rovere* halfway between Mango and Cossano in the heart of hearts of the densely occupied lower valley of the Belbo. So that Johnny proposed, more as a wish than a suggestion, to cut straight to the crest a little before Mango and to walk there directly, crossing four hills to the never-forgotten river. Now it seemed it was sufficient for them merely to see it, the river, to have a glimpse, even a fleeting one, of its peaceful bank. But Pierre observed briefly that at this time of day the banks would be swarming with them unless they were idiots and they were giving ample proof of not being that. It would be atrocious, to say the least of it, to fall into their jaws just as they were setting foot on that bank they dreamt of.

'What's wrong, Pierre?' asked Johnny, puzzled by his voice. Pierre's voice had always tended a little towards querulousness but now, as never before, it grated and wavered.

'I must have a bit of a temperature.'

Johnny went and felt his brow but his fingers rendered insensible by the cold could not form a judgment. Yet 'You're certainly shivering,' he said.

Jackie intervened, very solicitously. 'Have you a temperature, chief? for goodness' sake, have you a temperature?' but Johnny said to him drily not to whine.

They stopped in the heart of the wood of Madonna della Rovere,

---

* The Madonna of the Oak.

dejected, Jackie tried pathetically to make himself useful, he wanted to do all the work that there was to be done, but there was nothing else to be done but to let themselves fall down and sit along a glassy trunk on the clotted earth. Then while they watched as if in a coma, after having held himself in as much as possible, anxious not to fall asleep on bad terms, he exploded.

'You are bright boys, all three of you. I've really been lucky to come across you.'

'But we're not,' said Ettore.

'At least admit I saved your lives. You were going into the jaws of the Germans. You can be certain that I won't do anything else stupid. Hunger, hunger sometimes finishes you and me off.'

'I wish hunger would shut you up now.'

'Please let me get it off my chest. I would like you to keep me with you after this. You will certainly make a good team. You're not the kind to give in.'

'We'll see,' Pierre gurgled.

'I won't disappoint you and won't make you angry, you'll see, I'll do whatever you order, having regard for and taking into consideration my damned age.'

'About your age,' said Ettore, 'why the devil did you become a partisan at this damned age of yours? To be frank, I tend to see in it the defect of partisans who aren't too young. Instinctively I don't trust them, to go on talking frankly, I see self-interest.'

'Self-interest? What self-interest? I don't know about the other partisans of about my age but I can say that I was and am a partisan because of the idea. And it is an old idea, when you were little kids I was already having problems because of the idea. But in these times it seemed to be too little to me and so I plunged into the partisans.'

'When?'

'Only at the beginning of October in the enthusiasm of the town and I admit it is very little. But I chose the worst time of the year for my age. But the idea is in me and stays there even if tomorrow I shall find myself with my face to a wall. So respect me, boys, trust me.'

'It sounds as if you aren't hungry any more, Jackie?'

'Right – because I am talking about my idea.'

Pierre was at the bottom of the deep well of sleep, a limp sack sobbing at the foot of a tree, and even the talkative Jackie was slipping down, slipping down until he stuck there motionless, crumpled. Ettore arranged himself as best he could against this trunk and said: 'Maybe you're right, Johnny, to go straight to the river.'

'Don't let's try our luck, Ettore. Tomorrow will be the same as today if we are lucky.'

'Lucky?'

'And then Pierre wouldn't make it over the four hills. Are you cold?'

'Damnably. The Fascists are more than is needed. Just being cold is killing us.'

His voice dropped, became sleepy, he was close to abandoning Johnny to his watch so that Johnny hastened to save himself by holding Ettore back on the edge of narcosis. With an infantile urge he asked him to talk about the town.

'What about the town?'

'Anything you like – maybe about the times when we didn't even dream about anything like this . . .'

'The town is down there,' said Ettore *dreamily.*

'I know.'

'And it's full of them.'

'Yes, infested with them like lice.'

'That's right – infected with them like lice. But they are making us end up like lice, Johnny. They'll squash us all.'

He huddled with his back to the trunk, his knees supported his chin. 'Now I shall have a dream, I order myself to have a dream. I am at a table at a temperature of twenty-two degrees, a nice safe room, where I am eating my favourite menu and my mother is serving me personally.'

Johnny was not sleepy. As a last exercise against the cold – it had to last all night – he wandered about a little around that extinguished bivouac; then he returned to the three kicking, hissing and groaning in their squalid sleep which he envied them even so. But it did not come, it hovered over his head without ever alighting on it. Neither fear nor caution kept it away because it was a matter of total indifference; under the omnipotent wind the wood creaked and groaned so much that its sound would have drowned the *trampling* of a regiment. Nor did hunger keep it away – at the moment hunger was the mildest inhabitant of his body. He shook his feet and boots and saw them oscillate as light as detached feathers with no sawing bite into his calves. He lowered himself against a trunk, assumed the most passive position and that most favourable to sleep. He began to practise autosuggestion on himself, he would repeat a thousand times maybe Bunyan's interpolation: '*And as I slept I dreamed a dream. And as I slept . . .*'

At the end of the night Ettore wakened him, then said he had been shaking him for five minutes but evidently his numbed hands had neither weight nor grip. Jackie was getting up, only Pierre still stuck to the ground with fever in his eyes and on his lips.

Johnny went to observe the Belbo valley. The silence was perfect, no one was awake yet down there, not even a cock.

He came back, asked 'Which way shall we take?' of Pierre who was rising.

'Where there aren't so many swarms of them.'

'It remains to be seen where they aren't swarming so much.'

'Then let's wait for daybreak,' said Pierre lying back again. He was stammering because of his trembling.

After a while Johnny said they should set out for the crest at Mango to have clear and direct information at the feared and longed-for birth of the light. They set out groping in the dark, Pierre groping for two.

The light insinuated itself little by little, almost lamenting its nocturnal hemisphere, and amid that avarice of light they climbed up through the wood to the phantasmal profile of the crest. Then Jackie's eye, sharpened by hunger, detected a farmhouse, solitary, poor and hostile, on the edge of the big wood. He went forward first on tiptoe over the little courtyard which had no guard-dog, first he whispered then shouted to attract the inhabitants. The door and the little windows remained barred, but from the ruined corner of the house a woman advanced and confronted by their levelled weapons raised her hands to her mouth. They lowered them. Her young face was devastated by insomnia and fear, because of poverty she wore an ill-fitting childish skirt down to her knees which were covered by thick black wool.

'Fascists?' muttered Jackie.

'They came by yesterday morning and again yesterday afternoon.'

'They didn't do any damage as far as I can see.'

'They took away all the hens and rabbits, the calf and the piglet.

And they killed my dog which didn't like them with a rifle. They said they were taking it all away only because of the Germans who would come by, will come by after them. So I am out here waiting for the Germans. And please get out of my courtyard at once and go away.'

Jackie said: 'We haven't eaten for three days. Give us a little bread and cheese, signora.' She stretched out her arms as if she wanted to tear that little skirt of hers. 'They took away everything and as for bread I haven't baked for three days. Inside I have only a crust.'

'Right, throw me that crust,' said Jackie.

'Make him stop,' groaned Pierre and Johnny went and pulled Jackie away by the arm. But then the woman wanted to talk a bit more.

'Do the Germans have these famous sniffer dogs or not?'

'It's a story as far as I know.'

'People say they have them.'

'It's a story, signora.'

She sighed with relief pushing out her bosom which was her only riches: 'My husband and my father-in-law are hidden in the ground and I spread fresh manure over the hole so that if the dogs came their noses would be confused and they wouldn't pick up the smell of Christian flesh. Are they safe down there, my husband and my father-in-law?'

'Yes, they're all right where they are.'

They went on, the light was already flooding and in it they hastened towards the crest. At last they lay on it to keep out of the possible field glasses of some early-morning officer and looked to all points of the compass. The village of Mango, wrapped up in itself, seemed deserted but firing was already going on and lively in ravines in front of it and indicated not the suppression of some sort of defence but an eager and organised manhunt. And something of the same kind was going on on the peak of San Donato to their right but with none of those involved in sight. They turned round to look at the approach to the wood of the Madonna della Rovere and the first slopes were swarming with them, joyous and lively. As the light grew a whole column faced the wood and fanned out in a long line.

At Mango the firing was growing heavier so they had no other choice than the peak at San Donato. Up there the shots had stopped although the odds were that it was only a respite. They attacked the faded slopes of the gigantic naked hill, smooth and absolutely without corrugations at any point. Johnny looked back at Pierre, the imminence of the danger and the need to confront it had certainly put his slight temperature at the bottom of the list.

They climbed up, at times on all fours, in the gloomy conscious-ness of their nakedness and extreme visibility, halfway up they stopped to regain their breath.

One cheek sticking to the dew-bathed earth Johnny looked at that landscape of life and death. From that point he could look right over the crest at Mango and beyond the plain of Neive and Castagnole he could see the grey-blue mists that rose from the river. He sighed, he said that at least he had managed to see it but his heart felt a pang at the thought that they were trying at the risk of their lives to take the longest road to it. There was certainly a motive because now the firing in front of Mango was growing heavier and the serpentine head of two columns of smoke appeared over the ridge. They had no line of sight now into the Belbo valley but they knew that now the others were beating the wood of the Madonna della Rovere metre by metre, perhaps they had already examined the clearing where they had passed the night.

They got up again and climbed up to the knife-edge crest. At a hundred paces from the village, deserted, silent, necropolic, they stopped and sniffed the air. Then Johnny and Ettore went forward first. They ran on tiptoe across the last stretch and together went round the first hovel, suddenly eavesdropping on the interior of its mossy, saltpetred walls. The smell of the dew-drenched nettles and the fresh chicken dung was acute. But humankind was missing, buried or taken up into heaven, and the silence of the clump of houses shrieked. They went past the other corner of the hovel and had a better view of the place; two low rows of bolted and barred huts of the high hills and then, as backdrop, the dirty façade of the church with its door off its hinges. On all those walls blackened by inclement weather there shone in the sun, in rich extremely fresh black paint, big letters singing the praises of the Fascists and their Germans, adoring the Duce, promising lead and the noose for the partisans and a thousand deaths to Nord. They slipped back into the thin shadow of the first hut.

From the little door of the sheepfold the woman of the house barely appeared. She called them unfortunates, said she wouldn't like to be in their mothers' place . . . yes, they had just passed through, Fascists and Germans together, twenty minutes ago, they must still be on the little hill between the church and the cemetery, they had shot two partisans winkled out of the church against the cemetery wall. They should be careful about going down because the road the others had taken overlooked at almost every turn the immense naked slope.

They went back behind the bank of the crest to Pierre and Jackie. The two of them were very nervous because they had seen the forward troops of the Belbo valley column flashing on the edge of the wood. There was not a minute to be lost, the only thing to do was to get down to the foot of the Mango crest at full speed, down the slope that was like the palm of one's hand, hoping not to be seen by the column which was going down towards the road.

They had a fleeting view of them while they turned a bend in the road that bit into the slope. They were walking down as if on a school outing, the officers playing at being mates with the other ranks. When they disappeared round the bend, they threw themselves down the slope. Their speed assumed an almost giddy rhythm, very soon they were appalled at their mad uncontrollable flight, every time their feet touched the ground was a frightening risk. Johnny wished for anything except a sprain or a broken leg. Jackie's little legs were the first to give way, with a *gasp* he dived and somersaulted, then rolled down like a tree trunk. The tree-lined edge of the neighbouring valley seemed to rise towards him giddily like a wall being mechanically thrust upwards to make the crash more murderous. Johnny shut his eyes and threw himself down sideways. He felt the dunt of his side on the ground and almost simultaneously the short burst of fire let off by the Sten.

He landed between the legs of Jackie who had already arrived, huddled in a little green-lined hollow. Jackie was holding his head in his hands. 'You've done for us,' he whispered. 'They must have heard you and now they'll come this way.' Ettore and Pierre arrived and they too crowded into the little hollow, Pierre said only: 'You could have got it all in your body if the Sten had been turned towards you.'

But the surrounding hillocks did not become crowned by their helmets, the burst of fire had fitted well into the rifle fire which tore apart the invisible ravines of the Mango valley. Then they looked back at the very highest crest of San Donato, which was still deserted. (On the campaniles of all the villages round about it was striking ten with such a slight difference in timing that perhaps a hundred peals rang out to mark ten.)

Then they clambered up the steep slope towards Mango and buried themselves in its bushes.

The whole of Mango was there under their eyes. The village had not been set on fire, its lanes and open spaces all deserted and as if subject to an electric shock. On the slope opposite they were burning a big farmhouse which in previous months had served as mess hall for the partisans. The head of the column which had come down from San Donato had just arrived on the level ground and was watching that fire, admiring it and commenting on it. The evicted family was sitting on the edge of a ditch turning their backs to the flames, all with their heads sunk on their chests, blind to the passing Fascists who, as they passed, mocked and harangued them. The head of the family was in a field trying with all his might to tame two oxen which *stampeded wildly* at the smell of the fire.

Every road and path in the valley had its group of men scouring it, but on the point of relaxing with their weapons hanging down rather than levelled. There was no firing anywhere. Darker and thicker smoke rose from the gullies between Mango and Neive. Further down, as far as one could see, the plain at Neive was literally crawling with with them, in rank upon rank they were beating the under-growth and bushes along the railway. Johnny looked further over and beyond the plateau at Castagnole, he once again saw the blessed river shining a good deal in the sun, blue as it is only in spring. Johnny followed it far as he could to where a huge spur edged with haze cut off his view.

Then Ettore gave him a dig with his elbow and following his eyes which were popping from their sockets, Johnny saw behind them everything there was to see. The crest at San Donato was becoming peopled with them, ten, twenty, fifty, a hundred of them black against the sky, with the mechanical gestures and movements of marionettes on that lofty stage. Jackie sank his face in the soft cold earth. Pierre coughed, 'If they come down the hill,' Ettore began but did not finish. All four gave a last *squirm* the better to endure that long, corpse-like immobility – who knew for how long? 'They'll come down the hill,' Ettore said once more.

But for the moment they were not coming down, evidently they were regaining their breath and resting in what remained of the sacked village. Now there was nothing to be heard but the *drone* of a bad-tempered insect.

'They are coming down the hill,' said Ettore after a little without looking round.

Then Jackie could hold out no longer and turned his head round to check. Then he turned back and said with a weepy voice: 'It's not true – it's not true. There's not a soul on the hill nor on the crest. Why did you say that?'

At that moment a hoarse trumpet sounded in the heart of Mango and in their hearts. The hope that it was the signal for withdrawal pervaded them and shook them so violently that they all rose on their elbows heedless of the Fascists on the crest at San Donato. Yes, they had done with Mango, the patrols scattered over the countryside were regaining the village, with rapid and relieved steps. The trumpet repeated the signal but before the column had emerged from Mango, compact and stamping their feet, and made for Neive the campaniles had struck twelve. And the crest at San Donato remained deserted.

They went downhill slowly, the men turning round several times to look at what they had done, but now the head of the column was disappearing round the first bend; in ten mintues the rearguard would be swallowed too. Then Johnny looked back and on the crest at San Donato all the hundreds of men from the Belbo column appeared strung out as if for a surprise. They heard the trill of a whistle and the first of them leapt down the hillside, covering it all the way across, one man at least every ten metres.

'Do as I'm doing,' whispered Johnny with the most normal of voices. He began to crawl to the right and in no time was out of sight of the forward troops from San Donato and in full view of the rearguard from Mango which was going downhill two hundred metres away. He stood upright and began to walk comfortably in a carefree manner alongside the rearguard, measuring the distance from bush to bush with one eye and with the other seeing if anyone in the rearguard was looking in his direction. Behind him he heard the identical movement of the three others.

The big thicket which edged the big ravine east of Mango was at a hundred paces or so, as he took them Johnny audibly counted them one after the other. And meanwhile nothing happened, not a single shout or shot, nor the blind leaps of the other three behind him. At the ninetieth step he began to smile. At the ninety-fifth to laugh, diving into the blind shade of the thicket he gurgled with laughter. Then he turned round and the other three hugged his shoulders and lowered their heads into that well of arms like rugby players. Jackie was crying noiselessly. 'We shall reach the river,' said Johnny. 'Let's not start off again for a little,' said Ettore. It was still early, lethally early, the liquid shade of the scrub was deceiving them as to the real state and progress of the day. Jackie timidly said he didn't agree – why make for the river when the whole of their right flank was free? They persuaded him that it certainly wasn't free, going to the right they would stumble across the Fascists who were coming from Santo Stefano and carrying out the round-up. To the river, to the river, as soon as it began to get dark.

From among the bushes they watched the great slope of San Donato. The Fascists had already done a sweep of two thirds of it, but they were so sure that it did not contain any partisans that now they were trying to reach the next valley in leaps and bounds and carelessly. Then they would certainly enter Mango.

They decided to get reasonably far from the village and having crossed the ravine went to the village cemetery. There they stayed in the shelter of the low wall, two looking towards Belbo and two towards the river. Something was going on in the lower Belbo valley, sporadic and *ragged* firing. Meanwhile the column from San Donato had reached Mango but five minutes later was leaving it along the road to Neive which the first occupying force had taken.

They relaxed waiting for the dark. Now they felt at peace and so did not pray for the swift night, here there was safety, dusk would mark the resumption of *exertion* and danger.

'You're absolutely set on this river, really convinced?' insisted Jackie but weakly and they did not answer with even a single word. Ettore had lain on his back and was drowning his eyes in the greying sky. 'Now I can tell you what I felt like up on the crest between the firing from two sides. Yes I felt myself. My heart was beating like a piston but I couldn't have said exactly where. If I had been able to move I would have felt myself all over to catch it, stop it. That's it – I would have played at cops and robbers with my heat.'

So calm and relaxed at the last moment they saw the column from Santo Stefano advancing towards Mango in Indian file along the flat summit which branched off into the Belbo valley. They came silently and swiftly without gleams in the darkened air. The four threw themselves down the slope and got to the bottom without injury or being seen, but angry at themselves for their carelessness, with hearts they could no longer control, they did not stop there but in a flash climbed up to the brickworks at Avene and there threw themselves down not on the crest but into a row of vines overlooking the plain between Neive and Castagnole. The plain between the two places was swarming with them, in the fields and along the railway, their trucks came and went along the straight stretch of road. Only when they gloomily had had enough of the sight did they notice that Jackie was no longer with them. 'We must have shaken him off during the run,' said Pierre, but turning round they could no longer see any trace of him either on the Avene slope or down below at Sant'Ambrogio. Up there the long file of Fascists was advancing along the slope which was already blurred because of the twilight towards the village of Mango.

'He'll find us again,' said Ettore of Jackie with regret in his voice.

XXVII

With evening gliding in, the low breath of the wind of the plain began to stir all round them. They were in a dip in that plain right behind the metalled railway line, still kneeling before the gods of the dark. The evening grew and grew, Fascist trucks passed each other on the straight stretch of road going to and from Neive and Castagnole, at a reduced speed, without headlights which shone feebly in the incomplete evening. They drove them slowly as if off duty and to pass the time, after a day of unchallenged triumph which was too exciting and tiring, of libertine despotism over men and territories.

The evening grew deeper, soon the heights before the river sank their soft profile in the nearest sky, some strong gleams of light among the houses of Neive and Castagnole indicated that they had camped there. A big patrol passed on the road; they were chatting so close by that Johnny could tell where its members came from by their intonations. It had scarcely passed than they ran bending low with several dives to some cover nearer the road less than fifty paces away. There the evening came of age and the idea of salvation correspondingly dawned in them. The road, that frontier of the Fascists' domain, was within reach of their feet. They were collecting themselves for the last spurt when a Fascist car announced itself gruffly with strong wide beams of light behind which it passed on phantasmally. Then they dashed in a wild race, scarcely touching the wrinkled tar with their feet, behind them the roar of a speeding car exploded; they had the exact time to dive into the ditch, the headlights just missed them. The machine shot on beyond Neive, they ran madly on in the soaking grass receiving in their buzzing ears the *ragged* echo of the others' camp-fire songs.

They were at the top of the last height, they turned round in cordial unison and threw a last glance at the frightening hills over which night was falling like a shroud. Then they looked ahead at the precipitous wooded descent, at the narrow and sinister strip of shore which appeared in bit by bit, at the river with its leaden heart and icy marrow, at the other bank. It lay in the dismal guard of night and winter but they greeted it like the gates of Eden.

Pierre guided them to the ferry at Neive as being the nearest, they walked towards it perilously but with an invincible impulse through wood and scrub, followed an intuitive path, from time to time directly overhanging the black and silent waters. On the march they heard beyond the ridge a couple of dampened explosions, Fascists on guard who were surely firing at shadows.

The boat was not in its place. Straining their eyes through and beyond the deceptive night mists they made out the old boat stranded further downriver in an inlet on the other bank; looking more closely they also discovered the cut cable, hanging sadly to fathom the depth of the river.

This was one of the only two ferries in the whole zone and they had perforce to think that the other too, the one downstream from Castagnole, had been sabotaged. If it was they were done for, lost on that impossible, untenable riverbank, and just in sight of the other bank so dreamt *and marched and hoped for*. They turned on their heels and walked to the other ferry with so many of their anxieties and hopes kept silent and repressed. It was a hard walk in the thickening darkness, along the river which grew more and more sinister, through labyrinths of cliffs and brush, with hopeful spurts of acceleration and pessimistic rallentandos. It took them more than an hour to arrive there and there was the other boat, undamaged and perfectly anchored, its long and powerful cable high and taut over the water, vibrating electrically in the night air.

They applauded silently and jumped into the boat. Pierre used the pole and the other two caught hold of the cable. The sense of escape was such that Johnny could completely enjoy the slow, heavy progress of the boat and the angry lapping against it of the rudely awakened waters and all the immense meaning of that tiny voyage. The other bank was approaching and in the total darkness it was as if it were lit up by the very solidity of its peace and safety. Nothing could be seen or heard on the nearby highroad and they felt themselves, and were, safe at last.

They disembarked and as a last warlike action cautiously app-roached the road; then they flew over the tar and within a second were already strolling in the soft country lane they had dreamt of for three days. Now they could walk and rest, light a cigarette and sing a little. From the sky a fine, powdery drizzle was distilled, delightful in its lightness and freshness, almost a delicious memento of the fact that they were alive and safe, and it was no dream.

A dog barked near them but mildly and from the direction of the sound they made out the white ghost of a little farmhouse, just the haven of peace and rest they had dreamt of. But Pierre remarked that it was still too near the road and they went on merrily, almost enjoying that delay in journey's end. Another dog bayed at them and a much bigger farmhouse loomed up at them with monastic walls but once more Pierre signalled to go on.

At last in the deepest shadow of the first overhanging heights beyond the river a farmhouse literally blocked their way and this was the right one. Small and tidy, with its courtyard flat and clean shining in a tiny gap in the clouds they made towards it without looking for the private path, crossing the grass which was so soaking that they shivered. They stopped to look for the guard-dog but there was none, they went forward over the courtyard on tiptoe. From the door they saw that the family had gone up to sleep. They went past the door and set hands on the ladder in the hayloft. Up on top they groped and felt about them, discovered that it was a hayloft that was shut in on three sides, a real bedroom with abundance of forage. They got rid of their weapons and ammunition, took off their massively heavy boots, then they dug down in the forage, lowered themselves into the hole and covered themselves with whole handfuls of hay, hardly leaving a filter for their mouths. Pierre begged them: 'Please don't let us fall asleep right away. Let's hold out and tell each other how it went. Let's try to go to sleep as late as possible.' And certainly it was wonderful to stay awake and knowingly enjoy each moment of that rest, every moment of that safety, but in a minute sleep crushed them under its black heel.

Next morning they were gradually wakened by the raking scrape of a metal tool, understood in a flash and like ghosts emerged from the tomb of forage and thus appeared to the terrified peasant at the top of the ladder. He was still young but bore the immense weight of someone who had accepted to the full the *husbandry* of married man and overseer, which conferred on his ordinary youth the grandeur of the patriarch.

'You are partisans,' he said, 'and you arrived here last night.' He scratched his head. 'You must come from over the river as many did but in the first days – not so late.'

Pierre inquired if there were Fascists in the neighbourhood.

'Will you believe me if I say I haven't ever seen one?'

'Lucky people. We haven't eaten for three days.'

'Is that possible?'

'Are you on our side?'

'Of course. I don't like the Fascists. Of course I am on your side. If you'll allow me, naturally.'

'What can you give us to eat?'

'My wife could tell you that better than me. But let's see – bread and bacon fat certainly and cheese as well . . . You see, I'm not rich, you see how small my house and land are.'

Pierre searched and finally produced a thousand lire note, immensely crumpled but very valid and offered it to him, 'Wait a minute,' said the peasant. 'I'm going down to waken my woman and . . .'

'But please don't go around talking and only call us when it's ready on the table.'

He went down the little ladder and ran to the kitchen while they stretched out again in the increased comfort of their confirmed safety, with a further safety deriving from the raininess of the day. Johnny and Ettore were smoking, looking round completely relaxed at the grey relaxed look of the sky, hearing *blankly* the scratching and shitting of the hens ranging in the courtyard. Then the man called to them from below, informed them that his wife was already at the stove, did they approve that he should take a look around as sentry, going as far maybe as the road?

They relaxed even more comfortably and sensually. As the man went off they could, without putting their heads out, see him walking along his familiar path towards the so-familiar surroundings, a sack on his head against the rain which was growing heavier and with the concentrated gait of a real patrolman. Then it cleared a little and through the films of drizzle the heights beyond the river appeared and then Pierre's mind and tongue addressed themselves once more to the Langhe, with an oppressive feeling of sadness he asked himself and the others if they would be themselves again, the units, the brigades and the headquarters, all re-formed, the whole network rewoven.

'Don't worry, Pierre,' said Johnny, 'we are invincible, indestructible, cannot be eliminated and that for me is the real lesson the Fascists are learning across the river. After all, what did they find when they finally closed their grip? Nothing or very little. In a couple of days it will all be like before. Don't worry, Pierre.'

At that moment a mouse eyed them through a maze of gear and hay and sat there motionless and terrified as if all its senses were *benumbed*. Ettore arched forwards making only a tiny rustle in the forage, seized a stick and was measuring the blow at the bewitched mouse when he halted his arm and then lowered it, while his eyes filled with tears and Pierre whistled to the mouse to rouse itself and escape.

The peasant came back and reported that it was a lunar landscape with nothing and no one on it. He had gone as far as the riverbank, the ferry lay empty and inactive, the other bank completely quiet and deserted. Then they came down and entered the kitchen and ravenously ate a fine spread, turning their backs to the fire that had been specially poked into a blaze. The woman of the house served them, a tiny woman but quick and able and sweet, having altogether a certain charm and ability which suggested some service in a house in town before her marriage. But she seemed a little overcome by the event and definitely alarmed at the silent presence of their weapons. Then they climbed up again to sleep.

Later when the dusk had gathered, after the peasant had gone back to the road and the bank for a new reconnaissance and the possible collection of news, they climbed to the first hill by safe paths between hedgerows, guessing that from up there they would have some sort of panorama of the other side of the river. In fact turning round on the top of the hill they saw them perfectly although apparently cut off by the threatening shadow, much higher than the modest heights by the river: the biggish hill at Neive and these more massive, lofty and desolate ones at Mango, grey-black in the distance and massive yet airy like enormous storm clouds anchored to the earth. Their wild crests were melting into the late sky and the rare, sinister trees on the ridge were slanting under the strong evening wind. And Johnny felt an unbearable nostalgia to be up there and walking on these ridges high up under that wind (*in the midst of its strength*). To the others too the sight suggested peace restored and Fascist rule over.

They went back to the house and awaited the return of the man. He came back and reported still not to have noticed anything or anyone but he had been able to form a legitimate impression of peace and of it being 'all over'. They had supper and went into the stable to sleep. The man was to wake them at five and promised to stay up all night on guard.

'We have to thank you.'

'Not at all, you make me feel young and daring and useful as I haven't felt for ages.'

They were awakened punctually and at first light walked to the river across the countryside which was still clotted in sleep, sniffing the air as if it might contain odours of peace or of tumult across the river. They crossed the tarred road and scouted on towards the bank through a large thicket. The boat was still on the opposite bank and the boatman was on board, fighting against the cold of dawn and water with firm steps on the echoing deck. They whispered to him and stood up high in the bushes so that he could see and recognise them. He saw them, certainly recognised them and pulling on the cable came across the river. So now everything was back to normal. He confirmed it the moment his boat touched the bank, a real giant dressed in a few but extremely heavy bits of cloth and he vomited into the raw air crude aromas of wine and garlic. By the way what had happened to the ferry at Neive? A Fascist squad had arrived in an attempted manhunt and guessing its usefulness to the partisans had cut the cable and pushed the boat out to crash against the other bank. Not only that but they had fired, without hitting him, at the ferryman who had come running up to shout to them not to wreck it, that it was only used for civilian purposes. 'You boys bring death down on us before our times, you boys,' he said but his voice was not tired or rancorous.

They had scarcely crossed the first ridge when they saw a boy partisan running across their path at full stretch, disarmed and with a big blue scarf fluttering in the air. And when he overtook them 'Watch out for the Reds,' he shouted. What was up with the Reds? What sort of news was this?

Brooding on this uncertainty they went on until they were in sight of the highest roofs of Castagnole which glimmered in the early sun. At last they came across a boy from Castagnole who in the past *hung about* their garrison and they asked him what all this was about the Reds.

'Rascals!' he shouted. 'The swine are disarming the Blue stragglers, all the Blues who come back from the river. They say they didn't fight as they should and that the men who come back from the river are just deserters. And they are disarming them.'

They were paralysed with amazement . . . anger deprived them of words. The other went on: 'I want to see the Reds when the Fascists attack them. And it's going to happen, isn't it? it's in the air. But meanwhile they are taking weapons from the Blues saying they can make much better use of them. Ones who are by themselves they strip away, the ones in groups they ask politely to come to their headquarters at Castigliole or Motta and there they are locked up and disarmed. Pay attention to me, Pierre and you others – if you meet them shoot first.'

They walked on in the grip of passion, longing to meet one of these hateful Reds. And indeed three hundred metres from the village there were three of them, positioned under the roadside bank, they emerged on the road and made a friendly signal and then came towards them in a friendly way. Two were boys recruited by the Communists in the countryside, both armed with rifles, their leader was a tall thin person with red, red hair which was very bright in the strong sunlight.

'Well then,' said Johnny very *slackenly.*

'You're coming back from the river, aren't you?' their leader asked.

'Yes, what business is that of yours?' said Ettore.

'None of mine personally but it might be important for my headquarters. You see, my headquarters needs to interrogate everyone who comes back over the river. A pure formality in everybody's interest.'

Ettore studiously turned to Johnny and asked as flatly as possible if he gave a damn for the Red headquarters. But Johnny could not reply in the same way because his mouth was trembling as was his whole body from unheard-of rage.

'Shut up about my headquarters, you with the moustache,' said the Red. But then he became nice again. 'A pure formality, I am telling you. And it's a kind of outing, along the river and through the gardens . . .'

Johnny suddenly covered him with his Sten, 'Hands up.'

'You're mad,' shouted their leader.

'I'm as mad as you are a swine.'

Pierre kept the other two covered with his machine-pistol and Ettore had stripped them of their rifles and thrown them away in the high grass. Their leader had a heavy pistol in his belt but his hands were stretched to the sky. He shouted: 'Either you're mad or I haven't made myself clear.'

The two boys had rushed off and now were running over the fields with infinite leaps and spurts.

'Let's talk about it for a moment,' said Johnny, his tongue dry, 'so you Reds are really convinced that you will face a new Fascist attack a minute more than our men did? Talk!'

'What are you talking about? I referred to a pure formality and what are you coming out with now? But comrade, brother –'

He gave him a blow with the Sten in the solar plexus, the red head staggered back and fell. Johnny was on top of him and beat him all over. He beat him with lucid blindness, with the utmost accuracy on the eyes and mouth. He had never felt so furious and destructive, so much in need of hatred and blood, needing other blood and other disfigurements even as the blood spurted and the disfigurement appeared. With his next blow he straightened the twisted head with ferocious care. And as he hit it he shouted that he was going to reduce his face to pulp and worked to that end with savage lucidity. From very far off the voices of Pierre and Ettore reached him saying that that was enough, that a few more blows would kill him, that was really enough now. But Johnny was still hitting him and replied in a friendly thoughtful way: 'No, I am not killing him, don't worry, I am only making him lose his human features.'

Then they dragged him away from that blind and bleeding mask, from that groaning throat and that body as motionless as if it had been run through, and Johnny could scarcely stand on his feet, exhausted by mortal fatigue and mortal shame. So that it was a limp robot and the most blushing of pilgrims who dragged himself along behind his silent companions towards the peaceful, sunlit village of Castagnole.

XXVIII

Nord was still in the saddle as they quickly learned from one of his bodyguards on a motorcycle who set them the task of re-forming the units in the triangle Castagnole, Neive, Mango.

They set to work in the plains and on the hills which were no longer swarming, among sceptical middle-class people, sulky and turned miserly, in the gloomy lenten period of the Indian summer and by the end of the month they had rounded up about fifty men between Neive and Castagnole who were on the point of giving up the ghost for lack of ammunition and funds. Fortunately the big garrison in the town did not make any large-scale move, being satisfied with its absolute control of the foothills, even if signs of its forthcoming *thrusts* were not lacking. Meantime the Fascist command had published by every means, especially through the omni-obsequious priests, its latest proclamation about surrender without fear of punishment, stressing the harshness of the winter that was coming on, the general Allied halt on their autumn positions and the well-known growth in power of the Fascist army. And they reaped their harvest because the valleys and crests seemed more and more depopulated and the comrade to whom you had got used in a certain way disappeared at any moment without a word or without handing over his weapon.

Instead members of families swarmed everywhere looking for and taking home – under the cover of that proclamation – the adolescents. And to reply to their questions was perhaps the chief task of Pierre and Johnny in these empty, gloomy days in the increasingly uncongenial village of Castagnole. Eight times out of ten it was their mothers because travel was now risky for men. They got about and arrived mostly on foot, some on bicycles, and some others had hired a horse and trap. And they were tired and fearless, tearful and determined. 'Do you know a boy from Alba or Bra or Asti called Aldo, Piero, Sergio?'

They shook their heads: 'Their baptised name is no use, signora, if you don't tell us their *noms de guerre*.'

'I never knew his *nom de guerre* but,' and here they beamed, 'I know this – his commander was called Nord.'

'Signora, Nord commanded thousands.'

Then she played her last card. 'A boy that wasn't eighteen yet – a good-looking boy with light eyes and curly hair.' Then the men followed them with their eyes for a long time as they resumed their pilgrimage.

They had no change of underwear, were in a desperate state as far as socks and shoes went, unwashed, their hair tangled and dull, their beards long, ill-fed and disastrously short of tobacco. And without a reserve of funds because there had been no more sign of Nord. They knew only from what people whispered that he had not set up a new headquarters but travelled about uninterruptedly in the valleys and hills surrounded by a hundred or so men. Soon Johnny and Ettore gave in and went to knock at the little villa but it was bolted and barred and empty. Elda had cleared out long ago, a big city like Turin – in view of the Nazi-Fascist lesson of the two previous weeks – seeming much more safe and peaceful than that little hamlet without a name. Over the village the epidemic of danger and a kind of contagion seeped night and day, every night they left to sleep outside the village in lonely farmhouses, changing every night. And Pierre studied these changes and variations as if they were a system for roulette. The peasants received them only with a gesture and a sigh, they pointed to the place and the straw – they no longer lent blankets – then they climbed up to the floor above to give courage to their wives who had had a heart attack. And anyone with a good ear could catch through the cracks in the ceiling their groans and talk about fire and death and the suffocated hushing of the men so that the partisans wouldn't hear and be offended. They wakened them at four in the morning and even earlier without offering of bread any more or even of warm water to unfreeze their stomachs with a splash, they put them out and left them in that impossible world of darkness and cold. 'They are tired of us,' sighed Pierre as they lay shivering under the scanty covering of straw with the animals already asleep and therefore giving off very little heat, 'tired, tired, tired'.

One day Pierre and Ettore set off together to carry out an inspection at Neive and Mango and they came back with grim faces reporting to Johnny that the phenomenon was even more serious than their blackest expectations. In the vast area which up to the end of October had been host to not less than five hundred men there remained perhaps eighty in all, reduced to the absolute bottom in terms of arms, ammunition and funds. More than one lad was shivering in the open in shorts and a summer blouse, the great Nazi-Fascist invasion had carried off an enormous quantity of livestock with a catastrophic fall in the standard of living: now the itinerant partisans were generally offered polenta and cabbage and often they were asked to do some work to earn that food.

At the very beginning of December the whole Fascist front sprang to the attack and the Red line was broken in half an hour.

It was six in the morning, Pierre and Ettore were warming themselves at the bakehouse with their backs to the wall of the oven. Johnny was coming across the icy desert of the square when the new great din burst out. At that the village woke and waking fell back as if dead. The two came out of their warm refuge and with Johnny went to the east gate which was the best sound stage. 'It's their turn this time,' said Johnny not without feeling and rancour. Pierre wondered if this time perhaps the Blues would be left in peace but Johnny thought that this went against the grain, of the Blues only those who were on the highest hills and not down in the alluvial plains could hope to remain undisturbed. As far as Santo Stefano, ten kilometres from Castagnole, the Fascists would certainly spread out and this time the town garrison could not fail to make a move.

The din of weapons was immense over the numbed countryside. Silent, sullen, their men had gathered behind them from every nook and cranny in the village and now gazed east with them. Johnny said in a low voice: 'Disband them, Pierre, or at least send them to Mango, high up.' Pierre hesitated, said that it was not on, supposing the Fascists didn't break through in their direction. 'They're sure to come. If they get to Santo Stefano they'll get here too. It's only a few kilometres and all flat and inviting. Disband them or send them up into the hills. If you like give them a rendezvous although I believe they will stay disbanded for weeks.'

The men behind them hardly breathed and with that very breath seemed to give weight to Johnny's words. Pierre read their eyes and sent them to Mango. They got ready to leave and it was only too evident that once they had left each one would take the road he liked best. There was no need for a special evacuation or for removing signs from the village, this having been the most fleeting and short-lived garrison in the history of the partisans. The three followed them with their eyes as they strode quickly off in the misty plain, then they returned to listening to the east.

The firing grew in spasms then in a minute fell away and was silent and half an hour later, in the suspense of that treacherous neutrality, the hum of trucks invaded all the surrounding roads. They hid behind the corners of the houses and were on their guard but it was Red columns in retreat. So they came out into the open and waited. The vehicles were overloaded with Reds, their caps drawn tightly down over their heads, silent and huddled, from the cabins flew hoarse voices asking the way to the river. So they had to act as traffic police and point out the river and the ferry. Part of them, a small part, was uncertain about the river and preferred to make for the high hills, towards the great Communist territory round Monforte. Big, heated diatribes blazed up directed at the departing trucks. There followed an hour of exhausting waiting, then a crowd of fleeing civilians indicated that the Fascists had entered Canelli without striking a blow and that the fate of defenceless Santo Stefano had already been signed that morning. In fact at ten a dense crowd of civilians in flight indicated that the Fascists were swooping on Santo Stefano to occupy it permanently. It was a hard blow even if foreseen; it was cruel to think of the fate of that village fairground. And Johnny after swallowing that bitter pill said: 'Let's go.' Pierre remarked that they would have a long march and they had empty stomachs. 'Ettore, go and dig out something to eat on the way.' Ettore left with all his notable gifts as someone who knew the ropes. The shop was bolted and barred and the pizzamaker was already buried in the burrow he had prepared, Ettore brought him back to life and made him serve him in the back shop. Then he reappeared with three monumental *sandwiches* of bread and anchovies. Biting into them they set out for

Mango but the anchovies were rancid and had not been desalted, they poisoned them with their bitter taste, but their hunger was too great, they threw away the anchovies and ate the bread, although it tasted horribly of putrid anchovies.

The countryside after Coazzolo was lunar: the earth seemed to have been virgin since the world began, the woods and undergrowth breathed freely, almost as if all the air was theirs alone. The dogs were silent, all the farmyard animals invisible. In these surroundings they climbed up, thoughtful and withdrawn, then Ettore complained of a stomach-ache because of eating those poisonous anchovies . . . The long shadow of danger fell on them and made them raise their heads.

It was them – more than two hundred, the furthest a hundred paces away, standing there motionless, taking aim carefully, now they were firing.

'We've no luck,' shouted Ettore.

Johnny felt a bullet tear a shoulderstrap. They were standing there, as if in a shooting booth, and aimed and fired at their leisure. He looked down at the ground again just in time to see the feet of the other two spin round and take off in the opposite direction followed by spurts of earth raked by fire, always longer and lower, like unrelenting greyhounds. Between shots the Fascists were now shouting and ullulating, one voice topping them all in clarity and sheer power. 'Surrender!' and a section of them was climbing over the embankment with their weapons raised.

Johnny dashed away to the right and, zigzagging, forded un-harmed through the stream of bullets aimed at Pierre and Ettore, and arrived exhausted and flat on his face on a bank of the river. They had seen him and now the dry naked branches over his head were being pruned by their careful fire. And to his ear a soft elastic sound of pursuing searching feet sounded like the fiercest and most lethal gallop. The central stream of bullets had dried up, Pierre and Ettore surely lay riddled with bullets on the great stretch of open ground, offering all their limbs to the satisfied inspection of the Fascists. Johnny was so sure of it and so terrified that he did not even turn round to make certain it was so on the flat expanse. He crawled on his stomach towards the river.

A soldier came into sight at fifty paces, but he hesitated, and waited for five or six of his comrades to join and support him, Johnny could see the little helmet resting askew on his big coarse peasant head, his bestial eyes rolling, his rifle shaking in his hands. He let himself slide down into the icy water which was a hand's breadth deep. At first the cold numbed him, then quickly reactivated and revitalised both him and his spirit of self-preservation. He lay for a second to listen to their discordant voices, the coarse voices of Northerners, one suggesting this way and another that, one urging them on and another holding them back. Then they began to fire their rifles haphazardly into the sparse bushes all around with one of them not joining in, keeping himself ready for a deadly shot.

He did not cross the river, he decided to go up it for a few metres to where the vegetation was a little thicker and the bed of the river grew a little deeper. So he waded along on his elbows dying at every widening ripple. There was a total silence – the seal of death or a glimmer of safety? Johnny raised his eye to the level of the bank and saw a whole lot of them appear at the farthest bend as if out for a walk, each with his left arm taken up with carrying that little piece of individual booty, some had a loop of sausages on their chests as well as the loop of their bandoliers. They were coming down the road not more than thirty paces away, in a flash he would have on him one of their absent-minded glances.

He got over the bank on his stomach, rose up and ran into the field, which was naked, endless. An uproar exploded behind him but it was only an uproar of shouts; Johnny ran and wondered when the first bullet would arrive. It arrived, and others as well, an infinite number of others, now from the side as well, from his primitive trackers, the whole world was full of their shots and shouts, shouts pointing him out, shouts of encouragement, of correction, curses. Johnny ran and ran, the distant crests flashing in his staring and almost blind eyes, he ran and the shooting diminished in his ears, as did the shouting, shots and cries drowning in a swamp between him and them.

He ran and ran or rather flew, overcoming body, fatigue and movements. Then running through new places, unrecognisable to his veiled eyes, his brain began to work again but not endogenously, purely receptively. The thoughts entered it from without, struck his forehead like stones from a sling. 'Pierre and Ettore are dead. Ettore had a stomach-ache, he couldn't run the way he needed to. They killed him. I am alive. But am I alive? I am alone, alone and it is all over.'

He was conscious of the solitude and the silence, but he still ran, kept on running, his brain had darkened again and his physical sensitivity returned but only to experience suffering and exhaustion. His heart beat at spots that were always different and all absurd, his knees gave way, he saw blackness and collapsed.

When he woke he found himself a few paces from the top of a hill. He reached it on his elbows, his legs refusing to support him. The limited sky was a tender grey, surely the evening of what had been a fine day and even the hills surrounding the town stood out clear. He had run over hill after hill, that was the hill at Treiso. The hamlet was on the left no less sealed and silent than its cemetery with the line of cypresses humming in the rising breeze. His head was working frantically now to dredge up, to pin down a memory, any memory. What was he supposed to remember? Ah yes, Pierre and Ettore were dead, killed, today.

Unconsciously, almost from inertia he was going down the slope. Where was he going? Into the thickets of the San Rocco valley, twisted and dark beneath him. But in that way was he not getting too close to the town, dangerously so? What did it matter? He had nowhere to go and so he went on down and down dazed but speedy.

'*Enough, enough, today I've had enough. Maybe they two are still alive, but they are dead, they both. Enough, enough I don't want to be shot at any longer, I don't want to have to fly for my life once more. Enough, enough, the proclamation. No, I don't want to consign, to give myself up, but I'll hide in any house, in a hut a cellar, I'll have myself maintained, I'll dress in civvies, I'll bury my Sten. Enough, I'll surely be patient until the end. I'm alone. Enough.*'

The valley became narrower, the vegetation grew darker, an hour later there than on the high hills, and so the track was already fading, as were the terrified faces of the rare farmsteads. So it was only at the last step that he noticed the bundle that blocked the road.

Johnny sat down beside it, on the rigid grass, sprinkled with blood. His face was hairless and serene, his hair well brushed in spite of the shock of the volley and the thudding fall to the ground. The blood that had spurted from all the holes in his chest had barely splashed the edge of his blue silk scarf worn round his neck like a cowboy and it was the only piece of clothing of a certain *shocking* luxury amid the general poverty of a partisan preparing for winter. Johnny turned his eyes away from his intact face, then fixed them on it again suddenly almost as if to surprise him, with the mad idea that the boy would half-close his eyes and then lower the lids again for his renewed attention. He lay in unbounded solitude which was accentuated by the single-voiced sound of the nearby stream. They had taken off his boots, Johnny examined his double stockings of thick, holed wool. And he thought that Pierre and Ettore were lying just like this, some millions of hills further back.

He felt he was being watched and pointed his Sten at a curtain of canes. A face was peeping out which then tried to hide, but there was a *jerk* in Johnny's arm which persuaded the man to stay there, petrified. Johnny pointed to the killed partisan and raised his chin questioningly.

'This morning,' said the man, 'the column that came out from the city.'

'Come down and talk to me,' Johnny ordered.

The man begged not to have to do so, he was in terror of the corpse and the sudden return of the Fascists. He advanced only enough to come round the clump of canes.

'I saw them do it. They forced me – me and my family and all the neighbours. He had managed to escape from one patrol but ran into another.'

'Why did they leave him here?'

'After the execution the officer told us not to touch him in any way, he said he would come back towards evening to see if we had obeyed him. Our parish priest was given precise orders not to bury him till tomorrow evening. But we are going to try to bury him tonight, the parish priest, me and my neighbours.'

'Where will you bury him?'

'Up there in Treiso, although it will be a hard job to climb up with a dead man on our shoulders in a night as dark as a wolf's jaws. But we will do it willingly. You are in a bad way, you partisans. Now go away, for goodness' sake, go away, because the Fascists might come back to check. And we are tired of seeing you killed, tired of being asked to be there, our pregnant women are all going to pieces. Go far away, I beg you. Do you want me to throw you a loaf of bread?'

The twilight in the valley was growing thicker, while the sky over the hills remained extraordinarily, silverly clear, almost like an effulgence from the crests themselves. He suddenly desired them and walked towards them. Halfway up that luminosity overhead was already lessening, giving place to an ashen emanation in which the white disc of the sun floated motionless. He made an effort and reached the crest. From a col he had a partial view of the town squatting in a loop of the river weighed down by mist and fate. That very evening they would receive the news of the death of Ettore and Pierre, Johnny imagined the way that mournful whisper would make its way through icy rooms, desperate hiding-places, in the desolate night. And he thought that perhaps a partisan would be standing upright like him on the last hill looking at the town and thinking the same of him and the news about him on the evening of the day of his own death. That was what was important – that there should always be one left.

He shook his head and gazed more sharply as if to see further and see more deeply, longing for the town and dislike of the hills seized on him together and together crushed him but it was as if his feet were rooted in the hills. *'I'll go on to the end, I'll never give up.'*

The sun was setting white, whiter than the moon ever was, a bird cried out and rustled the boughs behind him. He turned round in a flash but it had already disappeared, flying camouflaged against the darkened side of the next hill. He stirred himself, walked on, did not know where to go, his feet carried him to Cascina della Langa. And when he recognised it against the black sky he was happy and grateful to his feet and said that was just the place he wanted to reach. Great was the buffeting of the wind in the branches of the big old trees, tempest-tried. He did not arrive by the path but from the unusual angle of the courtyard and saw the courtyard to be deserted and the house calm. He advanced over the courtyard wondering where the bitch might be, hearing only under his soles and deep hard ruts left the German field-guns.

The door of the house opened and Johnny's Sten rose up like a penis to a vagina. But it was the old woman of the house, her smell floating over to him. From the distance she recognised him and mumbled his badly learned name.

'You're not dead, Johnny?'

'Ettore and Pierre are dead.'

She shook her head with a kind of flirtatiousness.

'They're dead?'

'They're dead.'

'Never mind,' she said. 'You must be destroyed with the great running and walking. Come in, go up to my own room and lie down at once in my bed.'

Swaying on his feet on the floor which was drowned in potatoes Johnny reached the stairs and as he climbed heard a rumble from the bitch who was at once quietened and calmed. When he went on someone held his breath, someone else struck a match and in that flame Johnny saw Pierre and Ettore sitting on the bed, silently laughing at him with the bitch stretched happily on their legs.

XXIX

The following morning they walked over to Mango athirst for news and to take stock of the situation. They walked along breathing the air which had recently been breathed by their mortal enemies, through the soles of their feet they felt the ground the latter had so long and triumphantly trampled. And that world of the hills they were crossing seemed to them more than ever provisional and imaginary, almost like an empty theatre at four in the morning. The Fascists had come and had cancelled out, had destroyed everything. The deserted state, the emptiness of the great hills, was so glaring that it hurt the eyes; the Fascists had reduced them from many thousands to a few hundreds. As for the missing thousands, thought Johnny, as they walked along, where had they taken refuge and hidden? The earth must have swallowed them up. Even Castino, the old headquarters, now stood there depopulated and neglected on the chalky ridge; everything had been removed – the living quarters, roadblocks, the telephone lines, all done away with. That immensely lively, colourful, *blatant* rebel life uprooted like a big, merry, tremendous *maypole*.

Pierre summed it up for them all: 'There will be one of us left on each hill. The Fascists have guessed that already and will deal with us very soon. They will send up a squad for each hill and on each of them they will finish one of us off. We shall all be dead by the spring.'

Now the road on the crest was caught between two steep, whitish frozen walls of clay which shut off any view round about along with any wind. Here they met two partisans who bore the signs of a long and depressed march. Their uniform however kept some of the brilliance of the summer and early autumn. They were armed only with pistols and seemed to be of the more educated and intelligent kind. To Pierre's question the most lined and nervous of the pair answered that they had come from Canelli through a labyrinth of roads and did not know where they were going.

'You got a mighty slap in the face too.'

'The biggest imaginable. They are strong – excessively strong. They will lord it all winter and none of us will wake up one morning next spring.'

'That's exactly what I was saying a minute ago,' said Pierre.

'Have you got a smoke?' inquired Johnny.

'I smoked my last cigarette before their attack. Now I am dying for one.'

At that moment Johnny discovered that his holster was undone and made a move to button it up again but a pistol flowered in the other's fist pointing straight at Johnny's heart.

'You're mad,' whispered Johnny.

'What were you doing with your pistol?' the other shouted *distracted.*

'I was doing up the holster.'

The other's fist slackened round the butt, 'God, I was within a hair's breadth of firing,' and emotion prevented him from putting it back in its holster.

'Boys, boys, let's keep our heads,' shouted Pierre.

They exchanged greetings and parted not without turning round reciprocally at the last moment as if to avoid a final surprise. Johnny said: 'From now on when we move we'll take the bitch with us,' and the two nodded. And Ettore said he had never met a partisan quicker than that one with his pistol. 'And he simply didn't look the type with that intellectual's face, did he?'

They entered Mango late in the snowy morning. There was rather a lot of life but very *hushed* and unobtrusive. At their entry a few shutters closed with scarcely a rustle, some retreating footsteps sounded sharply on the frozen paving-stones. Those people who had not had time to withdraw barely nodded in greeting, sober and reserved.

'Have any partisans gone through?' The old man sitting upright in his door cleared his throat. 'A few have gone through but none have stopped.'

'Nord?'

'I haven't seen him since the good old days. They say . . .

'What do they say, grandpa?'

'They say he moves about in the high hills, moves about day and night, without ever halting. And he is right because I heard with my own ears from the soldiers what they will do to him as if they take him.'

They went on into the heart of the village among thick, vivid Fascist inscriptions in black paint, incredibly rich and fresh and modern on the old saltpetred walls. Some women looked down from a window or a balcony and avoided their eyes with a wretched air when they returned the glance.

They turned off to the inn which had been their bar every day and Nord's room for reports and audiences in the good times, and which had played host to more partisans than any place like it in the hills. Now the bar seemed violated and sacked with the floor deeply stained and scored as if trampled on by men shod with corrosive heels, the shelves for the wine grinned emptily because of the way the bottles had been pillaged, the vast low kitchen was silent and frozen so near midday. They heard the noise of slippers behind them and turned round to see the host, who had aged by years in a few days.

They said they wanted to listen to the English radio, they had a tremendous need for news.

'Radio? so you don't know that just yesterday they were here and took it away. Radios were the first thing to be carried off, mine the very first. There's not a radio in the village any more except Constantino's – he rescued it by sheer good luck. Go to Constantino's.'

Pierre planted himself in front of him. 'Why have you changed so much?'

'We haven't changed, Pierre,' replied the host with tears in his eyes. 'It would be a mortal sin to change towards fine lads like you. We know you are better than them, that we know. But we are afraid, we live trembling all the time and that is why we are fed up with life, but we love it too and it is terrible to go to bed each evening without being sure to wake up in the morning. And we have wives and children and grandchildren, you know, and all the duties that go along with that. If that weren't the case I would be with you with my double-barrelled gun in spite of my age. And then there are the spies, we know they have left their spies behind and that they can be upon us with an hour's warning.'

Shock and incredulity silenced them, then Ettore said: 'If you discover any spies send your boy running to us and we'll be ready to kill him. We'll kill them all for you.'

Once outside Pierre went to the doctor to ask him about his temperature. Ettore who wasn't anxious to hear Radio London kept on walking up and down the deserted, windy lane. Johnny went to Constantino's.

Constantino said: 'I'll go down and dig out the set. I have this one socket here. No – don't apologise – I want to listen too. I missed the previous broadcast and my wife said it was important. It came from high up, she says, very high up.'

Constantino came up again with the set, placed it on its shelf but didn't plug in at once, it was still early; he knew the London timetable by heart. Meantime he laid out the ingredients and began to roll himself a cigarette. From it he then drew strange, greenish mouthfuls of smoke with a complicated medicinal taste. He smoke with marked reluctance and with invincible gusto and Johnny was so intent on him and on his herbal smoke that Constantino sighed and rolled another for Johnny from his scanty tobacco pouch. It was a mixture of rationed tobacco and a herb of recent invention and they shook the ash into an old conch shell. Then Drake's drumroll* sounded out in the house in the high hills and spread through one of the wildest and darkest corners of the Langhe. It was a very serious matter, they were repeating the appeal from General Alexander** to the Italian partisans: to surrender to the winter, to disband and go home or elsewhere one by one, to winter and meet again in the old places and under the old commanders for the last push in the coming spring. During all that time the Allied command would act as if partisans no longer existed.

'*Well done, general*,' Johnny whistled through his teeth.

---

* The signature tune of Radio London was in fact Lilliburlero.
** The notorious proclamation by Field-Marshal Alexander, Allied commander in Italy, was broadcast on 13 November 1944.

'He's done the right thing, hasn't he?' said Constantino, 'he said what had to be said, didn't he?'

'Yes – go home. Who has a home any more that isn't under observation by spies or surrounded by Fascists? And then how are we to get back into town? Whistling a tune and with our hands in our pockets? And who will be resting all winter in town if not the Fascists? And what clothes will we go back into town in and with what faces? *Well done, general!*'

Outside he found the other two already looking for him. Pierre said that for the time being his ailment wasn't anything serious but was liable to become serious with time and neglect. 'The doctor says I need to go into hospital.'

Said Johnny: 'Then he is of the same opinion as General Alexander' – and he repeated the gist of the broadcast. They called him imbecile and idiot then it was all *sighed and grinned off.* They set out again for their base with all eyes in the village following them like a te deum. But the little children were still in school and as they passed they clearly heard them reading syllable by syllable. Ettore said this was the last chance for months to look at a decent woman and went up to the school window and looked in towards the teacher's desk. But he saw a poor young woman teacher as ugly as a woman can allow herself to be with a thick dark growth of hair on her cheeks and upper lip. She noticed Ettore's special gaze and returned it, offering him all her blush of hope and distress, her ugliness and her immense awareness of it. And Ettore withdrew saying that fortune had truly abandoned him all along the line.

They returned to the farmhouse and passed an empty afternoon there, to begin with playing to the full with the willing bitch, then sitting uselessly on the cold stones, one hand in the other, looking at the empty sky, up and down the empty landscape, feeling the cold and the breath of winter, the long absence of the sun, all the tomorrows and passivity and the nearness of their death and the astronomical distance of the spring. Then Pierre felt ill again and withdrew into the stable very early because of the cold and his shivering.

In the dusk, in spite of the confusing wind in the branches, they heard a special swishing noise, and shouting to waken Pierre they ran out with their weapons to the courtyard gate, preceded by the leaping bitch, but it was only an advance party of Nord's making sure that the way was clear and after them the rest of his group appeared; two trucks, some thirty guards and half a dozen exhausted and complaining women. And they wrought indescribable havoc in the abandoned farmhouse, the arrogant, vulgar, intolerable bodyguard. But Nord was understanding and smiling with them, although he was suffering atrociously from an infection in one hand and had need of a surgeon that could not be delayed. He was wearing a tremendous English officer's greatcoat with gold buttons* and an astrakhan collar and the splendid chromed parabellum which he used to entrust to the nearest bodyguard he held tightly in his arms. And the woman of the house gave him an indescribable *fluster* of admiration and service, her old, dirty, worn femininity wakened by the presence of this incredibly handsome man. Nord said right away that he was no longer able to pay for the disturbance; she said, with a smile that was scarcely less broad, that she could give him credit till the spring. Nord smiled and sighed: 'The spring.'

Then a guard presented himself, one of the old deserters from the Veneto, and with an *indereliquenda*** formality saluted and reported to him that the places he knew of had been looked for and found, they were very suitable, also because there wasn't a civilian soul in sight. Then Nord signalled to all the men to set to work. It was a question of burying the heavy collective weapons and their ammunition and of hiding the two big headquarters trucks. Johnny and Ettore helped, the spot had been chosen in the big, tangled, sinister wood downhill from the house. The weapons were already greased and wrapped up, they were buried and the care of the deserters from the Veneto and their fantastic variations to camouflage the tombs better were interminable and touching. As for the two trucks, they lowered them with ropes into the heart of the wood and on the radiators and sides they fixed big placards signalling that the vehicles were mined and would blow up even if they were merely touched. This more than anything to prevent their discovery and jackal looting by civilians. During the work the feeling of

---

* Brass – more likely.
** Latin – which cannot be abandoned.

liquidation was so acute that it had the effect of being exciting and perhaps positive.

The woman of the house had meantime prepared a huge supper and Nord invited the three of them along with the leader of the guards. Nord said: 'Let's stop playing at being men – now and for a long time to come we will play at being dormice. It is beastly, wears one out rapidly, but is necessary.'

Ettore let the question escape him where he personally would find a hiding place but Nord quickly pursed his lips and his commanders darted sharp glances at Ettore. Then Johnny said that the three of them were staying in the house, they would always find them there, if necessary. Nord noted this but remarked that he didn't like the house too much, so solitary and high up it acted as a natural magnet; he had to confess that he would not have felt at peace there. At which the woman of the house protested with a certain gaiety.

Pierre was visibly shivering in the light of the carbide lamp. He asked Nord to be excused and withdrew into the stable. This reminded Nord of his own malady: 'It must be cut without delay – I don't want to risk losing a hand just when I shall need more than two next spring.'

'We shall be your hands, boss,' said the leader of the deserters with blind devotion.

Half an hour later as the dark was thickest, Nord left for weeks and perhaps months, such was the darkness that after they had gone a metre you could not tell whether they had turned north or south. And then Ettore and Johnny realised the full meaning of the word 'disband' and ran into the stable to watch over Pierre, who was trembling on the straw, and to be more than two.

Three days followed, so empty and useless, with idle hands, exhausting guard duties, Pierre was getting worse so that Johnny was grateful to the women of the house for sending him for bread at the bakery at the crossroads. It was a delicious walk, reviving, with the shiver of walking on the main road exposed to Fascist raids and the delicious rest in the warm fragrant bakehouse, which was frequented by the remaining partisans – the two from the hill opposite – gathered there for the heat and the human intercourse. A clump of houses typical of the high hills hung over the crossroads and the bakehouse and a minimum of human contact was always assured.

Now people were allowing themselves to give better treatment to the partisans, perhaps because they had become so rare and because of the desperateness of their situation. So that at the bakehouse the conversations were friendly, relationships easy, and before going home the peasants let a loaf fall into the partisans' sack. Then the way back with on your shoulders the warm, crackling sack, and the magnificient, pioneering sensation of carrying a weapon and bread and at the end the welcome from the woman. And from the bitch, then Ettore's smiling-smile and Pierre's smiling-grimace.

On the fourth day Pierre was so bad as to frighten himself and the other two. Ettore wanted to run off to Mango for a doctor but Pierre prevented him, he knew very well that what he needed and what would suffice was a shelter and hope. And he went in search for them in Neive in his fiancée's house. 'I'm only telling you now that I am engaged to a girl from Neive. The people of the house know that their daughter will become my wife and they will welcome me like a son. But they won't let me in armed, I shall only take my pistol, well hidden on me. Now help me to grease and wrap up my sub-machine-gun.'

In the hoary white afternoon they climbed up to the wood, plunged into it, Johnny buried the bundle and Ettore cut a mark in the nearest tree. And at dusk so as to reach Neive at depth of night, Pierre and Johnny left with the bitch. They passed through the village of Trezzo, sinister and sealed up in its black hollow, then made for the short flat stretch before Neive. The bitch, now ahead of them and now behind, worked marvellously; padding along quietly on the safe straight stretches, she threw herself boldly ahead at the hint of a bend, took a look at the next straight stretch and then shook her tail in reassurance and *forwarding*. 'It is fantastic,' said Pierre. 'Listen to me and always take her along when you go out.'

When night had completely fallen they were near Neive, recognising the village by the irrepressible hum but certainly not by its physical presence, the air was ink-black, they could not even see the little patch of street on which they were putting their feet; it was as if they were standing on the clay banks of a wide black river, which was breathing deeply and quietly. Pierre said he was sorry but it was only for a week, then he waded into that black river, suddenly drowning there. Johnny waited ten minutes then he saw a door half-open,

357

letting out an extraordinarily yellow light; Pierre was silhouetted in it for a moment, then he disappeared and with him the light. Johnny snapped his fingers at the bitch and turned away.

Towards ten they were feeling their way near Trezzo. It was like going along an avenue in a cemetery at midnight; the animal began to whimper – rather unnaturally without waking the concert of guard dogs on the watch in the darkness of the hollow. Where the houses were thickest on the little square the dog gave a clear and alarmed bark and on the left the door of the inn flew open and from it came light and three or four armed men. The first, clumsy in the dark, cocked his Sten and said: 'What's wrong with that damned animal? I'll make it shut up . . .'

Johnny covered him with his Sten: 'I'll shoot you long before that. The bitch is with me. I am Johnny and the bitch is the animal from the Langa.' And as the weapons were lowered he asked where Geo was.

'I'm here,' said a calm and educated voice and Geo came forward, detaching himself from the vulgar group. 'It's a shock to see you without the other two.'

'Ettore is waiting for me at the house and Pierre I have just escorted to hide because of illness.'

The ox from before said sarcastically in the dark: 'But it's an epidemic. But it only affects the bosses.'

Johnny charged at him with the bitch charging along behind him, the men and the dog struggled a little in a perverse tangle, gasping and hissing, until Geo and some civilians begging for peace and quiet separated them. The ox apologised and smiled saying that student partisans were very touchy, as touchy as virgins. Then he invited Johnny into the inn to drink with him the wine that was a peace offering from the civilians. But Johnny walked on and Geo accompanied him to the edge of the little square. 'I won't give in,' said Geo, 'but I am fed up to the teeth with the company and the place. I need to be up on the hilltops and alone. One of these days I am going to leave but as a matter of conscience I want to wait till I really can't stand it any longer. And I am telling you that it only needs a drop for my cup to overflow.'

In the night an endless time after he had lain down on the straw beside Ettore, who was sleeping like the dead, the woman of the house wakened them and without a word, only with tugs and hisses, brought them out under the dark black pre-dawn sky, then not content with where they were took them further on across the path to the wood. At the edge of the wood she finally spoke, said that the butcher had wakened her specially at this impossible time and had warned her that the Fascists, a little squad, had burst into Treiso at one in the morning, had surrounded an isolated hut and had taken five partisans in their sleep. Their host had been shot in the yard, one partisan, a certain Geo, had been killed halfway to the town in an attempted escape, the other four taken into town to be shot that evening. All this a couple of kilometres away as the crow flies, with them asleep and unconscious, it could easily happen to them and to the house. 'And they were certainly guided by spies,' said the woman of the house, 'because they paid not the least attention to the village but made straight for the hut and finished it all off in a minute. And they say they were walking with their boots wrapped in rags.'

She was shaking with terror. 'We live among spies, the spies are among us Christians like so many demons. Kill, lads, kill them all, for God's sake!' Johnny had never seen her in this state, this indomitable and foolhardy woman. She wanted them to stay in the wood armed and on the alert; before going off she said: 'Johnny, from now on you won't take the bitch when you go out because everyone knows her as the bitch that belongs to this house – and it wouldn't take anything for the spies . . .'

Then a little before midday, reassured by the absolute emptiness of the landscape and the joyful clarity of the light, she called them back with a whistle to eat. The two repaid her by doing jobs, Johnny gathering and bringing in bundles of brushwood from the ravines round about and Ettore drawing from the well a series of buckets of water. Later on, in the afternoon, they saw to the animals following her instructions. The woman of the house gave them supper, then they left for a different sleeping place, making for the highest and wildest hills, and the woman of the house, knowing that they would find miserable accommodation, lent them an old saddle-cloth stinking of grease and urine. And in the frozen and incredibly starry night they went in search of a place to sleep, Ettore with the saddle-cloth wound round his head like a turban. And he said: 'Spies, spies exist. I had never believed it, not even in novels or the cinema. But they exist. I'd like to discover one and you can be sure that whatever

359

death I caused him I wouldn't be satisfied with it. And you know I'm not bloodthirsty, Johnny. What do you say, Johnny? Did you follow my argument?' He had followed him but had not been able to reply being entirely possessed by imagining what he would do to a spy.

This farmhouse was no use, too exposed, too near the main road, this other shack was no use either, situated in a ravine which was completely wild but which opened out too soon on to the road in the Belbo valley. Until they stopped in front of a shack, the smallest and most miserable in all the hills, hardly more than a shed for gear. This one satisfied them and they knocked. A man lived there with a woman, the most miserable since the expulsion from Eden, the man, young and shabby, in a medieval condition of serfdom, gave them a good welcome in the hope of tobacco. But when they said they hadn't seen any for ages he was scornful and threw open the door of the stable for them with crazy violence. It was a little box of a stable with a big window without glass or a piece of cloth, open to the sky which grinned down with starred teeth of frost. As it did not have a piece of straw nor the smallest ox, only a couple of trembling lambs and from the mess they had made they realised that half the space was taken up by thorny bundles of firewood.

They lay down uncovered on the tiles, abandoning themselves to long, detailed and waking dreams of warmth and softness, food and tobacco, interrupting them with groans and gasps. Until sleep came bringing with it real dreams of terror and death.

At the last dregs of night without the man having to call them they got up and went out, exhausted, and yet walking energetically towards the Langa which now seemed like a king's castle. The woman of the house gave them boiling water with in it a spoonful of something sweetish which ran down *ruthlessly* into their empty insides. Then once again off and away, looking carefully at whatever countryside emerged from the mists which were so slowly being defeated and calculating the innumerable hours needed for high noon to arrive. Now the air was as dull as at vespers and pervaded by an opaque whiteness that promised snow very soon and the pollen and perfume of the snow was on the wings of the rising wind. They knelt down mentally, prayed for the snowfall, so much snow that it buried the world, blotted out every road and path, in this way encapsulating every living man in a hole, inaccessible to the human race.

XXX

They had lost sense and count of time and regained them more or less because of the way people were talking about Christmas. Once, returning from a very secret sleeping-place Ettore suddenly said: 'You know, Johnny, if I didn't know you I'd be afraid of meeting you.' 'Is that how I look? I haven't seen myself in a mirror for ages. Can you smell me, by any chance, Ettore?' 'No – really not.' 'Nor I you.'

Then a serious ailment gripped Ettore's throat and fever because endemic throughout his solid body. Rapidly he became almost voiceless and unable to swallow. He lay for a long time in the stable with anxiety and panic on the part of the woman of the house because rumours of spying were flying about on the hills more and more widely and intensely. So when the peasants reported that a partisan was lying mysteriously killed on one of the least public paths Johnny decided to see him and have a good look at him, and in the absence of Johnny the woman of the house wanted Ettore to get out of the stable and wait for him in the thickest part of the wood, she would give him as many blankets as he wanted. But Ettore refused bluntly, indeed he tunnelled further into the straw, he only asked Johnny to leave him the Sten which he laid at his side in the straw.

So with ugly forebodings and under a sky which inspired still worse ones, Johnny went to Sant'Elena in the wilds of the ravines to see the killed man. Ivan, the partisan from the hill opposite, was already bent over him, examining, noting details and making deductions while coughing without cease. Behind there stood a row of peasants, absorbed but *squirming* with eyes and feet, their ears pricked up at each gust of wind in the low branches. And they all shook their heads while Ivan asked questions: 'You really heard nothing? Not even a shot? And didn't see anything either? Someone running away at full speed?'

The boy was lying on his face and in his back from two holes the blood shone, already crystallised. 'Do you have a cigarette, Johnny?' said Ivan sceptically. 'It doesn't matter. This is the death that I have seen that impresses me most. This death changes the whole situation, do you understand, Johnny?'

The boy was an acquaintance of Ivan, quick-witted and bold, not easily tricked, with a perfect knowledge of the ground, capable of escaping from pursuit by a battalion, and he was not wearing anything that unequivocally stank of the partisan, he was somewhere between peasant and skier. A woman asked Johnny to turn the dead man over, and take a look at his beautiful face, and it really was as the woman described it: the pink of the cheeks had not yet completely vanished, the youthful brightness of the features had not yet sunk into the unfathomable age of death nor were they too sharp from the strain of the desperate life he had led at so early an age.

'Such a good-looking boy,' the woman lamented, 'I'd have been proud to be his mother. And now here he is, killed like a rabbit.'

Said Johnny: 'Yes, Ivan, this changes the whole situation. The man who killed him was someone whom he did not know and whom he absolutely did not suspect. A man who met him perhaps with a smile and a greeting and two steps later drew his pistol and shot him in the back.' 'That's how it was,' said Ivan, 'and he could have been dressed up in any way as a peasant, a beggar, a tramp. It's very possible that the dead man greeted and smiled to him.'

They left the boy who had taught them this important lesson, the people who remained promising that at nightfall they would carry him to the cemetery at Rocchetta with all the necessary respect and prayers.

Ivan went a bit of the way with Johnny. 'How come that you are going this way, Ivan?'

'This evening I am not going to stop at Benevello – I'm going further on. In the Beria valley there is a girl of a good well-off family who has taken a fancy to me and warms me up and feeds me. Her family gives me a very sour smile but the girl is so strong, she is the strongest of them – and she keeps me warm. There's nothing as warm as under a woman's skirt, Johnny. But tonight I won't make her make love, tonight I want her to pray for snow.'

They were about to separate on the road on the crest, the wind was so strong that it made the pebbles flow like a stream with a little noise that cut the heart-strings. 'By the way,' said Ivan, 'I saw Nord a few days ago. He was coming back from Cortemilia where they had operated on his hand. He had his toughest people round him and we had a little talk about spies. You know, Johnny, his people have already dealt with one, a teacher. I asked if they were perfectly sure about him and his dirty trade. Very sure, they replied, and they would have done the same to him even if they were only eighty per cent sure. "Because," Nord said, "this is the new law," from now on and until further notice. When in doubt kill. He did not actually say kill but the equivalent.'

'When in doubt put them down,' suggested Johnny.

'Exactly. When in doubt put them down. That's the new law.'

Ettore was lying in the straw, immersed in a shadow that was already nocturnal, and from down there he mimed that his sore throat had got worse. Johnny knelt beside him with one fist on the Sten. 'I saw the dead man, Ettore, and learned an important lesson. Certainly we two will always be together but if anything should happen to me you will know what to do. That man was killed from behind by someone whom he did not know and whom he did not suspect. Someone met him, greeted him, passed him and then shot him in the back. A spy, a Fascist dressed as a peasant or farmer or beggar etcetera.' Ettore followed him with his burning eyes and his head nodding all the time. 'So for now on, call halt to everyone you meet and aim at them and make them come forward with their hands clasped on their heads. Above all speak to them in dialect and make them answer in dialect. At your first doubt or at the first false move shoot, shoot, because we can't afford the luxury of being finished off in this terrible way.'

Then Johnny went out to eat, the woman of the house was curiously incurious and unfeeling, then Johnny went to work in return, wood and water, with all his weapons on him, on his shoulder and at his belt. The bitch was not tied up and spent all her time of freedom following Johnny and running about the open space and gullies round about without ever a bark.

Then Johnny kept guard for all the interminable night with the bitch as enthusiastic companion in the incessant torrent of the wind in which panic and safety were so easily and closely mingled. Every so often he went into the stable to take a look at Ettore, the last time he found him awake. Laboriously Ettore asked him to go next day to Mango to get something for his sore throat. Johnny nodded and went off for another spot of guard duty. But towards dawn, precisely when the need to be awake was greatest, he felt sleepy, treacherously drugged and could barely get back into the doorway.

When he woke, he had an immediate, half-waking sensation of snow but then he saw the mist. But such a mist as he had never seen on the most favourable hills: a universal mist, an ocean of curdled milk which narrowed the frontiers of the world to those of the courtyard, indeed much closer than that. The invisible bitch was padding a couple of paces away and it was a struggle to find one's bearings and reach the kitchen door. The woman of the house was greatly pleased at the thick mist, she felt very safe and comfortable, said that if Johnny came back from Mango at a reasonable hour he would have something better than the usual scanty rations for supper. But she did not let him take the dog.

Then Johnny went into the stable and took a last look at Ettore. He was sleeping deeply and beneficially but he was lying with his whole weight on his pistol. Johnny, as gently as he could, turned the belt round till the pistol came out from under him and was within reach of his hand without Ettore waking up.

He found the road by feeling for the corner of the house with his hand and went on following the relative smoothness of the ground. Where the mist was less compact he could just see his feet floating dreamlike on a distant sea of earth and frozen grass. Undoubtedly the mist was equally thick everywhere and he would know when he had arrived at Mango only when he heard his feet trampling on the familiar cobbles. At a certain moment he was conscious only of walking, walking, weary of the road but without pain. The path kept smooth and familiar under his intuitive feet. Then at a point where he guessed he was at least halfway there he stopped short. The ground was strangely rugged and sloping under his narcoticised feet and the fear of having lost his way hit him hard. He searched cautiously with his foot all round him, now with the fear too of the ravines and deep ditches, then his extrordinary knowledge warned him that he had lost the road to Mango and was wandering about on the immense precipitous slopes above the Belbo valley. Then he wept: all the weeping he had within him for a thousand tragedies burst out because of this trifle of having taken the wrong road, he wept unrestrainedly and bitterly, with his feet motionless on the unhelpful ground. The damp furrows of his lost tears madly irritated his desiccated skin as if it had grown thin. His wrinkled hardened handkerchief made the skin worse. Then he turned his back to the steep slope and climbed up towards the lost path; to try to recognise it he climbed bending forward. He found it with a *gasp* and walked slowly along it. An age later, it seemed to him, he was clattering on the paving-stones of Mango and was amazed to smell in the narrow streets, which were brimful of mist, the odour of midday, and it was exactly twelve, he had taken six hours for a walk normally of two.

He went into the pharmacy. The shelves were three quarters empty and the shop did not smell of medicines any more but like an ordinary family room. From the back shop came the smell of a rich minestra and light music on the radio. The doctor listened to the request, shook his head and then offered him a little box of potassium pills with a sceptical grin. 'Naturally I can't pay,' said Johnny. The other waved a hand, that old gesture now had the fresh intensity – an expression of the utmost comprehension and compelling need.

'Thank you. And, doctor, what are the symptoms of scabies?'

'Have you got it?' he blurted.

'No, I was asking by way of preventive knowledge.'

His back was almost screaming out of the need for a massage, a pummelling seemed to him to be the peak of sensual desire.

The doctor gave him a list of symptoms.

'If I get it can I turn to you?'

'Well – I don't even have a bottle of ointment left. But there's no need to shed tears over it. I wouldn't be the slightest help, with the kind of super-scabies you partisans are liable to get.'

He came out from behind the counter and let a cigarette fall into Johnny's hand. It was a splendid cigarette, bulky all and soft, with seamless paper and tobacco of the same colour all through and mild. The pharmacist made to light it but Johnny drew aside: 'Forgive me but I haven't smoked for ages. This one I want to smoke reverently.

Lend me a couple of matches and forgive me again.'

He smiled, gave him a handful of matches and said: 'This is from my last stock-up in town.'

Johnny stood there open-mouthed – this man had recently been in town; the pharmacist sketched a gesture of extreme, frightened disgust. 'I swore not to put foot in it again till the end of the war. Life is so impossible and death only too possible. Very strict curfew at five, a whole lot of patrols everywhere, with tense faces and levelled guns. And every night their firing squads are at work in the cemetery, my friends told me, every night.'

Johnny went on, slumped on the last step of the pharmacy and lit the cigarette with delicate care, taking pains to bathe in an accurate flame the round tip of the cigarette. He smoked with long slow intakes of breath and the smoke he breathed out disappeared quickly into the mist. But halfway through the cigarette he was already *surfeited* by the smoke because his head and stomach were too empty. So it was a rather long stub that he threw away as he rose to go back.

Although still thick and heavy to the point of immobility the mist now had in it a few moving and active cracks, and its immense mass now seemed to sway clumsily to and fro under the growing force of the wind which would disperse it by evening after holding heavy sway for a whole day. The road seemed much more visible and traceable than in the morning, yet he thought he would not get back till four.

Round about that time in fact he was walking, somewhat feebly, on the crest of the last hill less than a kilometre from home. Here the mist was in a state of crisis and huge areas of cold landscape rose up and stretched out before his eyes seemingly stupefied by their long burial and even more by this resurrection. Birds were timidly, hoarsely, crying in the nearby pines which had just been dis-entangled from the mist. And in that field of vision Johnny caught sight of a group of men whom he recognised at once as the inhabitants of the nearby farmhouses: they were standing with one foot on the side of the road and the other on the hillsides as if ready to flee, to disappear in a flash. They too recognised him in a way that suggested that it was him they were waiting for, but they made no sign to him to hurry. There were women too constantly touching their stiff skirts as if out of despair and nerves and full hearts.

'Stop here, partisan, wait before going back to the house.'

'Tell me the end,' said Johnny.

'The Fascists were here this morning when the mist was worst.'

'Did they shoot him on the spot?'

'No, they took him and carried him to town as a prisoner. And the woman of the house and the wolfhound, and all the animals, big and small. They made a cartload of everything and everybody and yoked the oxen of the house to it. What could your comrade do, seeing them, damn the mist, only when they were sticking their rifles down his throat.'

Said Johnny: 'And to think of the blessings we called down on the mist this morning.'

He felt in his pocket, took out the pillbox and offered it to a woman: 'Keep it for your children for when they get a sore throat.'

The woman took it and said: 'So you're left all alone, alone on the whole hill. They smashed the whole house, you won't find even a crust of bread. This evening, after dark, come to us for supper. Ah, you'll all end up like that, boys. But it's the work of spies, I swear, going on under the eyes of God.'

Johnny went into the middle of the road and stood there to adjust his weapons about him.

'What are you going to do?'

'I am going to have a look.'

'Wait. They certainly left a while ago but you never know. And you are so alone and so out of your mind.'

Johnny asked if they had gone beyond the house and if they had gone down into the big wood. They made a gesture of No and it said very clearly that they knew about the buried trucks.

He plunged into the wood and made his way through it to reach the house from the most unexpected side. But he moved forward without particular caution, distracted by the thought of Ettore, which was at one and the same time blunt and lacerating, about how far he had gone down the path of capture and death, trying to imagine what shut and guarded room he had now entered after the wild freedom of the hills. He arrived at the fence which had been broken down, the courtyard was immensely deserted, there was not the slightest sound of poultry scraping and chirping. Total death had followed the tumult of life which had death as its corollary and objective. From outside already he could see that the interior had been completely sacked and broken up.

He pushed down the barbed wire and jumped on to the courtyard. He sniffed the air almost as if it might retain the diabolical stench of the men who had captured Ettore like thieves. He inspected the stable – empty; the kennel – empty; the entrance – stripped of carts and harness. He burst into the kitchen. It and the rooms beyond had been sacked, then from the threshold they had madly fired bursts at the old, shoddy furniture, riddling it with bullets. And his feet crunched horribly on the layer of smashed pottery which covered the tiled floor.

He went out into the yard again and made for the abandoned oven, thrust a hand into its mouth and felt the cold and dusty stones, until his fingers touched and gripped something metallic. It was Ettore's pistol – that was why they had not shot him on the spot. But would they do it that night or one of the next ones? Ettore could not prove that he was not a partisan. And he would not even try or want to; he was proud and unyielding, so ready to pay the great price, but in his humble and always deprecating manner.

He weighed the pistol in his hand, then thrust it into his belt. Out of the corner of his eye he caught a furtive movement beyond the barbed wire, he wheeled round and pointed his Sten, but they were only the same men as before.

He went towards them, weapon and head lowered.

'What will you do?'

'Oh, let him do what he wants,' said another.

Johnny set off at a run, darted behind the house, reached the crest and from up there contemplated the number of crests and valleys, the number of houses, the vague twilight distances. Nord could be in one of them but which? He threw himself down the woody slope while the confused cries of the men clashed and faded in his wake.

He rushed down into the Belbo valley over slopes devoid of human beings, seeking a lucky meeting with some remaining partisan, if possible one who had information and was involved, to learn where Nord actually was and if he still had Fascist prisoners for an exchange. After half an hour of giddy descent he was in sight of the hamlet of Campetto, just beyond the river, the old rendezvous where the partisans had swarmed, now shrouded in empty solitude and evening twilight, the evening was gathering strength to blow on the waters of the river, increasing its icy murmur. He waded the river, which was cold enough to take one's breath away and strike at the heart, and made for the inn on the other bank weakly indicated by shafts of light that were afraid of themselves. He threw open the door and from the threshold asked about partisans. The host and the few customers made negative gestures with the air of asking whether they would have been so calm with partisans in the inn at this unlucky evening hour.

He ran to Rocchetta in a whirling wind that was sometimes favourable and sometimes contrary along the shadowy road. The village was lightless and bolted; absolutely deaf and dumb. The partisans, if there were any, must be in their most secret recesses and their trembling hosts would deny their presence to him even if it cost their lives. Fatigue and despair weighed on him while he went through the bilateral length of the entire village. Then at the very end of his search he caught sight by chance of the face of a partisan looking at him from the badly lit frame of a little window almost level with the ground. Johnny crouched down and knocked on the sill and on the grating. The man was one of Nord's bodyguard and was having something mended by a young girl, his weapon ready on the table in the meantime.

At Johnny's knocking the man scowled and the girl trembled.

'You know me,' said Johnny. 'Tell me where Nord is.'

'I don't know,' he answered and made a sign to the girl to go on working.

'You must know.'

'I know you but I can't say – I'd risk my head.'

'But it's a matter of life and death.'

'And it must be for Nord too it seems.'

'At least tell me if Nord still has any Fascists for an exchange.'

'Not a single one. That I can tell you for sure. I was part of the squad that was outside the town for the last exchange.'

'It was for Ettore. They took him this morning.'

'Ah.'

'Can't you tell me if there's a partisan with a Fascist prisoner? Even twenty, thirty, forty kilometres from here?'

He said no, he didn't give a damn about Ettore, for him the conversation was finished.

But Johnny could read clearly what his hard sarcastic face was saying. 'If you don't give a damn ... if you like him so much, try direct action. There are whole regiments of Fascists in Alba and Canelli. In Alba or Canelli, you can choose. Run along and catch one.'

He went off and meantime answered himself: 'Yes, I'll go tomorrow. I'll try at Canelli. If not I'll find one in Alba.'

He crossed the river again and began to climb, weakness, distress and the dark made it an ordeal. Near the top he instinctively turned off towards the house where he had been promised food but then he thought that replenishing would be more useful next day before he left for Canelli. So he set off again for the Langa, to which the previous day's events gave a more marked *hue* of ghostliness and ill-omen. He entered the courtyard past the kennel, past the kitchen, horribly aware of their deserted state, and went into the stable which was icy because emptied of animals. Nevertheless he took off more things than he had ever done before and lay down in the manger, his weapons hanging from the hay-rack. Under the hay he waited for sleep, his mind quietly busy with the next day's programme: what man would he meet tomorrow on the outskirts of Canelli, what rank, what size, how armed ... Then he slept like a stone in an unhealthy jumble of dreams from which Ettore was missing but full of food and *comfort*.

XXXI

He woke up in the pitch dark. He took his weapons and went staggering in the ravines towards the house with the promised food which was already awake to judge by the little shafts of light and the curling smoke from the chimney. The guard dog became furious, the woman appeared in her vest, quieted the animal and beckoned to him to come in. She would give him a bowl of milk and a fried egg. Meantime she set the bread in front of him but Johnny found himself to be so weak that he could not manage to break it and then the woman cut it for him and as she did so said: 'I understand, you know, what you are going off to do. But remember that two deaths are much worse than one . . . and three days before Christmas.' Johnny only said that he didn't have a handkerchief any more and could she lend him one. The woman did not have one but she went and cut a piece with her scissors from a fine bit of linen.

The special food had fortified him and even made him optimistic so he went off with a firm step and a mind at peace. He cut diagonally across the immense slope then down above Cossano and continued towards Santo Stefano, walking along in the cover of the rachitic vegetation on the bank of the river which ran parallel to the road in the valley.

The big village was silent and shut down, even its constant distinguishing mark – trading – had died away. He cast a glance at the big, empty greyish square beaten by gusts of wind under a dirty white sky, pregnant with snow that refused to be born. All the chimneys were smoking thick and solid against that sky. He went forward in the cover of the houses, keeping close to those that looked on to the river, and finally found himself in the middle of the village two hundred paces from the bridge at the railway station. He stopped under the cover of a back-stairs to make up his mind. He decided to cross the ridge, wade the river between the church and the station, then make straight for the outskirts of Canelli by way of the hill.

The man who was looking curiously at him from a little back window was the barber from the square and he seemed deeply worried. 'What are you wanting? Don't you know that Santo Stefano is a trap for people like you? They are at Canelli four kilometres from here. Just think how long they take to get here by truck. You scarcely hear the swish and they are here. The San Marco Batallion,* in great shape and pitiless. Take my advice – get away at once and far away because I feel that today is a visiting day.' On the contrary Johnny climbed up a couple of steps to get on the same level as the barber who was seized by panic: 'And once they are in the square what do they usually do? Do they scatter and go about separately or stay together?' 'Not at all, I catch what you mean. They'll trap you because they never take the least time off – are always on the watch. They arrive – fifty or a hundred of them – get out and go about and work elbow to elbow. If you have come fishing this is the worst pool you could choose. We don't want to be called out by the Fascists to see you dead or taken alive and slaughtered.'

The man disappeared but Johnny felt that he was still eyeing him from some unknown chink to see what he would end up doing. Then with a new fresh feeling of confidence he walked off coming a little closer to the bank of the river. It ran through the *treeless* levels in stony flatness glinting with pools of weedy, icy water. The hill opposite was enormous and rugged, each of the houses scattered across its bosom sent curling up whitish, plump smoke against the black flank of the hill and the opalescent sky. It would be a waste of breath and bad for the lungs to have to escape by running in that direction. He went forward, his feet very uncomfortable and noisy on the gravel, feeling on his back more than one look directed at him from the back windows of the houses on the river.

At that moment from the other side of the village there was born, spread and flew over the Canelli road a whistling thread** and the

---

* A unit in Mussolini's Republican Army notorious for savagery in its anti-partisan role.
** A signal rocket.

already minimal noise of the village fell to perfect silence. In which the rumble of the trucks rose to a diapason, in two minutes they braked with an immense din in the large square and Johnny could also hear the banging of doors, the thud as they debussed, the first harsh orders, a laugh, their quick trampling to their appointed posts. He ran to a tiny piece of cover right down on the water's edge looking with repugnance at the icy water he would have to cross in a minute. Less than five hundred paces from him a strong patrol of Fascists came on to the bridge to set up a machine-gun there. And Johnny waded over and *s'enfonça** in the fairly thick vegetation on the other bank. But what shape was he in? That short run had upset him, it had rent his heart and lungs. He took a hold of himself, got down on his knees and looked back at the bridge. The machine-gun had been aimed at the smoky hill with eight or ten men behind it. Two, sitting on the ammunition boxes, were looking to the weapon, the others were now walking up and down the bridge, smoking, chatting, pointing things out to each other, occasionally shouting taunts at the nearest barred windows. After a little a comrade arrived with a can of something warm. Later still an officer came to inspect the post immediately stopping their tentative salutes and began to look round with an air of bored confidence and to hear with the shadow of a smile the flattery of the men. He was young, of medium height, a little plump, with blond hair that was dull in the dull atmosphere. Merely a little lieutenant, thought Johnny, but exactly the man who would weigh the same in the scales as Ettore.

He waited, still watching, then shook his head: they seemed rooted to the bridge, none of them would move away by himself, if he did so it would be for a very short distance covered by the eyes and weapons of his companions. Then he decided to skirt the bottleneck of the bridge by way of the hill, cross the river again beyond the station, and then make for Canelli. So by a perpendicular ravine he got all the way up the pyramidal hill and from up there took a long look at the Lilliputian Fascists garrisoning the toy-bridge. Walking up and along the serpentine paths of the mid-slope he met some peasants who were looking down from behind tree trunks at that same spectacle below, staring and hating. 'Look at the black

* plunged.

swine. When will we kill them once and for all?' 'Next spring.' 'The way you say it it seems further off than Doomsday. Next spring. Have you any tobacco, partisan?' 'I was going to ask you for some.' 'God, the black swine. But it's some sort of consolation to think that we'll still be in the world smoking when we feel like it and they'll be underground, full of worms.'

Walking on he felt himself to be full of subtle and quiet happiness to find that he, the nervous, slim townsman, had become more patient than the peasants, who were as patient as the most patient of their oxen. He had covered the mid-slope and was now going down directly to the station whose façade of faded Pompeian red was the *main feature* of that neutral landscape. He had already had enough of the day although he knew it was not yet ten. On the level ground he crossed the rusty rails, then over the empty meadows he went to wade the river, then he clung to the hill once more for a useful look at the road to Canelli. He placed himself behind the thin, just-sufficient trunk of a poplar, his legs were hurting because of the water. On the main road just up from the iron bridge a good number of Fascists were meeting between two of their motionless trucks. And a long line of them, just in the act of spreading out, were attacking the slopes of the nearby hill. So there was nothing to be done in that direction, he had come up against the most lively and active day for the garrison since it had established itself in Canelli the previous December.

He did an about-turn and walked away beyond the station and along with a new icy wind slipped into the valley going towards the station at Calosso and Boglietto, an arctic canyon, sinister, patched with soot.

By midday he was at the big crossroads at Boglietto. There was a certain windy movement of women shopping and the noisy iciness of the plain which was spreading everywhere. With the Sten hidden as well as possible under his jacket he went into the baker and grocer's, its woman owner worried but not saying anything, and went in silence to lean against the wall of the oven. He stayed there feeling his back thaw, nebulously thinking that that kind of heat definitely was not good for him but enjoying it to the full. Meanwhile he watched with veiled eyes the coming and going of the housewives, as silent as the owner, because of him, ordering and being served by gestures. Quarter of an hour later the shopkeeper asked if he wanted anything, Johnny shook his head against the warm wall, the woman sighed and began to cut bread and pork fat for him. They heard the bell ring and the door half-open but no one came in and the shopkeeper complained and uttered a loud reproof for that ring of the bell. Then the customer came in and went up to the counter. It was a very old peasant woman, lantern-jawed and bald, reduced to looking almost like a man. At the counter she croaked: 'Once we had a whole lot of partisans and almost always sitting idle but now at the moment of need where you can find one? So we have to see a Fascist soldier walking calmly through our countryside and not a partisan to make him pay for it. A hundred grammes of jam. The blackguard is walking towards Castagnole all alone like a king.'

Johnny, although befogged by the heat, had taken it all in. He went out quietly and was on the frozen tar. The road ran straight for a short time, but the Fascist was no longer there, he was walking on round the corner. Johnny went on at a run, his footsteps sounding extremely loud on the tar and as he passed a half-shut door a quarter of a man emerged to make a sign to him for more speed and a capture. He turned the corner and saw the man – it was no mirage and not much more than a hundred paces ahead. He was very tall, like Johnny, a short greatcoat fluttered wildly round his thighs, he was walking at a tremendous pace, always staring ahead. He was armed, he carried a weapon under his arm, but from the distance Johnny could not tell what it was.

Since the tar drummed out his running too loudly he began to walk and walked his best, but he was doing too little to wipe out the other's start. Then he jumped into the ditch alongside and in it ran crouching, when he re-emerged the man was still sixty paces ahead of him, still striding out and staring ahead. He had passed someone on the road and this man was now coming towards Johnny – an old peasant, who recognised Johnny straight away. He stopped, laid his two baskets on the ground and waited for Johnny. 'So this is it?' he said with a *luscious* grin. 'What kind of gun has he?' 'A rifle.' 'Sure?' 'Sure – but watch out, he has a determined look.'

He walked faster and nibbled away another thirty paces. Then for the first time the soldier turned round and automatically Johnny took on a country gait, sturdy but clumsy and gangling, looking with peasant interest at the countryside and the fields. The soldier had no suspicions, he walked on and more strongly. Johnny glanced behind him in his turn and saw the old man still standing there among the baskets he had laid on the ground, staring at the two of them and their race. Now Johnny was not gaining a metre and the outskirts of Castagnole were already appearing whitely among the green in the more luminous air. Johnny did not want it to happen in the village and pulled himself together to walk more quickly. Now he had half uncovered the Sten and if he turned round the solider could notice it. So he went off the road, went round the first farmhouse and from the corner in the wall saw he was ahead of the soldier; he hid behind a heap of poles and listened to the other's steps. And when the soldier passed, staring ahead as always, he leapt across the ditch and thrust the mouth of the Sten into his back.

The man collapsed, Johnny had to hold him up by his collar, then he turned him round; his eyes and brows were trembling, his eyes rolled, his country boy's face white and in spasm. Johnny slipped off his gun and ordered him to take off his greatcoat helped by Johnny because he could not manage alone. Johnny searched him and in the pocket of the greatcoat found a hand-grenade which he unwillingly burdened himself with. Then Johnny signed to him to cross the tarred road and go into the fields but the other did not move: 'I'm not leaving the road, you'll kill me the moment I'm off the road.' Then Johnny pushed him over the ditch into the field and stopped him from getting down on his knees. He ran no risk of dying, he said, he would be exchanged for a friend, a comrade of his who was in prison in Alba waiting to be executed. Not only would he not kill him but he wouldn't harm a hair precisely out of love for the complete safety of his friend. Meanwhile he would see that he got food and rest. 'Have you understood properly – everything?'

As his only reply the soldier collapsed on a bank out of sight from the road because of thin already wintry bushes, and burst out crying with his face in his hands. 'Even if it is as you say I'm finished just the same – I'm dead. It's all over with me!' Johnny gave him a good shake, asked again whether he had really understood what he said.

But: 'I'm finished, I'm dead just the same! Not because of you but them! Because I am a deserter – I was deserting when you took me. I escaped from Asti last night from the bunker on the bridge where I was on guard.'

Johnny flopped down beside him – above them a couple of sparrows chirped without fear.

'So you were a soldier at Asti?'

'I had to be – they rounded me up and put me in uniform.'

'Don't lie.'

'Well, I was frightened and reported when I was called up. But now I was deserting and had managed it all by myself and you come and capture me halfway there.'

'Why halfway where? Where are you from?'

The man named his village and Johnny ordered him to speak in dialect and he had indeed the very narrow 'e' of the way they spoke in that village.

'Please, set me free and on my road.'

But Johnny shook his head and roughly, to hide his own sadness, ordered him to get up and walk. 'I'll get you exchanged in Alba as soon as possible. The officers in Alba won't know yet that you are a deserter because the headquarters at Asti can't communicate by wire or phone and certainly won't risk a mission for an ordinary soldier like you.' 'I wish I were something less than an ordinary soldier,' the boy wept. 'They'll shoot me the moment they know I have deserted.'

They were climbing up the pleasant dry hill to Coazzolo. 'Do you see the campanile? Under it there is a priest who will speak about your exchange with the officers in Alba.' But the boy wept and walked on without seeing the road. Out of shame and misery Johnny did not look at him except for a quick uncomfortable glance at the thickset coarseness of his body in the skimpy, cheap, *manreducing* Fascist uniform. A boy from the village had caught sight of them from behind a hedge and having grasped the situation wanted to come closer and have a better look and perhaps ask questions but Johnny angrily chased him back into his hiding-place. 'You're safe for days,' he said then to that long back, 'before Alba knows from Asti that you deserted the way things are today. And one of these days you can desert again and from a base much closer to your home than Asti. Yes, listen to me, desert as soon as possible and cross the river at Roddi or better still further upstream. But pay attention – get yourself a civilian suit. In Alba people will give you one, because if a partisan catches you again who doesn't have my need to exchange you, this time you will end up killed – deserter or not.' By the heaving of his back he expressed gradual agreement and gratitude and black despair. Then he turned round with a suddenness that made Johnny level his Sten again. 'But after the exchange the officers will interrogate me,' he said, 'they'll want to know where and how I was captured. And what will I say? They know perfectly well that you people are hiding and keeping your heads down and are absolutely finished everywhere. What answer shall I give the officers?'

A fit of anger shook Johnny out of sheer fatigue and pity. 'I'm fed up with you. I've had enough of you. You're a chicken, as wet as a chicken. It would have been infinitely better if I had come across one of the bravest of the brave on the road. You're so chicken-hearted that I am ashamed of having attacked and taken you. What answer will you give? I don't give a damn. It's up to you to answer. Make something up. Somehow or other you slipped into that filthy uniform. It means shame and disgrace and now you are having to put up with that disgrace. And from now on shut up and think up your excuses. Understood? Not another word. Get on.'

The village came into sight with its *one-storey* way of clinging to the naked flat crest with the tiny, airy noise of its hidden existence, the prisoner spoke again but only to beg Johnny to be good and understanding with him as he had been earlier, not to insult him and make him feel uncomfortable any more. 'You are a partisan with the idea in your head and a town boy, I am a soldier against my will and only a country boy.'

Two o'clock was striking on the campanile when they entered the village one behind the other. Here too everything was deserted and bolted but Johnny's expert ear caught through the walls whispers and a minimal fiddling with shutters and vibrations of windowpanes. He directed the man to the inn, the lowest house of the very low houses on the right. Then from the uneven flagstone like a mirage ominously barring the way, Flip rose up. And seeing him the soldier shook and took refuge behind Johnny. And Johnny sighed and his heart fell, exhausted by the day, by the wandering, by that shameful capture and pity for the prisoner. Flip's bulk blocked the alleyway and his animal eyes shone with untimely drunkenness. He was not a bad lad nor a bad partisan, Flip, because he had always happily donated his notable physical strength to every laborious partisan task, rejoicing and glorying in his superior strength, more than one truck extricated and mountains of ammunition carried on his back. But God had made him from the commonest of clay and then his breath of the spirit had barely touched him. However drunk, he had rapidly sized up the relationship and the situation, the Fascist grey-green acting as the most effective smelling salts to clear his mind.

He gave a hoarse greeting. 'Well done, Johnny, well done. I'm not asking because it's your business. But now get out of the way. He's mine as much as yours, isn't he? You've done the best part of the job and now I'll do the rest. Get out of the way so that I can do him over a little.' He came forward, rolling up his sleeves on his thick arm.

The prisoner swayed behind Johnny who felt his hot, flustered breath on the back of his neck. 'Keep off, Flip. He's not to be touched. He's not mine nor yours. He is Ettore's. You know Ettore, he was a mate of yours in the good days, wasn't he? Well, he's been captured and condemned to death and I have captured this one to exchange him. So keep off and keep calm.'

'You keep calm, Johnny, I'm not going to kill him,' said Flip with the oily sweet tone of the drunk. 'I'm just going to do him over a little. Get out of my way, I'm telling you . . .' He did not get out of his way and Flip got angry. 'I hadn't ever thought of laying a hand on you but I didn't think either that you'd become such a swine. A swine who won't let me punish a Fascist, a swine who has already forgotten that the Fascists shot a brother of mine.' His thick, naked forearms danced in front of Johnny's eyes. 'I haven't forgotten that they shot a brother of yours, I just don't want you to touch him, because I need him to stop Ettore from meeting the same end as your brother. Think of Ettore.'

'I don't give a damn about Ettore!'

Johnny was covered by the sinister blackness of his hurtling mass, he shut his eyes and kicked him hard, seeking the bone in one leg, and then kicked him again in the stomach. Now he was lying flat in the gutter, gaping, and Johnny hit him to knock him out for a little, when he became aware that two other hands were pummelling at the body along with his own. 'Don't you touch him,' he shouted at the Fascist but it was Diego, the innkeeper's son who was hitting with a concentrated and *businesslike* face. The prisoner had gone to lean against a wall with his fingers in his mouth out of terror. Diego stopped knocking Flip unconscious accompanying his last blows with a whistling voice but one without rancour. 'I've had it in for you for a while, I've had it in for you for a while.' Then he stood up and with Johnny and the soldier docilely behind them, took him into the stable for a sleep on the straw. 'You can talk to him in dialect,' said Johnny to Diego about the soldier who was holding the door open to let them through, 'he's from our parts.' 'Oh the bastard,' said Diego but with a light voice, full more of bitterness and surprise than of outrage. Then Diego went off for food.

It was agonising to see how the soldier behaved at table, serving Johnny, waiting for him, rigorously observing precedence and respect, exactly in the relationship of slave to master. Johnny told him not to overdo it and to take the biggest portion. 'I had a good meal this morning. Have you got a cigarette instead?' He had a whole packet from the Fascist ration and gave them all to Johnny. 'I don't smoke. I took the ration because it was mine by right and above all to give them to the civilians in Asti, with them I bought company and comfort. I had such a need to be with civilians.' He was eating voraciously. 'In barracks I ate three times a week.' 'Are they really so short of food?' 'No, no, they have plenty of everything – even of meat. But I didn't feel like eating. My throat was tight from fear and homesickness and the shame of this uniform. I was always desperate. I woke up desperate and went to sleep desperate.' And the thought of sinking back into that despair made him weep again, his tears in his plate.

Diego had been at the presbytery, he came in again shaking his head. 'I knew it beforehand but I wanted to try. My parish priest refuses. He is seventy and really can't get to Alba without something to take him. He says to try the curate at Mango – he's young and can cycle for any number of kilometres.'

They got up to take the road to Mango. Diego confronted the soldier in sober seriousness. 'I saved you from the punches and gave you food. Don't thank me. I only ask you to forget me and my house and my village. Can I be sure that you won't come back guiding a Fascist column which will hang me and set fire to my house?' 'No, no, not me,' stammered the man. 'He won't,' said Johnny. 'What will you do with Flip when he comes round?' 'Nothing, if he toes the line. But if he plays the bull I'll kick in his guts.'

They walked to Mango, the prisoner asking the direction at the crossroads, along pleasantly deserted paths, under a whitish grey sky which made all the hills, and the one at Mango more than any other, look bleak. Johnny was smoking the cigarettes from the Fascist ration, thinking of the partisans he would find in the village, of their responsibility and willingness to take on that exchange – along with the curate who was always ready. He quietly considered the man's back and said to himself, yes, for him they would give Ettore back.

The village looked more deserted and bolted than Coazzolo and the saddest spot was precisely the alley leading to the entrance with the pre-evening wind which was raging there in a vain search for more dust to scrape away and whirl up. They stopped near the hut with the weighbridge and knocked at all the windows and doors. Then a man peeped out of the archway, his whole person withdrawn into a hiding-place. Johnny made a sign to him, then a whistle and the man came out of his cover with open repugnance and walked stiffly towards them. 'You know me,' said Johnny, 'I know you well but I was watching you and couldn't make out whether you were the captive or the captor,' and he sniggered *distressedly*. Johnny asked if there were any partisans about in the village and who they were. He replied Franco and Gatto and that was a good thing because they were – especially Franco – dependable boys. Johnny sent the man to find them and while they waited they sat on the tree trunks near the weighbridge. The soldier dropped his head into his hands once more. 'You're leaving me like this?' 'I have to, but don't be afraid, you'll see with your own eyes, I'm leaving you with good lads. I have treated you well, haven't I, after all?' The man nodded wearily with his head buried. 'Well, they'll treat you even better because they're better than me.'

Franco and Gatto came down the avenue, slow and not very interested. A minute later Gatto ran off to the presbytery to warn the curate. And Franco looked at the soldier coldly. 'Oh, he was a chicken,' said Johnny. 'Yes, but you didn't know that when you tackled him.' Franco took the rifle, the hand-grenade and the overcoat, for the use of the unit he intended to form when the new season started on 31 January. Gatto came back with the curate's assent, he was happy to help Ettore, had by now quite a bit of experience with exchanges, the Fascist officers knew him from afar and he would go down into town the very next day.

Johnny turned to the soldier for the last time. 'I'm sure that in town you'll find good solution to your problems and in a couple of days you'll be home. Thanks for the cigarettes.'

'I wish you weren't leaving me,' stammered the soldier.

'Don't worry, these two are better than me and I didn't treat you badly. Don't worry – have supper and then a good sleep.'

He walked towards the distant Langa a little light in the head and swaying a little, dreamily greeting and enjoying the flatter stretches. There was, at the beginning of his walk, a certain sweetness in the air and in the colour of the earth, even in the wind, but Johnny was scarcely aware of them. And when the house appeared to him black against the darkened sky Johnny longed for the old beams of light from the windows, so visible from afar, and then had dark doubts whether Ettore would be ransomed.

XXXII

In the night he started up horribly with the choking sensation of encirclement and capture. He seized his dangling belt with the two pistols and dived headfirst at the door of the stable and the Fascists outside, the sight of them and their firing, and vast death and the slenderest chance of deliverance. The door burst open and before his eyes could see his naked feet as they sank in the snow, already a hand's-breadth deep, fresh and soft. Under the snow the yard was deserted and friendly. The whole world immersed in a heavenly peace and in such silence that one could almost catch the landing of each single flake of snow. The cold which rose up columnarly from his feet had immediately extinguished the tumult of his mind and body and now there he was smiling, letting the belt with the pistols hang down round his naked belly, moving his feet imperceptibly in the cold but so *cosy* hollows in the snow. He was smiling. '*You're coming, snow. We need you and you do come. Please go on coming down our fill and yours,*' and he bent down to stroke it with his hands, its surface soft-hard in the process of crystallising. Now his feet were boiling with the cold and he laughed at it and laughed at the pistols hanging across his thin, tense belly. He withdrew into the stable with an absolute, very first sense of peace and safety as if he had been given a safe conduct from on high. He bent over the manger and began to rub his feet on the straw, *babbling nonsense*, compliments to the snow. '*You must have come for Christmas, you are Christmas.*' He did not want to fall asleep again right away, some sort of celebration was incumbent on him; besides he felt as good and happy with his eyes open, lying on his back in the straw, thinking in every sense of the snow. He thought he ought to smoke as a celebration and festival; he found the soldier's last cigarette but the necessary match refused to turn up. He looked everywhere with increasing anxiety. He reached such a peak of exhaustion and sensitivity that the simple fact of not finding a match could make him go mad. At last his two fingers came across it, the last of the handful from the pharmacist in Mango, hiding in the seam of his pocket. He dug it out and scratched it with frozen fingers. Then he smoked quietly to the end, letting his mind drift in a pond of safety and isolation.

He woke up and got up in the late morning – he had never been so late. He went out expecting great things from the snow, which had not been damaged by his nocturnal acquaintance with it. The snow had risen to his knees, perfectly crystallised and moderately brilliant under the embryonic sun. Joyfully, sportively, he ploughed through the snow to the gate and managed to reach the corner of the building for a wider view. All the world of the hills was shining white with the extraordinarily abundant snow which it bore like a feather. Absolutely no trace of road, lane or path remained and the trees in the wood rose up white from head to foot, the trunks extremely black, almost freakishly mutilated. And the houses all round had a *funny look* of happy acceptance of the blockade and the isolation. It felt like a day unlike any other, removed from the context of the war, a day from before or after it.

He thrust his hand into the hard snow – it was compact and cellular, lasting, it would not let itself be sent away by a little sun or wind from the sea. The weak sun caused a stronger reflection from the snow, adding levity and liveliness to the scene. He turned, catching his breath, to the Alps as the greatest gift of that extra-ordinary morning but he was disappointed; they were disappearing opaquely in a ragged, lower curtain of dull mists.

A constant rustling sound and loud and liberated shouts from children punctuating the whole flight of that rustling noise made him turn to the nearby slope. The urchins from the peasant houses were sliding down at will on rudimentary hay-sledges. Some were practising on real skis, home-made, made by their fathers, short and wide and clumsy. They went down like lightning and then took a good quarter of an hour to regain the summit, expending in shouts, gasps and fatigue their prodigious reserves of breath. Johnny sat on the snow and stayed there watching them, knowing they would not get quickly tired of it. From there he could see the gigantic intakes of breath of their tiny chests, the heightened rosiness of their cheeks, the formidable muscularity of their little legs fighting the snow and the slope. And he loved them as children, accepted their being so young and so much not part of the war, and hoped they would later on rapidly and totally forget that war in which they had marginally scampered about with their innocent feet, wished them good things and good fortune in that afterworld which he knew he had so little chance of sharing with them. The day was so full of peace that the peasants had decided to set free the guard dogs and there they were flying back and forwards among their infant-masters with the same inventiveness and capacity for enjoyment.

The smoke of dinner curled up thicker and richer than ever from the chimneys, then the mothers leaned out to call their children to table with the loudest of imperative voices. The slope was quickly empty and dark as if the sun had stopped shining on it.

He went back into the house, taking advantage of the earlier footprints, but it had never seemed to him so desolate and violated. He set out in search of some sort of food through the length and breadth of the house. They could not have carried off and destroyed every single thing, something must have escaped them. Crunching over the desert of crockery, he rummaged the kitchen meticulously, throwing open the bullet-torn cupboard doors. The cupboard was completely scraped bare. The pantry once opened let off a horrendous sour stench, like certain animals in peril of their lives. Johnny *gasped* and ran off across the crackling crockery. He went into the room under the stairs where they usually kept the produce of the soil: potatoes and apples and hazelnuts. Everything had been taken and swept away, only at the back of the room on a pyramid of sorghum stalks there shone, like a chalice, an apple perfect in form and colour. He went forward catlike, as if it were something that could move, escape, then his fingers clutched it and sank into its frozen pus. He threw it out of the window and splashed on the walls the drops of icy, rotten juice. In a corner he found some hazelnuts, less than six of them, so dry that they resisted his teeth and he had to crack them with his heel, with much spoiling and scattering.

Smoking would dull his stomach. He sat down and relaxed in the most comfortable and calming position. Then he began the search with his finest and most sensitive fingertip all the remains of tobacco in all his pockets. Slowly he extracted and heaped tiny little segments and atoms of tobacco mixed with crumbs of old bread and threads from the cloth. Now he had in his palm enough for a cigarette. He went back into the stable to look for the stub of the previous night and found it. With it he would contrive a robust and well-filled cigarette. Then he looked for paper, a product scarcely known in the house. He looked around and rummaged until he found an old pamphlet, wrinkled and yellowed with time, on agriculture and housekeeping. He tore a page into a square and began to roll it. Working at it with infinite care and suspense, he realised how coarse his hands had become, how unadapted to these delicate tasks. If the cigarette turned out to be decently shaped at one end it remained formless at the other; at a certain moment the tobacco slid down on to the tiled floor. He shut his eyes and clenched his teeth: 'Don't lose your head. It's nothing. In any case you wouldn't even have a match.'

He went out. The day had become corrupted from its morning brilliance to evening grey, making that sea of snow look leprous and yellowish just as in the old days at Mombarcaro. And the immanent comparison of the different periods made him think of the length of the whole business, and he sobbed and kicked at the snow out of hatred and contempt.

Then he walked through the virgin snow to the panoramic crest because voices were reaching him from below, travelling easily through the motionless and lifeless air. Something was going on at the crossroads at Manera. A dozen peasants, grouped round a rudimentary snowplough, were arguing with a couple of partisans, Ivan and Luis. He realised that the people wanted to clear the snow for reasons that affected their lives and the partisans, for similar reasons that affected their lives, were opposed to it. The spokesman for the peasants was almost writhing about beside the snowplough in the intensity of his oratorical display but Ivan harshly signalled No from his full height. In the end the peasants turned back home with their powerful pairs of oxen, leaving the snowplough alone and useless, while Ivan and Luis apparently pursued them with harsh words.

He went back inside. The snow, as it turned to ice under the newly-born arctic wind, bit at his boiling-hot knees. And before evening he received in the house a delegation of peasants from his hill, all of them old. The spokesman was a man of medium height whom Johnny recognised as the sharecropper from Serra dei Pini. Under his working trousers he wore grey-green puttees taken from the army at some time or other. Johnny invited them into the house out of the wind but they were unwilling to see the spoilation and wreckage and so the conversation took place in the courtyard. 'We have come to ask for authorisation because we know our duty and we don't give a damn for your skin.'

'Clear the snow as much as you want and wherever you want.'

Everything was already settled but peasants cannot refrain from an argument that has been turned outside in and thoroughly dealt with.

'Of course,' said the sharecropper from Serra dei Pini, 'roads cleared of snow are easier and more attractive to the Fascists, but we and our families, how shall we live blocked up? The children can't go to school and that would be the least of it. But almost all of us have let our bread ovens go out and how can we get to the public one? And what shall we do for wood?'

'Clear as much snow as you like.'

'So we can go and harness the oxen to the machine?'

'And you,' the sharecropper insisted, 'how would you get out for something to eat? We know very well that those robbers left nothing in the house. With the roads cleared you can go about and reach our houses to eat with us, one day here and the next day there, eh?' and he looked round his comrades, taking their consensus.

He went down with them to a crossroads where the oxen and the snowplough stood with a child sitting on its nose. They began; during the work one of the peasants, the only young one, stopped and rolled himself a cigarette with dark shag. Then he looked up and caught the gleam of desire in Johnny's eye and quickly made another, offering it with blackened and deformed hands. Johnny inhaled and a cough shook him furiously. The other laughed. Johnny was all red in the face, he was having difficulty in recovering. Then he said: 'I thought I was one of the greatest smokers.' The sharecropper from Serra dei Pini came up to him and looked at him with an almost medical air; in a low voice he said that it was too much, he shouldn't miss meals 'with decent people everywhere you turned'. 'I feel very well and then I don't want to put on weight.' 'Weight? That we are poor we can shout to the heavens without fearing that the Lord will strike us with lightning or bring down punishment on our children's heads – but a loaf more or an egg more – come down to my house this evening to begin your round. By then you'll find the path already cleared.' The man with the cigarette grinned again and Johnny heard an older one admonish him in a low voice: 'Stop it, idiot, it can look like an insult and taunt and you never know how it will end up with these young people carrying guns.'

After nightfall he went down to Serra dei Pini on the path that had been cleared of snow, armed only with one pistol in his belt.

The children had already eaten and now were playing far from the table. The smallest ones were playing, with only the slighest hint of quarrelling now and again, at a kind of tombola with beans and maize seeds (to be put back in the open sacks against the wall) while the older girls and boys amused themselves by playing a mouth-organ made from an old comb wrapped in tinfoil.

Johnny ate the coarse and abundant fare slowly and attentively, almost as if following a medical prescription. The guard dog growled every so often but perhaps only to draw to its master's attention that he was keeping watch as was his duty and was not dreaming or snoozing. Johnny rose from the table and went over to the children to watch them play. They looked up at him with a timid little smile and Johnny realised that he was disturbing them greatly. He went back to the table while the woman cleaned the plates and glasses in a sink under a little window with a formidable grating. The man wanted to talk but waited in vain for Johnny to give him an opening and then he made up his mind with that kind of peasant ponderous dislike of starting a conversation.

'You are a special kind of partisan, without wishing to offend the others. What do you think about spies?'

'They exist.'

'And are they people like us?'

'Italians, yes, if that is what you mean.'

'Mother of God! It seems impossible. For me it's easier to think of a parricide than a spy. And what are they?'

'Fascists.'

'Civilians or –'

'Very often they are soldiers, disguised as tramps or beggars or

388

even partisans who go about, take notes, report, when they don't do the nasty work themselves.'

'But they have a nerve.'

'Yes, they have.'

'Because apart from you people, we ourselves, men of peace, people who don't come into it, if we found them we'd tear out their hearts and guts.'

Johnny looked round at the children at play and said: 'Whatever happens, take care of them. Understood? Think of them first. And leave us to our fates. Think only of them. You will not feel remorse as time passes, you will be at peace.'

The man was looking doubtfully at his wife, who had turned round from the sink and looked at the man with an old-established need for consent, for permission to start. 'Must I tell him?' The man nodded and sat looking elsewhere in the peasant way when leaving the stage to others. But the woman quickly got confused, stammered and called for help from the man, who took the whole situation in hand.

'The day it is important to talk about,' he said, 'I was away, I was at the fair in Coasano, the kind of fair there are these days. So the woman was left alone in the house apart from the children and was cooking, because it was the time when, as we had agreed, I was coming back over the river. She was cooking and had necessarily to stand in front of that little window,' and he pointed to the grated opening. 'Looking up by chance she saw a face, a man's face, framed exactly in the window.'

'I almost died of fright,' the woman interjected, 'and then had to sit down and couldn't recover and when he came back no meal was ready.' The man at the window was a trader in rabbit skins from Alba and asked if the woman had skins to sell for he could offer a good price. On the spot the woman lied, saying they had sold them all although they had half a dozen laid out in the stable. The man confined himself to smiling and saying that he would maybe be luckier another time; there was neither regret nor ill-will in his voice. He said goodbye politely and went off very calmly. Their eldest son, a reliable boy, went out to watch him go, but only saw that he had a bicycle and was well dressed and well shod against the cold and the mud.

'The woman,' said the sharecropper, 'will have seen a hundred of

389

these skin traders but never one with a face like that. And she was sure he was a spy, one of their soldiers disguised. Probably an officer to judge by his face, and what frightened her most was his smile.'

'What kind of smile?' asked Johnny but the woman indicated that she was simply not capable of describing it.

The man spoke: 'He smiled to her in a way that terrified her, fit to freeze her blood, that's the kind of smile. For nights we have talked about it in our room, at dead of night, with our children fast asleep. And he had a bit of a squint, says the woman, but very slight, a defect in one eye that made him good-looking and not ugly, says the woman, and although he was very young, about your age, partisan, he had a white lock in the midst of his other dark black hair.' 'I got a good look at it,' said the woman, 'because owing to the heat of the climb he had pulled his balaclava back a little.' Then Johnny asked if he had spoken in dialect and the man hit the table with his fist. 'He spoke to her in Italian* and I just wish I had been there to hear him. Because I could have told more or less which part he came from, because when I was in the army I got used to every kind of Italian. Imagine a skin-merchant from these parts who speaks Italian. The only ones to speak Italian – but that was thirty years ago – were the oil-merchants from Liguria who went around selling olive oil but the second time round they already said the kind of oil, the weight** and the price in our dialect.'

So it was him, a spy, thought Johnny. A cold desire for him, an icy programme, *mastered* him to the point where he trembled: that must be his man, his plan and his specific prey for the whole war, out of this world with either him or Johnny. And mentally Johnny prayed for him to return, to think once more of coming back, in search of him and certain destruction, to come back smiling and remain there killed dead by him, Johnny.

'What do you think of that now, can you tell us?' said the man very anxiously.

'Eh,' said Johnny. 'Oh, yes, I say it's odd. No, it's not odd, I say he's a spy.'

At the word the sharecropper hammered with his fist on that table,

---

* Not in dialect but in standard Italian.
** Olive oil was measured by weight and not volume.

more scandalised than angry. And Johnny sank back again into the thought that the killing of this man from hell would make up for the whole winter, would adorn all this immense squalor once more with the crown of victory and merit.

'And suppose he comes back?' asked the man.

'He will never come back.' He rose up and thanked them for the meal and the company.

The man accompanied him to the beginning of his private path. 'You could stay and sleep in my house,' the man uttered the words as best he could in the great wind. 'We feel safe with all this snow around us.'

He said no. 'Tell me instead – are all the roads clear of snow as far as Mango? I want to go there to get information about my prisoner and Ettore in prison. I can't live without knowing.'

'Yes, you will walk easily as far as Mango. The whole road must be free of snow, because we in the country have an agreement and none of us is stupid enough not to respect it.'

Very slowly he made his way along all the glassy, wind-*ravaged* path to the Langa, thinking all the time with calm intensity about the Fascist with the odd smile and the streaked hair, walking along with his own deadly step and burden of initiative and courage and death, and had to take a hold of himself to prevent his excessive desire from suffocating him and exhausting him before he got home.

XXXIII

In the wreckage of the house Johnny had collected an old pair of scissors and had been busy for hours freeing his feet of the dead and ruined skin which so much walking had formed in layers under and round them. He stopped when the point ran into sensitive tissue which was painful and bled a little. He put the double pair of socks which he had been wearing since the days in Castagnole on again, then his mountain boots, which had become so impressive to look at, being so much a part of him that it made him feel queasy to see them empty and torn off, lying on the ground, with all their leathery appearance lost, inflexible, stony.

'What next? What next?'

After Christmas he had passed four miserable days as full of cravings as a pregnant woman, with a mad need for tobacco, for something sweet to suck very very slowly, for a wash with a real piece of soap, for the stupidest songs on the radio, forcing himself to go on sleeping again, and visions and nightmares peopled those miserable snatches of sleep. '*What next? What next?*' His heart was rent by longing for the old community, the quarrelsome and at times repellent community, and for the old battlefields and for the company of the living, of the dead, of the prisoners, of Pierre, of Michele, of Ettore. He yearned for the re-formation of the partisan forces, for that he would have given half his blood. He talked to himself out loud as happened more than often: 'Where is Nord? What is he doing and thinking? Nord, 31 January is an absurd date for us to meet. That morning you will get up and call and only the silence of the hills will answer you.'

Beyond all those hills that fall down to the lowlands, all of them proudly glowing because of the extent and thickness of the ice, from the plain round the city echoed roars and rumbles. Even yesterday he had heard them – a whole series of noises, at one spot and spaced out. Again now: it could only be mortar fire, thought Johnny, but for what reason, at whom? He went out on to the courtyard and then on to the ridge to hear better that dull, dark rolling noise. As he walked he felt, somewhat painfully, the new sensitivity of his feet: up to this morning he had felt as if he had been walking for a long time with someone else's feet. He sat on the frozen ledge, lonely, high and dark, and sun and snow made an unbearable background, and sat for a long time listening to the rumbling noise from the town. When from the last bend in the road there emerged a cart, drawn with infinite slowness by a pair of oxen, and on the driving seat there sat a woman in black with men around her, peasants, in attitudes at once of help and reverence. Johnny rose on tiptoe and shaded his eyes against the sun. It was the old woman released from prison in the town. Going downhill at perilous speed he wondered where the big bitch could be. The woman recognised him quickly, then raised her arms in fear and entreaty, for at that moment Johnny slipped and came down hard on the ice. His hands were bleeding from the sharp edges and as he waved them in greeting the blood spurted far.

'Did they let you go? Did they let you go?'

She held her greasy hands out to him, her features were bold and optimistic as always only in her eyes could one see a new, frightened, cautious animality.

'As I told these good men who have escorted me thus far it was pure nastiness on their part not to set me free for Christmas so that I wept the whole of that holy day. Ah, they are bad, Johnny.' The man at the shaft of the cart said they had always been bad and that feeling their end drawing near were worse.

'What about Ettore?' asked Johnny leaping up on to the driving seat.

'They tried us together – I'll tell you the whole story of the trial just as I have told it to these good men from my hill. Ettore has been sentenced but is still alive and we cannot ask more from the Lord. I'll tell you everything, Johnny, I'll tell you all day long until it's dark and when it's dark I shall still have things to tell.' She turned to the men. 'Now you can go, men, and take the thanks of God and of the poor woman of the Langa who was taken by the Fascists. You can go now,

now I have my partisan with me, my personal partisan, who is taking me home, to my poor house, Johnny, go and take the shaft.'

The men had withdrawn, Johnny was guiding the animals with all his weapons hanging about him, and asked about the bitch, with a pang in his heart. The Fascists had kept her, they wanted her for themselves, for their evil ends, for their round-ups on the hills. 'Think of the wolfhound helping them to find and kill you! They are bastards, Johnny. You should have seen me leaving with my cart and my oxen and them laughing after me because the beast naturally wanted to come with me. She was tied round the neck with a double rope and wept and groaned as I left so much that I thought she was giving up the ghost. Because she had spirit, our dog, Johnny. Drive the oxen more firmly, harder, don't be afraid to hit them over the nose, or we'll not take this narrow bend. That's the way, that's the way, that's the way.'

They went into the last, narrow steep ramp before the house and the woman prepared herself with all her strength for the sight. 'Tell me, my house is all in pieces, isn't it?' 'You know it is, you saw them breaking it up, didn't you? Think of your life.' 'I am completely ruined, Johnny – with nothing, not a grain of wheat or an ounce of meat and not even a plate to eat from.' 'Don't distress yourself, your neighbours – I heard them – are competing to help you most.' 'But I am ruined just the same. Whatever they can give me it is not enough – some gear and something to eat but they won't give me money. I am ruined if Nord doesn't pay me good money. I am his creditor but he can very easily deny me the money and I would be ruined with my only solution to throw myself down the well.' Johnny assured her that Nord would undoubtedly pay her – and several tens of thousands of lire, he would see to it, at the beginning of February, that Nord paid her several tens of thousands of lire.

He unyoked and stabled the oxen then rejoined the woman in the kitchen. She was still standing on the threshold, hunched up and sniffing. And Johnny felt deeply sorry that he had not on any one of those days of solitude and boredom thought of finding a brush and gathering up that layer of broken crockery. 'Johnny? Will you still remember me, even when it is all over and you are a big man in town?'

The news had spread like lightning over the great hill and Johnny could already hear the voices of the visitors drawing near and their scraping on the ice. He went out and saw them coming up from all directions with gear and parcels and bags, even with children, and he signed to them all to go in. The old woman had picked up the least damaged of her chairs and now was sitting enthroned, a handkerchief to her nose and her eyes turned away from the door. The people came in, in silence they showed and deposited their gifts and aid, then spoke with calm voices and sober glances. 'It isn't much but you know what it is like these days as well as we do. Please show us a serene and relieved face because a woman of your age and experience doesn't need to be told that it is life that counts not things, things you can get again, and your life is safe now.'

'I have been through so much,' she sighed, 'I have been through everything, I can say. They tried me and dared to say I deserved a death sentence. Only because I gave shelter and food to so many good lads like this one here. How much I went through!' 'Now you've got away from all that,' said an old man. 'And later on they'll give you a medal.' 'What does a medal do for a ruined woman?' The sharecropper from Serra dei Pini spoke up. 'Don't talk like that, mistress, because you are almost blaspheming. Think of all those who for having done exactly the same as you have had their houses burnt down and their people killed.'

Then the women *jerked out* the men and began to sweep, clean and tidy. The woman had made to get up and join in the work but the others nailed her down. 'And cheer up because now it's all over.' 'I can't, I simply can't cheer up. It is all so like when I was left a widow.'

They finished and left, leaving everything clean and tidy, the *gaping* nakedness of the pillaged room becoming even more striking. The women had also left food prepared and of that the two ate by themselves. 'If only I had my bitch now! Johnny, take your pistols and look around to see if everything is calm as far as your eyes can see.' He took them and went out, he circled round the top of the hill, looking hard into each ravine, looking up at each crest: everywhere from close at hand to the distant plains hidden by cold thick, thick mists, the silence and peace were absolute, almost holy. He came slowly back and all the way he too felt greatly the lack of the dog.

It was pitch dark, all encompassing, and they had supped on what was left from midday and the woman still had not spilled everything out.

Yes, Ettore had been so brave at the trial but she who was at his side all the time could see that his eyes were starting from their sockets and his heart beating in his throat. No, he had not been beaten at least not the bits you could see. And it was so difficult for him to answer because of his sore throat which had got worse. Call it a trial – everyone was on their side, judges, prosecutor and defence lawyers, all the officers, and they went through with the trial as if it were a game, laughing and smiling a lot. As for her she had had trouble right away with their Italian, said she understood little or nothing, they replied that she was pretending, that she was a nasty treacherous country witch, then got angry with her, and her defence lawyer shouted at her. They handed her out eight years, Ettore got the death sentence but not immediate execution, then she and Ettore were at once separated. She was taken to the Smaller Seminary ('just think the use they are making of a seminary, Johnny') where she stayed for her whole time in prison. All round her there were ordinary soldiers, almost all not nasty, some of them very nice, but she suffered horribly thinking about her house, about her age and fate, and Ettore who had been condemned to death. Besides she was very uncomfortable with all these men because at the moment when they took her she had not yet put on her knickers. The guards weren't nasty and were very willing to speak, some of them sighed and glanced at her in great uncertainty, as if they had decided to open up to her but every time they said nothing and put it off. She learned that the other ranks were very fond of their colonel and trembled for him and her. The colonel – she saw him once during an inspection – was an old man with very fine white hair, sad eyes and a desperate mouth. His son had been killed in Lombardy by Lombard comrades of Johnny's, it was he who signed the orders for execution by firing squad and the posters that gave notice to the citizens that the execution had been carried out. But the soldiers said he was the best of commanders and of men, a gentleman, head of a family, but his days were numbered and the other ranks trembled at that when they didn't weep about it. The junior officers, along with a captain and a major, judged him to be too weak and protocol-bound. They had accordingly made accusations about him to the high command and he would be replaced one of these days and the whole command would pass into the hands of that major and that captain. Two tigers according to the soldiers who didn't want them and trembled if they merely went past. 'You should try to kill that major and that captain, Johnny.' And one soldier, from Como or thereabouts, had then become close to her and called her granny, quite seriously, and saw that they did not ill-treat her or dishonour her or mock her in the mess, she simply asked him to tell her when the partisan Ettore would be shot and he promised but up to the last day he had given no information so that Ettore must still be alive.

As for the food it was the same as their own and of the same quality but you could die of cold. 'The fire was no help, Johnny, it is the place, the building itself. Now I understand why half the clerics end up consumptive before they are ordained. I suffered so much from cold and yet wood wasn't scarce, just think they had cut down all the trees round the walls. If you looked at the town now, Johnny, you would see it is as ugly and unhappy as a raped girl.'

'Maybe you can tell me something about these explosions we have been hearing up here for two days now.'

'They are firing, Johnny.'

'I know they're firing but what at?'

'They're firing at the ice on the river because the river has frozen over and the ferry doesn't work any more. So they set to with the mortars firing at the ice. Please, Johnny, take another look round outside.'

Peace and evening and the ice as it faded *glowing disgracefully and drearily*, but peace.

For the last two days she had been transferred to the college. Johnny must certainly know the place and it was as cold and draughty as the seminary and she wasn't happy at the move. First of all because she was racking her brain and trembling to understand the reason, and secondly because there were some partisans there condemned to death and each one waiting for his particular night. She didn't shut an eye all night, she snatched some sleep only in full daylight, the guards didn't tell her off for that, praying all the time that up in the hills Johnny and his comrades wouldn't put a Fascist to death. 'Because otherwise we were all done for. There was one of your comrades, Johnny, with raging toothache and a jaw so swollen that I felt ill just looking at it. But he was so intent on the thought of his own execution that he could put up with that tremendous pain pretty well. Every so often a soldier came in from the medical service and gave him a painkiller and a pat on the shoulder. But one night, my second last night, a sergeant came to take him away and he got up, said goodnight to all of us who were left and in the door turned round and said, "In half an hour my toohache will be quite cured." And all of us burst out weeping because the most of them were old, hostages from the town and country folk like me guilty of giving food and lodging. All night long you heard people groaning and coughing under that damned lamp which was always lit.'

The shadow had grown so dark that the plate was no longer any more than a whitish, frightening blotch, and Johnny got up and lit one of the candles brought by the neighbours. He sat down again and asked her to go on. Her eyes became even more staring, catching all the light of the candle. 'I could go on telling you my story all night and still have enough till midday. But what is the use of telling it? You personally, the best thing you can do is not get caught. I tell you this as well. I always had my mind on my oxen and my cart and kept asking the soldiers about them. They replied that they were in the stables along with their own horses and being treated very much better than their mistress deserved. About the dog I wasn't particularly worried because I knew they were all mad about her, officers and soldiers, even that major and that captain, and at mess-time they gave her kilos of stuff to eat. But I missed her a lot specially when it got dark and those bastards always took her out away from me for their games and fun. Until this morning comes and an NCO wakes me and takes me into the courtyard. I understand it all at once because as we went down I saw my cart ready with my oxen harnessed to it and facing the way out. They signed to me to get up into the driver's seat and start up the oxen, which I did as if in a dream and under the eyes of their officers in the balconies and a guard armed to the teeth opened the carriage gateway. Two soldiers escorted me to the checkpoint – one, after having called more names than you can imagine, went ahead to make the beasts go faster and the other who was still at the side of the cart found time to whisper to me: "Stamp my face in your mind, signora, and save me from the partisans and put in a good word for me and shelter me. It doesn't matter if the partisans beat me till I'm disfigured, if I chance to come your way, so long as they don't take my life. I've had enough specially now that the colonel is leaving and in a few days I'll desert." I barely nodded yes and immediately went through the checkpoint with all of them shouting names at me behind me including the one who had just asked me for a favour.'

She got up but so shrunken that her hair almost caught fire from the candle. 'But why did they give me eight years then?' Johnny replied that they would track them down and make them pay for it if they won the war. 'Mary Mother of God, and will they win it?' Johnny laughed No. 'What are you going to do now, Johnny?' 'I am going out, I'm going to sleep elsewhere.' 'I'm sorry but it is really best, you know. Next time they would really shoot me.'

He was standing in the unhinged door, confronting the deathly cold, the great windy chaos. 'It's cold enough to kill you,' she said. 'I'm not in a condition to lend you a rag of a blanket any more and you weren't born to these hardships. Where will you sleep, Johnny?' 'Down towards the river. In a farmhouse where I know the guard dog is dead and they haven't replaced it yet. So I shall climb up into the hayloft without calling out and the people won't get a fright.' She said to come back next day for a mouthful of dinner and to help her a little, only if he looked round him at every step. And Johnny entered the ice and the darkness and the *mainstream* of the wind. The steel of his weapons burnt his hands, the wind pushed him on from behind with a hand that never relented, scornful and dismissive, his feet danced perilously on the sharp ice. But he loved it all, night and wind, dark and ice, and the distance and the wretchedness of his destination because all of them were living and solemn attributes of liberty.

In the morning he woke and his frozen arms did not manage at the first go to lift the mountain of hay under which he had lain all night. He repeated the effort and could see the dirty beams of the hayloft and the sky. It was of a grey from Limbo, which had no faith in itself or in life, a day that its Creator would throw into the wastepaper basket. Then he felt an exceptional dryness in his throat and an intolerable tightness in his chest. He tried to cough to shake it off but he did not manage to break the grip; he felt in his chest a sticky juxtaposition of what felt like metallic diaphragms: outside, his chest felt as if they had been punching it all night. I'm finished, he thought, I'm going fast towards TB. 'But I'd like to have TB and be put in hospital.' And he imagined the place, a sanatorium halfway between Switzerland and heaven and so powerful was the vision that he had to lie down again on the hay, pressed down by it gently but firmly. He dreamt of his little room, delightfully painted pale yellow, no bigger than a cabin on a boat and with only one opening like a porthole, highly transparent and double-glazed, temperature at four degrees, his pyjamas of purple silk and his slippers of fine white leather; a gramophone with ten records and a couple of books, Malory* and Propertius. The door opened silently and in floated the blonde nurse, asexual . . . who smiled to him to be ready for a delicious injection, hence the wonderful *company-making* touch of fever. His internal diaphragms rubbed together horribly, his throat croaked from pure dryness, then something crashed and clattered inside him as if his body was entirely composed of old iron. His watch had stopped but it must be after six although the sky was completely devoid of clues. Then a harsh noise of sawing came to his ears and looking down to his left he saw a man sawing frozen wood with a frozen saw in the most frozen corner of his frozen courtyard.

The man noticed his presence and that he had stayed the night only from his thud on the ground, *grinned* impotently towards the partisan, asked for no explanations and arched his back over his saw again. Johnny wandered a little on the crackling sheets of ice, fed up with it as much as with the sky and the day. 'Can I give you a hand?' he then asked the peasant. The man stopped, distrust and avarice were interwoven in his voice. 'You're hoping to get food in return? You will understand I . . .' 'No, no, I just want to get rid of the cold a little. Can I?' He went over and with both hands sawed with the man a little mountain of wood so frozen as to be almost mineralised. Every so often he glanced at the poor house, he could catch at the little window the hard stare of a young woman devastated by poverty who held high in her arms a living little bundle of wool.

It was nine, the sky greyer, when Johnny left that courtyard and began to climb through the woods towards the Langa, often turning aside to delay his arrival. His lips, which were swollen and *sear*,

* Thomas Malory's *Le Morte d'Arthur*.

troubled him terribly, he wet them continually to the point of nausea. At last eleven struck in the campanile of Benevello and he adjusted his watch, then he circumspectly made for the house, on its roof a thin scarcely visible little curl of smoke. He did not cross the courtyard but from the road on the ridge looked in at the little kitchen window. 'It's me. All well?' 'Take a good look round, Johnny, then come in. I had a terrible night. I dreamt everything I told you all over again. Everything, would you believe it? Every single bit.' She was cooking lavishly, thick slices of meat were roasting in abundant nut oil of which the neighbours had given her whole bottles. 'I have had a good look round and there's nothing there. Must I draw water from the well for you?'

He began to draw water – he had turned the pulley round so as to be facing the road and his weapons weighed on his shoulders as he worked. He was carrying his fourth bucket to the stable when he was overwhelmed by heavy breathing and the drumroll of paws and he caught sight of the bitch passing him like a whirlwind, giving a single bark, as loud and sudden as the noise of a claxon, then skidding on the ice it burst into the kitchen from which a cry at the miracle arose. Johnny dropped the pail, rushed into the kitchen and threw himself along with the old woman on to that mixture of skin and excitement and hugging the animal they hugged each other and his hands ran without making any distinction over the coat of the dog and the hair of the old woman. 'She escaped from them!' she cried at a pitch of joy and faith. 'She escaped from them! My little wolf didn't take the wrong road, the true God guided her. My heart told me so, Johnny, but I never revealed it out of superstition. My little wolf, now I'll give you the meat that's for roasting,' and she made to get up and serve the dog but then she sank on her knees again, not having fulfilled her need to hug and welcome it. And Johnny took possession of the front paws, swollen and scratched from hours of galloping, and put them to his cheeks out of love and gratitude. 'Everyone must learn about the miracle of my bitch,' said the old woman, 'everyone in the hills,' then she had second thoughts and said it was better if only those knew about it who had seen her galloping home. Then she took a slice of meat and laid it beside the muzzle that lay on the tiled floor; the beast was still panting as if in a coma, but she was overcome by happiness and triumph, with half-shut eyes glancing at the rich meat close by but without stretching her lips out a millimetre. Johnny and the woman also remained on their knees exhausted by the surprise and love and only then noticed that the bitch was wearing a magnificent brand-new collar of leather and metal certainly bought for her by a Fascist officer in a shop in town. And the housewife said she would always leave it on her neck as a memento, as a decoration and because it was such an expensive one that she would never be able to buy one like it.

They all ate at three. Johnny getting up every so often to look about all round and the bitch was already so recovered as to be ready to follow him every time he went out.

After a reign of chaotic clouds the sun, which was as distant as could be, was making immense efforts to grant a drop of light to this unfortunate son of a day, almost as if it wanted to baptise it before it died. So the light did not shoot shafts but transformed itself into a diffused kind of harsh brightness which made the ice shine with a constant grey-blue halo, hard and peaceful. After the big celebratory dinner the bitch had curled up but when Johnny went out on to the hill on sentry-go and to pass the time she suddenly got up and set off behind him, as if to follow on from the enormous freedom she had enjoyed all day. And Johnny got permission to take her with him on condition that he went to the wildest and most deserted places. Johnny gave an undertaking saying he would come back when the first darkness fell.

They set off towards the very high *pastry-looking knoll* of the Boscaccio and on the way Johnny talked a lot to the dog and asked her questions and loved her for her return and her company and the way she carried her head and tail. They did not climb to the very top but went round the summit to reach a little col from which the view was exactly the same as from the top. Johnny stopped and looked all round with the animal not appearing to enjoy the halt. And so the whole scene took place under his eyes.

XXXIV

They appeared round the last bend on the road from Berria, a score of Fascists, grey-green dwarfs wrapped in grey-green cloaks and walking like puppets on the icy surface. Johnny watched from up above and after his first feeling of excitement was intrigued by the tiny size of the company and the unusual direction it was taking. It could only be a detachment from the strong garrison which since November had been moved to Cravanzara to cut in two the partisan territory and as for their destination, it could easily be either the town or a walk to counter the wintry numbing of body and spirit, so much had they become the lords and masters of the hills. Johnny scarcely had time to snap his fingers at the bitch for it to take cover like himself because on the road which ran at right-angles to the one the Fascists were on and hidden by a snowdrift, two partisans came into view, certainly Ivan and Luis and a third person, a child or a dwarf. In spite of the distance Johnny could clearly see the two joking with the little person and encouraging it to walk on, seeming to have great fun with that extraordinary company. Ivan, given his longer stride, was five paces ahead of the other two and five paces further on was about to come round the snowdrift which hid the Fascists advancing unaware but on the alert. There was no use firing a burst in the air to give the alarm and besides Johnny could not do so before he became frozen by the terrifying geometric dimension of what was happening. Ivan stopped for a moment to let the other two catch up with him and they re-formed a gay knot, their hands nowhere near their weapons as they came round the drift.

The child screamed. Ivan fired first, with his pistol and one of the Fascists toppled over like a toy figure with lead feet that has just been hit. Luis fired with his pistol, the Fascists all fired together, the child

403

screamed, Ivan and Luis shouted, the Fascists shouted too. The little figure was already a *squirm* on the snow. Ivan and Luis were still standing with their knees giving way only by degrees. Still shouting the Fascists fired again, remaining with their heads thrust forward parallel to their levelled guns, then raising them when the two partisans lay long and motionless on the snow.

Now they scattered in all directions on the road, at the pitch of success and fear, looking all round and up at the hills as if obsessed, pointing their weapons everywhere with abrupt mad gestures. Their officer looked fleetingly at Ivan, went on to Luis and gave him the *coup de grâce*, then went over to the child who began to scream and kick. Then the soldiers came and bent over the two dead men to take their weapons and every possible partisan emblem, then re-formed in a compact electrified body.

The bitch came and rubbed against Johnny's legs with such an impatient and affectionate impulse that she almost knocked him over into the snow. The silence which had fallen was horrible and fascinating, the distance from down below was such as to make the Fascists look like nothing but concrete ghosts on a background of white moss. Johnny blinked his eyes and the Fascists became slightly more concrete and more concrete than Ivan and Luis. Now the cries of the child reached him like the brief tune of a fleeing blackbird. The Fascists were still drunk with success and fear, the officer had gone over to his man wounded by Ivan who was sitting on the snowy roadside nursing his arm. Then encouraged by the officer they formed a column, there was some sort of consultation, then they went back the way they had come; their feet only for a moment taking on the normal marching pace then all together they burst into a real run, looking madly back and around with the child shouting after them.

Johnny threw himself into the lateral snowfield, it was hard enough not to sink into, then he ran to one side to try to see them in perspective beyond the bend which had hidden them from sight, but they had already crossed the brief stretch in his view. He threw himself downhill towards mid-slope but here he sank in snow up to the knees, the dog up to her chest. He made his way back to the harder snow and worked out the most direct and easy way down. The silence was absolute but the deadly volleys still hung over everything as if embodied in tiny icicles hanging in mid-air. 'Go home, dog, you know the way,' and he patted her behind to send her on her way but she paid no attention and followed him downhill.

He zigzagged down, aiming at the black heap, two thirds of it motionless and the remainder threshing about against the intensely white background and when the descent became steeper he set his course by the groans of the small creature. The silence was deeper than ever but Johnny's expert ear could extract from it the slow furtive arousal of all the peasants round about. One of them was looking out from a hurdle in a courtyard.

He jumped on to the road, the bitch behind him. The child stopped groaning and suddenly turned its head to him. It was not much more than ten years old but its face made it look much older because of the freckles, the wrinkles caused by hardship and the hard, knowing eyes. A bullet had gone through his calf and the blood was dribbling down on to the black woollen stocking.

'You are a partisan!' he shouted. 'Keep away from me. Those two got me wounded and now you'll get me killed. Go away,' and he cursed like a grown-up. Johnny went and knelt down to look at Ivan and Luis. The wind was licking against the tufts of grass that emerged from the blanket of snow with an extremely dry sound. The child had begun to groan again but Johnny paid no attention to him, being entirely absorbed in contemplating the other two with an increasing capacity to identify himself with them. '*You've been so clever,*' he whispered and they had indeed been clever in those few seconds when they could do something, the last thing they could do. The child was calling for help but not from Johnny's direction and a slow step could be heard approaching over the ice. It was the peasant who had come out from the hurdle. Johnny straightened himself and ordered him to get a cart. 'I haven't got one and my house is along way away.' 'Go to the nearest one and get out a cart. If they don't want to threaten them in my name.' The peasant went off and Johnny turned to the child.

He was shouting: 'Fascists and partisans, I'll wither the balls of all of you.' He felt his pocket and produced his metal tobacco box knocked out of shape by a bullet. 'I'd like to see my father scold me for smoking now. It would have been all up with me if I didn't have this vice – the tobacco box protected my heart. Oh, do something for my leg.'

Something crackled high above and in front of him and Johnny saw on the topmost crest three men from Benevello, squatting there motionless. He signalled to them to come down and help, they came down and the first to arrive, the miller from Manera, asked first of all if they had at least fought back. 'Of course, they fired first,' said Johnny drily and ordered them to wait for the cart. He went to have a look at the road taken by the victorious Fascists. His heart, faced by the white emptiness of that last bend, *heaved and swelled* with the desire for blood. From that last bend the wind slipped away like a deadly hissing serpent. He turned back and then saw the cart coming out of the ravine, the man with the dark head was urging on the animal in a hoarse, terrified voice. The child had been lifted up from the ground, now he was in the capable arms of the miller. The bitch was bounding all round and now was making for the cart as it arrived. Johnny put the Sten behind him and clasped Ivan's long, bony, tremendously heavy body. A peasant helped him and Ivan was the first to be laid on the cart, then Luis, all the work of the miller, who was rather *grimly* triumphant at his physical strength and expert handling of corpses. Now the child was in a state, he didn't want to be put on the cart with the dead men, he cursed and demanded that these big strong men should carry him on their shoulders. Said the miller: 'They're dead, they won't bite you, and we're all here with you,' and put him on the cart on a layer of straw. 'How the devil were you walking about with two partisans in these times and on these dangerous roads?' 'We were going the same way. I had run away from home and was going to Borgomale to play at cards with my mates.' He felt in his pocket and produced a dirty pack of cards, his own personal pack. 'You know they're terrible at cards, at any kind of game of cards, and down there in Borgomale I have my suckers. Today I needed money for tobacco.'

The cart pulled itself clear, as they moved on Johnny looked up at the high banks and crests, they were lined with motionless peasants, hard and dark and as feeling as poles in a vineyard. The miller had seen to getting the cart under way and now joined Johnny in the rear. And said: 'One of you must be keeping a score. So you will know that you have a frightening debit balance to write off. Can I have a word with you later, Johnny?' 'You can,' said Johnny. 'As for the debit balance, we know all about that. The others can take us and kill us without restraint and without scruples. We can't – the lucky one we happen to take we have to keep alive and well-looked after to exchange him for those of our comrades who are imprisoned and condemned to death in town.' The brat had reached a pitch of impudence and bravado. 'Can one of you open my tobacco box with the bullet hole and make me a cigarette with the stub inside it.' One man tried but the flattened lid did not open. Johnny was shaken by a tremendous fit of coughing that left him red and exhausted. 'I'll have a word with you later,' said the miller.

Benevello came into sight, the bulk of the church black in the evening light like a frightening prow and a rigid, motionless crowd lined the windy parapets. Some men came down to meet them so as to be the first to see and help. At the path to his house the boy was unloaded and carried shoulder-high while the men of the escort applauded him and wished him well.

The cart arrived in the square, up and across sheets of bomb-proof ice, the women were already coming down from the balconies to add a touch of mourning. They unloaded them under the entrance to the municipality and laid them out on the beams and trestles stood there for traders. The secretary to the commune, a young man with lint-white hair, bespectacled and stammering, said they would be placed in coffins as soon as possible. 'The commune will pay for the coffins, naturally. Once they are in their coffins we'll carry them into the church for the proper ceremonies.' He threw a timid glance at the two bodies which the growing darkness was now submerging. The women sighed, wept and lamented in whispers. The miller, so big, so active, so much in command, said to the women: 'You'll catch your deaths of cold here, women. Go back home while we put them in their coffins. When they are in church we'll send for you and you will show some sorrow for them but be a little more sheltered, all right?' The women obeyed but slowly and lingeringly, then he pushed them homewards with the pressing urgency of his arms which were at once powerful and gentle and as he did so stumbled over the bitch. 'And what is this? Isn't it the big dog from the Langa? It can't be – the Fascists kept it in town.' 'It got away,' said Johnny. 'Amazing – but it was just the sort to do it. I always had a weakness for this wolfhound. So you got away from them, eh, wolf? At least you did – you who are only an animal.'

The secretary came to Johnny again, addressed himself to him, he said, as being the only partisan present and available. 'I think your two comrades have no family near here. If I am not mistaken no one here even knows their real names and addresses for which reason we are not in a position to inform their families of the burial. In the present state of affairs, and I am concerned only about the safety of this village, I should like to suggest that they are buried this very night. Naturally they will not be kept *short* of any and every formality and rite.' Johnny agreed and the secretary sent off to appeal to one of the best families in the village who would certainly receive both of them in their family tomb until the morning when victory dawned.

A new step echoed on the ice. It was Puc, one of Nord's men, half bodyguard half dispatch rider. He identified Johnny and came up to him. 'Nord sends me. Are they really dead, Ivan and Luis?' Johnny pointed to the doorway, Puc went over, took a close look, swore under his breath and came back. 'Tell Nord I saw them being killed and if necessary I shall give him a report at the first opportunity. And tell Nord that 31 January is an absurd date.' 'What do you mean?' 'Don't worry. Nord will understand.'

Johnny leant against a pillar in the porch and the miller came over to ask what he was thinking about. 'About how lucky I am, how undeservedly lucky!' Up to now fortune had so turned out that he had not become part of that scheme of things. He too had gone about and had stopped at places, had been here and there, had slept and lain awake, unconsciously chosen such and such a road and such and such a time rather than another, just like Ivan and Luis exactly like all the other dead of the winter and the decision to disband. Well, the deadly insect had barely fluttered over their heads and had stung to death . . . those others.

'You really are lucky, Johnny, whether you don't deserve it I don't know. But you are intelligent enough to realise that luck too runs out. This is the nub of what I talked to you about. But not here out of respect for the health of your lungs. Come down to my mill and call the dog after you.'

The kitchen at the mill was the warmest place Johnny could remember ever having entered, the women were preparing supper, they were putting wonderful, silky lasagne into a rich, thick broth, and suddenly the bitch began to besiege the table to the great annoyance of the miller's wife. She was thin and complaining, the opposite of her husband. The two men sat with their feet on top of the stove where the snow sizzled and faded away at once.

'I'm ignorant, I know,' the miller began, 'and since we have a little time I'll try to explain to you how little I know and why. I was born into ignorance and was raised in it till I was a child. But from when I was a boy I didn't want to stay there like all those who are born and live on these high hills but rebelled and fought against it and am still fighting. All I need to tell you is that although I follow this wretched trade and live in these wild spots, I have never missed reading the newspaper every day, naturally so long as the post-bus worked. Every time I reread the same page three times to get out of it ideas about men and things that were going on and about the world.' Here he threw a polemical and provocative glance at his wife. 'Just to tell you that within my limits I am a man of commonsense and you must weigh and think over the consequences of my present words which, above all, really come from the heart.'

Johnny was in a state of complete mental vacuum, practically deaf, completely confused in that high temperature and the aroma of that rich minestra*. . . . 'They're knocking you off the branch like sparrows. And you're the last sparrow on these branches of ours, aren't you, Johnny? You admit yourself that you have been lucky up to now but luck runs out and will certainly run out before 31 January. So why are you still going about in uniform and armed, eating nothing and with your teeth chattering? It almost looks as if you want it, as if you are getting ready to be their prey.' He clasped his powerful hands calmly. 'Pay attention to me, Johnny. You have done your bit and your conscience is certainly at rest. So give it all up and go down into the plain. Not to hand yourself in, God forbid, and in any case it is too late. But go down and a lad like you must surely have relations and friends who will hide you. A hiding-place to stay in till the war is over, just eating and sleeping and enjoying the cosiness and . . .' he grinned and lowered his voice, 'and getting a visit every so often from some woman friend you trust, the only one to know your address.'

* There is a short gap in the text at this point (Editor).

The wife with all the kitchen gear in her hand was watching them, Johnny and her husband, out of the corner of her eye with an angry but contained air of disapproval, she was certainly calling her husband names under her breath. Johnny could follow her train of thought as if it were written on her brow; 'What the devil is that idiot of a husband of mine blethering about without weighing his words and without being asked and then asking him here. You never know how they'll react, these wild boys with the guns. The devil take my idiot of a husband and that nasty armed youth who has managed to get into our house.' Johnny gave her the shadow of a smile so that she would calm down and be quiet but the smile landed on the nose of the miller who returned the smile at his imminent success and continued with even more rotund eloquence. 'I see you take my point. What would be the use anyway? You know better than me although I never miss a broadcast by Radio London, not one . . . the Allies are stuck in Tuscany with snow up to their knees and the situation allows the Fascists to knock you off like sparrows on the bough, as I said before. When the thaw comes the Allies will stir themselves and then they'll strike the big blow – the winning one. And they'll win without you. Don't be offended – but you partisans are by far the least important piece in the whole game, you must agree. So why kick the bucket waiting for a victory that will come in any case without you – quite apart from you.'

The man was undoubtedly speaking from the heart and perhaps to spare himself the grief, not to mention the effort, of handling Ivan and Luis. And that evening at the burial he would certainly be one of the most active and demonstrative. So Johnny only smiled at him and called the bitch. The man followed him to the door in a great state of excitement. 'What do you say, Johnny?' Johnny lifted his chin. 'I have given an undertaking to say no to the end and this would be a way of saying yes.' 'And it is just that,' shouted the miller. 'It is, it is a way of saying yes.' Beyond the door the icy night waited like a wild beast in ambush and the dog thumped him between his legs. 'At least have a bite of supper with us,' said the miller but Johnny was already swallowed up by the mist.

An arctic wind from the ravines to the left swept his road forcing him to resist with all his might against being thrown into the ditch on their right. Everything – including the bite of the cold, the fury of the wind and the abyss of the night – came together to immerse him in a resonant feeling of pride. 'I am the sparrow that will never fall. I am that one and only sparrow.' But he was quickly sorry for it and *soberised* when he felt he saw in a circle of daylight the grey, stony cheeks of Ivan and Luis relax almost imperceptibly into a mildly critical, *knowing* smile. Then he shouted to the wolfhound which was wandering playfully on that nocturnal hill and pushed on forwards almost bent in two towards the atoms of light which starred the black mass of the Langa. The woman of the house had known for hours what happened and looked gloomily and in silence at the steaming dog: 'No one saw it,' Johnny lied. 'I know what's going through your mind. They're tightening their grip, they're tightening their grip and next time it will be me. Don't worry, I'm going to sleep a long way off and tomorrow I'll keep away all day. Chain the bitch and try to sleep.'

XXXV

A week passed of eternal wandering and disastrous malaise. His forehead painful and feeling like a naked bone, his chest bruised, his bouts of coughing exploded from crest to crest, to his feverish eyes even the slightest gleam of the embryonic light on the rusty snow felt intolerable. Every hour in the twenty-four was tyrannised by a most intense cold and all he could get to protect himself better was a pullover which was given him in a house in a ravine, home-made, of goat's-wool with strands as harsh and thick as ropes, besides it was of not much more than child-size, the first time he slipped into it made him feel as if he had been cast in plaster, suffocated. From the plain by the town there rose, dull and punctual, the roar of the mortars on the frozen river; it sounded like a drum-march to the scaffold, a giant was about to be beheaded. The hours stretched out to biblical dimensions.

He threw a last glance at the campanile of Benevello, a grey castrum* rising up from the equally grey snow, there Ivan and Luis slept, not to be wakened even momentarily by the shout of victory on some hot, bright spring morning. Then he coughed harshly and went on towards the Langa which was surmounted by a light, grey curl of smoke like a mourning band. He stopped at the edge of the wood and whistled to the house awaiting the bounding appearance of the bitch. But she did not appear and Johnny whistled more loudly. Then the old woman came out, visible from afar, so worn out and trembling, so changed from the old, merry and intrepid *vivandière!* 'What do you want?' she shouted to him. 'Nothing, I was passing almost by chance. Where is the bitch?' The beast was on heat, she

---

* Latin – a fort.

412

said, and at dawn had gone to her lover, a red-coated mongrel on the other side of the Boscaccio; she had gone off to him for three days and each time her absence was longer. 'She won't pay any attention to you but if you happen to catch sight of her try to bring her home for me. I can't be without her these days!'

Very vaguely but no less bitterly Johnny felt the absence of the bitch, the fact that she had her own personal business that was hers alone, when he and the old woman had such great need of her. He passed his finger over his lips which were swollen but felt dead. 'I have nothing to do and don't know where to go. I shall climb up beyond the Boscaccio and see if I can see and catch her.' She said to come back after dark and whistle and she would come out with something to eat in her hand. 'I'd ask you in now, Johnny, you are in a terrible state, but I daren't by day – I'm sorry.'

He set out for the crest. Nine was striking murkily on some campanile and he checked his watch. His wrist was growing visibly thinner – at a point of feminine slenderness but hard as iron the leather strap was now falling to pieces. He tore it off and slipped the watch into his breastpocket among the folds of his blue scarf. That watch had marked his conscious hours: he had glanced at it when Monti was talking about the Stoics, when Corradi dropped Oriani to give the extracurricular lesson on Baudelaire, when Captain Vargiu had announced 25 July, Johnny had consulted it when he was waiting for the Roman boy with the civilian clothes some days after the Armistice.* He shook his head – past and present were totally, equally incredible. And a cry flashed through his head: 'Johnny, what is the aorist of *lambano?*'**

As he walked along he searched and searched without finding her again. Then he forget about it; now he felt grateful to the bitch for having given him an aim and a goal that frozen, chaotic morning. Finding her he certainly would not ill-treat her but stroke her and make her return as nicely as possible.

He chanced to look down and saw the sharecropper from the Serra dei Pini dragging himself along the path lower down as if he had just

---

* References to Johnny's schooldays and army service. The armistice of 8 September found him deserting from the army in Rome and looking for civilian clothes.
** Greek verb – to catch.

stopped running for his life or had a bullet in his chest. He watched him a little longer then clapped his hands at him. He looked up immediately in the right direction and his arms leapt out as if in invocation or an attempt to make him draw near as quickly as possible. Johnny threw himself cross-country in the snow and ended up near the man. He was panting and stammered: 'The tramp, the spy, the one with the skins.'

Then Johnny's heart gave a bound. 'He passed by our house only minutes ago and was making for Rustichello. I wanted to send my eldest boy to you but then I thought it best to keep the boys out of this.' Johnny told him to lend him his cape. He did not understand and Johnny tore it off his shoulders. 'Don't ask me anything. Go home – not straight but go round about a little,' then he threw the cloak round his shoulders and set off running along the path with the man whispering after him words which were lost to his ears.

Ten minutes later he was looking down on to the courtyard of Rustichello and the path that led to it: everything deserted and peaceful – he had clearly gone on without knocking. He was wondering which way to go when he glimpsed his man, he was just coming out of a look-out point, pushing his bicycle towards the path which gave on to the road along the crest. He was calm and confident, he was climbing uphill with his head lowered, effortlessly.

Johnny's palpitations gave way to a normal speed, only his tongue had in a flash become entirely dry. He drew back behind a snowdrift with his back to the wood and waited. The man would pass in five minutes. He turned his head to and fro to breathe in as much air as possible, was aware of the perfect silence and of the absolutely deserted landscape all around. He took the Sten from under his cloak and cocked it slowly millimetre by millimetre. But when it was cocked doubt seized him. He could not fire on a pure assumption after so many blots he could not forget *fair play*: one is born like that. Suppose he were not a spy, were really, however scantily possible, a fur-trader? Anselmo's wife had so changed, so inflated reality: you can expect anything, in terms of imagination, from those hill-women who pass their lives in fecund loneliness, in the lonely and stimulating company of the deceptive wind. He felt that his soul, his fate were at stake in those few minutes which were so slow and headlong. He could stop him, tie him up, perhaps exchange him for

414

Ettore. But no – Ettore could not and must not be exchanged if that man was what he was. Then he thought he caught the man's heavier breathing at the top of the hill and even the rustle of the tyres on the frozen mud.

Then the man appeared on the crest and stopped to rest with one elbow leaning on the saddle. The brand-new metal parcel-racks on the handle-bars gleamed their utmost in the scant light of the sun.

A lump of catarrh rose tempestuously into Johnny's throat and spitting hard he leapt on to the road. The man started, then slowly raised himself, and surprise gave his voice a sarcastic tone. Johnny showed him his left hand which held the pistol and ordered him to pull back the hood of his cape.

'Why?' he asked in Italian* with a grating voice.

Johnny aimed at his chest. 'Pull it back.'

The white streak shone in the bed of the rich, raven hair.

'Now smile.'

'What do you want me to do?'

'To smile. Smile.'

The man smiled and spoke at the same time – a rush of words of which Johnny did not catch one.

'Shut up. Just smile.'

The man said he couldn't manage . . . 'I can't manage it. You have a face . . .'

'Smile!'

Then he smiled, a wide smile which bared all his teeth, frozen and freezing.

Then Johnny smiled at him and the man smiled more easily and in a friendly tone of voice asked him why he was making all these experiments. 'As you see I am a merchant. I trade in rabbit skins and squirrel ones too, when I find them. Now I'll let you see,' and he stretched his hand towards the parcel rack but Johnny threw him such a glance that the other suddenly withdrew his hand.

'Tell me instead why you let it slip just now that you are going back to barracks?'

He smiled blankly: 'Barracks? What barracks? What are you talking about, partisan?'

* i.e. not in dialect.

'To your barracks.'

'What barracks! Thank God I am out and about and far from barracks. What barracks are you talking about?'

Johnny had a rising sensation that Anselmo was hidden somewhere near and an incredible sense of shame seized hold of him and made him lower his voice. 'You've got to understand that you're not going back to barracks.'

And with his left hand he brought the pistol out again but with a loose and clumsy grip. And the man glanced at the swaying mouth of the weapon and judged the distance, fifteen paces and the chances. 'Think it out, think it out and make up your mind,' he begged him in his heart and then he said out loud: 'You are a spy, pray if you feel like it . . .' The man's hand dived voraciously into the metal container on the handlebars, *blowing* the furs, Johnny touched his Sten under his cloak and heard its immensely long trusty crackle. The man collapsed over the bicycle, the magazine was already empty, then he fell to the ground entangled in the frame, kicking his last in the wheels.

The echo of the burst of fire was still galloping away through the depths of the Belbo valley. Johnny ran over to the heap, pulled the man free of the machine and rolled him to the bank at the roadside and then down the hill towards the wood, frantically. The body rolled smoothly on the hard snow, bounced at a hummock and then disappeared into a depression.

Johnny returned to the bicycle and thrust his hand into the metal carriers, extracting from it a P38 and three magazines, full and well oiled. He arranged them all in his belt and sighed with a sense of liberation and relief. Then he looked and listened in every direction but nothing was to be heard or seen. But he felt that Anselmo was very close by but not the need to call him. Then he crossed the road to reach the corpse in a hollow beyond the slope. He climbed down, imprinting footsteps exactly on the drops of blood, blending them into an indecipherable grey-brown stain. Then he stood on the top of the last slope, looked at the corpse where it had landed and sat down.

He had never killed a man like that and now he had to bury him, something else he had never done. The snow crackled behind him but he did not even turn round so certain was he of Anselmo's presence. The peasant knelt down on the ridge looking at the corpse with his bulging eyes. With a calm and grateful voice Johnny said: 'He was precisely what you said.' 'So? And you weren't sure that he was a spy and I had never doubted it. You did a good job. I have to tell you that I was worried about you, Johnny, but when I heard the burst I knew you were winning and he was dying. How are you now?' 'Well, I feel well.' He was calm and sweating. 'You know it's the first man I have killed looking him in the face.' 'I believe you,' said the peasant. 'But the bicycle is still on the road.' 'Go up and get it and dump it in the thickest part of the wood.' 'Johnny,' stammered Anselmo, 'won't you give it to me? I would like it for my eldest son when he is big.' 'You really want it? That bicycle?' 'Yes, for my children when they are big and for use only when it's all over.' 'Take it then but I'm warning you. If they find it in your house it's as good as a death sentence.' 'Don't worry, I'll hide it where even the angels won't find it.' He rose, wrapped himself in his cloak, and climbed up to take possession of the bicycle. From up there he informed Johnny that he would be back in twenty minutes with a shovel and a spade. 'Good,' said Johnny, 'we'll have a good bit of digging to do. A metre of snow and as much again of earth.'

Anselmo loaded the bicycle on his shoulders and then set off at a run for the steep hillside. And Johnny turned round again to watch over his own corpse. It was very cold, but it felt to him as if the winter (and perhaps his war as well) was over and done with.

XXXVI

The man next to Johnny burst out laughing. 'Do you know? it seems we've all had the worst cold in our lives.' And it was true, they all looked washed out, dripping and shivering, the hundred men who answered the appointment of 31 January on the hill at Torretta.

When Johnny arrived from the Langa there were already something like fifty men, rigid with cold or walking about on the mortally cold hillside, under a covered and very low sky. They did not exchange words except for quickly exhausted requests for tobacco. Some peasants passed nearby on their way to market or manual work and as they passed they left sombre good wishes and a few *grim* but heartfelt references to good luck this time, to the coming spring. One man stood sentry scanning the stretch towards Mango and another was doing the same to the east watching the Belbo valley and the arrivals from it, including Nord himself.

Johnny strode from one sentry to the other, renewing his ties with comrades but essentially waiting for Pierre and Nord. Meanwhile he tried to discover the winter secrets of these men, secrets which clung to their bodies, clothes and weapons. One of them was telling out loud one particular winter adventure and his story was punctuated by bursts of incredulous laughter.

Then a hurrah burst out in the west to salute the men from Mango, Pierre at their head. They ran to embrace, then Pierre stood back to take a look at the whole of him once more and remained contrite and perplexed, for he clearly understood that his face was not like Johnny's. 'Here we are together again and to the end,' said Pierre with a slight hesitation and Johnny was glad, happy, but felt that the tide of joy left him untouched and dry, in an untouched state that could not be flooded by the tide because of the long winter solitude. Then

Johnny asked if he knew about Ettore. Pierre sighed that he knew it all. 'Let's hope he stays a prisoner till the spring.' 'But it will be terrible for him. I feel that our first success will be his misfortune. If we win somewhere Ettore will be shot. And we have to begin to win in a few places.' In his hiding-place in Neive Pierre had learned a lot of things about the garrison in the town. 'The old colonel, not that I am sorry for him, has been sent away. Now the whole command is in the hands of a major and a captain. The first, they tell me, is a tiger, the second a hyena. And it seems they don't accept exchanges neither in town or outside – the men who fall prisoner are abandoned to their fates, lost, both ours and theirs.' So the last hope of ransoming Ettore was lost and from that mournful realisation the roar of welcome to Nord, who was arriving from the east, roused him. From what could be glimpsed through the tight circle of bodyguards he was wearing the prestigious English officer's greatcoat with its Persian fur, but how worn and shabby it was, speaking at first sight of the marches and the times of hiding, the climbing up and down in stables and haylofts. On his head he wore with a *certain coquetry* a naval officer's cap. He looked round the assembly – now there were one hundred and fifty of them – and made towards the orator's high bank.

There he pushed his cap back and 'What did you think of the winter, lads?' he said. 'Wasn't it something great, tremendous? It was, I can tell you, and it is what we shall boast about most. Isn't that so? You are looking wooden and numb. So courage! Next winter we shall be in peacetime, perhaps in a fine room, twenty-two degrees of heat, perhaps in our dressing-gowns, perhaps in slippers and perhaps, think of that, married. Think what a tragedy, what slapstick!' and all the men laughed loudly and *strainedly.* 'I wager my head,' Nord went on, 'that then a barbarous nostalgia will assail us for this terrible winter and we shall weep over its memory. So hurrah for this winter.'

The men *hurraed* and in the silence that followed Johnny's neighbour said with a loudish voice: 'He's right. What the devil shall we do next winter when we don't have to save our skins, and don't have any more Fascists to deal with?' And a great shudder ran through the questioning empty space.

Nord continued: 'Today we are one hundred and fifty, the best, the pillars of the house, the great old winter guard,' the men applauded themselves, 'tomorrow we shall be three hundred, within the month,

419

I guarantee you, we shall be a thousand. In the first week of March we shall be two thousand and we shall have arms and equipment for five thousand.' Here a wild cheer echoed fit to be heard beyond the Belbo and beyond the Bormida and it was followed by another burst of applause, less amazing but just as deeply felt, and Johnny turning round saw the lower crest entirely lined by peasants waving their hands. And Johnny blessed the winter which had gestated in its lethal cold the heat of this necessary day.

A man burst out of the ranks and drew near to Nord's natural platform; he was low-built and brown, an ex-officer of the army and a Southerner of the lowest type. 'Commandant,' he cried, 'you talk about the winter as being over. But I am reminding you that there are still a few months of it in these terrible Northern places.' The assembly roared with laughter. 'I am talking,' he went on, 'I have the honour to talk in the name of my fellow-countrymen from the South, of us who suffer atrociously from cold and will suffer from it till 21 March.'

Nord laughed. 'Leo, am I to blame, are we to blame if you are dirty, shivering Southerners?' And again a burst of laughter roared out and the North had never been so loved by the South and vice versa. And on the surrounding hurdles the peasants laughed in blind sympathy.

'Let me tell you a couple more necessary things because I too am getting fed up with this speech. I said we will have arms and equipment for five thousand men. Now I'll tell you why. A new English mission, the biggest and most complex in history, has been parachuted into Lampus' territory. It will stay up there long enough to fit him out with an unprecedented series of drops then they will come down here to us.' A roar exploded mixed with some singing from strained throats. 'Have you all understood clearly? Johnny, I am talking to you in particular. You know the work that is waiting for you. We will have thousands of men in uniform, we'll site a Bren every ten metres on our front, we'll cancel from the face of the earth their garrisons at Alba and Asti. And we will have all the rest – cigarettes, medicines, chocolate, underwear, boots.'

At last both the speech and the gathering were over. Nord was getting ready to go into the Belbo valley once again for his new headquarters. He turned to Johnny once more: 'You're dead, Johnny, if your English is a bluff.'

Then Pierre came to Johnny and informed him that the old system of garrisons was being revived. Johnny barely shook his head, opaquely, more in indifference than in a spirit of criticism. 'As could be foreseen,' said Pierre, 'I have been posted to Mango once again. From Nord I asked for you and Franco and you have been granted to me. Naturally I shall let you go the moment your work with the English comes along.' He looked around with embarrassment and said: 'We need twenty-five men from those present. Help me to choose them.'

The men were chosen and formed up. Johnny and Franco marched them to Mango to get them settled in while Pierre climbed up to the Langa to dig up his machine-pistol. From the new ranks Johnny followed him with his eyes as he hastened on his short and strenuous legs towards his winter realm and made an effort to love him as much as before. But that *patch* would never be cancelled out or submerged.

Johnny was lost – that *patch* far from being cancelled out became bigger. He could no longer put up with, do things in common, he shunned collectivity, reconnaissances and guard duty. Pierre let him live and be idle with a sort of sour understanding, with a certain querulous solicitude and with Franco took on himself all the work of reorganising the garrison. In less than a week it resembled the old garrison but with men who were more tried. More had joined them, the last to emerge from the winter maelstrom, so that now the garrison counted some fifty men. The civilians too seemed to have returned to the old solidarity and willingness to help, so that Johnny was even more profoundly wounded by the realisation that he alone of them all was no longer in step with them as before. Moreover he felt perhaps more than any other that normal, too normal progress towards the spring and its great abnormal realities.

The situation with regard to ammunition was the worst of all the discouraging situations in partisan history; in a serious action the best supplied of the men would run out in ten minutes, for Johnny personally there remained one Sten magazine. Almost every day a runner left Mango for Nord's headquarters to ask about the English and the drops. The English were still lingering near Lampus and no one could foresee the time when they would come down to Nord. And almost every night they could hear on the high hills to the south the rumble – like that of a *bourru bienfaisant** of the English four-engined planes and in the morning some sentries swore to have caught sight, at a particularly favourable moment, of the light of the signal fires on the ground in the hollows receiving the drops and even the luminous play of the lights in the bellies of the planes. The wait was so exasperating that some men threatened to go over to the Communists. 'We know perfectly well,' they said, 'that the Red Star does not get drops. But at least with them you are at once at peace in your heart and aren't eating it out.' And another without referring to desertion: 'Lampus is certainly a big boss and I will always stand to attention in front of him but let me say that he seems to me to be a bit too good to himself.'

The next day an alarm *sobered and frowned* men and things. Civilians in flight from the hills warned that the Fascists from the town were making a thrust towards Trezzo and Neviglie and Mango. Pierre drew up his few men – some were in the trenches with a mere pistol – and they waited under the hoary sky in the icy wind. Another flock of refugees informed them that they had already penetrated into Neviglie and were turning it upside down with *grim* silent meticulousness. They took note and kept their eyes on the dim crest of Neviglie planted with cypresses. There was nothing to be seen. However two prominent citizens of Mango climbed up to their position to ask if they were capable of defending the village reasonably if the Fascists *thrusted in*. Without looking them in the face Pierre said that the men had more or less a magazine a head. Said the prominent citizens: 'In that case the village hopes you will let them in without firing. If you do not fire they will occupy the village but probably won't do anything to us. Nothing in terms of lives, we mean. As for the things, we're already hardened to that.' Pierre nodded without saying anything and the prominent citizens left again while they gazed at the crest at Neviglie. Very long and black was the shadow of the cypresses on the grey and corrupted snow. Until their vanguard slipped along it, crouching and excited, searching and sniffing all round like animals. But the main body did not come into sight and after a little the patrolling troops turned back, nasty, black, antennaed animals on the lightless earth.

* French – a grumbling benefactor.

In the afternoon they detached a man to Nord to explain to him the risk today and to beat the big drum for weapons and ammunition. The English mission had almost finished with Lampus and Nord meantime was collecting a load for Mango: a Bren and various types of ammunition. At night Pierre and Johnny and Franco went to Constantino's to listen to the English radio. The bulletin did not interest them, they were all intent on the special messages to the partisans of the North which had been resumed and tonight they were very frequent, douching them with alternating anger and hope and frustration.

The load was late, the Fascists were more punctual. A big semi-motorised column came up from Asti and without stopping and without hold-ups aimed directly at Mango. The trucks had been stopped three hundred metres from the village and now the men were advancing towards their objective, which was desolate and extinguished and passive on a black-and-white morning, with infernal black rags of scattered clouds on a milk-white bed, the sky a perfect mirror of the earth below, with its patches of intact snow and uncovered earth. The partisans escaped towards the right, lazily, with many halts, sometimes in full view with their empty weapons dangling and their fists thrust into their pockets, without a straight line in their entire profile. Pierre hinted at possible mortar fire from the others but this did not hurry the men on even a little. And as the Fascist vanguard were entering the alley to the village, the last lingering partisans were exactly halfway between the invaders and Pierre's main body. Franco grumbled: 'Does it really look to you as if we had re-formed again? This is worse than when we disbanded last December.' They joined the others in a hollow, the true abode of cold and ice, and they sat for hours shivering in the wind and on the soaking earth. Hours passed and from the occupied village there did not rise a column of smoke nor an explosion nor screaming; as one of them observed they looked like the relatives in the anteroom to an operating theatre while their loved one is under the knife. Then some men, unable to stand any more, got up with broad applications of mud on their thin buttocks, and looked nauseously over the parapet of the hollow at the village under torture.

Johnny covered his eyes to blind himself to the misery of the day. How much he had dreamt of their reassembly in the loneliest days of

December and January and this was the dreamt-of achievement, the dreamt-of joy? He dreamt he was already with the English, already far away from these companions with whom he was still in contact, elbows and thighs, operating with those English, no longer with these ones. He horribly resented feeling himself elbowed, but it was simply Franco who was pointing out to him the Fascist column evacuating Mango. They were strung out serpentwise on the road to Sant'Ambrogio, wiggling their hips, their knapsacks bobbing up and down in march time, then the bend swallowed them and they reappeared only much later on the road to the crest. One man swore and sat down on the mud again, almost plunging his behind into it. 'Don't expect me to go back into the village. I haven't got enough cheek. Please don't expect that of me.' Franco saw the unease in Pierre's eyes and shouted to him to get up and not be stupid, everyone repeated to him not to be stupid. But meantime Pierre had taken complete control and ordered Johnny and four other men to keep close to him, to make sure they really had cleared off, that it was not just a trick.

They rushed down the slope towards the main road, with the fresh footprints of the Fascists extremely clear in the muddy patina. In the village civil life was being reborn, re-emerging, very cautiously: one man more daring than the others was the first to go on to the street and demanded with eagerness and pessimism what on earth they were going to do now and Johnny did not reply but saw the face of one of his companions, a frozen, square face, furrowed by the hot tears of shame and desire. Meantime something must have happened uphill because from up there people were shouting to them and making signs. Intrigued they moved halfway uphill and the whole main body of the garrison was coming downhill round a cart full of ammunition. Pierre said: 'Up to now we have been ashamed of ourselves but the afternoon will be different. Let us follow them, let us engage their rearguard and let's do a few of them in.' 'We can and must do it,' said Franco. The bulk of the men had thrown themselves on the cart and now were pillaging it with greedy hands and blind eyes. Johnny too threw himself on it but at that moment he was called over by the officer who had commanded the escort of the cart. 'You are Johnny? Come to headquarters at once with us.'

'I shall come this evening,' said Johnny.

'An order from Nord. Come up with us immediately.'

'What's new?'

'The English mission is arriving. It will be with us at two. Orders from Nord. In command is a certain Major Hupp.'

'Hupp!?'

'Hup, hop, hip, or hap! The essential point is that he is an English major and has a transmitter.'

Johnny looked round, the men had already all kitted themselves out and were becoming excited about the pursuit.

'Tell Nord that I shall come this evening without fail.'

'This evening Nord will tie you to the stake.'

'This evening, come what may. I shall justify myself to Nord.' And he threw himself on the cart again but it had been stripped clean and Johnny was left with his one old magazine.

He took his place in the column and Franco looked at him questioningly. He was knotting his blue handkerchief on his brow. 'Very probably it will end up in a mess,' said Johnny, 'but it has to be done. The wheel has to be set in motion again even if it is us its first teeth will grind to pieces.'

Pierre said to Johnny: 'Go up ahead and get off at the double.'

Johnny obeyed and in a minute his legs were already working madly with the overwhelming sensation of the ground slipping away under his feet like a velvet guide. He led on like this for a couple of kilometres and the village of Valdivilla was already in sight. He turned round for a second and saw behind him Tarzan and Settimo who were following him well, Pierre striding along half-running and behind him the column which had already totally crumbled. They penetrated into the village and a few, tremulous individuals informed them that the Fascists had stopped for a little to halt and rest, in a muddy space they could clearly see the imprints of the base-plates where the mortars had rested. One man calmer than the others shook his head at their plan and prophesied that in his opinion they would never achieve it, at this hour the last Fascists had already crossed the crest of San Maurizio and were comfortably descending on Santo Stefano.

But Pierre shouted to march on and Johnny resumed that murderous pace, every so often turning round to look back, the column more and more split up, some stopped at the mounds of gravel, doubled up, burst. Pierre was still floating on those waves of disintegration and exhaustion. Johnny *braced* and marched more strongly still.

After a last bend the summit of the hill appeared, idyllic even under that severe sky and in its grey bleakness. To the left was a cluster of weatherbeaten old houses leaning on each other as if for mutual help against the elements of nature and the bewitched solitude of the high hill, to the right of the street, at the same height as the houses stood a poor gas-burning truck with barrels of wine on the back. Johnny slowed down and sighed, everything seeming to him to block off hope and pursuit, the signal for return with empty hands. He turned and saw down below odd bits of the column, with faces contorted and gasping for breath. Suddenly a big, complex salvo from the houses blasted the road and Johnny dived into the ditch to his left so long as that interminable salvo lasted. He landed in the mud, unhurt, and thrust his face into the viscous slush. He had flattened himself out as much as possible, he was the nearest to them, at not more than fifty paces from the houses which were belching fire. A first series of hammerblows from a semi-automatic rifle reached him and he shouted making bubbles in the mud, then another whole series of *ranging* shots and he wriggled like a dying snake. Then the semi-automatic *ranged* elsewhere and he raised his face and dashed the mud from the corners. Then firing and shouts exploded behind him, clearly his comrades had taken up positions on the round crest of the hill on his left, the Bren was spraying the windows of the houses and the whitewash leapt like fireworks. All that firing and that shouting intoxicated him while in a bewildered way he prepared for action with open eyes. He picked himself out of the mud and stretched out his arms to the steep muddy bank to take his place in the battle, in the *mainstream* of the firing. He made some progress thanks to tufts of grass which stood up to his weight and tugging, but the automatic turned back to him, he seemed to see the last of his body slip into the sticky grass like a grey snake, so he let go and fell back into the ditch. Then he saw the Fascist, by himself and furtive, surprised by the attack in a meadow beyond the road, with one hand he held his rifle and with the other he was holding up his trousers, and he was watching out for the right moment to get back to his own people in the houses. The man took a look, then he

426

crouched down, he straightened up shaking his head at the situation. Johnny gripped the Sten but it felt wobbly and inconsistent, a wind-vane rather than a moulded mass of steel. Then the man jumped over the ditch and Johnny fired the whole magazine and the man crashed on the gravel and behind Johnny other partisans fired at him, crucifying him.

Johnny sighed with fatigue and peace. The burst of fire had been so violent that Johnny had almost felt the weapon fly out of his hands.

The shouting rather than the maximum volume of firing deafened him, the barricaded Fascists shouted at them 'English swine!' with voices that were very shrill but almost exhausted and tearful, from outside the partisans were shouting: 'German swine! surrender!'

Johnny grasped the cold sharp grass once more. The automatic turned on him but with only a single shot, almost as if only by way of interdiction, and Johnny this time did not fall back into the ditch, he took another two handfuls of grass and leant with his belly on the edge of the bank. There were his companions in groups and in echelon, lying down or sitting, Pierre in the centre, mixing economical bursts from his machine-pistol with the general firing. Johnny smiled to Pierre and to them all, they were twenty paces away but he felt he would never reach them as if they were kilometres away or a pure mirage. Yet he got over the top of the slope and was in the thick of the battle with his whole body. The fire from the Bren flew over half a metre above him, the semi-automatic was *ranging* on him again. He shut his eyes and stayed there like a lump, a fold in the ground, holding tight to one side the empty Sten. A shout to surrender roared in his ears, he leapt to sit up in the steel-clad air, brandishing his pistol towards the road. But it was two partisans running for cover behind the truck from there to enfilade certain fire-spewing windows and as they ran they shouted to the Fascists to surrender.

The fire of his companions scorched his neck and lacerated his eardrums, as if in a dream he made out Pierre's voice, shouting and close to aphony. He threw a glance at the houses but saw only a Fascist bent over the window-sill with his arms already rigid and stretched out as if to retrieve something from the courtyard. Pierre's voice battered at his ears incomprehensibly. He *braced and called up himself*: this was the last, the only possibility of becoming part of the general reality. Sliding in the mud he made for Pierre while a machine-gunner opened fire from the windows on their line and Franco stumbled right over it and fell with a flood of blood erupting from his blue handkerchief and lay in Johnny's path. Johnny avoided the body, slowly, laboriously like an ant trying to get round a boulder and arrived exhausted beside Pierre. 'They must surrender,' shouted Pierre with foam at his mouth, 'now they are surrendering.' And he shouted to the houses to surrender, desperately. Johnny shouted to Pierre that he had no ammunition and Pierre was horrified and cried out to him to escape, to slip off and away. But where was Franco's rifle? He turned round on the mud and slithered in search of it.

Now the Fascists were no longer firing at the hill but were almost all replying to the sudden and deadly fire that the two partisans had opened up from behind the truck. The barrels were riddled and the wine spilled out like blood on to the road. Then from the house the Fascist officer came reeling to the door, pressing his breast with both hands, and now was shifting them giddily to wherever he received a new bullet, shouting he reeled to the side of the courtyard facing the partisans while from within his men called to him desperately. Then he fell like a stone.

Now the little hill was returning and receiving the general fire once again. Johnny stopped looking for Franco's rifle and crawled back towards Pierre. He shouted to the Fascists to surrender and to Johnny to withdraw while he put his last magazine in his sub-machine-gun. But Johnny did not withdraw, he was completely dazed, kneeling in the mud, facing the houses, his Sten on his shoulder, his hands gloved with mud spiked with grass. 'Surrender,' shouted Pierre with a voice close to tears. 'We won't get them, Johnny, we won't get them.' The Bren too sprayed for the last time, only the semi-automatic seemed to be inexhaustible, it *ranged* precisely, meticulously, lethally. Pierre threw himself face down in the mud and Tarzan took it full in the chest, he was motionless for good. Johnny lowered himself down completely and slid across to his rifle. But at that moment mortar fire exploded, distant and probing, aimed only at informing the Fascists of the *relief* and the partisans of their defeat. From the houses the Fascists shouted in triumph and revenge, on the last bend of the top of the hill a first truck appeared, packed with shouting and gesticulating Fascists.

Pierre swore for the first and last time in his life. He stood upright and gave the signal to retire. Other trucks appeared one after another at the bend, a few more scattered mortar bombs, the partisans were evacuating the little hill, slowly and as if bewildered, deaf to Pierre's shouts. They were no longer shouting from the houses, so happy and pleased were they to be liberated.

Johnny rose up with Tarzan's rifle and the semi-automatic . . .

Two months later the war was over.